N

X

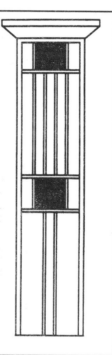

Night Road

Also by Kristin Hannah

Night Road

Kristin Hannah

ST. MARTIN'S PRESS

New York

This is a work of fiction. All of the characters, organizations, and events portrayed in this novel are either products of the author's imagination or are used fictitiously.

NIGHT ROAD. Copyright © 2011 by Kristin Hannah. All rights reserved. Printed in the United States of America. For information, address St. Martin's Press, 175 Fifth Avenue, New York, N.Y. 10010.

www.stmartins.com

LIBRARY OF CONGRESS CATALOGING-IN-PUBLICATION DATA

Hannah, Kristin.
  Night road / Kristin Hannah.—1st ed.
    p. cm.
  ISBN 978-0-312-36442-7
  1. Stay-at-home mothers—Fiction.   2. Foster mothers—Fiction.   3. Biological children of foster parents—Fiction.   4. Foster children—Fiction.   5. Teenagers—Fiction.   6. Life change events—Fiction.   7. Motherhood—Fiction.
8. Domestic fiction.   9. Psychological fiction.   I. Title.
  PS3558.A4763N54 2011
  813'.54—dc22

                                                                    2010041204

First Edition: April 2011

10   9   8   7   6   5   4   3   2   1

Dedication

I cannot deny that I was a helicopter mom. I went to every class gathering, party, and field trip, until my son begged me to please, please, stay at home. Now that he is grown and a college graduate, I can look back on our shared high school years with the wisdom that comes from distance. His senior year was without a doubt one of the most stressful years of my life, as well as one of the most rewarding. When I think back on it—and those memories were the inspiration for this novel—I remember so many of the highs and the lows. Mostly I think how lucky I was to live in a tight-knit, caring community where we supported one another. So, here's to my son, Tucker, and all of the kids who streamed through our house, lighting it up with their laughter. Ryan, Kris, Erik, Gabe, Andy, Marci, Whitney, Willie, Lauren, Angela, and Anna, just to name a few. And to the other moms: I honestly don't know how I would have survived without you. Thanks for always being there, for knowing when to lend a hand, when to offer a margarita, and when to tell me a hard truth. To Julie, Andy, Jill, Megan, Ann, and Barbara. Last, but certainly not least, thanks to my husband, Ben, who was always by my side, letting me know in a thousand different ways that in parenting, as in everything else, we were a team. Thanks to you all.

Night Road

Prologue

2010

She stands at the hairpin turn on Night Road.

The forest is dark here, even in midday. Ancient, towering evergreens grow in dense thickets on either side, their mossy, spearlike trunks rising high enough into the summer sky to block out the sun. Shadows lie knee-deep along the worn ribbon of asphalt; the air is still and quiet, like an indrawn breath. Expectant.

Once, this road had simply been the way home. She'd taken it easily, turning onto its potholed surface without a second thought, rarely—if ever—noticing how the earth dropped away on either side. Her mind had been on other things back then, on the minutiae of everyday life. Chores. Errands. Schedules.

Of course, she hadn't taken this route in years. One glimpse of the faded green street sign had been enough to make her turn the steering wheel too sharply; better to go off the road than to find herself here. Or so she'd thought until today.

People on the island still talk about what happened in the summer of '04. They sit on barstools and in porch swings and spout opinions, half-truths, making judgments that aren't theirs to make. They think a few columns in a newspaper give them the facts they need. But the facts are hardly what matter.

If anyone sees her here, just standing on this lonely roadside in a pocket of shadows, it will all come up again. They'll remember that night, so long ago, when the rain turned to ash . . .

Part One

Midway upon the journey of our life
I found myself within a forest dark,
For the straightforward pathway had been lost.

—Dante Alighieri, *The Inferno*

One

2000

Lexi Baill studied a Washington State map until the tiny red geographical markings shimmied in front of her tired eyes. There was a vaguely magical air about the place names; they hinted at a landscape she could hardly imagine, of snow-draped mountains that came right down to the water's edge, of trees as tall and straight as church steeples, of an endless, smogless blue sky. She pictured eagles perched on telephone poles and stars that seemed close enough to grasp. Bears probably crept through the quiet subdivisions at night, looking for places that not long ago had been theirs.

Her new home.

She wanted to think that her life would be different there. But how could she believe that, really? At fourteen, she might not know much, but she knew this: kids in the system were returnable, like old soda bottles and shoes that pinched your toes.

Yesterday, she'd been wakened early by her caseworker and told to pack her things. Again.

"I have good news," Ms. Watters had said.

Even half-asleep, Lexi knew what that meant. "Another family. That's great. Thanks, Ms. Watters."

"Not just a family. Your family."

"Right. Of course. My new family. It'll be great."

Ms. Watters made that disappointed sound, a soft exhalation of breath that wasn't quite a sigh. "You've been strong, Lexi. For so long."

Lexi tried to smile. "Don't feel bad, Ms. W. I know how hard it is to place older kids. And the Rexler family was cool. If my mom hadn't come back, I think that one would have worked out."

"None of it was your fault, you know."

"Yeah," Lexi said. On good days she could make herself believe that the people who returned her had their own problems. On bad days—and they were coming more often lately—she wondered what was wrong with her, why she was so easy to leave.

"You have relatives, Lexi. I found your great-aunt. Her name is Eva Lange. She's sixty-six years old and she lives in Port George, Washington."

Lexi sat up. "What? My mom said I had no relatives."

"Your mother was . . . mistaken. You do have family."

Lexi had spent a lifetime waiting for those few precious words. Her world had always been dangerous, uncertain, a ship heading for the shoals. She had grown up mostly alone, among strangers, a modern-day feral child fighting for scraps of food and attention, never receiving enough of either. Most of it she'd blocked out entirely, but when she tried—when one of the State shrinks made her try—she could remember being hungry, wet, reaching out for a mother who was too high to hear her or too strung out to care. She remembered sitting for days in a dirty playpen, crying, waiting for someone to remember her existence.

Now, she stared out the dirty window of a Greyhound bus. Her caseworker sat beside her, reading a romance novel.

After more than twenty-six hours en route, they were finally nearing their destination. Outside, a steel-wool sky swallowed the treetops. Rain made squiggling patterns on the window, blurring the view. It was like another planet here in Washington; gone were the sun-scorched bread-crust-colored hills of Southern California and the gray crisscross of traffic-clogged freeways. The trees were steroid-big; so were the mountains. Everything seemed overgrown and wild.

The bus pulled up to a squat, cement-colored terminal and came to a wheezing, jerking stop. A cloud of black smoke wafted across her window, obscuring the parking lot for a moment; then the rain pounded it away. The bus doors whooshed open.

"Lexi?"

She heard Ms. Watters's voice and thought *move, Lexi,* but she couldn't do it. She looked up at the woman who had been the only steady presence in her life for the last six years. Every time a foster family had given up on Lexi, returned her like a piece of fruit gone bad, Ms. Watters had been there, waiting with a sad little smile. It wasn't much to return to, maybe, but it was all Lexi knew, and suddenly she was afraid to lose even that small familiarity.

"What if she doesn't come?" Lexi asked.

Ms. Watters held out her hand, with its veiny, twiglike fingers and big knuckles. "She will."

Lexi took a deep breath. She could do this. Of course she could. She had moved into seven foster homes in the past five years, and gone to six different schools in the same amount of time. She could handle this.

She reached out for Ms. Watters's hand. They walked single file down the narrow bus aisle, bumping the cushioned seats on either side of them.

Off the bus, Lexi retrieved her scuffed red suitcase, which was almost too heavy to carry, filled as it was with the only things that really mattered to her: books. She dragged it to the very edge of the sidewalk and stood there, perched at the rim of the curb. It felt like a dangerous drop-off, that little cliff of concrete. One wrong step could break a bone or send her headlong into traffic.

Ms. Watters came up beside Lexi, opening an umbrella. The rain made a thumping sound on the stretched nylon.

One by one, the other passengers disembarked from the bus and disappeared.

Lexi looked at the empty parking lot and wanted to cry. How many times had she been in exactly this position? Every time Momma dried out, she came back for her daughter. *Give me another chance, baby girl. Tell the nice judge here you love me. I'll be better this time . . . I won't forget about you no more.* And every time, Lexi waited. "She probably changed her mind."

"That won't happen, Lexi."

"It could."

"You have family, Lexi," Ms. Watters repeated the terrifying words and Lexi slipped; hope tiptoed in.

"Family." She dared to test out the unfamiliar word. It melted on her tongue like candy, leaving sweetness behind.

A banged-up blue Ford Fairlane pulled up in front of them and parked. The car was dented along the fender and underlined in rust. Duct tape crisscrossed a cracked window.

The driver's door opened slowly and a woman emerged. She was short and gray-haired, with watery brown eyes and the kind of diamond-patterned skin that came with heavy smoking. Amazingly, she looked familiar—like an older, wrinkled version of Momma. At that, the impossible word came back to Lexi, swollen now with meaning. *Family.*

"Alexa?" the woman said in a scratchy voice.

Lexi couldn't make herself answer. She wanted this woman to smile, or maybe even hug her, but Eva Lange just stood there, her dried-apple face turned into a deep frown.

"I'm your great-aunt. Your grandmother's sister."

"I never knew my grandmother," was all Lexi could think of to say.

"All this time, I thought you were living with your daddy's people."

"I don't have a dad. I mean, I don't know who he is. Momma didn't know."

Aunt Eva sighed. "I know that now, thanks to Ms. Watters here. Is that all your stuff?"

Lexi felt a wave of shame. "Yeah."

Ms. Watters gently took the suitcase from Lexi and put it in the backseat. "Go on, Lexi. Get in the car. Your aunt wants you to live with her."

Yeah, for now.

Ms. Watters pulled Lexi into a fierce hug, whispering, "Don't be afraid."

Lexi almost hung on too long. At the last second, before it turned embarrassing, she let go and stumbled free. She went to the battered car and wrenched the door open. It rattled and pinged and swung wide.

Inside, the car had two brown vinyl bench seats, with cracked seams that burped up a gray padding. It smelled like a mixture of mint and smoke, as if a million menthol cigarettes had been smoked within.

Lexi sat as close to the door as possible. Through the cracked window, she waved at Ms. Watters, watching her caseworker disappear into the gray haze as they drove away. She let her fingertips graze the cold glass, as if a little touch like that could connect her with a woman she could no longer see.

"I was sorry to hear about your momma passing," Aunt Eva said after a long and uncomfortable silence. "She's in a better place now. That must be a comfort to you."

Lexi had never known what to say to that. It was a sentiment she'd heard from every stranger who'd ever taken her in. Poor Lexi, with her dead, drug-addict mother. But no one really knew what Momma's life had been like—the men, the heroin, the vomiting, the pain. Or how terrible the end had been. Only Lexi knew all of that.

She stared out the window at this new place of hers. It was bold and green and dark, even in the middle of the day. After a few miles, a sign welcomed them to the Port George reservation. Here, there were Native American symbols everywhere. Carved orca whales marked the shop fronts. Manufactured homes sat on untended lots, many of them with rusting cars or appliances in the yard. On this late August afternoon, empty fireworks stands attested to the recent holiday, and a glittering casino was being built on a hillside overlooking the Sound.

Signs led them to the Chief Sealth Mobile Home Park. Aunt Eva drove through the park and pulled up in front of a yellow and white double-wide trailer. In the misty rain, it looked blurred somehow, rounded with disappointment. Plastic gray pots full of leggy, dying petunias guarded the front door, which was painted Easter-egg blue. In the front window, a pair of plaid curtains hung like fabric hourglasses, cinched in the middle with strands of fuzzy yellow yarn.

"It isn't much," Aunt Eva said, looking ashamed. "I rent from the tribe."

Lexi didn't know what to say. If her aunt had seen some of the places Lexi had lived in her life, she wouldn't have made excuses for this pretty little trailer. "It's nice."

"Come on," her aunt said, turning off the engine.

Lexi followed her aunt across a gravel path and up to the front door. Inside, the mobile home was neat as a pin. A small, L-shaped kitchen sidled up to a dining area that held a yellow speckled Formica and chrome table with four chairs. In the living room, a plaid loveseat and two blue vinyl La-Z-Boys faced a TV on a metal stand. On the end table there were two pictures—one of an old woman with horn-rimmed glasses and one of Elvis. The air smelled like cigarette smoke and fake flowers. There were purple air fresheners hanging from almost every knob in the kitchen.

"Sorry if the place kinda smells. I quit smoking last week—when I found out about you," Aunt Eva said, turning to look at Lexi. "Secondhand smoke and kids is a bad mix, right?"

A strange feeling overtook Lexi; it was birdlike, fluttery, and so foreign she didn't recognize the emotion right away.

Hope.

This stranger, this aunt, had quit smoking for her. And she'd taken Lexi in when obviously money was tight. She looked at the woman, wanting to say something, but nothing came out. She was afraid she might jinx everything with the wrong word.

"I'm kinda outta my depth here, Lexi," Aunt Eva finally said. "Oscar and me—he was my husband—we never had kids. Tried, just din't. So, I don't know about raising kids. If you're gonna be—"

"I'll be good. I swear it." *Don't change your mind. Please.* "If you keep me, you won't be sorry."

"If I keep you?" Aunt Eva pursed her thin lips, gave a little frown. "Your momma sure did a number on you. Can't say I'm surprised. She broke my sister's heart, too."

"She was good at hurting people," Lexi said quietly.

"We're family," Eva said.

"I don't really know what that means."

Aunt Eva smiled, but it was sad, that smile, and it wounded Lexi, reminded her that she was a little broken. Life with Momma had left its mark. "It means you're staying here with me. And I guess you'd best just call me Eva from now on, 'cause that Aunt bit is gonna get old fast." She started to turn away.

Lexi grabbed her aunt's thin wrist, feeling the velvety-soft skin wrinkle in her grasp. She hadn't meant to do it, shouldn't have done it, but it was too late now.

"What is it, Lexi?"

Lexi could hardly form the two small words; they felt like a pair of stones in her tight throat. But she had to say them. Had to. "Thank you," she said, her eyes stinging. "I won't cause you any trouble. I swear it."

"You probably will," Eva said, and finally, she smiled. "You're a teenager, right? But it's okay, Lexi. It's okay. I've been alone a long time. I'm glad you're here."

Lexi could only nod. She'd been alone a long time, too.

Jude Farraday hadn't slept at all last night. Finally, just before dawn, she gave up even trying. Peeling back the summer-weight comforter, taking care not to wake her sleeping husband, she got out of bed and left her bedroom. Opening the French doors quietly, she stepped outside.

In the emergent light, her backyard glistened with dew; lush green grass sloped gently down to a sandy gray-pebbled beach. Beyond it, the Sound was a series of charcoal-colored waves that rolled and rolled, their peaks painted orange by the dawn. On the opposite shore, the Olympic mountain range was a jagged line of pink and lavender.

She stepped into the plastic gardening clogs that were always by the door and went into her garden.

This patch of land was more than just her pride and joy. It was her sanctuary. Here, hunkered down in the rich black earth, she planted and replanted, divided and pruned. Within these low stone walls, she had created a world that was wholly defined by beauty and order. The things she planted in this ground stayed where she put them; they sent out roots that ran deep into this land. No matter how cold and bitter the winter or how driving the rainstorms, her beloved plants came back to life, returning with the seasons.

"You're up early."

She turned. Her husband stood on the stone patio, just outside their bedroom door. In a pair of black boxer shorts, with his too long, graying-blond hair still tangled from sleep, he looked like some sexy classics professor or a just-past-his-prime rock star. No wonder she'd fallen in love with him at first sight, more than twenty-four years ago.

She kicked off the orange clogs and walked along the stone path from the garden to the patio. "I couldn't sleep," she confessed.

He took her in his arms. "It's the first day of school."

And there it was, the thing that had crept into her sleep like a burglar and ruined her peace. "I can't believe they're starting high school. They were just in kindergarten a second ago."

"It's going to be an interesting ride, seeing who they become in the next four years."

"Interesting for you," she said. "You're in the stands, watching the game. I'm down on the field, taking the hits. I'm terrified something will go wrong."

"What can go wrong? They're smart, curious, loving kids. They've got everything going for them."

"What can go wrong? Are you kidding? It's . . . dangerous out there, Miles. We've been able to keep them safe up until now, but high school is different."

"You're going to have to let up a little, you know."

It was the sort of thing he said to her all the time. A lot of people gave her the same advice, actually, and had for years. She'd been criticized for holding the reins of parenthood too tightly, of controlling her children too completely, but she didn't know how to let go. From the moment she'd first decided to become a mother, it had been an epic battle. She had suffered through three miscarriages before the twins. And there had been month after month when the arrival of her period had sent her into a gray and hazy depression. Then, a miracle: she'd conceived again. The pregnancy had been difficult, always tenuous, and she'd been sentenced to almost six months of bed rest. Every day as she'd lain in that bed, imagining her babies, she'd pictured it as a war, a battle of wills. She'd held on with all her heart. "Not yet," she finally said. "They're only fourteen."

"Jude," he said, sighing. "Just a little. That's all I'm saying. You check their homework every day and chaperone every dance and organize every school function. You make them breakfast and drive them everywhere they need to go. You clean their rooms and wash their clothes. If they forget to do their chores, you make excuses and do it all yourself. They're not spotted owls. Let them loose a little."

"What should I give up? If I stop checking homework, Mia will stop doing it. Or maybe I should quit calling their friends' parents to make sure the kids are going where they say they're going? When I was in high school we had keggers every weekend, and two of my girlfriends got pregnant. I need to keep *better* track of them now, trust me. So many things can go wrong in the next four years. I need to protect them. Once they go to college, I'll relax. I promise."

"The right college," he teased, but they both knew it wasn't really a joke. The twins were freshmen in high school and Jude had already begun to research colleges.

She looked up at him, wanting him to understand. He thought she was too invested in their children, and she understood his concern, but she was a mother, and she didn't know how to be casual about it. She couldn't stand the thought that her children would grow up as she had, feeling unloved.

"You're nothing like her, Jude," he said quietly, and she loved him for saying it. She rested against him; together they watched the day brighten, and Miles finally said, "Well, I better get going. I have a surgery at ten."

She kissed him deeply, then followed him back into the house. After a quick shower, she dried her shoulder-length blond hair, put on a thin layer of makeup, and dressed in jeans and a boatnecked cashmere sweater and faded jeans. Opening her dresser drawer, she withdrew two small wrapped packages; one for each of her children. Taking them with her, she walked out of her bedroom, down the wide slate hallway. With morning sunlight streaming through the floor-to-ceiling windows, this house, constructed mostly of glass and stone and exotic woods, seemed to glow from within. On this main floor, every viewpoint boasted some decorating treasure. Jude had spent four years huddled with architects and designers to make this home spectacular, and her every dream for it had been realized.

Upstairs, it was a different story. Here, at the top of a floating stone and copper stairway, it was kidland. A giant media room, complete with big-screen TV and a pool table, dominated the east side of the house. Additionally there were two large bedrooms, each with their own en suite bathroom.

At Mia's bedroom door, she knocked perfunctorily and went inside.

As expected, she found her fourteen-year-old daughter sprawled on top of the blankets in her four-postered bed, asleep. There were clothes everywhere, like shrapnel from some mythic explosion, heaped and piled and kicked aside. Mia was actively engaged in a search for identity, and each new attempt required a radical clothing change.

Jude sat down on the edge of the bed and stroked the soft blond hair that fell across Mia's cheek. For a moment, time fell away; suddenly she was a young mother again, looking down at a cherubic girl with corn-silk hair and a gummy grin who'd followed her twin brother around like his shadow. They'd been like puppies, scrambling over each other in their exuberant play, chattering nonstop in their secret language, laughing, tumbling off sofa and steps and laps. From the very start, Zach had been the leader of this pair. He'd spoken first and most often. Mia hadn't uttered a real word until after her fourth birthday. She hadn't needed to; her brother was there for her. Then and now.

Mia rolled over sleepily and opened her eyes, blinking slowly. Her pale, heart-shaped face, with its gorgeous bone structure—inherited from her father—was an acne battlefield that no amount of care had yet been able to clear. Multicolored rubberbands looped through her braces. "Hola, Madre."

"It's the first day of high school."

Mia grimaced. "Shoot me. Really."

"It'll be better than middle school. You'll see."

"Says you. Can't you homeschool me?"

"Remember sixth grade? When I tried to help you with your math homework?"

"Disaster," Mia said glumly. "It could be better now, though. I wouldn't get so mad at you."

Jude stroked her daughter's soft hair. "You can't hide out from life, Poppet."

"I don't want to hide out from life. Just from high school. It's like swimming with sharks, Mom. Honest. I could lose a foot."

Jude couldn't help smiling. "See? You have a great sense of humor."

"That's what they say when they're trying to set up an ugly girl. Thanks, Madre. And who cares, anyway? It's not like I have friends."

"Yes, you do."

"No. Zach has friends who try to be nice to his loser sister. It's not the same thing."

For years, Jude had moved heaven and earth to make her children happy, but this was one battle she couldn't fight. It wasn't easy to be the shy twin sister of the most popular boy in school. "I have a present for you."

"Really?" Mia sat up. "What is it?"

"Open it." Jude offered the small wrapped box.

Mia ripped open the box. Inside lay a thin pink leather diary with a gleaming brass lock.

"I had one when I was your age, and I wrote down everything that happened to me. It can help—writing stuff down. I was shy, too, you know."

"But you were beautiful."

"You're beautiful, Mia. I wish you saw that."

"Yeah, right. Zits and braces are all the rage."

"Just be open to people, okay, Mia? This is a new school, make it a new opportunity, okay?"

"Mom, I've been going to school with the same kids since kindergarten. I don't think a new address is going to help. Besides, I tried being open . . . with Haley, remember?"

"That was more than a year ago, Mia. It doesn't do any good to focus on the bad things that happen. Today is the first day of high school. A new start."

"Okay." Mia tried gamely to smile.

"Good. Now get out of bed. I want to get to school early today, so I can help you find your locker and get you settled into first period. You have Mr. Davies for geometry; I want him to know how well you did on the WASL test."

"You are *not* walking me into class. And I can find my locker by myself, too."

Intellectually, Jude knew that Mia was right, but Jude wasn't ready to let go. Not yet. Too many things could go wrong. Mia was fragile, too easily flustered. What if someone made fun of her?

A mother's job was to protect her kids—whether they wanted it or not. She stood up. "I'll be practically invisible. You'll see. No one will even know I'm there."

Mia groaned.

Two

On the first day of school, Lexi woke early and staggered down the narrow hallway to the bathroom. One look in the mirror confirmed her worst fears: her skin was pale, a little sallow, even, and her blue eyes were puffy and bloodshot. She must have cried in her sleep again.

She took a quick, lukewarm shower, careful not to waste her aunt's money. There was no real point in drying her hair. The waist-length black strands would curl and frizz and do whatever they wanted to, so she pulled it all into a ponytail and went back to her room.

There, she opened her closet door and stared at the few articles of clothing she owned. There were so few choices . . .

What did kids wear here? Would Pine Island be like Brentwood or the Hills, where kids dressed like avant-garde fashion models? Or East L.A., where rap-star wannabes and grungoids filled the classrooms?

There was a knock at her bedroom door, so quiet Lexi barely heard it. She made her bed quickly and then opened the door.

Eva stood there, holding a cotton-candy-pink sweatshirt with a rhinestone butterfly bedazzled onto the front. The kidney-shaped wings were purple and yellow and shamrock green. "I got this for you at work yesterday. I figured every girl should have something new to wear on the first day of high school."

It was the ugliest thing Lexi had ever seen, better suited to a four-year-old than a fourteen-year-old, but she loved it instantly. No one had ever bought her something special for the first day of school. "It's perfect," she said, feeling a tightening in her throat. She'd only lived with her aunt for four days, and every hour she felt a little more at home. It scared her, that settling in. She knew how dangerous it could be to start liking a place. A person.

"You don't have to wear it if you don't want to. I just thought—"

"I can't wait to wear it. Thanks, Eva."

Her aunt gave her a smile so bright it bunched up her cheeks. "I told Mildred you'd like it."

"I do."

Eva bobbed her head in a little nod and backed into the hallway, closing the door behind her. Lexi put on the pink sweatshirt and stepped into a pair of faded Target jeans. Then she filled her hand-me-down backpack with the notebooks, paper, and pens Eva had brought home from work last night.

In the kitchen, she found Eva standing by the sink, dressed now for work in her blue Walmart smock, lemon-yellow acrylic sweater, and jeans, drinking coffee.

Across the small, tidy space, their gazes met. Eva's brown eyes looked worried. "Mrs. Watters worked hard to get you into Pine Island High. It's one of the best schools in the state, but the school bus don't come over the bridge, so you'll have to take the county bus. Is that okay? Have I already told you all this?"

Lexi nodded. "It's fine, Eva. Don't worry. I've been riding buses for years." She didn't add that she'd often slept on their dirty seats when she and Momma had nowhere else to go.

"Okay, then." Eva finished her coffee and rinsed out her cup, leaving it in the sink. "Well, you don't want to be late on your first day. I'll drive you. Let's go."

"I can take the bus—"

"Not on the first day. I got the late-shift special."

Lexi followed her aunt out to the car. As they drove toward the island, Lexi studied her surroundings. She'd seen all of this on maps, but those little lines and markings only told so much of the story. For instance, she knew that Pine Island was twelve miles long and four miles wide; that it was accessible by ferry to downtown Seattle and by bridge to mainland Kitsap County. On the Port George side of the bridge, the land was tribal. Pine Island, she saw now, was not.

She could tell by the houses that the people who lived on the island were rich. The houses over here were practically mansions.

They turned off the highway and drove up a hill to the high school, which was a collection of squat redbrick buildings huddled around a flagpole. Like many of the schools Lexi had attended, Pine Island had obviously grown faster than expected. A collection of portables ringed the main campus. Eva parked in the empty bus lane and looked at Lexi. "These kids are no better'n you. You remember that."

Lexi felt a rush of affection for this careworn woman who had taken her in. "I'll be fine," Lexi said. "You don't have to worry about me."

Eva nodded. "Good luck," she said at last.

Lexi didn't say that luck was useless at a new school. Instead, she forced a smile and got out of the car. As she waved good-bye, a school bus pulled up behind Eva, and kids poured out of it.

Lexi kept her head down and started moving. She'd been the new girl often enough to know the tricks of the camouflage trade. The best tactic was to blend in, disappear. You did that by looking down and moving fast. Rule one: never stop. Rule two: never look up. By Friday, if she'd followed this pattern, she'd just be one of the kids in the freshman class, and then she could try to make a friend or two. Although it wouldn't be easy here. What could she possibly have in common with these kids?

When she made it to Building A, she double-checked her schedule. There it was. Room 104. She merged into the crowd of students, all of whom seemed to know one another, and let their tide carry her forward. In the classroom, kids slid into their seats and kept talking excitedly.

Her mistake was to pause. She looked up just long enough to get her bearings, and the classroom went quiet. Kids stared at her; then whispering began. Someone laughed. Lexi felt her flaws keenly—her thick black eyebrows and crooked teeth and frizzy hair, her lame jeans and lamer sweatshirt. This was the kind of place where every kid got braces at adolescence and a new car at sixteen.

In the back of the room, a girl pointed at her and started to giggle. The girl seated beside her nodded. Lexi thought she heard *nice butterfly,* and then: *did she make it herself?*

A boy stood up, and the room went quiet again.

Lexi knew who he was. Every school had a guy like him—good-looking, popular, athletic, the kind of boy who got what he wanted without even trying. The football captain and class president. In his aqua blue Abercrombie T-shirt and baggy jeans, he looked like Leonardo DiCaprio, all golden and smiling and sure of himself.

He was coming toward her. Why? Was there another, prettier girl behind her? Was he going to do something to humiliate her, to make his friends laugh?

"Hey," he said. She could feel everyone looking at them, watching.

Lexi bit her lower lip to hide her crooked teeth. "Hey."

He smiled. "Susan and Liz are bitches. Don't let them get to you. The butterfly's cool."

She stood there like an idiot, dazzled by his smile. *Get a grip, Lexi. You've seen good-looking guys before.* She should say something, smile; *something.*

"Here," he said, taking her arm. At his touch, she felt a little jolt, like an electrical charge.

He should have moved, led her somewhere. That was why he was touching her arm, right? But he just stood there, staring down at her. His smile faded. She couldn't breathe all of a sudden; the whole world drained away until only his face was left, only his amazing green eyes.

He started to say something, but Lexi's heart was pounding so fast, she couldn't hear his words, and then he was being pulled away from her, led away by some beautiful girl in a skirt that was smaller than a dinner napkin.

Lexi stayed a moment too long, staring at his back, still feeling out of breath. Then she remembered where she was and who she was: the new girl in the bedazzled pink sweatshirt. Tucking her chin into her chest, she bolted forward, made her way to a seat in the back row. She slid onto its slick surface just as the bell rang.

As the teacher droned on about the early days of Seattle, Lexi replayed that moment, over and over. She told herself it meant nothing, the way he'd touched her, but she couldn't let it go. What had he been going to say to her?

When the class ended, she dared to look at him. He moved with the crowd of students, laughing at something the girl in the miniskirt said. At Lexi's desk, he paused, looked down at her, although he didn't smile or stop. He kept moving.

Of course he didn't stop. She rose slowly and walked to the door. For the rest of the morning, she tried to hold her head high as she moved through the crowded halls, but by noon, she was lagging, and the worst was yet to come.

Lunch in a new school was hell. You never knew what was in and what was out, and the whole social order could be upset if you dared to sit where you weren't supposed to.

At the door to the cafeteria, Lexi paused. Just the idea of walking in there, being scrutinized and judged, was more than she could bear today. Normally she was stronger than that, but Mr. Popular had unbalanced her somehow, made her want the impossible, and she knew firsthand how waylaid one could be by longing. It was a waste of time. She walked back outside, where the sun was shining. She dug through her backpack, found the lunch Eva had packed for her and a well-read copy of *Jane Eyre*. Some kids had stuffed animals or special childhood blankets. Lexi had Jane.

She walked idly through campus, looking for a place to sit down and read while she ate her lunch. Across the campus, she spied a pretty little tree growing up from a triangular patch of grass, but it wasn't the tree that caught her attention. It was the girl sitting cross-legged on the grass beneath its green canopy, hunched over a book. Her blond hair was divided into a pair of loosely twined braids. Dressed in a delicate pink tulle skirt, a black tank top, and black high-tops, she definitely made a statement.

It was a statement Lexi understood: I'm not like you. I don't need you.

Lexi had spent a few years dressed the same way herself, back when she hadn't wanted to make friends, when she'd been afraid of being asked where she lived or what her momma was like.

She took a deep breath and walked toward the girl. When she drew near, Lexi paused. She wanted to say the right thing, but now that she was here, she didn't know what that would be.

The girl looked up from her book. She was fragile looking, with acne-blistered skin and green eyes that were rimmed with too much purple eyeliner. Brightly colored rubber bands accented her braces.

"Hey," Lexi said.

"He's not here. And he's not coming."

"Who?"

The girl gave a disinterested shrug and went back to reading. "If you don't know, it doesn't matter, does it?"

"Can I sit with you?"

"Social suicide," the girl said without looking up.

"What?"

The girl looked up again. "It's social suicide to sit with me. Even the theater kids won't hang with me. Yeah. It's that bad."

"You mean I won't make the cheerleading squad? How tragic."

The girl looked interested in Lexi for the first time. A smile quirked her mouth. "Most girls care about stuff like that."

"Do they?" Lexi dropped her backpack onto the grass. "What are you reading?"

"*Wuthering Heights.*"

Lexi held out her own book. "*Jane Eyre.* Can I sit down?"

The girl scooted sideways to make room on the small patch of grass. "I haven't read that one. Is it good?"

Lexi sat down beside her. "My favorite. When you're done with yours, we could trade."

"That would be awesome. I'm Mia, by the way."

"Lexi. So what's the book about?"

Mia began talking slowly, stumbling over her words, but when she started talking about Heathcliff, she kind of took flight. The next thing Lexi knew, they were laughing as if they'd been friends for years. When the bell rang, they got up and walked toward their lockers together, still talking the whole way across campus. Lexi didn't keep her head down anymore, didn't clamp her books to her chest or purposely not make eye contact with anyone. Instead, she laughed.

Outside the door to her Spanish class, Mia stopped and said in a rush: "You could come to my house after school today. If you wanted to, I mean." She looked nervous as she asked it. "I know you probably won't. No worries."

Lexi felt like smiling; only nervousness over her teeth kept her in check. "I would totally like that."

"Meet me at the flagpole by the admin building, okay?"

Lexi went into her classroom and took a seat at the back. She eyed the clock for the rest of the day, willing time to speed up until finally at 2:50, she was at the flagpole, waiting. Kids swarmed around her, jostling one another as they made their way onto the buses lined up outside.

Maybe Mia wouldn't show. Probably she wouldn't.

Lexi was about to give up the whole thing when Mia came up beside her. "You waited," she said, sounding as relieved as Lexi felt. "Come on."

Mia led the way through the hive of students, toward a shiny black Escalade parked out on the main road. She opened the passenger door and climbed in.

Lexi followed her new friend into the leather-scented beige seat.

"Hola, Madre," Mia said. "This is Lexi. I invited her home with me. Is that okay?"

The woman in the driver's seat turned around, and Lexi was stunned by her beauty. Mia's mom looked like Michelle Pfeiffer with her perfect, pale face and sleek blond hair. In an obviously expensive salmon-colored sweater, she looked like she belonged on the Nordstrom catalog cover. "Hello, Lexi. I'm Jude. It's nice to meet you. And how is it that I don't know you?"

"I just moved here."

"Ah. That explains it. Where did you move here from?"

"California."

"I won't hold that against you," Jude said with a bright smile. "Will your mother mind if you're not home right away?"

"No," Lexi said, tensing for the inevitable next question.

"I could call her if you'd like, introdu—"

"Mo-*om*," Mia said, "you're doing that thing again."

Jude flashed Lexi a smile. "I'm embarrassing my daughter. Something I am sadly wont to do these days, just by breathing. But I can hardly stop being a mother, can I? I'm sure your mom is just as embarrassing, right, Lexi?"

Lexi had no idea what to say to that, but it didn't matter. Jude laughed and went on as if she hadn't asked a thing. "I'm supposed to be seen and not heard. Fine. Buckle up, girls."

She started up the car, and Mia immediately started talking about a book she'd heard about.

They drove away from the school and onto a pretty little main street. The traffic was stop-and-go all the way through town, but once they made it onto the highway, the road was clear. They followed one curvy, tree-lined, two-lane road after another until Jude said, "Home sweet home," and turned onto a gravel driveway.

At first there was nothing but trees on either side of them, trees so tall and thick they blocked out the sun, but then the road curved again and they were in a clearing full of sunlight.

The house was like something out of a novel. It sat proudly amid its landscaping, a soaring structure made of wood and stone, with windows everywhere. Low stone walls delineated magnificent gardens. Behind it all was the blue Sound. Even from here, Lexi could hear waves hitting the shore.

"Wow," Lexi said, getting out of the car. She had never been in a house like this before. How should she act? What should she say? She would do the wrong thing for sure and Mia would laugh at her.

Jude slipped an arm around her daughter and they walked ahead. "I bet you girls are hungry. Why don't I make you some quesadillas? You can tell me about the first day of high school."

Lexi hung back instinctively.

At the front door, Mia looked back. "Lexi? You don't want to come in, do you? You've changed your mind."

Lexi felt her insecurity dissolve, or perhaps more accurately, it joined with Mia's and morphed into something else. They were alike; impossibly, the girl who had nothing was like this girl who had everything. "No way," Lexi said, laughing as she hurried toward the door.

Inside, she slipped out of her shoes, seeing a second too late that her socks had holes in the toes. Embarrassed, she followed Mia into the magnificent house. There were walls of glass that framed a stunning ocean view, a stone fireplace, gleaming floors. She was afraid to touch anything.

Mia grabbed her hand and dragged her into a huge kitchen. There were gleaming copper pots hanging from a black skeletal thing above the eight-burner stove and fresh flowers in several places around the room. They sat down at a long black granite counter while Jude made quesadillas.

She just walked right up to me, Madre. And I told her it was social suicide to sit with me, but she didn't care. Is that cool or what?

Jude smiled at that, and started to say something, but Mia kept talking. Lexi could hardly keep up with Mia's steady stream of stories. It was as if Mia had been holding observations and thoughts inside of her for years, and now they were coming out. Lexi knew about that, about holding things inside and being afraid and trying to stay quiet. She and Mia compared opinions on high school, boys, classes, movies, tattoos, belly button piercings, and they agreed on *everything*. The more they agreed on, the more Lexi worried: what would happen when Mia found out about Lexi's past? Would Mia want to be friends with a drug addict's kid?

At about five o'clock, the front door banged open and a group of kids burst into the house.

"Shoes," Jude yelled from the kitchen without looking up.

Nine or ten kids surged forward, boys and girls. Lexi could tell they were the popular kids. Anyone would have recognized them—pretty girls in low-rise jeans and midriff-baring T-shirts, and boys in PIHS blue and yellow sweats. They'd probably come here from football and cheerleader practice.

"My bro is the one in the gray sweats," Mia said, leaning closer. "Don't judge him by the company he keeps. Those girls have the brains of breath mints."

It was the guy from first period.

He peeled away from the crowd with the ease of one who knew how popular he was and sidled up to Mia, putting an arm around her shoulders. The resemblance between them was startling; Mia's face was a feminine, sculpted version of his. He started to say something to his sister, and then he noticed Lexi. His gaze sharpened, grew so intense that she felt that fluttering start in her chest again. No one had ever looked at her like that before, as if everything about her was interesting.

"You're the new girl," he said quietly, pushing the long blond hair out of his eyes.

"She's my friend," Mia said, grinning so wide her braces were a multicolored blur.

His smile faded.

"I'm Lexi," she said, although he hadn't asked her her name.

He looked away from her, disinterested. "I'm Zach."

A girl in tiny shorts and a midriff-baring top moved in behind him, draped herself along his side, and whispered something in his ear. He didn't laugh, barely smiled in fact. Instead, he backed away from Lexi and Mia. "Later, Me-my," he said to his sister. Slinging an arm around short-shorts girl, he led her toward the stairs and disappeared into the crowd of kids running upstairs.

Mia frowned at her. "Is something wrong, Lexi? It's okay if I say you're my friend, right?"

Lexi stared at the empty place where he'd been, feeling unsettled. He'd smiled at her, hadn't he? At first, for a second? What had she done wrong?

"Lexi? Is it okay if I tell people we're friends?"

Lexi let out the breath she'd been holding. She forced her attention away from the stairs. Seeing Mia's nervousness, she realized what was important here, and it wasn't a guy like Zach. No wonder he confused her. He would always be incomprehensible to a girl who'd grown up in the weeds. What mattered was Mia and this fragile beginning of their friendship. "Of course," she said, smiling. For once, she didn't care about her teeth. She was pretty sure Mia wouldn't care. "You can tell everyone."

※

The media room was full of kids, as usual. Some women might be overwhelmed by the noise and mayhem, but not Jude. Years ago—back when the twins were starting sixth grade—she'd made a conscious effort to make her house welcoming. She wanted the kids to hang out here. She'd known herself well enough to know that she didn't want to be dropping her kids off into other women's care; she wanted to be the one in charge. To that end, she'd designed the upstairs carefully, and it had worked. Some days, there were fifteen kids here, eating their way through her snack provisions like locusts. But she knew where her children were and she knew they were safe.

Now, as she unlocked the great room's series of wood-framed pocket doors and opened them wide, she could hear movement upstairs; the floors groaned and footsteps thudded through the house.

For once, Mia wasn't hiding out from all that horseplay in the media room, she wasn't locked in her bedroom, watching *The Little Mermaid* or *Beauty and the Beast* or another of her Disney comfort movies. She was out on the beach, sitting on the sandy edge with Lexi beside her. A heavy woolen blanket wrapped them together; black and blond hair tangled together in the salty air. They'd been sitting out there for hours, talking.

Just the sight of it, of her daughter talking to a friend, made Jude smile. She had waited so long for this, hoped for it so fervently, and yet now that it had happened, she couldn't help worrying just a little. Mia was so fragile, so needy; it was too easy to hurt her. And after the thing with Haley, Mia couldn't take another friend's betrayal.

Jude needed to learn a little bit about Lexi, just to know who her daughter was hanging out with. It was a parenting choice that had yielded good results over the years. The more she knew about her kids' lives, the better mother she could be to them. She stepped out onto the patio. The breeze immediately plucked at her hair, whipped strands across her face. Without bothering to step into any of the shoes that lay cluttered outside the door, she walked barefooted across the flagstones, past the collection of dark, woven outdoor furniture. At the edge between the grass and the sand, a giant cedar tree rose tall and straight into the pellucid blue sky. As she approached the girls, she heard Mia say, "I want to try out for the school play, but I know I won't get a part. Sarah and Joeley always get the leads."

"I was totally scared to talk to you today," Lexi said. "What if I hadn't? It's no good to be afraid of stuff. You should go for it."

Mia turned to Lexi. "Would you come with me to tryouts? The other theater kids . . . they're so *serious*. They don't like me."

Lexi nodded, her face solemn with understanding. "I'll come. Definitely."

Jude stopped beside her daughter. "Hey, girls." She put a hand on Mia's slim shoulder.

Mia grinned up at her. "I'm going to try out for *Once upon a Mattress*. Lexi's gonna come with me. I probably won't get a part, but . . ."

"That's wonderful," Jude said, pleased by this development. "Well. I better take Lexi home now. Your dad will be home in an hour."

"Can I come with?" Mia asked.

"No. You have a paper due on Friday. You might as well get started on it," Jude answered.

"You're already checking the Web site? It's the first day of school," Mia said, her shoulders slumping.

"You need to stay on track. Grades matter in high school." She looked down at Lexi. "You ready?"

"I can take the bus," Lexi said. "You don't have to drive me."

"The bus?" Jude frowned. In all her years of parenting on this island, she had never had a child make that offer. Most said they could call their moms; none ever offered to take the bus. Where would one even catch a bus around here?

Lexi unwound herself from the red and white striped wool blanket. When she stood up, it slumped to the sand. "Really, Mrs. Farraday. You don't need to drive me home."

"Please, Lexi, call me Jude. When you say Mrs. Farraday, I think of my mother and that's not a good thing. Mia, go tell Zach I'm starting the drive. Ask him who else needs a ride."

Ten minutes later, Jude started up the Escalade. Five kids shoved their way into the plush interior, talking over one another as they buckled up their seatbelts. In the front passenger seat, Lexi sat quietly, staring straight ahead. Jude admonished Zach and Mia to start on their homework and then drove away. The route was so familiar she could have driven it in her sleep—left on Beach Drive, right on Night Road, left on the highway. At the top of Viewcrest, she pulled into her best friend's driveway. "Here you go, Bryson. Tell Molly we're still on for lunch this week."

He mumbled some kind of answer and got out of the car. For the next twenty minutes, she drove the standard route around the island, letting off one kid after another. Finally, she turned to Lexi. "Okay, hon, where to?"

"Isn't that a bus stop?"

Jude smiled. "I am not putting you on a bus. Now, where to, Lexi?"

"Port George," Lexi said.

"Oh," Jude said, surprised. Most of the kids at Pine High lived on the island, and, really, the other side of the bridge was a whole different world. Geographically, only about three hundred feet separated Pine Island from Port George, but there were many ways to calculate distance. Port George was where nice, upstanding boys from Pine Island went to buy beer and cigarettes at the minimart, using fake IDs they made on old magic cards. There was all kinds of trouble in the schools there. She drove out to the highway and headed off the island.

"Turn there," Lexi said about a mile from the bridge. "In fact, you can let me out here. I can walk the rest of the way."

"I don't think so."

Jude followed the signs to the Chief Sealth Mobile Home Park. From there, Lexi directed her down a winding road to a tiny plot of land, overgrown with weeds and grass, where a fading yellow double-wide sat on concrete blocks. The front door was an ugly shade of blue and cracked up the middle, and the curtains inside were ragged and unevenly hemmed. Rust inched like caterpillars along the seams. Deep, muddy ruts in the grass showed where a car was usually parked.

Jude parked at the edge of the grass and turned off the engine. This was hardly what she'd expected. "Is your mom home? I hate to just drop you off. I'd actually like to meet her."

Lexi looked at Jude. "My mom died three years ago. I live with my Aunt Eva now."

"Oh, honey," Jude said. She knew how it had felt to lose a parent—her father had died when Jude was seven. The world had become a dark and frightening place, and for years she'd been unsure of her place in it. "I'm so sorry to hear that. I know how difficult it must be for you."

Lexi shrugged.

"How long have you lived with your aunt?"

"Four days."

"Four days? But . . . where were you—"

"Foster care," Lexi said quietly, sighing. "My mom was a heroin addict. Sometimes we lived in our car. So I guess you don't want me hanging around with Mia anymore. I understand. Really. I wish my mom had cared who I hung out with."

Jude frowned. None of this was what she'd expected. It did worry her, all of it, but she didn't want to be that kind of woman, the kind who judged a person by his or her circumstance. And right now Lexi looked as beaten as any teenager Jude had ever seen. Everything about the girl radiated defeat; no doubt she'd been disappointed a lot in her life.

"I'm not like my mom," Lexi said earnestly. The need in the girl's blue eyes was unmistakable.

Jude believed her, but still, there was potential danger here. Mia was fragile, easily led astray. Jude couldn't simply ignore that, no matter how sorry she felt for this girl. "I'm not like my mother, either. But . . ."

"What?"

"Mia is shy. I'm sure you already know that. She doesn't make friends easily and she worries too much about being liked. She's always been that way. And last year, she had her heart broken. Not by a boy. It was worse than that. A girl—Haley—befriended her. For a few months, they were inseparable. Mia was as happy as I've ever seen her. But the truth was that Haley had her sights set on Zach, and he fell into her trap. He didn't know how it would upset Mia. Anyway, Haley dumped Mia for Zach, and when Zach lost interest, Haley refused to come to the house anymore. Mia was so hurt she stopped talking for almost a month. I was really worried about her."

"Why are you telling me this?"

"I guess . . . because if you're going to be her friend, she needs to know she can count on you. I'd like to know that, too."

"I would never do anything to hurt her," Lexi promised.

Jude thought of all the dangers this friendship could pose to her daughter, and all the benefits, and she weighed them, as if this decision were hers to make, although she knew it wasn't. A fourteen-year-old girl could make her own friends. But Jude could make it easy for Mia and Lexi to stay friends, or difficult. What was best for Mia?

When she looked at Lexi, the answer came easily. Jude was a mother, first, last, and always. And her daughter desperately needed a friend. "I'm taking Mia into the city on Saturday for manicures. A girls' day. Would you like to join us?"

"I can't," Lexi said. "I haven't got a job yet. Money's tight. But thanks."

"My treat," Jude said easily, "and I won't take no for an answer."

Three

2003

The last three years had both worn Jude down and sharpened her. She hadn't known how terrifying life could be until the first time she handed Zach and Mia car keys and watched them drive away. From that moment on, she'd begun to be afraid for her kids. Everything scared her. Rain. Wind. Snow. Darkness. Loud music. Other drivers. Too many kids in a car.

She'd issued her kids cell phones and instituted rules. Curfews. Accountability. Honesty.

She paced when they were minutes late and didn't breathe easily until they were safely in bed. She'd thought that was the worst of it, the freedom that came with a driver's license, but now she knew better.

It had all been a prelude to this: senior year of high school. The semester had just begun, and already it was a pressure cooker, a Rubik's Cube of deadlines and paperwork. College loomed on the horizon like a nuclear cloud, tainting every breath of air. Years of driving back and forth to sporting events, practices, play rehearsals, and performances was nothing compared with this.

On the wall above her desk she had two giant calendars, one marked ZACH and the other MIA. Every college deadline was written in red ink; every test date was in bold-face type. Jude had spent years studying admission statistics and reading about the various universities, gauging which would be best for her kids.

Getting into college would be a cakewalk for Zach. He had entered senior year with a 3.96 GPA and a perfect SAT score. He could go almost anywhere he wanted.

Mia was a different story. Her grades were good but not great; same with her SAT. Even so, she had set her heart on the prestigious University of Southern California drama school.

Jude had begun to lose sleep about it all. She lay in bed at night, going though admission statistics and criteria in her head until she felt sick. She was constantly figuring out how to make her daughter's dream come true. It wasn't easy to get *one* kid into an ultracompetitive school, and Jude needed to get two in. The twins had to go to college together; any other outcome was unthinkable. Mia needed her brother beside her.

And now, as if all that pressure weren't bad enough, the word she'd been dreading had just been said aloud.

Party.

Jude drew in a deep and steadying breath.

She was seated at the dinner table, with her family gathered around her. It was a Friday night in early October; the sky was the color of bruised plums.

"Well?" Zach said from his place at the table. "Can we go or not? Molly and Tim are letting Bryson go."

Mia was beside her brother. Her blond hair had been braided wet and dried into crimpy zigzags. In the past three years, she had blossomed into a true beauty, with flawless skin and a smile that was marquee bright. Her friendship with Lexi had stayed as true as magnetic North, and it had given Mia a new confidence. Her daughter still wasn't brave or extremely social, but she was happy, and that meant the world to Jude. "What about you, Mia? Do you want to go to this party?"

Mia shrugged. "Zach wants to go."

It was the answer Jude had expected. They were a pair, these two, in every way. Where one went, the other followed; it had been that way from the moment of their birth and probably before. One could hardly breathe without the other.

"Did you hear that, Miles?" Jude said. "The kids want to go to a party at Kevin Eisner's house."

"Is there a problem with that?" Miles asked, pouring hollandaise sauce on his grilled asparagus.

"The Eisners are in Paris, if I'm not mistaken," Jude said, seeing the twins flinch in unison. "Small island," she reminded them.

"Kevin's aunt is there, though," Zach said. "It's not like no adult is around."

"Totally," Mia added, nodding.

Jude sat back. She'd known this moment was coming, of course. She'd been a teenager herself, and senior year was the Holy Grail of teenhood. So, she knew what it meant when seniors wanted to "party."

She'd had endless conversations with the kids about alcohol, told them repeatedly how dangerous it could be, and they swore not to be interested in drinking, but she wasn't a fool. Neither was she the kind of woman who pretended her children were perfect. What mattered to her was protecting them from the risks associated with adolescence, even those of their own making.

She could say no. But they might defy her, and wouldn't they be more in danger then? "I'll call Kevin's aunt," she said slowly. "Make sure an adult is supervising the party."

"Oh my *God*," Mia whined, "way to totally humiliate us. We're not *children*."

"Really, Mom," Zach said. "You know you can trust us. I'd never drink and drive."

"I'd prefer it if you'd promise never to drink," she said.

He looked at her. "I might drink one beer. It won't kill me. You want me to lie to you? I thought that wasn't how we rolled in this family."

Her own words thrown back at her, and with deadly accuracy. The price for honesty with your kids was that often you learned what you'd rather not. The way Jude saw it, there were two parenting choices: ask for honesty and try to roll with unwanted truths or stick your head in the sand and be lied to. Zach's honesty was a reason to trust him. "I'll think about it," she said in a forceful enough voice to end the conversation.

The rest of the meal passed quickly. As soon as they cleared the table, the kids put the dishes in the dishwasher and then ran upstairs.

Jude knew they were getting ready for the party. They assumed victory—she'd seen it in their eyes.

"I don't know," she said to Miles. They stood side by side at the picture window, staring out at the darkening night. The Sound had turned graphite and the sky was a deep bronze color. "How do we stop them from drinking and keep them safe?"

"Chaining them to a wall would work. Too bad the state frowns on that."

"Very funny." She looked up at him. "We can't stop them from drinking—you know that. If not tonight, then some night they'll get drunk. That's just the way it is. So, what do we do to protect them? Maybe we should have a party here. We could take the kids' keys and make sure everyone stayed safe. We could make sure they don't drink too much."

"Uh. No. We'd be risking everything we own. Not to mention, if someone got hurt, we'd be responsible. And you know teenagers, they're like bacteria. They multiply too fast to see and you can't keep them in your sights. I can't believe you'd even suggest it."

Jude knew he was right, but it didn't help. "Do you remember high school? Because I sure do. Keggers at Morrow Farm were a weekly occurrence. And we drove home."

"You have to trust them, Jude. Let them start making some decisions. Mia's smart, and she sure as hell isn't a party girl. And Zach would never let anything bad happen to her. You know that."

"I guess." Jude nodded, thinking it all through for the thousandth time. There seemed to her to be no good answer. No indisputably right way to go.

For the rest of the evening, Jude wrestled with the question of how to be the best parent in this situation. She was still trying to figure it out at nine o'clock when the kids came running down the stairs.

"Well?" Zach said.

She looked at her kids. Zach, so tall and handsome and steady in his low-rise jeans and striped American Eagle sweatshirt, and Mia, in tattered blue jean capris, white T-shirt, and blue silk men's tie, knotted off to the side. She had her hair drawn back in a ponytail that geysered at the top of her head. She'd come out of her shell since meeting Lexi, but she was still fragile, a little needy. She could get her heart broken so easily, could make the wrong decision because she was afraid of being laughed at.

They were good kids. Honest kids who cared about their futures. They'd never given Jude any reason to mistrust them.

"Madre?" Zach said, smiling, reaching for her hand. "Come on. You know you can trust us."

Jude knew he was manipulating her, using her love to his advantage, but she was helpless to resist. She loved them both so much and she wanted them to be happy. "I don't know . . ."

Mia rolled her eyes. "This is like the witch trials. Can we go or not?"

"We said we won't drink," Zach said.

Miles came up beside Jude, slipped an arm around her waist. "We can count on your word, then?"

Zach's face split into a huge smile. "Absolutely."

"Your curfew is midnight," Jude said.

"*Midnight*?" Zach said. "That's so lame. Like we're middle schoolers. Come on, Mom. Dad?"

Miles said "Midnight," at the same time Jude said, "One o'clock."

Zach and Mia surged at her, drew her into a fierce hug.

"Stay safe," Jude said nervously. "If there's *any* trouble, call me. I mean it. If you drink—and you shouldn't—but if you do, call home.

Your dad and I will pick you up, and any of your friends. I mean it. No questions asked, no getting in trouble. I promise. Okay?"

"We know," Mia said. "You've told us for years."

And with that, they were off, running for the sporty white Mustang she and Miles had bought for them last year.

"You should have held firm at midnight," Miles said when the car door slammed shut.

"I know," she said. It was so easy for him. When Miles said no, they gave up. When she said no, they tried harder, boring through her resolve like boll weevils through corn, until there was nothing left between them and what they wanted.

Miles frowned as the red taillights of Zach's car disappeared into the darkness. "Senior year isn't going to be easy."

"No," Jude said. Already she regretted the decision to let them go. There were so many things that could go wrong . . .

❦

On a warm autumn night like this, Amoré was packed with customers. Summer was ending and everyone, locals and tourists alike, knew the cold season was moving their way.

Lexi had worked part-time at this ice cream shop since sophomore year. Every penny she earned went into her college fund. She and her boss, Mrs. Solter—a sixty-year-old widow with steel gray hair and a penchant for layering beaded necklaces—worked the counter in perfect synchronicity, one ringing sales while the other scooped ice cream.

Tonight, even though the place was busy, Lexi kept watching the clock. The party at the Eisners' place started at nine, and Mia and Zach were picking her up.

Zach.

He was the only fly in the ointment of her new life. In the past three years, Lexi had found a place where she belonged. Aunt Eva cared for her deeply; it was obvious, even though the woman wasn't demonstrative. Mia had become Lexi's other half, her sister. They were inseparable. And the Farradays had welcomed Lexi into their family with open arms, never judging her. Jude had become like a mother to her, so much so that on Mother's Day, Lexi always bought two cards—one for Eva and one for Jude. She always wrote *thanks* across the white space.

Only Zach held back.

He didn't like Lexi. That was all there was to it. He never stayed in a room alone with her longer than was absolutely necessary, and he hardly ever spoke to her. When he did say something to her, he looked away, as if he couldn't stand making eye contact. Lexi didn't know what she'd done to offend him, and no amount of reparations had helped. The worst part was that it hurt her feelings every time. Every time he looked away or walked away, she felt a little pinch of loss.

But it was a good thing; that was what she told herself. It was good that he didn't like her because she liked him too much. And one thing she knew for sure, had known from the beginning: Zach Farraday was off-limits.

At just past nine, she heard the Mustang drive up outside. She whipped off her multicolored apron and ran to the employees' bathroom for her purse. Snagging it off the wall, she glanced in the mirror just long enough to see that her makeup was still okay, and then headed for the front door, waving to Mrs. Solter as she passed.

"Be good," Mrs. Solter said with a happy little wave.

"I will," Lexi promised. She ran out to the Mustang and climbed into the backseat. The stereo was blaring so loudly that no one could talk.

Zach backed out of the parking stall and headed out of town. In no time at all, they were turning onto a long gravel driveway. At its end sat a quaint yellow Victorian, with a pitched shake roof and a big white wraparound porch. Lights hung from the eaves, illuminating baskets of flowers.

When they got out of the car, Lexi could hear the distant buzz of conversation and the music, but there were very few kids visible. They were probably down at the beach, where the neighbors were less likely to see them and thus less likely to complain to the local police.

Zach came around the car and stood by Lexi. She tried to act casual.

As usual, she couldn't manage it. She turned slightly and caught him staring down at her.

Before she could think of anything cool to say, Mia came up beside Lexi, held her hand. "Will Tyler be here?"

"Probably," Zach answered. "Let's go," he said, walking off.

Lexi and Mia followed him through the tall grass. When they reached the front yard, they saw the party. There were probably seventy-five kids in the yard; most were gathered around the fire. The sweet smell of pot filled the air.

Mia grasped Lexi's hand, yanked her to a stop. "There he is. How do I look?"

Lexi scanned the crowd until she saw Tyler Marshall. He was a tall, gangly kid with skateboarder hair who wore his baggy pants so low on his hips he was constantly yanking them up. Mia had had a crush on him since the end of junior year.

"You are beautiful. Go talk to him," Lexi said.

Mia's cheeks turned bright red. "I can't."

"I'll go with you," Lexi said, squeezing Mia's hand.

"You, too, Zach Attack?" Mia said.

Zach shrugged, and the three of them walked deeper into the party. They made their way past a pair of silver kegs and walked up to Tyler.

"Hey, Mia," Tyler said, giving her a bright grin. He held out a half-empty bottle. Raspberry vodka.

Mia reached for the bottle and took a drink before Lexi could even react.

"I guess that makes me the designated driver," Zach said. Then he added, "Be careful, Mia."

"You wanna walk on the beach?" Tyler asked Mia.

Mia gave Lexi a *wow* look and followed Tyler toward the beach.

Lexi was acutely aware of Zach beside her. He stood there, saying nothing, and yet she felt something in the quiet between them. Unable to help herself, she turned and looked up at him. "Why don't you like me?"

"Is that what you think?"

She didn't know how to answer. There seemed to be something going on she didn't understand. She wished she'd never asked the stupid question in the first place.

"Lexi—" he started.

Amanda Martin appeared in front of them as if by magic, holding a half-empty pint of Captain Morgan spiced rum. She was a leggy redhead with full lips and eyes that slanted gypsylike. Zach's latest girlfriend.

"There you are," she purred. "Took you long enough." She wrapped her arms around him and melted against him.

Lexi watched them walk away, all tangled together—he was kissing Amanda now—and felt a familiar sense of disappointment. Sighing, she wandered down to the beach. There, she met up with some of the kids from the drama club. For years, Lexi had been hanging out with these kids, watching them all rehearse with Mia. They sat around on the sand, talking. Of course, college came up. It was the big topic these days. From the very start of senior year, they'd been talking about deadlines and applications and admission stats. Every day, another university representative was in the library, talking to any senior who was interested. Weekend campus visits were becoming the norm. And the students from Pine Island didn't just go to downtown Seattle to check out schools. Oh, no. Their parents flew them all over the country.

"Lexster!" Mia's voice rose above the noise.

Lexi turned and saw Mia lurching toward her.

"I doan know how I got this drunk," Mia said, swaying dangerously. "Lexi, how did I get this drunk?"

"Drinking, maybe?" Lexi got up and put a steadying arm around Mia.

"I love you, Lexi," Mia whispered, but it was a drunk's whisper, stagey and slurred. She put an arm around Lexi. "You 'n Zach Attack are my bess friends."

"You're my best friend, too."

Mia slumped to a sit on the cold sand. When Lexi joined her, they leaned together. "Tyler said I'm pretty," Mia said. "Do you think he means it?"

"He'd be a fool not to."

"We danced," Mia said, her voice dreamy. She swayed for a moment and then went still. "I can't feel my lips. Are my lips still there?"

Lexi burst out laughing. "I think we better get you home. Let's go find Zach."

Lexi helped Mia to her feet and led her friend through the crowd. They found Zach in the shadows by the side of the house. Amanda was throwing herself at him. At least Lexi thought she was.

"Zach?" Lexi dared. "Mia's not in good shape. I think she needs to go home."

At that, Mia doubled over and vomited into the grass.

Zach rushed to Mia's side. "Are you okay?" he asked, putting an arm around her.

Mia swayed unsteadily, wiping her mouth. "I doan feel so good."

"Amanda?" Zach said. "Can she stay at your house? I can't bring her home like this."

"As if," Amanda said, making a sour face. "I'm not leaving the party this early. It's barely midnight." She gave Zach a long kiss and then walked away, flipping her hair as she headed back toward the keg.

"Mia can spend the night at my house," Lexi said. "Eva will be asleep by now."

Zach looked at her. "Really?"

"Sure."

Zach guided Mia back to the Mustang and put her in the backseat. It was like trying to make cooked spaghetti stand, and by the time he was finished, Mia was laughing uproariously and spread out across the seat. Snapping her seatbelt in place took forever.

Lexi got into the passenger seat while Zach started the engine. He backed up slowly and drove out to the main road.

As they sped down the highway toward the bridge, his fingers tapped out a rhythm on the leather-covered steering wheel. The music coming through the stereo was unfamiliar to Lexi, but its beat was strangely addictive. Mia was humming in the backseat, out of tune, as usual.

At the trailer, Lexi got out of the car, and Mia was right behind her, stumbling out, laughing as she fell to her knees in the damp grass. "Less go to our hill," she said, staggering back to her feet.

Zach rushed to his sister's side, held her up. "Hey, Mia," he said gently, "maybe you should go to bed."

Mia smiled drunkenly. "Yeah. Tha would be good."

Zach looked at Lexi. "I'll wait until she's in bed to leave, okay?"

"You don't have to do that. I know you want to get back to Amanda."

"You have no idea what I want."

Stung, Lexi went to Mia, took her from Zach. "Let's go, Mia." She guided her best friend across the damp grass and up into the mobile home. In the living room, Mia collapsed to the floor, giggling and moaning. "Sshh," Lexi said.

"I'll jus sleep for a sec . . ."

Lexi left Mia on the carpeted floor for a minute and went back outside. From the porch, she stared at Zach. Slowly, she moved toward him. He was looking at her now, *watching* her even, and his attention made something in the pit of her stomach flutter. "S-she's fine," she said.

"What's your hill?" he said.

"Mia and I hang out there. It's nothing."

"Can I see it?"

"I guess."

Lexi was aware of his footsteps cracking on twigs and branches as they pushed their way through the heavy salal and brush. The path was so thin you could only find it if you knew where it was. When she emerged into the open again, it was onto a high bluff of untended land that overlooked a busy strip of the highway, the glittering casino, and the black Sound beyond. "I come out here all the time," she said.

"It's cool." Zach sat down on the soft ground.

Lexi reluctantly sat beside him. They were so close she could feel his leg against hers.

She waited for him to say something, but he didn't.

Silence stretched out, turned uncomfortable. "So you guys are checking out colleges next weekend. That's cool," Lexi finally said. It was all she could think of.

He shrugged. "Whatever."

"You don't sound very excited about it."

"Mia says she'll die if we don't go to USC together. Don't get me wrong, I want to go to school with her, too, and I want to be a doctor like the old man, but . . ." He looked out over the casino and sighed.

"But what?"

He turned to her, caught her looking at him. "What if I can't cut it?" he said so quietly she barely heard his voice above the distant drone of highway noise.

She had known Zach for more than three years now, adoring him from a distance; she'd studied him like an archaeologist, culling through his words for hidden meaning. And never had he said anything like this to her. He sounded vulnerable and confused.

The night seemed to fall quiet; the buzz of the cars faded. All Lexi could hear was the beating of her heart and the even strains of their breathing. She was reminded of all the times she'd waited for her mother's return, only to be disappointed, discarded. If there was one emotion she understood profoundly, it was uncertainty. Never in her wildest dreams had she imagined that Zach could feel the same way. It made her feel connected to him, in tune. For one split second, he wasn't Mia's brother; he was the boy she'd seen on that first day of school, the one who'd made her heart speed up. "I didn't think you were ever afraid."

"Oh, I'm afraid of something." He leaned the slightest bit toward her. Maybe he was just shifting his seat on the hard dirt; she didn't know— she just knew how it felt to be afraid, and the way he was looking at her made it hard to breathe. Without really thinking, just feeling, she leaned toward him for a kiss.

She was just about to close her eyes when he jerked back. "What are you doing?"

The magnitude of what she'd almost done knocked the breath from her. He didn't even like her, and, worse than that, he wasn't available for her. Jude had made that clear; so had Mia. And Mia was what mattered, not some useless, baseless crush on a boy who fell in love with a different girl every week.

Horrified, she mumbled an apology, got to her feet, and started running through the brambles and bushes for the relative safety of her mobile home.

"Lexi, wait!"

She ran into the mobile home and slammed the door shut behind her. Mia lay at her feet, singing a song from *The Little Mermaid*.

Lexi stepped over her best friend and peeked out from between the curtains.

Zach stood there a long time, staring at the closed door. Then he finally went back to his car and started it up.

It wasn't until Lexi had brushed her teeth and put on her pajamas and crawled into bed with Mia that she let herself really think about what she'd almost done.

"You're an idiot, Lexi Baill," she said into the quiet.

"No you're not," Mia said; then she started to snore.

The next morning, Lexi stood at her bedroom window, staring out at the falling rain, feeling sick to her stomach. She couldn't believe that she'd almost kissed Zach last night.

What an idiot.

What should she do now? Tell Mia the truth, throw herself on her best friend's mercy and apologize for a moment of lunacy? But what if it ruined everything? And Zach would never tell. Or would he? Did he hate Lexi that much?

"I feel like crap."

Lexi heard the mattress creak against the wood-slatted bed frame. There was a pinging sound as Mia maneuvered to a sit. Lexi turned slowly around, feeling a fresh wave of shame.

Mia pushed the tangled blond hair out of her eyes, which were a little dazed looking, unfocused. A red scratch marred one pale cheek. Lexi had no idea how Mia had gotten the injury. No doubt Mia didn't either. "Man," she said. "I got roasted last night."

"You did." Lexi went back to the bed and climbed in beside her best friend.

Mia leaned against her. "Thanks for taking care of me. I swear I didn't drink that much." She banged her head back against the wall. "God, I hope my mom doesn't hear about this."

Lexi couldn't take it; the truth was corroding her from the inside out. She *had* to be a good friend to Mia. She had to be. "Speaking of last night. I did a really stup—"

Mia sat up suddenly. "Tyler asked me to the homecoming dance."

Lexi stopped. "What?" She and Mia usually hung out together on dance nights. Neither one of them had been asked to any of the dances last year. She felt vaguely jealous that this time she'd be sitting out the dance while Mia was having fun.

"You can come with us. Really. It'd be a blast. We could triple date with Amanda and Zach."

"Uh. No. And about Zach . . ."

"What about him?" Mia kicked back the covers and got out of bed. She stood there, a little unsteady on her feet, looking around the room for her pants.

"They're in the dryer. You puked on them last night."

"Gross." Mia padded out of the bedroom and headed down the hallway. The trailer shuddered at the weight of her steps.

Lexi followed Mia, stood in the hall while her friend slipped back into her jeans. She was about to bring up Zach again when Eva came out of her bedroom.

"Hey, Eva," Mia said with an obviously forced smile. "Thanks for letting me spend the night last night."

Eva said, "You're always welcome. Did you have fun last night?"

Mia smiled again, but it was ragged; her skin was a little gray. "We did. It was great." She put an arm around Lexi. "I don't know what I'd do without Lexi. She's the *best* friend ever."

Outside, a car horn honked.

"That'll be my mom," Mia said. "She texted me last night. We're going to visit my grandmother today. I better go."

Lexi followed Mia to the front door. In her mind, she blurted out her secret several times, and they laughed about it; in truth, she said nothing, just stared at Mia's long blond hair.

At the front door, Mia hugged her fiercely. "Thanks, Lexi. I mean it." She drew back, looking a little uncertain. "I'm sorry, you know. I shouldn't have lost it like that. You'll come to the dance with Ty and me, right?"

"Like I'm not lame enough already," Lexi said.

"Don't say that. We'll have a blast."

Outside, the car horn honked again.

"She's so OCD," Mia said, opening the door.

The white Mustang was parked out front, its engine purring, exhaust melting into the fog.

Zach got out of the car and stood there, staring at Lexi over the Mustang's white roof. Rain pelted his face, made him blink.

Mia flung her hoodie over her head and ran down to the car, getting in.

Lexi was certain she saw Zach shake his head slightly, as if to say, *it never happened . . . it can't happen.* Then he got back into his car.

Lexi watched them drive away, then went back into the trailer, closing the door behind her. He didn't want her to tell Mia. Was that what he'd meant?

Eva sat at the kitchen table, her hands cupped around her mug. "His car woke me up last night," she said, looking up. "So I went to the window. I din't expect you to come home."

Lexi tried to imagine the scene Eva had witnessed: Lexi practically carrying Mia up the stairs; Mia collapsing on the floor, singing. "I thought we'd be staying at the Farradays'."

"I'm pretty sure I know why you din't."

Lexi sat down across from Eva. "I'm sorry," she said, too ashamed to make eye contact. Aunt Eva would be disappointed in her now, maybe she'd even wonder if Lexi was like her mother after all.

"You want to talk about it?"

"I didn't drink anything, if that's what you think. I saw . . . my mom drink, so I'm . . ." She shrugged. There was no way to put all of that emotion into a few careful words. "I didn't drink anything."

Eva reached across the table and took hold of Lexi's hands. "I'm no warden, Alexa. You wouldn't know it to look at me, but I remember what it's like to be young, and I know how the world works. A girl can get in real trouble when she's in that condition. She can make a bad decision. I would hate for you to get hurt."

"I know."

"I know you know. And one more thing: Mia and her brother aren't like you. Those two got choices you don't. They'll get breaks you won't. You understand me?"

Lexi knew that; she'd known it from the first time she walked in the Farraday house. Mia could afford to make mistakes. Lexi couldn't.

"I'll be careful."

"Good." Eva looked at her. "And about that boy. I seen the way he ran after you. You be careful there, too."

"He doesn't like me. You don't have to worry about that."

Eva studied her carefully. Lexi wondered what she saw. "You just be careful around him."

$\mathcal{F}our$

Jude loved her garden in October. It was a time of organization, of planning for the future. She lost herself in the work of planting bulbs, imagining how each choice would alter the garden next spring. And she needed that now, to find a kind of peace.

The past five days had been stressful for her, although she couldn't exactly say why. She hadn't wanted the kids to go to the party, but they had, and it had gone uneventfully. Zach had come home right on time, and she'd hugged him tightly (smelling his breath) and sent him to bed. She'd seen no evidence of drinking, and Mia had spent the night with Lexi and come home smiling the next day. Apparently, nothing had gone wrong. So why did she think something had? Maybe Miles was right, and she was seeing problems where none existed.

She sat back on her heels and clapped her hands together to release the dirt clinging to her gloves. Tiny black particles rained down, creating a lacy pattern on her thighs.

She was just about to reach for the clippers lying in the dirt beside her when she heard a car. She looked up, tented a gloved hand across her eyes, and saw sunlight glint off the silver hood of a brand new Mercedes.

"Crap," she muttered. She'd forgotten about the time.

The car pulled up in front of the low stone wall that outlined her front garden.

Jude pulled off her dirt-caked gloves and stood up as her mother got out of the car. "Hello, Mother."

Caroline Everson walked around her bullet car and into the vibrant garden with the bearing of an ice pick. She was dressed, as always, winter or summer, in a pair of black wool pants and a fitted blouse that showcased her toned, fit body. Her white hair was drawn back from her angular face; the severity of the style offset her bottle-green eyes to perfection. At seventy, she was still a beautiful woman. And successful; that was what mattered to Caro. Success. "Have you agreed to be on the garden tour yet?"

Jude wished she'd never revealed that little dream to her mother. "It's not ready yet. Soon, though."

"Not ready? It's beautiful."

Jude heard the derisiveness in her mother's tone and tried not to let it wound her. Caroline saw no point in hobbies. The end game was what mattered to her mother, and until Jude showed this garden on the island tour, she would somehow be a failure. "Come inside, Mother. Lunch is ready." Without waiting for a response, Jude led the way toward the front door. On the porch, she slipped out of her gardening clogs, brushed the dirt off her pants, and then went inside.

Sunlight poured through the home's twenty-foot-tall windows, made the exotic wood floors glow like burnished copper. An immense granite fireplace dominated the great room, which was decorated in soothing neutrals. The real star of this room was the view: soaring glass panels captured a swatch of emerald grass, a layer of steel blue Sound, and the distant Olympic Mountains.

"Can I get you a glass of wine?" Jude asked.

Her mother set down her purse so carefully it might have held explosives. "Of course. Chardonnay, if you have it."

Jude was glad for the excuse to leave the room. She passed through the dining area, created by a long bird's-eye maple table and ten chairs, to the open kitchen beyond. The only time she couldn't see her mother was when she opened the wood-paneled door of the Sub-Zero refrigerator.

When she returned to the great room, her mother was standing at the end of the sofa, looking up at the huge canvas that hung above the fireplace. It was a gorgeous, abstract work of art—swiping, curling streams of amber and red and black that somehow managed to convey a buoyant happiness. Mother had painted it decades ago, and Jude still had trouble reconciling the work's glorious optimism with the woman standing in front of it now.

"You should replace that piece. The gallery has some lovely work now," her mother said.

"I like it," Jude said simply, and it was true. This piece had been her father's favorite—she remembered standing with him as a little girl, her small hand tucked in his bear-paw grasp, watching Mother paint it. *Look at the way she does that, it's magic,* he'd said, and for a time Jude had believed it, believed there was a kind of magic in their home. "I remember watching you paint it."

"A lifetime ago," her mother said, turning her back on the painting. "Why don't you go clean up? I'll wait."

Jude handed her mother the glass of wine and then left the room. She took a quick shower and changed into a pair of comfortable jeans and a black V-necked sweater and returned to the great room, where her mother was seated on the sofa, her spine straight, sipping at the wine like a hummingbird.

Jude sat opposite her mother. A large stone coffee table separated them. "Lunch is ready anytime you're hungry," Jude said. "I've made us a Waldorf salad."

At that, they lapsed into their usual silence. Jude couldn't help wondering why they continued this pretense. Once a month, they met for a meal—trading locations back and forth as if it mattered where they were. During a lunch of healthy food and expensive wine, they pretended to have something to talk about, a relationship.

"Did you see the article in *The Seattle Times*? The one about the gallery?" her mother asked.

"Of course. You sent it to me. You said how important motherhood is to you."

"And it is."

"Nannies notwithstanding."

Mother sighed. "Oh, Judith Anne. Not that old whine again."

"I'm sorry. You're right," Jude said, and not because it was the only response that would end the conversation. It was true. Jude was forty-six years old. She should have forgiven her mother by now. Then again, her mother had never asked for forgiveness, never thought it necessary, even though she'd checked out of motherhood as if it had been a cheap motel. Fast and in the middle of the night. Jude had been seven years old and suddenly upended by grief, and yet, after her father's funeral, no one had thought to reach out for her, certainly not her own mother, who went back to work the very next day. In all the years that came after, her mother had never stopped working. She'd given up painting and become one of the most successful gallery owners in Seattle. She nurtured young artists while entrusting her daughter's care to one nanny after another. They'd had no relationship whatsoever until about five years ago, when Caroline had called and scheduled lunch. Now, once a month, they pretended. Jude didn't even know why.

"How are the children?" her mother asked.

"Wonderful," Jude said. "Zach's grades are phenomenal and Mia has become a talented actress. Daddy would have been proud of her."

Her mother sighed. It didn't surprise Jude, that small exhalation of breath. Dad as a topic was off-limits. Jude had been a daddy's girl; neither one of them wanted to acknowledge that now, all these years after his death, although Jude still missed him and his bear hugs. "I'm sure you're right," her mother said, smiling tightly. "I assume Zach can go to any school he wants. I hope he continues with his plans to become a doctor. It would be a shame if he quit his studies."

"I suppose that's another reminder that I quit law school. I was pregnant and Miles was in medical school. We hardly had a choice."

"You lost the baby," her mother said, as if that was what mattered.

"Yes," Jude said quietly, remembering. She'd been young and in love, and honestly, for most of her life, she'd been afraid of motherhood, afraid that she would discover in herself some genetic anomaly that had been passed down from Caroline. She and Miles had gotten pregnant accidentally—too soon, when they weren't ready—and Jude had discovered from the inception how profoundly she could love. The very *idea* of motherhood had transformed her.

"You have always loved your children too much. You care too much about making them happy."

Parenting advice from her mother. *Perfect.* Jude smiled thinly. "It's impossible to love your children too much. Although I wouldn't really expect you to understand that."

Her mother flinched. "Judith, why is it that you give that girl from the trailer park the benefit of every doubt, and you give me none?"

"Lexi—and you certainly know her name by now—has been like a part of this family for the past three years. She has never disappointed me."

"And I have."

Jude didn't answer. What was the point? Instead, she stood up. "How about we have lunch now?"

Her mother rose. "That would be nice."

They spent the rest of the appointed time—exactly two hours, from twelve to two, talking about things that didn't matter. When it was over, Mother kissed Jude perfunctorily on the cheek and went to the entry, where she paused. "Good-bye, Judith. Today was lovely. Thank you."

"Good-bye, Mother."

Jude stared through the open door at her mother's slim figure, walking fast through the garden, not bothering to look at any of it. As hard as she tried to feel nothing, Jude experienced the free-form depression that always accompanied these lunches. Why was it that she couldn't quite stop wanting her mother's love? The Mercedes came to life with a throaty purr and drove slowly up the driveway.

On the entry table, a cordless phone lay next to a glass bowl filled with floating roses. Jude picked it up and punched in her best friend's number.

"Hello?"

"Molly. Thank God," Jude said, leaning against the wall. Suddenly, she was exhausted. "The wicked witch was just here."

"Your mother? Is it Wednesday?"

"Who else?"

"You want a drink?"

"I thought you'd never ask."

"Twenty minutes. Dockside?"

"See you there."

⁂

On Friday, after school, they went shopping for dresses. Jude was ridiculously pleased about the whole thing. She knew it was just a dance, nothing earth-shattering, but it was Mia's first real date, and Jude was eager to make the whole experience perfect for her daughter. To that end, she'd set up manicures and pedicures for both of them—and Lexi, of course—and an evening of shopping at the mall.

She heard her bedroom door open and she turned. Miles stood in the doorway. He leaned against the doorjamb, wearing a pair of well-worn Levi's and an Aerosmith T-shirt. In the pale autumn light, he looked ruggedly handsome. A gray stubble had grown out during the day, giving his face a sculpted look. "I come home from work early and you're leaving?"

Smiling, she went to him, let him take her in his arms. "Why is it, Dr. Farraday, that you don't shave and your hair starts going gray and you manage to look more handsome, but if I forget makeup for one day, people mistake me for Grandma Moses?"

"They only call you that behind your back."

"Very funny."

He touched her jawline, a featherlight caress. "You're beautiful, Jude, and you know it. It's why things go your way."

It was true for both of them. Miles had been golden from childhood. Good-looking and brilliant, with a ready smile, he seduced people without even trying. His nickname at the hospital was Doc Hollywood.

"Take Zach out for dinner. I'll be home as soon as I can. Maybe we can sit on the beach tonight and have a glass of wine. We haven't done that in a while."

Miles drew her in for a kiss that meant something. Then he swatted her butt. "You better go before I remember how much I like afternoon sex."

"As opposed to morning sex and evening sex, which you hate?" She twirled playfully out of his grasp and headed upstairs.

At Zach's bedroom door, she knocked, waited for a "come in," and opened the door. He sat in that expensive new game chair of his, playing something on his Xbox. She touched his head, scratched his hair. His hair was still damp from football practice. He lifted up into her touch, straining like a flower toward the sun.

"We're going to the mall to buy Mia a dress for the dance. You want to come?"

He laughed. "I'm not even going to the dance, remember? Amanda will be in L.A. with her family."

Jude sat down on the bed. "I hate that you're not going. It's senior year. And Mia tells me you're a shoo-in for homecoming king."

Zach rolled his eyes. "Big deal."

"You should take a friend to the dance. Someday you'll look back—"

"If I care about that crap in the future, shoot me. Really."

Jude couldn't help smiling. "Okay, fine. But at least come shopping with us. It would mean a lot to Mia."

"I thought Lexi was going."

"She is. What does that have to do with it?"

"Mia has a friend with her. And I am *not* sitting outside a dressing room while my sister tries on dresses. No way."

"Okay, but I'm not giving up on the dance."

"There's a shock," he said with a grin. "You're not giving up on something. And do *not* buy me jeans again. I mean it, Mom. You don't get what I like."

"Fine. Fine." Jude scratched his head one last time and turned away from him.

She left Zach's room and met Mia in the hallway. Together, they went out to the garage. In fifteen minutes, they had picked up Lexi and were on their way to the mall.

At the first store, Mia wandered among the racks, looking a little confused and overwhelmed, and then suddenly she pulled out a dress. "Look at this one," she said, holding up a floor-length salmon-pink dress with lacy sleeves and a tiered skirt. "What do you think?" she asked Lexi.

Lexi smiled, but it was a little distracted. "It's great. Try it on."

"Only if you'll try one on, too. Please? I can't do it alone. You know I can't."

Lexi sighed. She went to the rounder, found an aquamarine-blue gown with a beaded, strapless bodice, and followed Mia into the dressing rooms.

When they came out, Jude was stunned by how beautiful they both looked. "Those are perfect," she said.

Mia studied her own reflection as she spun around. "These are definitely our dresses for homecoming, don't you think, Lexster?"

"I'm not going to the dance," Lexi said. "I don't have a date."

Mia stopped twirling. "Then I'm not going either."

Lexi muttered something under her breath and walked back into the dressing room. When she came back out, she was dressed in her jeans and T-shirt. "No more dresses for me," she said. "I can't afford one anyway."

"Come on, Lexi," Mia pleaded. "You're my best friend. If you don't go to the dance, I won't go."

"She could go with Zach," Jude said.

Mia shrieked. "That's a *great* idea, Mom. We can totally double-date."

Lexi gasped. "I am *not* going to force your brother to take me to a stupid dance." On that, she walked away from them.

Tears immediately brightened Mia's eyes. "Did I hurt her feelings, Mom? I didn't mean to."

Jude watched Lexi leave the store. "You didn't do anything wrong," she said softly. "We all just . . . forget sometimes that Lexi doesn't have the same opportunities that you do. We should have been a little more sensitive. Come on." They walked over to the register, where Jude paid for both dresses. She had the clerk box up Lexi's. "Go get dressed, Poppet. I'll take care of Lexi."

Jude walked out of the small boutique and into the busy mall, carrying a shopping bag. Everywhere she looked, she saw packs of girls, no doubt armed with their parents' credit cards. No wonder Lexi was out of sorts. It had to be difficult to be different from all the kids you knew, from your best friend, who just expected to get what she wanted.

Jude saw Lexi sitting on the bench outside the bookstore. She was slumped forward, with her long black hair falling across her downcast face.

Jude went to her, sat down. Lexi scooted sideways to make room for her.

"Sorry for the rant," Lexi mumbled.

"I should have been more sensitive. I know those dresses are expensive."

"It's not that."

Jude tucked the hair back behind Lexi's ear so she could see the girl's face. "I didn't mean to embarrass you."

"It's cool. I shouldn't have made such a big deal out of it."

Jude sat back. Her heart ached for Lexi; she knew how hard life had been for the girl, how hard it still was sometimes. While most of the island kids—like her own—were looking all over the country for the perfect college, Lexi was planning on going to the local junior college after graduation. She worked too many hours at the ice cream shop, saving every cent she earned. Her pie-in-the-sky dream was a full scholarship to the UW, but those were few and far between. It pained Jude to think that Lexi would miss the rite-of-passage senior year homecoming dance. "I hear Zach has a good chance of being homecoming king."

"He will be."

"And Kaye Hurtt is a shoo-in for queen."

"It could be Maria de la Pena."

"But Zach won't be there because Amanda's going to be out of town."

Lexi tilted her face to Jude. If Jude hadn't known better, she would have said Lexi looked scared. "I didn't know that."

"I don't want either one of you to miss the dance. Zach would never take a real date, not while he's with Amanda, but you're his sister's best friend. Amanda wouldn't mind. And then all three of you could have fun at the dance. You'll always remember it."

"I don't think it's a good idea," Lexi said quietly. "What about what happened with Haley?"

"Oh, honey. You would never do something like that to Mia. This is a whole different thing." Jude smiled. She knew how sensitive Lexi was to overstepping her welcome, but this would be good for everyone. "How about if we let Zach decide?"

Lexi stared at her for a long time, saying nothing.

"It's not a sympathy date, Lexi. It's a night out for friends. And I really think Zach should be there when he's named homecoming king, don't you?"

Lexi sighed. "Yeah."

Jude held out the shopping bag. "I bought the dress for you."

"I can't accept that," Lexi said. "It's too much."

Jude saw Lexi's gratitude, but there was something else in the girl's blue eyes, a dark, smoky shame that broke Jude's heart. "You're part of the family, Lexi. You know that. Let me do this for you, okay? I know you want to go to the dance. Let Zach take you."

Lexi looked down at the tile floor. The hair behind her ear fell free again, shielded her profile from Jude. "Okay, Jude," she finally said, softly. "If Zach wants to take me, I'll go with him. But . . ."

"But what?"

Lexi shook her head; her hair shimmered at the movement. "Don't be surprised if he says no."

Five

"Okay. Open your eyes," Jude said, putting her hands on Lexi's shoulders.

Lexi drew in a deep breath and did as she was told. In front of her was a big mirror surrounded by tiny globe lights. For a split second, she saw a stranger—a girl with sleek, glossy black hair, layered now around her face, and perfectly arched eyebrows. Carefully applied violet eyeliner had enhanced her blue eyes, given her a smoky, sophisticated look, and blush highlighted her high cheekbones. She was almost afraid to smile, in case it was an illusion.

Jude leaned closer. "You're beautiful."

Lexi slipped out of the chair and turned around. "Thank you," she said, hugging Jude tightly.

Later, on the ferry home, she and Mia sat in the backseat of the Escalade, with Jude in the driver's seat. Lexi kept sneaking looks at herself in the mirror. She wanted to believe it would make a difference somehow, this transformation, that Zach would finally look at her and think she was pretty. But she knew better.

Tonight was not going to go well. Honestly, she couldn't fathom why he'd agreed to take her to the dance—probably because Jude and Mia had pressured him mercilessly, and one thing was always true: Zach hated to disappoint his sister.

If only Lexi hadn't almost kissed him. None of this would be a problem if she'd never turned to him that night. Or if she'd told Mia the truth. If only . . . if only. It was a list that went on and on, and she'd reread it so many times in her mind that she felt sick to her stomach.

It had been a week since the party—since the hilltop. Lexi had repeatedly intended to tell Mia the truth, but she hadn't. She couldn't, and now, for the first time, when she saw her best friend, Lexi felt like a liar. And every time she saw Zach, she ran like a track star. She was terrified that she'd ruined everything, that when her secret came out, she'd lose Mia's friendship and Jude's respect. Everything that mattered to her.

"I should have said no," Lexi muttered later, as she and Mia bounded up the stairs at the Farraday house to get dressed. "This has disaster written all over it."

"I don't get you," Mia said, closing the door behind them. "I really don't."

Lexi immediately felt guilty. "Sorry. It'll be fun. I can't wait." She went to Mia's overflowing closet, where both dresses hung between sheets of plastic. They dressed and studied themselves in the oval mirror by the desk. Only occasionally could Mia's black-and-white Converse high-tops be seen under her hemline.

"I think I look okay," Mia said, turning to Lexi. Her green eyes held worry. "Don't I? Will he think so?"

"You look gorgeous. Tyler will—"

A knock at the door interrupted them. There was a pause, then it opened. Jude stood there, holding a silver camera. "Tyler is here."

Mia looked nervously at Lexi. "How do I look?"

"Totally hot. He's lucky to have you."

Mia threw her arms around Lexi and hugged her tightly. "Thank

God you're with me. I don't know if I'd have the guts to go downstairs without you."

Holding hands, they left the bedroom and walked down the big curving staircase.

Zach and Tyler were in the living room, standing together, talking. Both were wearing blue suits. Zach's hair was still wet—the football game had just ended and he'd raced home to get ready.

He looked up and saw Lexi. She saw the way he frowned as she came down the stairs. Her heart started beating so fast she felt light-headed.

Be cool, she thought.

She'd say she was sorry right away, laugh it off, that stupid near-kiss. Maybe she'd say she'd been drunk and didn't remember any of it. Could she pull that off?

As she neared him, Zach stepped forward, offering her a blue-tipped white carnation in a clear plastic box. "Thanks," she mumbled.

"It's got, like, a rubber band on it; it goes on your wrist," he said. "Amanda says they're the best kind."

"Thanks," she said again, not daring to look at him. He'd mentioned his girlfriend; she got the point.

"Okay, picture time," Jude said. Miles came up beside her. "We'll need fingerprints from you, Tyler," he said.

"*Dad!*" Mia shrieked, blushing.

Lexi moved awkwardly into place beside Zach. He put an arm around her, but didn't pull her close. They stood like images from an Old West photograph, stiff and unsmiling.

Flash. Click.

The photographs went on and on, until finally Zach said, "No more, dos amigos. We're outta here."

As they started for the door, Lexi pulled away from Zach. She stepped into the entryway, where she'd left a brown shopping bag by the table. Reaching inside, she pulled up a small green plastic container that held a potted purple petunia.

"This is for you," Lexi said to Jude, feeling her face grow hot. It was such a little gift—she'd found it on the half-price counter at the local nursery. It was probably totally the wrong thing, but it was all Lexi could afford. "I know you don't really need anything, but I looked . . . and you don't have any petunias, so I thought . . . anyway, thanks for the dress."

Jude smiled. "Thank you, Lexi."

"Come on, Lexster," Mia said from the doorway.

Lexi walked to the door with Jude, and then followed Mia out to the Mustang.

"One o'clock curfew," Jude yelled from the doorway.

Zach didn't seem to be listening. He walked on ahead to the Mustang, which was parked out front. He opened Lexi's door but didn't wait for her to get in. Instead, he walked around to the driver's side.

When Mia and Tyler were settled in the backseat, Lexi took her place beside Zach. He started up the car and cranked on the music.

All the way to the high school, Mia and Tyler whispered together. Zach kept his eyes on the road. He seemed pissed off at Lexi, or at the fact that she was his date. She could hardly blame him. In the school lot, he parked close to the stairs, and the four of them merged into the colorful river of kids streaming into the gymnasium, which had been transformed into a tacky version of New Orleans, complete with streamers and fake moss. The Mardi Gras theme continued when they walked into the gym, where a chaperone handed them a handful of brightly colored bead necklaces.

The song playing was "Hella Good," and the dance floor was overflowing.

They got their pictures taken first—each couple alone, then the girls, then Mia and Zach.

Lexi could see how stiff Zach was. Every girl in the senior class seemed to be watching them. No doubt Amanda had asked for a full report, and Zach wasn't going to do anything to hurt his girlfriend's feelings. He wouldn't even look at Lexi.

Finally, he took her hand and led her out onto the dance floor. As they got there, the music changed, slowed down. He took her in his arms.

Lexi stared at his chest, tried to move with him and not step on his feet. Honestly, she had no idea how to dance, and she was so nervous, she couldn't breathe. Finally, she looked up and found him staring down at her, his eyes unreadable. "I know you didn't want to take me to the dance, Zach. I'm sorry."

"You don't know anything."

"I'm sorry," was all she could think of to say.

He grabbed her by the hand and pulled her through the crowd. She stumbled along behind him, trying to keep up, smiling at the people she pushed past so it didn't seem weird that Zach was pulling her off the dance floor.

He kept going, past the punch bowl and the row of parent/teacher chaperones and through the big doors to the football field. There, everything was black and still. The stars overhead joined with a bright moon and set the goalposts aglow.

Zach finally stopped. "Why did you try to kiss me?"

"I didn't. I lost my balance. It was stupid . . ." She sighed and looked up, immediately wishing she hadn't.

"What if I wanted you to?"

"Don't mess with me, Zach," she said. Her voice cracked, betraying her. She knew his reputation. He probably said things like this all the time. He went through girlfriends like she went through lip gloss. "Please."

"Can I kiss you, Lex?"

In her mind, she said no, but when Zach looked down at her, she shook her head, unable to find her voice.

"If you're going to stop me," he said, pulling her close, "this would be the time."

And then he was kissing her and she was falling and flying, twisting into someone else, some*thing* else. When he finally drew back, he looked as pale and shaky as she felt, and she was glad of that, because she was crying.

Crying. What an idiot . . .

"Did I do something wrong?"

"No."

"So, why are you crying?"

"I don't know."

"Zach!"

Lexi heard Mia's voice and she lurched away from Zach, wiping the stupid tears from her eyes.

Mia ran up to them. "They're crowning the homecoming king and queen. You better get in there."

"I don't give a shit about that. I'm talking to Lexi—"

"Go," Mia said.

Zach looked at Lexi again, frowning; then he walked off, headed for the gymnasium.

"What were you two doing out here?" Mia asked.

Lexi started walking toward the gym. She didn't dare look at her best friend. "He wanted to tell me something about the game tonight." She forced a laugh. "You know me. I don't know jack about football." She winced. Another lie to her best friend. Who was she becoming?

It was the last time that night she and Zach were alone together until he walked her up to the front door of the mobile home, and even then, Mia was in the car, watching them.

At her door, Lexi had no idea what to say to him. Everything felt off balance; she was like some prey animal, frozen with fear, her senses acute. The kiss had rocked her world, but had it even made a ripple in his?

He stared down at her, his golden hair turned silver by the moonlight.

She wanted to scream *say something* but managed only a shaky smile. "Thanks for letting me be your sympathy date, Zach."

"Don't say that," he said.

"Curfew," Mia yelled from the car. "Mom will have a cow if we're late."

Zach leaned down, kissed Lexi's cheek. It took all her effort not to respond, not to put her arms around him, but she just stood there, feeling his lips on her skin like a branding iron.

She stood there a long time, long after they'd left. Then, finally, she went into her house and turned off the lights.

Lexi didn't go to school on Monday. How could she face either Zach or Mia after what had happened?

By Monday night, though (and he hadn't called, of course he hadn't, why would she think he would?), Eva had threatened to make a doctor's appointment—something they definitely couldn't afford.

So, on Tuesday, Lexi went back to school. Out at the bus stop, she huddled under the narrow shelter's overhang, watching rain turn the world into a blue and green kaleidoscope.

She would just be cool.

She'd smile casually at Zach and keep walking, as if the kiss meant nothing. She wasn't a complete idiot. It had just been a kiss from a boy who kissed girls all the time. Lexi couldn't let it mean anything to her.

At school, she easily avoided Zach—they hardly moved in the same social circles—but there was no way to avoid Mia. Their lives were too braided together. After the last bell, Mia walked Lexi to work.

All the way downtown, Lexi kept a smile on her face as she listened to Mia's dance play-by-play. Again. But the word *liar* screamed through her mind over and over, and every time she looked at her best friend, she felt sick to her stomach.

"We made out. Did I tell you that?" Mia said.

"Only about a million times." Lexi stopped in front of Amoré, where a sweet, vanilla-scented air enveloped them. She meant to just say *later* and go inside, but instead she paused. "What was it like?"

"At first I thought his tongue was kinda slippery and gross, but I got used to it."

"Did you cry?"

"Cry?" Mia looked confused, then nervous. "Should I have cried?"

Lexi shrugged. "What do I know about kissing?"

Mia frowned at Lexi. "You're acting weird. Did something happen at the dance?"

"Wh-what could have happened?"

"I don't know. Something with Zach, maybe?"

Lexi hated herself; she wanted to tell the truth, but the thought of losing Mia's friendship terrified her. And what would be the point, really? It had just been a single kiss, not the start of anything. "No, of course not. I'm fine. Everything's fine."

"Okay," Mia said, believing her. And that just made Lexi feel worse. "Later."

Lexi walked into the ice cream shop. It was brightly lit, with a long glass and chrome ice cream counter and a small area that contained a few tables and chairs. In the warmer months, this place was hopping busy, but now, in mid-October, business was pretty slow.

Her boss, Mrs. Solter, was standing at the register when Lexi walked in. A bell tinkled over the door at her entrance.

"Hey, Lexi," Mrs. Solter said brightly. "How was your dance?"

Lexi forced a smile. "Great. Here. I brought you some necklaces." She held out the Mardi Gras beads from the dance. Mrs. Solter lit up at the sight of them and swooped in like a magpie for the shiny necklaces.

"Thank you, Lexi. That was thoughtful of you." Mrs. Solter immediately put all the necklaces around her neck.

Lexi spent the rest of the day and into the evening waiting on customers. At nine o'clock, when business had slowed down to almost nothing, she set about cleaning the counters and getting ready to close up. She was coming out of the back room, carrying a container of Windex and a soggy rag, when Zach walked into the shop.

The bell tinkled gaily above him; she could barely hear it over the sudden acceleration of her heartbeat.

He *never* came here alone. Amanda was always with him, hanging on to him like that Louisiana moss you saw in horror flicks. Lexi slipped behind the counter so there was something between them.

"Hi," he said, moving toward her.

"Hi. You . . . want ice cream?"

He looked at her intently. "Meet me at LaRiviere Park tonight."

Before she could answer, the bell tinkled again and the door flew open. Amanda rushed into the shop and sidled up to Zach, putting her tentacle-arm around him. "Hey, Lexi. Thanks for keeping an eye on Zach for me. At the dance, I mean."

Lexi couldn't smile, even though she wanted to. "You want ice cream?"

"No way. It's too fattening," Amanda said. "Come on, Zach. Let's go." She moved toward the door.

Zach stayed where he was. *Ten o'clock,* he mouthed. *Please.*

Lexi's heart was pounding as she watched him follow his girlfriend out of the shop.

Ten.

She would be an idiot to think he really meant for her to meet him at the beach. He was dating Amanda, the human Post-it note. They were the most popular couple in school.

And it would hurt Mia if she found out. A kiss at the dance was one thing, almost understandable even, ordinary. This—sneaking out to be with him—would be something else. A bigger lie.

Lexi couldn't do it. Shouldn't do it.

She glanced over at her boss. *Don't do it, Lexi.* "Uh, Mrs. Solter? I was wondering if I could leave a few minutes early. Maybe nine-fifty?"

"I'm sure I can handle closing up by myself," she said. "Hot date?"

Lexi hoped her laughter didn't sound as nervous as it felt. "When have you ever known me to have a hot date?"

"Those boys at your school must be blind, that's all I'm saying."

For the remainder of her shift, Lexi refused to think about the decision she'd made. She focused on her job and did it to the best of her ability. It wasn't until later, when she left the shop, that nerves got the best of her.

She was an idiot to do this, but she kept walking.

Main Street was quiet on this chilly autumn night. Lights glowed through restaurant windows, but there were few patrons at this hour.

She passed the brightly lit Island Center grocery store and kept going, past the ferry terminal, past the Windermere Real Estate office and the Lil Ones Nursery School. In less than five minutes, she was out of town. Here, black stained the sky; a bright blue moon glowed above the towering treetops. There weren't many houses out this way, and the few that were here were mostly summer homes for Seattleites, and their windows were dark.

At the entrance to LaRiviere Beach Park, she paused.

He wouldn't be here.

Still, she followed the winding asphalt road down to the sandy stretch of beach. Moonlight shone on the tangle of giant driftwood piled up on the coarse gray sand.

There were no cars in the parking area.

Of course there weren't.

She walked out to the beach. The pile of giant driftwood—whole trees washed up onto the shore and tangled together—lay like giant toothpicks on the sand. A brightly lit ferry chugged through the Sound, looking like a Chinese lantern against the black water. Behind it, the Seattle skyline was a tiara of colored lights.

"You're here."

She heard Zach's voice and turned. "I didn't see your car," was all she could think to say.

"It's at the end of the other lot."

He took her by the hand and led her to a place where he had a blanket spread out on the sand.

"I guess you've brought a few girls here," she said nervously. She needed to remember that. What was special for her was ordinary for him.

He sat down and pulled her gently down beside him. She immediately took her hand back. She couldn't be smart when he was touching her, and she needed to be smart. This was her best friend's brother.

He said, "Look at me, Lexi. Please," and she was helpless to resist. He tucked a curly strand of hair behind her ear. It was the gentlest touch she'd ever felt, and it made her want to cry. "I know we shouldn't be together. Do you want to be, though?"

"I shouldn't," she said quietly. She closed her eyes, unable to look at him. In the darkness, she heard his breath, felt it against her lips, and all she could think about was how often she'd been hurt. Lexi thought about her druggo mom, who'd told her all the time how much she loved her. She'd hold Lexi so tightly Lexi couldn't breathe, and then suddenly it would be over. Her mom would get pissed and storm off and forget she even had a daughter. The only time Lexi remembered ever being happy before Pine Island was when her mother went to prison. Lexi had been with a nice family then, the Rexlers, and they'd tried to make her feel as if she belonged. Then her mother had come back.

Usually Lexi tried not to remember those last days with her mother, when Momma had been high all the time and pissed off and mean. Lexi had learned the truth about love then, how close it could be to hate, and how it could empty you out.

"Mia's friendship means everything to me," she said, finally looking at him. She saw how her words hurt him, and she understood at last. All that hostility of his, all that looking away; it had been an act. "You pretended not to like me because of Mia."

"From the start," he said with a sigh. "I wanted to ask you out, but you were already her friend. So I stayed away . . . or I tried to. I never could, though, not really. And then, when you tried to kiss me . . ."

Lexi's heart felt like taking flight. How was it possible that she could be so happy and so sad at the same time? "We shouldn't talk about this anymore. We should just forget about it. I couldn't lose Mia or your family. I couldn't. I've already been hurt enough, you know?"

"You think I haven't already thought all of that?"

"Zach, please—"

"I can't stop it anymore, Lex. I've been thinking about you for three years. Maybe if you hadn't kissed me back . . ."

"I shouldn't have."

"But you did."

"I had to," she said quietly. It was impossible to lie to him. How could she? She had loved him from the second she first saw him. She started to smile and thought about her teeth and bit her lip.

"I love your smile," he said, leaning toward her. She felt the distance between them closing, smelled the peppermint of his breath.

The kiss started slowly, gently. She felt his tongue touch hers, and her heart seemed to take flight. When he took her in his arms, she gave up, gave in. The kiss went on and on, deepening until she thought she couldn't stand for it to end. Behind them, the waves whooshed along the shore, and it became a song. Their song. Their sound.

Desire came from somewhere deep inside of her, radiating outward, tingling, aching. She started to tremble so hard he drew back, looked at her. "Are you okay?"

No, she wanted to say, *no I'm not,* but when she saw herself reflected in his eyes, she was ruined. She wanted him with a ferocity that terrified her. It was dangerous to want anything in this life, but his love maybe most of all. "I'm fine," she lied. "Just cold."

He pulled her into his arms. "Can we come here again tomorrow night?"

They were going down a bad road here; she should hit the brakes now, tell him it was too bad that they loved each other and let it go. Now, while she still could. She should tell him no, say she wouldn't do anything to jeopardize her friendship with Mia, but when she looked at him, she had no strength to turn him away. He made everything inside of her stop hurting.

Dangerous, Lexi, she thought, *say no. Think of your best friend and what matters.* But when he kissed her again, she whispered, "Okay."

Six

J ude sat in bed with her husband, listening with half an ear to the
late-night news. An expensive down comforter, covered by a cus-
tom silk duvet, floated like a cloud around them. In the past few
days—since the dance, in fact—her mommy radar had been emitting a
strong signal. Something was wrong with Zach, and she didn't know
what it was. Nothing bothered her more than being out of the loop in
her kids' lives. "Zach broke up with Amanda," she said finally.

"Uh-huh," Miles said.

She looked at him. How was it that no matter what drama unfolded
in this house, he never seemed to worry? He accused her of being a helicopter parent, all noise and movement, hovering too close to her children, but if that were true, he was a satellite, positioned so far up in the
sky he needed a high-powered telescope to track the goings-on in his
own home. Maybe it was the medical school training. He'd learned how
to suppress his emotions a little too well. "Is that all you have to say?"

"I could have said less, actually. It's hardly an event."

"Molly said Bryson said Zach was acting weird after football prac-tice. I don't think he's handling the breakup as well as it appears. You should talk to him."

"I'm a man. He's a teenage boy. Talking is hardly our best sport." Miles smiled at her. "Go ahead."

"What do you mean?"

"You're dying to ask him what's going on. You can't help yourself. So, go. Just listen to the kid and believe him when he says Amanda doesn't matter. He's seventeen. When I was seventeen—"

"Your horndog past is not comforting." She kissed him on the cheek and climbed over him to get out of bed. "I won't be gone long."

"Believe me, I know."

Smiling, Jude left their bedroom.

The second floor was ablaze with light. As usual, neither of her intel-ligent children had mastered the incredibly complex hand-and-eye co-ordination necessary to turn off a light switch. She paused outside Mia's door, listening. She could tell that her daughter was on the phone. No doubt she was talking to either Lexi or Tyler.

Jude made her way to Zach's room. At his closed door, she paused. She would *not* batter him with questions or bury him under advice. This time she would just listen.

She knocked and got no answer. Knocking again, she announced herself and opened the door.

He was in his game chair, wielding the black remote as if he were a fighter pilot, which, on-screen, he was.

"Hey you," she said, coming up beside him. "What are you doing?"

"Trying to beat this level."

She sat down on the black shag rug beside him. This room had been decorated once by a professional and redone over the years by Zach. Expensive chocolate-colored wallpaper had been covered by movie posters. The bookshelves were an archaeological display of his child-hood: a graveyard of action figures, a tangled heap of plastic dinosaurs, stacks of video game cases, a dog-eared copy of *Captain Underpants*, and the five Harry Potter novels.

She wanted to say, *Can we talk?* but to a teenage boy (or most any male), one might as well say, *May I please rip out your spleen?*

"Let me guess," Zach said. "You think I'm doing drugs? Or spraying graffiti? Maybe you're worried that I'm a girl trapped in a dude's body."

She couldn't help smiling at that. "I am so misunderstood."

"You *do* worry about the weirdest shit. I mean stuff."

"Do you want to talk about Amanda? Or how you feel? I've been through a few broken hearts in my time. Keith Corcoran in high school almost ruined me."

He put down the controller and looked at her. "How did you know you loved Dad?"

Jude was pleasantly surprised by the question. Usually she had to pry this kind of conversation out of her son. But maybe he was growing up, or maybe he'd actually been hurt by Amanda.

There were so many things she could say, memories she could share, and if she were talking to Mia, she might have done just that. But this was Zach. She didn't want to ruin this moment by talking too much.

"The first time I saw him, I knew. I know it sounds crazy, but it's true. When he said he loved me, I believed him, and I hadn't believed anyone since my dad. Until Miles . . . and you kids, I used to worry that I was like my mother. Your dad reminded me what love felt like, I guess, and when he kissed me for the first time, I cried. I didn't know why then, but now I do. It was love and it scared the bejesus out of me. I knew I'd never be the same again." She smiled at her son, who for once was soaking up every word. "Someday you'll meet the right girl, Zach. I promise. Only you'll be grown up and she'll be a woman, and when you kiss her, you'll know you belong with her."

"And she'll cry."

"If you're lucky she will."

❦

In the next two weeks, Lexi learned about keeping secrets. When she was with Zach, her love for him was overpowering, a wave that knocked her sideways so hard she couldn't tell which way was up. Later, when she was with Mia, guilt smacked her just as hard. Mia knew something was up with Zach, but it never occurred to her to look to Lexi for answers.

That was the worst of it, the broken trust. More than once Lexi had almost blurted out the truth, desperate for absolution, but she hadn't done it, hadn't opened her heart to her best friend. And why not?

Love. She couldn't deny Zach anything, it seemed, and he wasn't ready to tell his sister about them. Lexi wasn't even completely sure why; she just knew that Zach was afraid to tell Mia, and if Zach was afraid, Lexi was more so.

Every night, he picked Lexi up from work and drove them out to "their" beach. There, they lay on a blue plaid woolen blanket, talking. Lexi told him about her early years, what it had been like with her mother, how it felt to be forgotten and abandoned; Zach listened and held her hand and told her she was the strongest person he knew. He told her about his dreams for medical school and the expectations of success that sometimes crushed his spirit.

The stars overhead became their private universe. Zach pointed out the constellations and told her the stories that went along with each one: tales of gods and monsters, love and tragedy. His voice in the cold darkness became the home port she'd never known; in his arms, she discovered peace. She saw a side of him she'd never imagined. He felt things so deeply that sometimes he was afraid of his own emotions, and he worried that he would disappoint his parents. His surprising insecurities only made her love him more.

Tonight, they lay together, looking up at the giant universe. He took her in his arms and rolled over, covering her body with his own. She kissed him deeply, pouring every piece of her heart into the kiss, as if she could somehow meld their souls with the sheer force of her love.

When his hand slid inside her shirt, up her bare back, she let him go. It felt so good to be touched like that by him.

He unhooked her bra. She felt the soft cups slip away from her breasts, and then he was touching her there.

She dragged herself sideways, slipped out from underneath him. Breathing hard, aching for his touch, she lay there.

"Lex? Did I do something wrong?"

She refastened her bra and then rolled over to face him. In the moonlight, he was so handsome she could hardly breathe for wanting him. But she'd seen her mother give her body away too many times to be reckless with her own. She sat up, back on her heels, and bowed her head. Was this what love did to a person, twisted them up and emptied them out until there was nothing left but need? If so, how would she survive it? "What are you doing with me, Zach?"

"What do you mean?"

Lexi steeled herself. If she'd learned anything from her mother, it was that nothing good grows in the dark. "I'm not going to be your secret, Zach. If you're ashamed of me—"

"Ashamed? Is that what you think?"

"You don't want to tell Mia about us . . . or your family."

He shook his head. "Ah, Lex . . . I love you. Don't you know that?"

"You do?"

He sighed, and something in the sound reminded her how damaged she was, how certain she was that no one could love her. "You don't know what it's like being a twin. I love Mia, but I want you to be mine. And my mom jumps into my life like it's a swimming pool. She'll have an opinion on this, believe me."

"I love you, too, Zach. So much I can't believe it. But I can't be just yours. Mia's my best friend. We have to tell her. And your parents are important to me, too. I need them to like me."

"I know. But I don't want to hurt Mia. If she thinks I stole you . . ."

"I can belong to both of you," Lexi said solemnly. "I already do."

He kissed her one more time and took her by the hand, pulling her to her feet. In a silence that suddenly felt ominous, they gathered up the blanket and stood beneath the stars, facing each other. The burden of their decision felt unbearably heavy, and Lexi almost wanted to take it back, to say, *let's keep it secret a little longer.* What if she lost him because of it? She didn't fool herself. It was possible. If Zach had to choose between Lexi and his family, it would be no contest. He would always choose Mia, who was as much a part of him as the green of his eyes. The bond that connected the twins ran deep. Last year, Zach had been hurt on the football field, and Mia had known instantly; she'd felt her brother's pain.

"Tomorrow," he said.

"What if—"

"Don't say it. She'll understand. She has to."

The next day, as Lexi sat in one class after another, supposedly listening to her teachers drone on about this or that, all she could think about was telling Mia the truth. She imagined the conversation over and over, polishing each remorseful word like an agate. And still, when the last bell rang, she had the urge to just run away.

What if Mia didn't forgive her? Lexi could lose everything that mattered.

If only she'd done the right thing the first time and told the truth. She, of all people, should have known better. She'd grown up on a diet of lies; she knew the bitter taste they left in your mouth.

After class, she joined the throng of kids in the hallway. On either side of her, lockers clanged open and shut; students were laughing, talking, shoving one another. Mia met her outside of her last-period class, and together they walked toward the flagpole.

Zach came up alongside Lexi and slung an arm around her as if it meant nothing, but at his touch, her whole body came alive. She was attuned to his smallest movement; the breath he took, the hair that fell across his eyes, the finger that stroked her upper arm.

She pulled away. It was meant to be a casual move, but she overdid it and stumbled into Mia.

"Hey," Mia said, laughing. "You new to walking?"

Lexi looked at her best friend. "I need to talk to you." She didn't dare look at Zach, but she felt his gaze on her, hot as a touch. "Privately."

"Me, too," Zach said.

Mia shrugged. No hint of worry crossed her face. Why would it? She trusted these two more than anyone else in the world. Mia led the way to a grassy spot by the admin building, not far from the tree where she and Lexi had met on the first day of school. "Okay," Mia said. "What's up?"

Lexi couldn't speak. She felt exposed suddenly, a liar. She would lose her best friend now. And maybe the boy she loved.

Zach reached out, took hold of Lexi's hand. "We wanted to tell you we're together."

"Uh. Duh. I can see that." Mia looked back at the row of buses. "Do you see Ty?"

"We're *together*," Zach said again.

Mia slowly turned, looked at them, frowning now. "Together? As in hooked up? You two?"

Lexi nodded.

The color drained from Mia's face. "Since when?"

"She almost kissed me after the party at the Eisners' cabin," Zach said.

"That was weeks ago," Mia said. "Lexi would have told me. Right, Lexster? You tell me everything."

"Everything but this," Lexi admitted. "I didn't think it would ever happen. I met Zach on the first day of high school—before I met you, even—and I thought . . . no, that isn't what I want to say. I always liked him, that's the point, but I never thought he'd like me back. I mean . . . he's Zach and I'm . . . me. And I didn't tell you because I didn't want you to think . . . I was one of those girls who'd use you to get to him. Like Haley. It isn't like that."

"It isn't?" Mia said, her mouth trembling. "Why isn't it?"

"I love her, Me-my," Zach said. "And we love you."

"L-love? So all this time, you've been sneaking around behind my back? I kept asking Zach what was wrong, and he said nothing. Neither of you said anything. Were you laughing at me the whole time?" Mia said, stricken.

"No," Zach said. "Come on, you know us better than that."

"Do I? You're both liars." Mia's eyes filled with tears. She spun on her heels and ran for the row of school buses, climbing aboard just as the doors closed.

Lexi saw Mia on the bus, staring at them through the cloudy window, her pale face streaked with tears, her hand pressed to the glass.

Zach put his arm around her. "It's okay, Lex. She'll be okay with this. I promise."

"What if it isn't?" Lexi whispered. "What if she never forgives me?"

❧

For the next several hours, Lexi sat in her lonely bedroom, staring into a future without Mia's friendship.

Yeah, she loved Zach. With all of her heart and soul, but she didn't love Mia any less. It was a different emotion, rounder and softer and more comfortable; maybe it was more solid and reliable, too. All she knew was that she couldn't trade one for the other. That would be like having to choose between air to breathe and water to drink. She needed both to survive.

She never should have kept this secret from her friend. She should have done the right thing from the beginning—if she had, none of this would be happening now. It was a truth she should have learned from her childhood. Always do the right thing from the start. Instead, she'd done the wrong thing and hurt her best friend's feelings.

She knew what she had to do. She left her small, tidy bedroom and walked down the narrow hallway to the living room, where she found Eva sitting on the couch, watching TV.

"Can I go to Mia's house?" Lexi said.

"At this hour? On a school night?"

"It's important," Lexi said. She didn't know what she'd do if her aunt said no.

Eva looked at her. "This about that boy of yours?"

Lexi nodded.

"You going to do the right thing?"

Lexi nodded again, realizing with a jolt of shame that Eva had known what was going on all along. "I have to tell Mia the truth."

"The truth is always a good thing." Eva set down the remote. The pleats in her careworn face were emphasized by a smile. "You're a good girl, Lexi."

Lexi hated how that made her feel. She hadn't been a good girl lately. She swallowed hard, smiled one time, briefly, almost desperately, and then she left the house.

In almost no time, the county bus had dropped her off on Night Road. She walked the last few hundred yards to the Farraday house, which was blazing with lights on this dark autumn night. She picked her way through the carefully landscaped front yard and went up to the front door. She hesitated for a moment and then rang the bell.

Long minutes passed and finally Zach answered. "Lex," he said, looking broken. "She won't talk to me."

"Are your parents here?"

He shook his head. "She's upstairs."

Lexi nodded and moved past him, going up the stairs. At Mia's room, she didn't even knock, just pushed the door open and went inside. Mia stood by the big oval mirror. Even in the shadowy light, Lexi could see how wounded Mia had been by them. "Mia," Lexi said, moving forward. She felt Zach come up behind her.

"I trusted you," Mia said, her mouth trembling.

Lexi would have preferred anger, screaming; anything would have been better than Mia's quiet heartbreak. "Mia, you're the best friend I've ever had. I love you like a sister, and I'm sorry if I hurt you."

"You did. You both did."

"I know. But I want you to know how much you matter to me. No one has ever mattered as much. You have to believe that. If you want me to break up with him, I will—"

"Don't say that," Zach said, stepping toward her.

Lexi ignored him. Her gaze stayed steady on Mia. "I'll break up with him, I will. But I can't stop loving him. I don't know how. I should have told you that a long time ago."

Mia wiped her eyes. "There was always something weird about the way you looked at each other. I thought I was being oversensitive . . . because of Haley." She sighed heavily. "I know how I feel about Tyler. If it's like that . . ."

"It is," Lexi said solemnly.

"You promise you won't dump me for him?" Mia said.

It was an easy promise to make. Lexi let go of Zach's hand and moved toward Mia. "I promise. And I'll never lie to you again. I swear it."

"And if he breaks your heart," Mia said steadily, "you'll still be my best friend? Because you'll need me then."

"I'll always need you," Lexi said. "I'd die if I couldn't come over here. Honestly. No matter what happens with Zach and me, you and I will always be bffs." She stepped closer. "Say you're okay with this, Mia. Please."

Mia sniffed. Lexi wanted her friend to smile, but maybe that was asking too much. "I'm scared," Mia said.

"I know," Lexi said. "And it sounds crazy, but you can trust me."

"Us," Zach added.

"I want you guys to be happy," Mia finally said. "What kind of person would I be if I didn't? I love both of you."

"And we love you," Lexi said. It was true; she loved Mia through and through. Her best friend was a lioness, as all of this proved. Mia had been hurt—two people she trusted had lied to her—and still she stood here, trying to smile, caring about their happiness.

"It'll be the three of us for senior year," Zach said, obviously relieved. "How cool will that be?"

"I wouldn't throw a party just yet," Mia said, looking at her brother. "We're gonna have to tell Mom tomorrow."

"She won't care, will she?" Lexi asked, frowning. "I mean, she likes me."

Mia finally smiled. "Are you kidding? Our mom cares about every-thing."

>❦

The next night, the Journey Through Senior Year meeting was held at 6:00 P.M. in the high school library. Most of the island parents showed up.

"We all know how special Pine Island is," said police officer Roy Avery from his place at the head table. "I know a lot of this year's seniors—my own youngest son graduated two years ago—and I've watched this class go from Little League to varsity. I've watched you protect them with car seats and helmets and airbags. Some of you might think that the biggest danger facing them now is that colleges will reject them, but there's a new threat; one some of you know all too well, and some of you know not at all.

"Partying. Some of you think that the island keeps your kids safe, away from big-city dangers. But danger is here, too. It's in every empty house and lonely stretch of beach. It's in bottles of beer and rum. Start-ing about now every year, the senior class starts to feel both edgy and bulletproof. So keep an eye on your kids. Don't let them outsmart you. Let them know how dangerous partying can be."

As the crowd began to ask questions, Jude looked out at the familiar faces.

She'd driven carpool with many of these women; together, over the years, they'd sat freezing at football games, decorated gymnasiums for dances, been classroom moms. They'd joined forces to raise their chil-dren in a safe community. Now there was a new enemy: drinking. She had no doubt that the mom patrol would join forces again and be on the lookout for potential trouble.

When Officer Avery returned to his seat, Jude stood up. "Thank you to Officer Avery for that important heads-up. And thank you to Ann Morford for her insight on the college application process. I'm sure we'll all be knocking on your door with more question as the deadlines approach. Now, as the head of the parent group, I get to talk about the fun part. Graduation night. As most of you know, Pine Island works to keep drinking and driving out of the graduation equation. To that end, we plan a fun-filled night for the senior class. They leave right after the ceremonies and board a bus. They'll get home at six A.M. the next morning. This year's festivities look great . . ."

For the next few minutes, Jude laid out the plan she and her committee had come up with. Because it was Pine Island, and everyone had an opinion, she spent another ten minutes answering questions and then sent around a sign-up sheet for chaperone volunteers. After that, she joined her best friend, Molly, and they walked out of the gymnasium in a stream of parents. As always, Molly was dressed in an effortlessly chic style—low-rise jeans, a fitted men's-style white shirt, and a necklace of hammered copper and turquoise. Her hair, cut short and dyed platinum this year, offset her dark eyes and ready smile. She and Jude had become friends more than a decade ago. Molly's son, Bryson, was the same age as the twins, so Molly and Jude had found themselves together at one function after another—class functions, field trips, Chuck E. Cheese birthday parties. They'd been friends ever since; Jude didn't think she would have made it through the tough middle school years without Molly and their Thursday margarita nights.

Together, they walked into the cold evening. Jude was just about to say something to Molly, when she heard:

"The party sounds great."

Jude turned to find Julie Williams beside her. "Hey, Julie."

"I hope Zach is feeling better," Julie said, buttoning up her coat.

Jude felt through the mess in her purse, looking for her car keys. "What do you mean?"

"Marsh says he sprained his ankle. He's missed practice most of the week."

Jude stopped and turned. "Zach missed football practice? Because of his ankle?"

"Oh, boy," Molly said quietly.

"All week," Julie said.

"I think he's better now," Jude said evenly. "In fact I'm sure of it. Tell Coach he'll be at practice tomorrow."

"Marsh will be glad to hear that," Julie said. "And I signed up to chaperone the grad party. Let me know if you need me for anything else."

Jude nodded distractedly. Actually, she wasn't even listening. Clutching her keys, she moved purposefully through the crowd, barely making eye contact with people around her. At the car, Molly stopped beside her. "I take it he doesn't have a sprained ankle."

"The lying little shit," Jude said. "He's come home from practice every day this week, right on time. He even had wet hair."

"So what has he been doing?" Molly asked.

"That's what I'd like to know." She forced a smile. "Lunch tomorrow?"

"Of course. I'll want to hear the scoop."

Jude nodded and got into her car. All the way home, she talked to herself, practicing the conversation she would have with Zach.

Once inside the house, she called Zach on his cell phone, got no answer, and left a message. Then she began to pace. She should have made the kids come home for dinner tonight.

This time of night, the view outside was all but gone. A dark sky had settled over a black body of water. Only a few bright lights shone out here and there from the opposite shore. In the orange glow of her porch light, Jude saw a Halloween version of herself trapped in the glass.

She was there, tapping her foot, staring at her own reflection, when the twins came through the front door like bank robbers, shoving each other out of the way, their voices climbing over each other to be heard.

"Zachary, I need to speak to you," Jude said.

They skidded to a stop and looked up in perfect unison.

"Huh?" Zach said, highlighting his mastery of the English language.

Jude pointed to the sectional in the great room. "Now."

Zach moved slowly, his body pouring like syrup onto the overstuffed sofa. "What?" Already his gaze was narrowing, his arms were crossing. A shaft of blond hair obscured one green eye.

Mia plopped down beside him.

"You may go, Mia," Jude said to her daughter, her voice brooking no disobedience.

"Mom, please—"

"Go," Jude said again.

With a dramatic sigh, Mia got up and flounced out of the room. Jude doubted she went far; her daughter was probably eavesdropping from the foyer.

Jude sat down in a chair opposite Zach. "What do you have to tell me, Zachary?"

"What do you mean?" he said, not making eye contact. "We went to Pizza Factory for dinner. You had that meeting tonight. You told us to eat out. It's not even late."

"This isn't about your dinner plans tonight. You have something to tell me, and we both know it," Jude said sharply.

"You mean football," Zach said, sounding both miserable and guarded. "Coach called you."

"On an island this size? You think that's how I find out things? Really, Zach? And what would Coach Williams have told me if he had called?"

"That I haven't been to practice in five days."

"You're injured, I hear. Funny that I haven't noticed a limp."

His rounded shoulders answered her question.

"You've lied to me."

"Technically, I didn't say—"

"Don't go there, Zach. It won't help you. Why have you missed practice?"

Mia came back in the room and sat down next to her brother. She held his hand. "Tell her," she said quietly. "We were going to tell you when you got home tonight, Mom. Honest."

Jude crossed her arms and leaned back, waiting. There was no point in dismissing Mia. Jude shouldn't have bothered with that. "Yes, please, Zach. Enlighten me."

"I've been with Lexi."

"What do you mean?" Jude asked.

"I'm in love with her," he said.

Love. Lexi.

Of all the excuses she'd imagined, that hadn't even made the list. Zach was in love with his sister's best friend.

Jude looked at Mia, who wasn't smiling but didn't look angry, either. "Mia?"

"It's cool, Madre," she said.

Jude wasn't quite sure how to respond, and here were her mirror-image kids, so alike they seemed to breathe in tandem, sitting slanted together, looking somehow both worried and defiant, waiting to hear her reaction to this news. They had hidden this from her, and it stung a little. "How long?"

"A couple of weeks," Zach said.

Mia flinched at that, and Jude knew she'd been hurt by this, a little at least.

Jude let out her breath. This could be ruinous. What would happen if—when—Zach broke up with Lexi? What if Lexi stopped coming around? Mia would be heartbroken.

She chose her words carefully. "Obviously, Zach, I'm not going to tell you who to date and who not to. But Lexi is important to all of us. You need to remember that she was Mia's best friend before you started dating her and she'll be Mia's best friend after it's over. And we don't keep secrets in this family. You know that. Okay?"

"Okay." He smiled brightly. As usual, he expected to get his way.

"And about football practice. You will be on time to every practice from here on, and you will be without a car for the next week. I don't appreciate being lied to."

Zach's smile fell. "That's bogus."

"As is lying," Jude said.

Headlights flashed through the living room window, illuminating Zach and Mia for a moment.

The front door opened and Miles walked into the house, with a jacket slung over his shoulder and a novel under his arm. He came around the fireplace and saw them standing there in silence. He recognized trouble and frowned. "What's up?"

"Nothing," Zach said. He looked at Mia and hitched his head. They ran upstairs and disappeared.

"What was that all about?" Miles asked, tossing his sport coat onto the sofa. He went to the elegant mirrored bar in the corner of the room. A moment later he handed Jude a white wine.

"Zach's dating," Jude said, thankful for the wine.

"Again?" Miles said. "That was quick."

"It's Lexi."

Miles took a moment to think about that. "Well. Okay."

"No. Not okay. He's been skipping football practice."

Miles sat down beside her. "I'm sure you had one of your come-to-Jesus talks with him. He'll be back on track tomorrow."

"But why did he go off track? Zach's been dating a new girl every month since freshman year. As far as I know, he's never skipped anything to be with a girl. Lexi must be special. He actually used the word *love*."

"Hmmm."

She bit her lip, worried it. "I see problems here, Miles. Lexi's practically one of the family. And jealousy can be brutal—remember how they used to fight over the Captain Hook action figure?"

"The Captain Hook action figure. Are you kidding me?"

She looked at him. "This is a delicate situation. A lot could go wrong."

He smiled, a little indulgently. "That's what I love about you, Jude."

"What?"

"You can see the dark side of *anything*," he teased.

"But—"

"They just started dating. How about holding off on an airstrike?"

Jude smiled at that. She knew he was right—she was overreacting. But a lot could go wrong with this new relationship. Hearts could be broken. Still, there was nothing she could do about it now. She went to her husband, put her arms around him, and looked up. "You are no help at all."

$\mathscr{S}even$

The next morning, Jude woke to a cool and surprisingly sunny day. While Miles showered and dressed for work, she stood at her bedroom window, sipping coffee, trying to imagine how she could improve the borders in her garden. The lines weren't quite crisp enough, and she really wasn't happy with some of the lighting. It was too bad she hadn't noticed that in September. Now it was autumn, the rainy season, and gardening pretty much required a snorkel and mask.

Miles came up behind her, reached for her coffee cup and took a sip, then handed it back to her. "Let me guess: you don't like the roses you planted last week and azaleas would be better."

She leaned against him. "You're making fun of me."

"Not at all. What are you going to do today?"

"Lunch with my mother."

He leaned down and kissed her cheek. "Don't let her bully you."

"Yeah, right. I just have to get through it." Smiling at him, she went into the bathroom and took her shower. Afterward, she kissed Miles good-bye and started her day. She corralled the kids to breakfast, cleaned up the kitchen after them, and sent them to school with hugs and kisses.

She was out the door only an hour behind them. She dropped off Miles's dry cleaning, picked up some paperwork from the college counselor she'd hired, got her nails done, returned the movies they'd rented, and stopped by the grocery store to order a fresh, free-range, organic turkey for Thanksgiving.

With all those island stops, she made it to the ferry terminal with seconds to spare, driving right onto the boat. The channel crossing took less than forty minutes. In downtown Seattle, she found a parking spot a few blocks from the gallery and pulled in at exactly 12:06. Only a few minutes late.

On the sidewalk out front, she straightened, stiffened her spine, and set her chin up, like a prizefighter about to face a bigger opponent. In taupe wool pants and a creamy cashmere turtleneck, she knew she looked good . . . but was it good enough for her mother's critical eye?

She sighed at that. It was ridiculous, all this worry about her mother. God knew Caroline didn't worry about Jude's opinion. She resettled her purse over her shoulder and headed to the gallery. On the wall out front, a discreet sign welcomed her to JACE.

She stepped inside. It was a big, brick-walled space, dotted with large mullioned windows. Gorgeous paintings hung one after another, illuminated with precision. As always, there was a sadness to the work that made Jude frown. It was all in greens and browns and grays.

"Judith," her mother said, coming forward. She was dressed in slim black pants and a rose-colored silk blouse. A gorgeous stone necklace offset her green eyes. "I expected you a few minutes ago."

"Traffic."

"Of course." Mother's smile was as brittle as old bones. "I thought we could eat outside today. It's so unexpectedly lovely." Without waiting for a response, she led Jude through the gallery and up to the rooftop patio that overlooked Alaskan Way. From here, the view of Elliott Bay and Pine Island sparkled in the pale autumn sunlight. Large sculpted evergreens grew from huge terra-cotta pots. A table had been set with silver and crystal. Everything was perfect, as usual. *Lovely,* as her mother would have said.

Jude sat down, scooting in close.

Mother poured two glasses of wine and then sat down across from Jude. "So," she said, lifting a silver lid and serving up the salad niçoise, "what are you doing with yourself these days?"

"The kids are seniors in high school. That keeps me pretty busy."

"Of course. What will you do when they go to college?"

The remark was unsettling. "I saw a master gardener class that looked interesting," she said, hearing—and hating—the anemic tone in her voice. Lately, she'd begun to wonder exactly the same thing. What would she do when her children were gone?

Her mother looked at her. "Would you ever consider managing JACE?"

"What?"

"The gallery. I'm getting older. Most of my friends retired long ago. You've a good eye for talent."

"But . . . the gallery is your life."

"Is it?" Her mother sipped her wine. "I suppose. Why couldn't it be yours as well?"

Jude considered that. She had watched her mother work this gallery for years, giving up everything else in her life. She'd even given up painting. Nothing mattered to her mother except the artists she chose and their work. It was an empty existence. And then there was the real problem: her mother would never quit, and the idea of working together was horrifying. They hadn't had an honest conversation in thirty-some years. "I don't think so."

Mother put down her wine. "May I ask why not?"

"I can't see us working well together. And I certainly can't see you actually retiring, Mother. What would you do?"

Her mother glanced away, looked out at the bay, where a boat was pulling up to the marina. "I don't know."

For the first time in years, Jude felt a kind of kinship with her mother.

Both of them were facing changes in life, the natural consequences of aging. The difference between them was that Jude had people she loved around her. In that way, her mother was a cautionary tale. "You'll never quit," she said.

"You're right, of course. Now, let's eat. I only have forty minutes left. Really, Judith, you should try to be on time for our lunches . . ."

They spent the next forty-four minutes making agonizing small talk; neither one really listened to the other. Long silences punctuated every comment, and in the quiet, Jude all too often recalled her lonely childhood. Years she'd spent waiting for a kind word from this woman. When it was finally over, Jude said good-bye and left the gallery.

Outside, she stood on the street, unexpectedly unsettled. Her mother had struck a nerve with that *what will you do?* sentence, and it irritated Jude that she even cared. She walked down the busy street toward her car. She was almost there when she glanced in a window and stopped.

There, in a glass display case, was a gorgeous gold ring.

She went inside, looked closer. It was stunning: a perfect combination of edgy and sophisticated, modern and timeless. The shape was slightly asymmetrical, with a triangular flap on the top edge. The artist must have somehow wrapped heated metal around a form and then twisted it just enough to give the wide band a fun little tail. The empty jewel prong was also slightly off center.

Jude looked up. In response, an elegantly coifed older woman made almost no noise as she crossed the store and stepped gracefully behind the counter. "Have you found something?"

Jude pointed at the ring.

"Ah. Exquisite." The saleswoman unlocked the glass case and withdrew the piece. "It's a Bazrah. One of a kind." She offered it to Jude, who slipped it on her forefinger.

"It would make a beautiful graduation gift for my daughter. What stone would you suggest setting in it?"

The woman frowned in concentration. "You know, I don't have children, but if I were buying my daughter a ring like this, I think I'd want to extend the experience. Perhaps you could choose the stone together."

Jude loved the idea. "How much is it?"

"Six hundred and fifty dollars," the saleswoman answered.

"Ouch."

"Maybe you'd like to look at something less—"

"No. This is the ring I want. And could you show me some watches? For my son . . ."

Jude spent another thirty minutes in the store, waiting for the inscriptions to be finished, then paid for her purchases and left.

She drove down to the waterfront and caught the three o'clock ferry. At just before four, she was back on Pine Island, turning onto Night Road.

At home, she found Mia seated at the dining room table, with her laptop open, watching something on the screen.

"I overacted in *Our Town*," Mia said miserably. "Why didn't anyone tell me? USC will hate this."

Jude went to Mia, stood beside her. "Go to that scene in *Streetcar*, when you were on the balcony. That'll blow them away."

Mia took out one CD and put in another.

"How was school today?"

Mia shrugged. "Mrs. Rondle gave us a pop quiz. So lame. And they announced the winter play. *Romeo and Juliet*, set during the Vietnam War. I can get the lead, which is cool. Zach is gonna take Lexi home after practice, but he'll be home for dinner."

Jude rubbed Mia's back. "What do you think about Zach and Lexi being together?"

"I bet it's killed you not to ask me that before."

Jude smiled. "A little."

Mia looked up. "It's scary . . . and sorta cool, I guess."

Jude thought about Mia before Lexi, when her daughter had been like a scared, fragile turtle with her head tucked deep inside her shell. Mia's only friends had been fictional. Lexi had changed all that. "Whatever happens between them, you and Lexi have to stay honest with each other. You have to stay friends."

"After Zach breaks up with her. That's what you mean."

"I'm just saying . . ."

"I've thought of it myself, believe me. But . . . I think he really likes her. He talks about her all the time."

Jude stood there a minute longer, trying to figure out how to best bring up the other thing on her mind. Finally, she decided to just do it. "There's one other thing . . ."

"What? You want to ask me again if Tyler and I are doing it? We're not." Mia laughed.

"I remember the first time I fell in love. Keith Corcoran. Senior year of high school. Just like you. I didn't know until Keith kissed me how falling in love could be like riding a waterfall into warm water." She shrugged. "No one talked to me about it. Grandma is a pretty buttoned-up woman. All she ever said to me about love was that it derailed a woman. So I learned on my own and, like everyone, I made some mistakes. And the world is more dangerous now. I don't want you to sleep with Tyler—you're too young—but . . ." She went over to the second drawer beside the stove, opened it. She took out a small brown bag and handed it to Mia. "These are for you. Just in case."

Mia peered into the bag and saw the word *condom* printed on a brightly colored box. She gasped and clamped a hand over the bag. "Mo-*om.* Gross. We haven't done anything."

"I'm not saying you'll need them. In fact, I hope you don't, but you know me. And I can see that you think you *do* love him."

"I don't need these," Mia mumbled. "But thanks."

Jude looked down at her daughter. Touching her chin, she forced Mia to look up at her. "Sex changes everything, Mia. It can be great for a relationship when you're ready—older—but it can be napalm when you're not ready. And baby, you're not ready. Just so you know."

By mid-November, every kid in the senior class was stressed out. The high school hallways were filled now with kids talking about colleges. Families spent weekends on the road, visiting campuses and talking to admissions counselors and trying to find the perfect fit.

Lexi's concerns—and stresses—were less complex. She didn't have some endless bank account from which to draw money, so her choices were limited to state schools. And sadly, since she'd fallen in love, her grades had dropped. It wasn't much, just a tenth of a point, but in the dog-eat-dog world of college admissions, that was appreciable. Lately, when she was at the Farradays' or out with Zach and Mia and Tyler, she felt like some visitor from another country, unable to really comprehend their conversations. They all talked about USC and Loyola and NYU as if they were shoes you could point to and purchase.

Lexi could hardly comprehend that kind of confidence.

She stared down at the paperwork in front of her. Columns of calculations taunted her. No matter how hard she tried, there wasn't going to be enough money. Not for a four-year school. If she didn't get a governor's full-ride scholarship, she was out of the race.

Down the hall, a door opened.

Lexi looked up, saw Eva coming her way. "You've been at that a long time."

"College is expensive," Lexi said with a sigh.

"I wish . . ."

"What?"

"How did I get to be this age with no money? I hate that I can't help you more."

Lexi felt a rush of affection for this woman who had changed her life, given her a place to belong. "Don't say that, Eva. You've given me everything that matters."

Eva looked down at her. She looked worried; the wrinkles around her mouth compressed into deep grooves. "I talked to Barbara today."

"How is your sister? Still knitting enough blankets for a third world country?"

Eva sat down across from Lexi. "She wants me to move to Florida with her—after you graduate, of course. I wouldn't even think of it, but . . . this weather is hell on my knees. We were thinking maybe you could come, too. There's a beauty school right down the road. That's a good trade. People always need their hair cut."

Lexi tried to smile. She wanted to, but couldn't quite find the strength. The idea of being without Eva was frightening, but Florida was so far away. How would she ever see Mia and Zach if she lived in Florida? And would she really have to choose between the people she loved? Was that part of growing up?

"I guess you're thinking of your young man. You goin' to school together, then?"

"No. We'll see each other on vacations, though. I'll be in Seattle and he'll come home to see his parents."

"So you got it all worked out."

"All worked out."

"You be careful, Lexi," Aunt Eva said quietly. "I know what happens when boys get ready to go off to college. That's when girls make bad choices. Don't you be one of those girls."

"I won't be."

Eva got slowly back to her feet. Lexi noticed how slowly her aunt moved now that the weather had turned cold. She patted Lexi's shoulder and headed over to the hook by the front door, where her blue Walmart smock hung, waiting. She slipped it on and then put on her coat. "Off to work," she said. "We got lots of Thanksgiving merch to display." She turned. "I'll get us a turkey. We can have a dinner with all the trimmings. Would you like that?"

"Love it."

Eva opened the door and went out into the rainy darkness.

Only a moment or so later, there was a knock at the door. Her aunt must have forgotten something and locked herself out.

Lexi went to the door and opened it.

Zach stood on the top step, holding red roses. "I thought she'd never leave."

"Zach! What are you doing here?"

He pulled her into his arms and kissed her until she was clinging to him like a drowning girl. "I had to see you," he said finally, his breath as ragged as hers. Then he picked her up and carried her down the hallway. The whole house shook, and somewhere she dropped the flowers.

He put her down on her narrow twin bed and covered her body with his, kissing her. When he pressed against her, she could feel his hardness through her jeans.

His tongue played with hers, and the feel of it pushed her toward something, a wanting—a needing—that was new and frightening and powerful. Without thinking about it, she pulled him onto her, so she could feel how much he wanted her.

He cursed and broke free, sliding off of her. At her confused frown, he tried to smile, but the look in his eyes was dark. She saw her own desire mirrored there. The difference was that he wasn't afraid. "It's better if we don't do that," he said shakily.

"I know," she said, pulling her sweater back down. Her eyes stung, and she didn't know why exactly, but she felt ashamed. She rolled onto her side, away from him. He tucked up against her, molded his body to hers.

"Why are you so afraid of me, Lexi? I don't mean sex. I mean *me*. Why are you so sure I'll hurt you?"

"Because I love you, Zach."

"But I love you, too."

She sighed. Zach's view of love had been painted by his family; hers was a little darker. She knew how it felt to be abandoned by someone who'd claimed love. "Just hold me, Zach," she said, settling deeper into his arms.

As they lay there, she stared at the floor. A single rose lay on the industrial gray carpeting, stepped on, its bright red blossom tattered and torn.

❧

With winter break came the first round of college deadlines. By the time classes ended on the twenty-third of December, Lexi had mailed in most of her applications, and the waiting game had begun. She often woke in the middle of the night, with her heart pounding, a nightmare of rejection still hanging in the back of her mind. Zach and Mia were stressed out, too, but it wasn't so bad for them. Sure, they wanted USC, but there were no bad answers waiting for them. The question for them wasn't *if* they'd go to a four-year school; it was which one they would choose. The only one who seemed totally whacked out about the process was Jude, who couldn't seem to have a conversation that didn't include some college reference.

Tonight, Lexi was at the ice cream shop, working late. The school vacation gave business a shot in the arm. Families came downtown to Christmas shop, strolling from store to store beneath trees outlined in sparkling white lights.

She was ringing up a quart of fig and goat cheese ice cream when the phone rang. Thanking the well-dressed woman at the register, she answered, "Amoré Ice Cream Shop. This is Alexa. May I help you?"

"Lex, it's Mia."

"You're not supposed to call me here."

"The Ottomans are gone for the weekend."

"So?"

"Kim's having a party. We'll pick you up at nine, okay?"

"Lexi," Mrs. Solter said firmly. "That's a business phone."

"Okay," Lexi said.

Mia said, "Later," and hung up.

Lexi went back to work. From then on, the minutes seemed to crawl forward on sore knees, but finally the ice cream shop was closed up and Lexi was outside in the cold, waiting. All around her, Christmas lights hung from eaves and wrapped around potted trees in front of the local businesses. Bright banners hung from the lampposts, fluttering in the night air, and a giant illuminated star hung above Main Street.

A red SUV pulled up in front of her. Mia opened the passenger door and leaned out. "Hey!"

Lexi hurried around to the back door and climbed in the backseat, where Zach was waiting for her.

"Hey, Lexi," Tyler said from the driver's seat.

"Hey," Lexi said, cuddling up to Zach.

"I missed you," he said.

"I missed you, too."

They'd been together last night, studying with Mia in the Farradays' big media room (and making out whenever Mia left them alone), but it felt like a long time ago.

"I called your aunt," Mia said. "She said it's cool if you stay at my house tonight."

Lexi leaned against Zach, rested her hand on his thigh.

She had to be touching him.

There were already about fifteen cars at the Ottoman house when they pulled up.

The four of them walked up the gravel driveway together. Noise from the party sounded muted and distant, until they stepped inside.

Music was playing at the edge of pain. The kitchen was wall-to-wall kids; a few more lay sprawled in the living room, making out, and through the glass pocket doors, they could see about ten more outside, standing around a fire.

Tyler pulled Mia into his arms and twirled her around, lifting her off her feet. Mia laughed and clung to him, and then they were kissing like crazy.

Zach took Lexi by the hand and led her out to the fire, where a group of football players were shotgunning beer.

"Zach . . . Zach . . . Zach . . ."

The crowd chanted his name as they approached.

Bryson stepped forward, holding a Coors Light. "Brewski, dude?"

"Tyler's the d.d.," Zach said. "Hell, yeah." He took the beer, jammed a pen into its side, snapped the cap, and guzzled the whole thing in one shot. Wiping his mouth, he grinned at the crowd around him.

"You want one, Lexi?" Bryson asked.

"No, thanks."

"Come on, Lexi," Zach said, rubbing her arm.

She couldn't deny him. "Fine. I'll have a beer, but no shotgunning. I do my own laundry."

Zach laughed and called out for another beer.

For the next two hours, the party roared forward; the crowd grew louder and sloppier and drunker. Every now and then, the air smelled like pot. Someone was always laughing, and then, suddenly, the music changed.

The soundtrack from *The Little Mermaid* started. Throughout the house, guys—including Zach—groaned. Lexi grinned. "I love it when a *girl* has the party."

Mia appeared out of nowhere. In her expensive pink terrycloth sweatpants and thick white hoodie, she looked rumpled and drunk, a little unsteady on her feet. "It's my song," she said, grabbing Lexi's hand, dragging her out onto the patio, where kids were dancing.

She hung on to Lexi, trying to move to the beat, but this close, Lexi could see how drunk Mia was, and how sad. "Mia? What happened?"

"Tyler is all over Alaina Smith."

"Maybe you're misreading the signs. You *are* pretty hammered."

"I only shotgunned a few beers. And I'm not overreacting." She leaned forward, whispered, "It's 'cause she does it. All the guys know it."

"If he loves you—"

"Yeah, yeah," Mia said. "The point is, I love him. So what am I waiting for?"

Before Lexi could answer, Tyler showed up and took Mia away, leading her off the makeshift dance floor. Lexi saw how pathetically happy Mia looked at his return. It saddened her because she knew how dangerous it was to love someone that much, and because she knew it was how she looked at Zach.

"My sister dumped you, huh?" Zach said, coming up behind her, taking her in his arms. "I would never do that to you."

She turned into him, kissing him. She tasted beer and something else, something sharp and metallic. The look in his eyes was a little bleary, as if he couldn't quite focus.

He kissed her again, deeply, and then, taking her hand, he led her through the party and down to the beach. He started kissing her even before they lay down. His hand slid up under her shirt, unhooked her bra. She knew she should stop him, but it felt so good, and when he touched her breasts, she felt as if she were floating, flying . . . She made a sound she'd never heard before. Behind them, distant now, the music changed, or went on, or even went off; she couldn't hear anything except her own heavy breathing and the way he kept saying her name and whispering that he loved her.

It took a Herculean effort to push him away. "Don't, Zach . . ."

He rolled away from her and lay there. She felt the loss of his touch as a physical pain, and she instantly regretted her move. "I'm sorry, Zach. It's just . . ."

"There you are," Mia said, stumbling toward them. In the moonlight, Lexi could see how glassy eyed Mia was now, almost as if she'd been crying. And she was unsteady on her feet. Her shirt was buttoned incorrectly; the way it hung on her thin frame made her look strangely bent. She plopped down beside Lexi.

Lexi tried to rehook her bra without anyone noticing.

Zach sat up, drew his knees in, and stared out at the black Sound. After a long silence, he said quietly, "Mia? I don't want to leave Lexi."

"We don't have to go," Mia said, leaning against Lexi. She looked at her watch. "It's not one yet."

"In August," Zach said. He looked to her for support, but she could offer none. She was suspended, in a dangerous position between these two, both of whom she loved. "Couldn't we all go to UW together?"

"I might not be able to go to the U," Lexi said to him. "It's so expensive. I might have to start at Seattle CC."

"We could do that, too," Zach said. "It would save Mom and Dad a ton of money."

Mia looked at her brother. "Now you don't want to go to USC with me?"

"I don't want to leave Lex," he said quietly.

Mia looked away, stared out at the water. "Oh," was all she said, but in that little half word, Lexi heard an ocean of disappointment.

They all knew Mia needed Zach at college with her.

Tyler stumbled over to where they were and collapsed into the sand. "Hey, Mia," he said drunkenly, reaching for her. "I missed you."

"Shit," Zach said. "He's drunk."

Tyler laughed. "Oh, yeah. Whoa. I can't drive, that's for sure."

Lexi got to her feet and looked at the party. Kids were sprawled everywhere. The few who were still standing staggered around. "What are we going to do?" she said, starting to panic. "We don't want your mom to know we were drinking . . ."

"Shit," Zach said again, running a hand through his hair.

"Madre said we could call anytime," Mia said, trying to get Tyler to his feet. "No questions asked, she said. No repercussions."

Zach looked at Lexi.

"We don't have any choice," she said. *This was bad.*

He cursed again and made the call. "Hey, Mom," he said, straightening, trying to sound sober and failing. "Yeah. I know. Sorry. But . . . we need you to pick us up . . . yeah . . . Tyler . . . I know . . . thanks." He closed the phone and looked at them. "She sounded pissed."

"It's one in the morning," Lexi said. If only she hadn't had that beer. *She* could have driven them home and spared them all what was coming.

They made their way back to the house, where kids were still huddled around the fire. All around, on the grass, more kids were making out, passed out.

In the driveway, they stood by Tyler's SUV. It seemed to take forever, but finally a pair of headlights appeared on the rise, turned toward them, and grew brighter.

The big black Escalade parked. Jude stepped out of the driver's seat and came around to them. She was wearing a heavy, floor-length cashmere robe over pajamas. Without makeup, she looked pale and tired. And pissed off. Her gaze narrowed as she looked them over. Lexi had no doubt that she saw it all: Mia's glassy eyes and misbuttoned shirt, Zach's unsteady stance, Tyler's droopy eyes.

Lexi couldn't make eye contact she was so embarrassed.

"Get in," Jude said with a sigh. "Put on your seatbelts."

The drive home was utterly silent. When they were all in the entryway, Jude said, "Put Tyler in the media room. He can sleep on the sofa. Now I'm going to bed." On that, she turned her back on them and walked down the hall. At her bedroom door, she paused, turned back. "Good job for calling," she said tiredly, and then she went into her room and closed the door.

Mia immediately giggled. Zach shushed her, and they all climbed the stairs to the second floor. Tyler fell a couple of times, yelling out curses. By the time they got him onto the sofa, he was already asleep.

At Mia's bedroom door, Zach kissed Lexi until she couldn't think straight, and then left her.

She and Mia crawled into the big king-sized bed. Moonlight spilled through the window, illuminating them.

"Your mom looked pretty pissed tonight," Lexi said.

"Don't worry about it. We did the right thing. She wouldn't want us driving."

Lexi lay back into the pile of soft pillows, staring up at the dark, peaked ceiling. "About what Zach said . . . about school . . ." She didn't know how to follow that up. The dream was too sharp to handle.

"The thing is . . ." Mia sighed. "I *want* to go to USC. I actually dream about it. You know? But I'm afraid to go without Zach. I wish I were stronger . . . but I'm not. I need him with me."

"I know."

Mia rolled onto her side and looked at Lexi. "I have a secret. About Tyler and me." She paused. "We did it."

Lexi rolled over to face Mia. "It? You did it?"

Mia's face was so close Lexi could smell the beer on her breath and the floral scent of her shampoo. Her green eyes were bright. "He said he loved me. I know it's true now."

"Details!" Lexi said, trying to keep her voice a whisper. As she listened to Mia's story, Lexi couldn't help thinking about Zach and how much she loved him, and she wished she hadn't pushed him away now.

"I guess you're officially the last virgin in our class," Mia finally said.

Lexi closed her eyes, feeling strangely adrift, as if she'd missed some boat that everyone else was on. What if Zach only *said* he understood her reluctance? What if someday he just . . . found someone else to love?

Beside her, Mia started to snore.

Lexi thought about sneaking out of bed and going to Zach's room. She'd never done that before—she'd promised both Jude and Mia that she wouldn't do it—and usually it was an easy promise to keep. But tonight, she felt his absence keenly. They had so little time together. It was late December already. No matter what they all said—what they dreamed aloud—they wouldn't be going to school together. Beginning in September, they would only see one another on breaks. If then.

She closed her eyes and dreamed of Zach, remembering the times on their beach . . .

"Lexi. LEXI."

She came awake with a start.

Zach was peering down at her, his blond hair falling forward. "Come with me."

She took his hand. It was just that simple. He pressed a finger to his lips, said *sshhh* as they tiptoed down the hall toward his room.

She could have stopped him, pulled back as she'd done so many times before, but suddenly all her reasons for holding back felt silly. Whatever he wanted, she wanted. She couldn't bear the thought that she might lose him. She wanted to be everything to him while she could, so he would keep on loving her.

She followed him up onto his big bed, with its impossibly soft sheets and the airy goose-down pillows. Moonlight spilled through the open window, pooling on the white cotton.

"Here," he said, handing her a small pink-wrapped box.

"Christmas isn't for two days. I don't have your present."

"We might not have another chance to be alone," he said.

Her hands were shaking slightly as she opened the box. Inside, on blue velvet, lay a thin silver band with a tiny sapphire chip.

"It's a promise ring," he said solemnly. "The lady at the store said it's what you give the girl you love. It means I want to marry you someday."

Lexi stared down at it, feeling tears start behind her eyes. He *did* love her. As much as she loved him. When she lifted her gaze, all the love she'd hoarded since childhood was in her eyes. She gave all of it to him, all of herself. "Do you have some condoms?"

"Are you sure this is what you want?" he said. "Because if you aren't—"

"I'm sure," she whispered, taking off his shirt. "Love me, Zach. That's what I want."

Eight

꧁

Jude had very few Christmas memories from her childhood. Here was what she remembered: quiet mornings in the big house on Magnolia Bluff, a fake tree decorated by professionals, a single designer stocking hanging from the mantel. Breakfast had been catered. There had been gift openings, of course—a short, silent affair with Caroline sitting perched on an expensive gilt chair, her foot tapping nervously on the hardwood, while Jude sat cross-legged on the floor. A few solemn thank-yous were passed back and forth, and then the whole ordeal was done. When the last gift was revealed, her mother had practically run for the door.

Once, when her father had been alive, she recalled writing a letter to Santa . . . but that kind of whimsy had died with her dad.

Jude did things a little differently in her own home. Since motherhood had surprised her with its powerful pull, she'd become a holiday junkie. She decorated from corner to corner, until the entire house looked like a catalog spread. But it was Christmas morning that she really looked forward to, when the family came together, their cheeks creased from sleep, to open presents. In those early morning hours, with her sleepy, grinning children settled around her, she could see the result of her efforts. Her twins would remember these times with fondness.

Now, though, the boxes and papers and bows were put away, and they were at the table, eating their traditional holiday meal—eggs Florentine with fresh fruit and homemade cinnamon rolls.

Last night, in a burst of holiday cheer, snow had come to the Northwest, and the view outside was a gorgeous tableau of white and blue.

Jude had always loved snow days, and when they came for the holidays, it was a double bonus. Today, after brunch, the whole family was going ice skating down at the pond on Miller Road. It would be a good time, she thought, to have a serious talk with the kids about what had happened the other night at the party. It had taken a superhuman effort not to rail at them, but she had managed it. Still, there was some talking to be done, some ground rules for senior year to be reassigned.

She was so deep in imagining how she would conduct this conversation, what she would say to them, that she hardly heard what Zach had just said.

She turned to her son, who was busily buttering one of the cinnamon rolls she'd made. "What did you say?"

Zach grinned. From across the glittering expanse of their formal dining table, with his blond hair messy from sleep, he looked about thirteen years old. "A promise ring."

Silence fell. Even Miles frowned. His hand paused midreach. "Excuse me?"

Across the table from Zach, Mother straightened. "Excuse me, did you say a ring?"

"It's really pretty," Mia said, pulling a frosted bit from her cinnamon roll. She popped it into her mouth. "Mom? Are you having a stroke?"

Jude had to force herself to remain calm. Her son—her not quite eighteen-year-old son—had given his girlfriend a *ring* for Christmas.

"And what exactly are you promising Lexi?" She felt Miles lean toward her. His fingers closed around her wrist.

"It means I promise to marry her someday."

"Oh, look. We're out of fruit," Miles said evenly. "Here, Jude. I'll help you get some more." Before she could protest—she still felt frozen—he led her out of the dining room and into the big kitchen.

"What the—"

"Shhh," he said, pulling her behind the fridge. "They'll hear you."

"No shit," she said. "I *want* him to hear me."

"We can't come down on him about this."

"You think it's okay for our son to give a promise ring to a girl he's been dating for three months?"

"Of course I don't. But it's done, Jude. A fait accompli."

She pushed his arm away. "Great parenting, Miles. Do nothing. What if we'd found out he was doing heroin?"

"It's not heroin, Jude," he said tiredly.

"No. It's love. Or so he thinks."

"It *is* love, Jude. You can tell that by looking at the kid."

"Oh, for God's sake."

"I'm not going to have this debate with you. If you want to throw yourself on the sword, go ahead, but don't expect me to suture you up when you start bleeding."

"But—"

"Don't make a mountain out of a molehill. He was in a jewelry store, shopping for a present for his girlfriend, and he got swept away by romance. That's all. It happens to men, too, unevolved as we are." He pulled her toward him. "Sadly, our son is an idiot. They should have told us this when he was born. That way we could have lowered our expectations."

"Don't you dare make me smile. I'm pissed at him."

"It's Christmas," he said. "Our last one with them living at home."

"Low blow."

She let him put his arms around her. "Let's not ruin this, okay?"

"JoJo, the idiot boy, promises to marry a girl—"

"Someday—"

"—and *I'm* the one who is endangering Christmas."

"Zach and Lexi are not going to school together, Jude. Stop worrying. This is nothing. I promise you."

"Fine," she finally said. "I will keep my opinion to myself."

"Yeah," he said, smiling indulgently. "And you're so good at that."

Jude sighed. "I'll try. But I'll tell you this, Miles. They *better* go to separate schools."

Moving with an uncustomary stiffness, Jude went back into the great room and returned to her place at the end of the table. Miles held out her chair for her and squeezed her shoulder as she sat down.

The mood had changed. There was no mistaking the sudden quiet. Mia and Zach were both looking at her with the wariness of the guilty.

She managed a tight smile and said, "Don't you just love it when it snows for Christmas?"

Someone answered—honestly, she barely knew who it was. Perhaps her mother, saying something about the weather.

Jude's hands were trembling just a little, and if she were a woman who had to worry about her blood pressure, she would have worried now. She understood suddenly why so many of her friends had warned her about the stresses of senior year. It was only December, and already their lives felt out of kilter, as if the warm water that had always buoyed them up had abruptly begun to drain away. There was danger in shallow water, unseen shoals. Like love and parties and children who lied to you.

"I need to return that pink sweater," Mia said at one point. "It's way too big. I want to get something to wear to Timmy's party on Saturday. You want to come to the mall with me, Mom?"

Jude looked up. "Timmy's party?"

"It's on Saturday, remember?" Mia said.

"You two are not going to a party on Saturday," Jude said, stunned that they would even think to ask.

Zach looked up sharply. "You said we could go."

"That was before you called me, drunk, at one-twenty to come pick you up."

"You said we should call you," Zach said. "I *knew* we'd get into trouble for it."

"You let them go to a party?" her mother said, her carefully arched eyebrows raised. "With alcohol?"

Jude drew a deep breath and exhaled it to stay calm. The last thing she needed now was parenting advice from a woman who'd handled motherhood as if it were radioactive waste. "You did the right thing by calling. I'm glad you did. But you also got drunk, and that's the wrong thing. We've talked about this."

"We learned our lesson," Zach said. "We won't drink again. But—"

"No buts. This is the last week of winter break, and I want to spend it as a family. We're going to Molly and Tim's tomorrow, and your grandmother's gallery is having a special show on Monday night. Ty and Lexi are welcome to come over as much as you want them to, but no party on Saturday."

Zach started to come out of his chair. Miles put a hand on his son's shoulder, guided him back down.

"I *knew* it," Zach muttered, slumping into his seat, scowling.

Jude tried to find a smile again and couldn't. Maybe God had designed senior year so that mothers like her could let their children leave home. If this kept up, it would be easier than she'd thought.

❧

In January, on the last day of winter break, precipitation began as an icy, misting rain but quickly transformed into lacy white flakes that frosted fence posts and telephone wires. Soon, the roads were thick with new snow and red safety cones appeared at the bottom of steep hills. Kids bundled up and went out to sled on the barricaded hills; their moms stood by in groups, talking among themselves and taking pictures.

Lexi and Zach were at her house, snuggled up together in her twin bed. On her bedside table, a scented candle burned brightly, dispelling the slightly damp-smelling air that always came to the mobile home when the windows were shut.

"My aunt will be home soon."

"Define soon."

She grinned at him and smacked his arm, then rolled away and got out of bed. "You promised your mom you'd finish your college apps today, and she's been so pissed off lately, I don't want to make her mad again. So move it." She got dressed and headed for the door. She meant to walk right out of her bedroom and go straight to the kitchen table, where the paperwork for college was arranged in neat piles.

At the last minute, she weakened and turned around.

He lay in her bed, naked, her tattered blue comforter across his hips, his bare feet stuck out from the end. His smile worked its magic; she moved toward him. When she got close, he reached up and curled his warm hand around the back of her neck, pulling her down for a kiss. Just before his lips touched hers, she heard him say, "I love you so much." It took all her willpower not to crawl back in bed with him.

"You're a sex maniac."

"Takes one to know one."

Something about his smile, or the green of his eyes and the love she saw, something caught her then. How could she let him go away to college? Just walk away from her?

"Come on. I want your mom to keep liking me, and I told her I would make sure you finished the USC app today. You know she's going to check."

"What if I just missed the deadline?" he said.

"You won't. Now get your ass up. You need to finish putting everything together."

"Our last day of break and we have to do stupid shit," Zach grumbled, throwing the covers back. He saw the way she reacted to his nakedness and he grinned wolfishly, but before he could say anything, Lexi left the bedroom and sat down at the kitchen table.

Zach slid into a seat beside her, propping his elbow on the table. "Lex?"

She looked at him. "What?"

"I want to go wherever you go. Really."

He leaned forward and kissed her, and she thought about how it would feel to let him go, to say good-bye. It was all well and good for him to say he wanted to be with her, but that was a distant cousin to *going* with her. To be with Lexi, he'd have to stand up to his parents and disappoint Mia, who was more than just a sister. It would never happen, so there was no point dreaming about it.

"Come on," she finally said. "I don't want to piss your mom off again. Let's finish up and get going. Mia says everyone is sledding on Turner Hill."

❧

In February, Zach and Mia turned eighteen. The magic number convinced them that they were adults; suddenly they questioned every rule and restriction. Curfews struck them as irrelevant now, unnecessary. They were constantly testing the limits and wanting more freedom.

As the weather warmed, class parties sprung up like mushrooms on the roadside. Blooming instantly. All it took was a phone call and a fake ID in someone's hand. *My parents are gone* became the class motto, the equivalent of a clan call. Kids arrived at empty houses or on the beach or in the woods with fifths and six-packs and Baggies of pot. Some parents chose to host the parties themselves, rigorously taking car keys, but if no "cool" parent could be found, well, the party must go on.

The whole scenario had exhausted Jude, worn her to a frazzle. She felt more like a warden than a parent, and the constant battling with her twins about safety and compromise and good choices had weakened her. She no longer believed them when they said they wouldn't drink. At first she had clamped down, denied them, but that had only driven them to sneak out, which led to more clamping down—and more angry rebellion. Every day felt like a mountain to climb, every night they spent at home a triumph.

On top of all that was the college pressure. It had become a cauldron that held them all, parents and kids; the water was heating up fast. One question was asked over and over: *have you heard?* It was asked mother to mother at Safeway, in line at the post office, or on the ferry.

Honestly, Jude was as nervous as her kids about it.

Even now, on this gorgeous March afternoon, when she should have been gardening, she was standing at the window, staring up the driveway. It was almost three-thirty. The kids had just gotten home from school. They'd torn through the kitchen like locusts and then gone upstairs.

"You're wearing a groove in the floor," Miles said from the living room, where he was reading the newspaper. He had had a surgery cancelled today and come home from the hospital early.

She saw a flash of white.

The mail was here.

She grabbed her coat and stepped into the garden clogs on the porch and headed up the gravel driveway. At the top of the hill, she pulled open the mailbox and saw what she'd been waiting for.

A nice thick envelope with the USC emblem on the upper left corner.

It wasn't absolute proof, of course, the thickness of the envelope, but everyone knew it took a lot of pages to welcome a student and only one to reject.

Then it struck her. One envelope.

She let out a sigh and reached for the rest of the mail.

And there it was. At the bottom of the stack.

A second thick envelope with the same logo.

Jude hurried back down the driveway. Once inside the house, she yelled out for the kids.

"Did something come?" Miles asked, taking off his reading glasses.

Jude tossed the heap of mail on the entry table and showed him the two special envelopes. "Mail call," she said, feeling suddenly nervous. She had to say it twice—yell it, really—and then the kids came hurrying down the stairs.

Jude handed Zach the envelope with his name on it.

Mia snatched the other envelope, ripping it open as she walked away.

Not more than ten feet away, she spun around. "They accepted me!" A grin burst across her face and then faded as she looked at her brother. "Zach?" she said nervously.

Please, Jude prayed. *Let it be both of them.*

Zach opened the envelope and read the letter. "They accepted me."

Jude's shriek could have shattered glass. She launched herself forward to sweep Zach and Mia into a family hug.

"I'm so proud of you guys." She waited for Zach to hug her, but he was too stunned to move. Finally, she stepped back, beaming at them. "Both of you at USC. It's your dream come true."

"We have to call Lexi and Ty," Mia said. She grabbed Zach's hand and pulled him toward the stairs.

"And the crowd goes wild. Come on, Mama Bear," Miles said, coming to stand beside her. "I'll pour us champagne."

Jude stared up the empty stairs. "Why are we the only ones celebrating?"

"We're not. They're upstairs calling all their friends with the good news."

"That blows," she said, looping her arms around his waist and looking up at him.

"Indeed. Most of parenthood does. But we can still celebrate." He kissed her lightly on the lips. "Maybe now you can relax."

❦

After last period, Lexi went to the counselor's office. It was a small narrow room lined on all sides with bookshelves. In those shelves, there were literally thousands of college manuals.

She sat in a blue plastic chair, waiting.

At just past three-thirty, the receptionist looked up from her desk. "Lexi, Mrs. Morford can see you now."

Lexi nodded and slung her heavy backpack over her shoulder. She walked down the narrow, college-poster-lined hallway and stepped into the office in the back. Through the window, she could see the gym and a pair of skinny kids—probably freshmen—playing Hacky Sack.

Lexi sat down opposite the large brown desk that dominated the room. Her counselor, Mrs. Morford, sat behind it.

"Hello, Lexi."

"Hey, Miz Morford." Lexi reached into her backpack and pulled out two thick envelopes. Inside were acceptances from the UW and Western Washington. She handed them to her counselor, who read the letters and then set them down.

"Congratulations, Lexi. Now, what can I do for you?"

"Both schools offered me scholarships. Two thousand dollars. But . . . look at the costs. The UW tuition is fifty-three hundred, room and board is sixty-two hundred, and books are another thousand. That's more than thirteen thousand dollars. How can I get more help?"

"We talked about this when your grades dropped last semester, Lexi. The UW and WWU are extremely competitive schools. There are several island scholarships you can apply for, though, and you could always take out a loan. They have some really good educational programs."

"I'd have to borrow ten thousand dollars a year. And even then I'd have to work all through school. I'd be in debt when I graduated."

"A lot of people go through college on loans, Lexi. It's a way of betting on your own future."

Lexi sighed. "I guess community college isn't so bad. I can go to the UW in two years."

Mrs. Morford nodded. "It's a great way to save money. Two years will go by fast. In no time you'll be back with your friends."

Not the ones who mattered.

Lexi thanked the counselor and walked down to her bus stop. All the way home, she worked and reworked the numbers, trying to magically refashion it all into a plan she could make work.

But there was no making it work. Short of borrowing a ton of money, she was not going to a four-year school.

By the time she was home, she was thoroughly depressed. Never had she felt as much of an outsider on Pine Island as she did now. She would have given almost anything for the choices most island kids took for granted.

At home, she went straight into her room and flopped onto the bed. The phone rang.

She answered. "Hello?"

"Lexi! Zach and I got into USC. Both of us. And Tyler got into UCLA. Isn't that *awesome*? Can you come out to dinner with us tonight? We're celebrating!"

"That's great." Lexi banged her head against the headboard. She should just drown herself. Tears stung her eyes. She wasn't one to feel sorry for herself, but why couldn't life go her way JUST ONCE? "Of course I'll celebrate with you."

Mia launched into another college story and Lexi couldn't take it anymore. She mumbled some excuse and hung up on her best friend.

A few minutes later, a knock at her bedroom door surprised Lexi. "C-come in," she said, sitting up in bed.

Eva walked into the small, cramped room. The walls were covered with photographs: there were pictures of Zach playing football, of Mia waterskiing, of the three of them at the homecoming dance. "These walls are paper thin. I heard you crying."

Lexi wiped her eyes. "I'm sorry."

Eva sat down on the side of the bed. "You want to tell me what's wrong?"

Lexi knew she looked awful. Her eyes were puffy and red from crying. "Zach and Mia got into USC."

"You didn't want them to get in?"

"No." Just saying it made her feel miserable and small. "I'm afraid that when he leaves . . ."

"You know, I met my Oscar when I was sixteen and he was twenty-eight. Ooh-ee, was it a mess, I can tell you. A sixteen-year-old girl isn't supposed to know what she wants, and a man that age ain't supposed to want her at all." She sighed, smiling. "My daddy woulda shot Oscar if he'd showed his face at our place, so we waited. Oscar was in the service, and he went away for a few years. We wrote letters back and forth. Then on the day I turned eighteen, I married him. During Vietnam, we were apart again."

"How did you make it through all that?"

"It isn't about being at the same school or the same town or even the same room, Lexi. It's about being *together*. Love is a choice you make. And I know you're young, but that don't mean a thing. Do you believe in how you feel? That's what matters."

"I want to believe in it."

"Is that the same thing? You might think on that." Eva patted her hand and stood up. "Well. If I don't head out now, I'll be late for the night shift. Do you have plans for tonight?"

"The Farradays want to celebrate tonight. They invited me to dinner."

"That isn't the most sensitive thing I've ever heard. You okay with it?"

"I have to be," Lexi said. When her aunt got to the door, Lexi said, "Thanks, Eva."

Eva waved a gnarled hand as if to say, *humpf!*, and left the room.

Alone again, Lexi looked at the pictures and clippings on her wall. Then, with a last tired sigh, she got up, made her bed, and headed down the hall.

Forty-five minutes later—right on time—she was sitting in the living room, waiting. She had put on her best dress and taken extra time with her hair and makeup. When she was done, no evidence of her emotional meltdown remained.

Outside, a car pulled up. Headlights shone into the living room and then clicked off.

She meant to get up, but she couldn't seem to move.

The knock on the front door rattled the whole mobile home.

Finally, she made herself rise, move, open the door. Zach and Mia stood there.

"Can you *believe* it?" Mia said, launching herself forward to hug Lexi, who did her best to reciprocate.

Lexi dared to look over Mia's shoulder at Zach, who looked as devastated as she felt.

"Congratulations," she said woodenly.

He nodded.

Lexi felt Mia take her hand, and she let her best friend lead her down the wooden steps and across the wet grass to the waiting Escalade, where the three of them got into the backseat, with Lexi in the middle, as usual.

"Hey, Lexi," Miles said, looking at her in the rearview mirror. "We're glad you could join us."

"I'd never miss a celebration like this," she said, managing a smile.

"We're *all* celebrating," Mia said. "Lexi got scholarships to the UW and WWU. It's a dream come true, right, Lexi?"

"A dream come true," Lexi agreed tiredly.

After they picked up Tyler, the conversation kicked into high gear. All the way to the restaurant, Mia and Jude talked about USC and Los Angeles and what it would be like to hang out on the beaches of Southern California. Every sentence began with some version of *It'll be so cool . . .*

Zach held Lexi's hand, squeezing it just a little too hard.

Finally, as they pulled up to the restaurant and parked, Lexi dared to look at him.

I don't want to go, he mouthed. But he would, and they both knew it.

May came to the Pacific Northwest like a favorite relative, bringing sunshine. Gone were the perennial gray skies and ceaseless, dripping rain. Overnight, it seemed, color returned to this misty landscape. All over the island, curtains that had long been ignored were thrown open, barbeques were wheeled out of their garage hideaways, and patio furniture was uncovered and scrubbed clean. It was a glorious leonine month always, a bright respite before the pale gloom of June, and this year it was particularly bold. The combination of an egg-yolk sun and a surprising heat brought kids pouring into beach parks and bike paths.

On Saturday, the fifteenth, Lexi woke early. It had been a restless night, full of bad dreams about planes that taxied down runways and rose into cloudy skies. She padded out of her bedroom and headed down the hall.

Eva was waiting for her in the kitchen, wearing her old white chenille bathrobe and a pointed metallic hat. On the table beside her were two glazed donuts on yellow paper plates; one had a twisty blue candle in it. "Happy birthday," she said, blowing on a noisemaker.

Lexi almost burst into tears. In all the college drama, she'd forgotten about her eighteenth birthday. But Eva had remembered.

"I got you two presents this year." Eva cocked her head to indicate the wrapped packages on the table.

Lexi couldn't help remembering her birthdays before Eva—long, unhappy days spent waiting alone for a mother who never showed. She kissed her aunt's wrinkled, velvety cheek and then took a seat at the table.

"Open it," Eva said, taking a seat across from Lexi.

Lexi enthusiastically started unwrapping the paper. Inside the box lay a sapphire blue cotton sweater with tiny silver buttons. She held it up, admiring it. "It's beautiful."

"If it don't fit, we can exchange it at the store."

Lexi would never return it, even if it were two sizes too small. It would always be in her top drawer, alongside the pink bedazzled butterfly sweatshirt she'd outgrown. "It's perfect, Eva. Thank you."

Eva nodded. "Open that one."

The other gift was about the size of a tablet of paper, and slim. Lexi opened it carefully and lifted the lid.

On the top was a four-color brochure for an apartment complex in Pompano Beach, Florida. "Fun in the sun," it promised, in big, bold type. Below it was a class catalog from Broward Community College.

"That's Barbara's apartment building," Eva said, leaning forward. "I got to thinking about your future, and I thought, hell's bells, why couldn't you come to Florida with me? Barbara's got two bedrooms, and her and I have shared a bedroom before. You could have your own room and go to classes during the day. You wouldn't have to pay any rent at all."

Lexi looked across the table at this woman who had done so much for her, and her throat tightened. "It looks great."

"I shoulda known you wouldn't want beauty school. Barbara told me as much. You're the first one of us ever to go to college. College," Eva said the word reverently. "We're so proud of you. And you need to get to know your other aunt. Her kids and grandkids are dying to meet you." She patted Lexi's hand. "I know you got your boy to think about, but he's goin' off somewhere with his sister. So I wanted you to know you had me to think about, too. You aren't alone anymore, Alexa. Not unless you want to be. Now, let's eat these donuts. I got to be at work soon. Make a wish and blow out your candle."

A wish.

Lexi stared into the small flame dancing above the twisted blue candle.

There was only one wish, and it wouldn't come true, but she made it anyway.

"Good luck, Lexi. I hope your birthday wish comes true."

After that, they ate their donuts, toasted her birthday again with glasses of milk, and went their separate ways—Eva to a Saturday shift at Walmart, Lexi to the ice cream shop. For the rest of the day, Lexi was in constant motion. On a sunny weekend like this, the shop was crazy busy.

She didn't slow down again until evening, when Zach and Mia picked her up from work.

Lexi did her best to be cheerful around both of them. She laughed and joked and talked at the dinner table, but when Jude brought out a cake with candles, her fragile veneer cracked a little and it took willpower not to cry or run away.

Next year, she would celebrate her birthday by herself. Mia and Zach would be in sunny Southern California, living the college dream. She wanted to be happy for them, she really did. But she kept glimpsing the future that lay like a storm cloud on the horizon. Oh, they talked about staying in touch and keeping their lives braided together, and their intentions would be as true as their emotions, but it wouldn't be enough. When she told them about Eva's Florida offer, they both groaned aloud and begged her not to go so far away. They wanted to see her on school breaks.

Easy for them to ask. But she wanted that, too.

"What's it gonna be like?" Mia asked that night as the three of them lay together on blankets on the beach. It was the first time one of them had dared to ask the question aloud.

They were holding hands, staring up at the stars.

"I've been dreaming about it for so long," Mia said. "But now that it's getting close, I'm scared."

Lexi heard Zach sigh beside her. Because she loved him, she knew what that sound meant: he was stuck in the middle. He loved Lexi—she knew that, believed it with every part of her soul—but he and Mia were more than connected. They were twins, with all that the word implied. They could read each other's thoughts. And really, one of the things Lexi loved most about Zach was how much he cared about the people he loved. He hated hurting anyone. Mia most of all.

That was why he was going to USC. No matter how much he loved Lexi, he loved Mia and his parents even more. He couldn't disappoint them. And he worried that Mia was too shy to make it at USC on her own.

"We'll still be friends forever," Lexi said. She wanted it to be true, needed it to be.

Beside her, she heard Mia draw in a breath and quietly start to cry.

"Don't cry," Zach said.

Sadness rose up in Lexi, and before she knew it, she was crying, too. "We . . . we're dorks," she said, wiping her eyes, and although it was true, and it made her smile, she still couldn't stop crying. She loved both of them and soon they'd be gone.

"I'm gonna miss you, Lexi," Mia said. She rolled over and hugged Lexi and then rolled over onto her back again.

Overhead, the night sky loomed, as incomprehensible as their futures; beneath it, Lexi knew how small they were.

Zach pulled his hand out of Lexi's grasp and said, "I'll be right back." Then he got up and hurried back to the house.

"You'll call me tons, right?" Lexi asked.

Mia squeezed her hand. "We'll be like Jennifer Aniston and Courteney Cox. Bffs forever."

"Sam and Frodo. Harry and Hermione."

"Lexi and Mia," Mia said. "Just think: someday we'll be old together and we'll laugh about how scared we were to go off to college."

"Cuz we'll still be friends."

"Exactly."

Lexi fell silent. She'd learned a long time ago that there were things she might want but would never have, and it hurt less if she tried not to want what was unattainable. Was this friendship like that? Was this just a high school friend version of first love that would diminish into a fond memory with time and distance?

Zach ran back, slightly out of breath. He stood above them, a silhouette against the moonlit waves. "Get up."

"What for?" Mia demanded.

Lexi didn't ask why; she just got up and took his hand. She loved the way his strong, warm fingers curled around hers.

He held out a Ninja Turtles Thermos. "I have an idea. Move your ass, Mia, and quit asking questions."

"Someone thinks he's the boss of me," Mia said as she got to her feet and brushed the sand off her backside.

Zach led them down to the big cedar tree that guarded their beach.

In the moonlight, he looked pale, almost ghostlike, but there was a brightness in his green eyes that shone like tears.

He held out the Thermos and opened it. "We'll put something in here and bury it." He stared at Lexi. "It'll be . . . like . . . our pact."

"For as long as this time capsule is buried here, we'll be best friends," Mia said seriously. "Going off to college won't change that. Nothing will change it."

"We won't be like everyone else," Lexi said, hoping her comment didn't sound like a question, but even now, in this solemn moment, she had trouble believing. Everything came so easily to these two. "We'll never *really* say good-bye."

Mia nodded. "Not as long as this is buried."

Zach held out the open Thermos. Moonlight caught a flash of the silver interior and made it glow. "Put something in here as proof."

At another time, in another place, it might have been funny or melodramatic or just plain silly, but not here, not now, in this darkness that felt weighted by the future that was bearing down on them like an eighteen-wheeler.

"I love you, Lex," Zach said. "College won't change that. We'll stay in love. Always."

Lexi stared at him. It felt like they were connected, drawing one breath back and forth.

Mia dropped a pair of expensive gold earrings into the Thermos.

Zach took off the Saint Christopher medal he always wore and dropped it inside.

All Lexi had was the string friendship bracelet Mia had given her in tenth grade. Mia had long ago lost the one Lexi had made for her, but Lexi had never taken this one off before. She untied it slowly and dropped it in the Thermos. Her memento made no sound when it landed; it bothered her, as if she were the only one of three of them that left no mark somehow.

Zach screwed the lid back on.

"I don't think we should ever dig it up," Mia said. Behind her, a gust of wind came up from the waves and ruffled her hair. "Digging it up would mean . . . like good-bye, and we don't want that. As long as it's here, it means we still love each other."

Lexi wanted to say just the right thing. The moment seemed magical, charged; she'd always remember it. "No good-byes," she said, meaning it.

The look that moved between them was heavy with emotion: in their eyes, they passed around the sad truth that they would be separating soon and that they loved one another, as well as the sweet truth, or hope, that in this coming future some things would survive, that three teenagers could stand in the moonlight and promise to be friends forever and keep that promise.

They knelt in the sand, far above the high-tide line, and at the base of the old tree, they dug deep, deep into the cold gray sand and buried their Ninja Turtles Thermos time capsule.

Lexi wanted to keep it going, to keep promising to search for a future that felt slippery, but when the capsule was buried, the sand looked undisturbed again, and the moment washed away.

Nine

I n early June, the garden was miraculous. This was the time of year that Jude—finally—could take a moment to sit back and enjoy the hard work she'd done. Everywhere she looked, she saw the rewards of her careful planning and judicious pruning. The beds were a riot of glorious color, with sugary pink saucer-sized roses, ruffled yellow peo- nies, spiked purple delphinium. The deep green English boxwood she'd taken such time with was well on its way to becoming the bones of the garden. Above it all, a lotus tree was in full golden bloom; it looked like a Monet painting, just slightly out of focus, against the vibrant blue sky.

She could see how it was all coming together, growing in. Soon, maybe even next year, she would be ready to reveal her pride and joy to the garden-tour attendees.

She peeled off her dirty gloves and got to her feet. The heady scent of roses captured her, made her stand there a moment longer than she'd intended. There was such peace for her here. Every plant, every flower, every shrub was placed according to her plan. If she didn't like the way something grew or spread or bloomed, she yanked it out and replaced it. She was the Red Queen of this realm, in complete control, and, as such, she was never disappointed.

But there was more to her current sense of well-being than that. She hadn't realized until the twins got accepted to USC how tense she'd been throughout senior year, how stressed out. She'd worried endlessly about the kids and for them. She'd worried that one or the other would miss a deadline or make an irreparable mistake or that they wouldn't have the chance to go to college together. Now, she could sleep again, and, amazingly, she was excited for them to leave home. Oh, she was still anxious about them, still concerned about the emptiness of her nest, but spring had lightened more than a gloomy sky; it had lightened her way. She could glimpse a new future for herself, a time when she could be the captain of her own journey. If she wanted to go back to school for landscape architecture, she could; if she wanted to open a garden accessories store, she could. And if she wanted to simply sit on a lawn chair for the whole summer, reading the classics she'd missed, she could do that, too. Hell, she could spend a summer reading comic books if she wanted to.

The thought was liberating and a little scary.

She glanced down at her watch. It was nearing three o'clock, which meant that the kids would be home from school any minute. If the pattern from the past month held, they'd come home in a swarm of seniors, all of whom seemed to be on a mild form of crack. That was what pseudo adulthood and impending graduation had done to the kids. They'd become amped up, superemotional versions of themselves. The boys laughed too hard sometimes; girls became maudlin at the drop of a hat, burst into tears over a bad hair day.

It was no wonder that emotion ran so high in these first golden days of summer. In the words of the great Sam Cooke, change gonna come, and everyone knew it, felt its hot breath drawing near. Most of the island kids had been together since grade school, and their friendships ran deep. They were torn now, wanting both to stay here, where life was safe and known, and to fly far, far away, testing the wings they'd just recently grown. Each passing day, each hour, brought the end of high school that much closer. They felt the need to make lasting memories together. That was what mattered most to them, getting together. It was the same thing that scared the parents. Parties were rampant.

To combat the whole party obsession, Jude had taken her cue from the plain old garden spider: she created an attractive web. She'd had Miles haul out the Jet Skis and the ski boat and ready them for use. She made endless trays of food for ravenous boys and set out bowls of chocolate-covered dried cherries for the girls. She made it easy for her kids' friends to spend the day and night here, under her watchful eyes. For the most part, it had worked. Also, she had learned to trust her kids. Sure, they snuck a few beers at parties, but they kept their word: someone always stayed sober to drive, and they had never missed a curfew.

She put her gardening supplies away—everything in its place—and paused in her greenhouse. There was the petunia Lexi had given her the night of the dance; it looked leggy and forlorn. She made a mental note to plant it, and then went back into the house. There, she showered and dressed in a pair of low-rise black pants and a fitted white T-shirt. She placed the movies she'd rented on the kitchen counter: *Along Came Polly, Starship Troopers 2,* and *Return of the King.*

She was just about to go to the garage for a Coke when the front door banged open.

Footsteps thundered across the wood floors of the great room and thudded up the stairs.

What the hell?

Jude put down her dishrag and walked out of the kitchen.

The front door stood wide open.

Jude closed the door and then went up the stairs. Zach's door was open; Mia's was closed.

She paused outside her daughter's room, heard the unmistakable sound of crying. Sobbing.

"Mia?" she said. At the silence that followed, she opened the door.

Her daughter lay sprawled facedown on her bed, crying into the stuffed pink puppy that had been her favorite childhood toy.

Jude went to the bed. "Hey, Poppet," she said quietly, using the nickname that had been lost along the way, tucked in somewhere alongside baby teeth and patent leather shoes.

Mia made a howling sound and cried harder.

Jude stroked her daughter's silky blond hair. "It's okay, baby," she said, over and over.

Finally, after what felt like forever, Mia rolled over and looked up at Jude through puffy, bloodshot eyes. Her face was damp with tears, and her mouth trembled unevenly. "H-he . . . b-broke . . . up with m-me," she said, bursting sobs.

Jude climbed up into the big bed beside Mia, who curled up against Jude's side like one of the potato bugs they used to hunt for.

Her bright, beautiful, almost grown daughter looked like a little kid again, curled up, crying, holding Daisy Doggy as if it were a talisman, and maybe it was. The mementos of one's past had serious magic.

Mia looked up, tears streaking down her face. "In *class*," she added, as if it somehow doubled his crime.

Jude remembered this pain. Every woman had felt some version of it: the end of first love. It was when you learned, for good and always, that love could be impermanent. "I know how much it hurts," Jude said. "Keith broke up with me the week before senior prom. The week before. He took Karen Abner, and I sat home and watched *Saturday Night Live* by myself. I cried so much I'm surprised the house didn't float away." She remembered that night with clarity. Her mother had come home late, taken one look at Jude and said, *Oh, for God's sake, Judith Anne, you're a child,* and kept walking. Jude looked down at her daughter's teary face. "A broken heart hurts." She paused. "And it heals."

Mia sniffled loudly. "No one else is gonna want me. I'm such a dweeb."

"Oh, Mia. You haven't even begun to find out who you really are, and, believe me, other boys are going to fall in love with you. If a guy can't see how special you are, he isn't good enough for you."

"It just hurts so much."

"It won't always, though. You won't always want to puke when you see him with another girl. And then one day you'll see another guy who makes your heart race and it'll . . . just fade. Your heart will stitch itself back up and only a tiny scar will remain behind, and someday you'll tell your daughter how Tyler Marshall hurt you."

"I never want to see him again. How can I go to the grad party if he's there?"

"It doesn't do any good to hide out in life, Mia. That's how you used to handle things. You're stronger now."

She sighed heavily. "I know. Lexi says I shouldn't care what anyone thinks."

"She's right."

"Yeah," Mia said, but she sounded unconvinced.

Jude held her daughter, remembering the whole of their lives in the blink of an eye. "I love you, Poppet."

"Love you, too, Madre. Can we go get Lexi now? I need her tonight."

"Of course. That's what best friends are for."

※

In less than ten days, they would be graduating from high school.

Lexi stood in a crowd of seniors, staring out at the sea of folding chairs that had been set up in the gymnasium.

Principal Yates stood beneath the basketball hoop, his arms extended, telling them how the ceremony would go, but only a handful of kids were paying attention. The rest of them were laughing and talking and jostling one another.

"You'll file alphabetically out of the gym and along the bleachers and onto the football field—if it's sunny. If not, we'll be in here," the principal was saying. "Now, let's try a walk-through, okay? Jason Adnar, you start us off . . ."

Lexi followed along as she was supposed to, finding her seat on the floor. The rehearsal took all of sixth period, and when it was over, they were released from school. The whole class burst out of the gym like some musical where the kids were starting summer break.

She and Zach found each other without really trying; it was like echolocation. Each just knew where the other was, and they couldn't stand to be apart. Everything felt so big these days, so momentous. Graduation. Summer vacation. College. Sometimes all Lexi could really hold onto was *now,* her love for Zach and her friendship with Mia. Everything else was changing.

Zach took her by the hand, and they walked across campus. At the student parking lot, he opened the Mustang door for her.

"Where's Mia?" Lexi asked.

"Mom is picking her up. They're having girl time after school."

"That'll be good for Mia." Lexi got in the car.

Zach slid into the driver's seat and looked at her. "I need to tell you something."

"What?"

"Not here."

Lexi tensed. Reaching over, she held on to his hand as if it were a lifeline, which it had been from the beginning. All the way through town and down to LaRiviere Park, she said nothing.

At the park, he pulled into their usual spot and turned off the engine. She waited for him to open his door, but instead he twisted around in his seat. His green eyes were bright with tears.

"What?" she whispered.

"I love you, Lexi."

He was going to break up with her. She should have expected this, been ready for it. She wanted to say, *I know you do,* but she couldn't do it. The words felt like broken glass in her mouth.

"I want to go to Seattle Central with you. We could get an apartment."

"Wait. What? You want to go to community college with me?"

"I don't want to leave you, Lex."

She actually shuddered with relief, made a little sound.

He kissed her damp cheek and wiped his eyes, looking embarrassed by tears that were more valuable to her than diamonds.

Holding hands, they left the car and walked out to their place among the driftwood and sat down together. Waves whooshed along the sand, sounding like first love to Lexi. When she looked at him, she almost started to cry again.

He began to spin the dream for her. He talked about their life and the apartment they would find and the jobs they would get. He meant it, all of it, and she loved him all the more for it, but wanting it wouldn't be enough.

"Mia," was all she had to say. She hated to remind him, but what kind of friend would she be if she didn't? She loved Mia as much as she loved Zach.

Zach sighed. "What do I do?" He stared past her, out at the Sound. Then he said it again, more softly, "What do I do?"

"I don't think we should even talk about this, Zach. What's the point?"

"But it could work. Why couldn't it? We could get an apartment in Seattle. The three of us. We could go to Seattle Central Community College for a year or two and then transfer to the U. I'll still get in a good med school. It's not like USC is the *only* good school in the world."

She felt like a kid hanging onto a balloon, being pulled effortlessly into the air. His vision was so buoyant; for a few precious moments, she let herself believe in all of it. Then he said, "I'm going to tell them what I want," and she lost her hold on the string and fell back to earth.

"Not yet," she said, burrowing as tightly against him as she could. Instead of saying anything, she strained upward, kissing him until the tears in her eyes dried up. She let her hands and her mouth communicate how much she loved him.

Afterward, they lay entwined, listening to the incoming tide, watching the cerulean blue sky begin ever so slightly to darken. Finally, as the day drifted toward a lavender evening, they had to leave their snow-globe world, where the view was always the same and no one else could get in.

Lexi held his hand all the way back to his house, afraid to let go. As they turned onto Night Road, her tension grew, until it was a pitchfork-jabs headache that wouldn't go away.

She loved Zach, but he didn't know anything about disappointment. Everything had always come so easily. He didn't expect anything else.

She saw it in his face, a steely determination that fit uncomfortably on his handsome features, like a boy stepping into his dad's oversized shoes and pretending they fit. "You ready to do this?" he asked, coming around to her side of the car.

"No."

He gave her a confident smile. "It'll be cool. You'll see. Come on."

She let him take her hand and lead her into the house.

Miles and Jude lay engtangled on the sofa, each reading a book. Mia lay stretched out on the sectional's other end, watching TV. In a pink terrycloth hoodie, baggy gray sweats, and rhinestoned flip-flops, she looked like a little girl playing dress up. It wasn't until you saw her bloodshot eyes that you knew how wounded she still was, how fragile.

Mia got to her feet. "Hey guys," she said, smiling a little too brightly.

Lexi's heart ached for her best friend; she saw how hard Mia was trying to be strong. She went to her, hugged her fiercely. "How are you?"

"I'm fine," Mia said. "Or I will be. You guys should stop worrying about me."

"Mom? Dad?" Zach said, coming forward. "I need to talk to you."

Jude looked up sharply. Lexi was reminded of one of those nature shows where the prey animal steps on a twig and the predator suddenly looks up. That was how Jude looked now—on alert. "You want to talk to us? What's wrong?" She got up quickly, moved toward her son.

Zach took a deep breath. "I'm not going to USC. I want all three of us to go to Seattle Central CC. Mia? We could get an apartment."

Jude froze.

"What?" Miles got to his feet. "We paid your tuition deposit. It's nonrefundable. Damn it, Zach—"

"I never asked you to pay it," Zach yelled back.

"You never asked us *not* to," Miles said harshly. He stood beside Jude, who'd gone pale. "Well, I'll tell you this, I'm not paying for any damn apartment. If you want to throw opportunity away, you can do it on your tab. See how much fun college is when you have to work full-time and pay your own bills."

"That's not fair," Zach said. "You can't—"

"Stop," Jude hissed, holding up a hand. She looked shell-shocked, a little dazed. "I don't understand. Talk to us, Zach."

"Zach," Mia said, frowning. "You won't go to school with me?"

"I can't leave her," he said, looking miserable.

"And you can leave me? *Me?*" Mia said, starting to cry.

"No. I want you to come with us. I said that," Zach answered. "Come on, Mia—"

"What choice do I have?" Mia cried, looking from Zach to Lexi. "I guess this is you being my friend, too, huh?" Then she ran for the stairs.

Zach followed his sister from the room and up the stairs.

Lexi felt Jude's gaze on her, judging her, blaming her, and Lexi felt a rush of shame. This family had done so much for her, given her so much, and now she was to blame for this. It took all her courage to look up into Jude's disappointed face. "Don't be mad at me," she whispered, wringing her hands. "Please."

"You don't understand what you've done," Jude said. Her voice was shaky and her face was pale.

"I didn't do anything. It's not my fault."

"Isn't it?"

"I didn't tell him to do this . . . to want this."

"Think of Mia instead of Zach. Instead of yourself. You know how talented she is, and how shy. How would it be if the three of you lived together—really. How long before you and Zach started to ignore her?"

"That would never happen."

"Really? It looks as if it just did." Jude paused; her face seemed to soften at that. "I'm sorry. I hate to tangle you up in all of this. But if they don't go to USC they'll regret it, and sooner or later they'll blame you."

Lexi hated the truth she heard in those words.

"Talk to them," Jude said, clutching Miles's hand so tightly her fingers were white.

Lexi wanted to say no, at least to be uncertain about what to do, but she wasn't. Some courses of action were obvious. She had done the wrong thing once before, risked her friendship with Mia and her place in this family. Then, as now, love and longing had blinded her. It was a mistake she refused to repeat.

She turned her back on Miles and Jude and made her way across the room—bigger suddenly, an endless sea crossing—and went up the stairs. They were in Mia's room, standing like a pair of matched statues, staring at each other.

"Hey," Lexi said.

They turned at the same time, wearing identical expressions.

"I wish I were stronger," Mia said.

"You're stronger than you think," Lexi said, moving into the room. Zach reached out for her but she sidestepped him. "But that's not what this is about."

Mia started to cry. "I've dreamed of USC for so long."

"You could go by yourself," Zach said, and Lexi loved him for saying it, but she heard the crack in his voice, saw the regret already filling his gaze.

"I'd kill to go to USC," Lexi said quietly. "I'd give *anything*." She swallowed, looked from one face to the next, struck by how alike they were, mirror images. "You guys can't give up everything just because I don't have it. I won't let you."

She could see how hurt Zach was by her words, and how relieved. She drew in a shaky breath. Yes, he loved her. But he loved his sister, too, and he wanted to make his parents proud, and to secure his future. All of that, he could do at USC. Lexi forced a smile. "Enough of this. You two are going to USC. I'll be rocking SCC. We'll see each other every vacation."

"We have a whole month at Christmas," Mia said. At another time she might have smiled, but now she looked as broken as Lexi felt. Was this adulthood, this pruning of dreams to be practical?

"We'll miss you," Mia said. Zach just stood there, looking pissed and relieved and a little desperate. Cornered.

"It won't change anything," Lexi said, and they all knew it was a lie.

The decision had been made. There was nothing more to say.

Ten

For the next few days, Jude felt a little unsteady, adrift. A bullet had been dodged, there was no doubt about that. Lexi had somehow convinced Zach to follow through on the plans that had been made. It should have been a more than satisfactory conclusion, and it was, but like all compromises, something had been lost by everyone. There was a fissure in this house now, a resentment that was new. Jude couldn't remember when Zach had been so angry at her. Zach, her pliable, lovable boy, had become a surly, angry teenager who slouched in his chair and mumbled his sentences. He was pissed at his sister and his mother—and maybe at Lexi, who knew?—and he wanted everyone to know it.

Jude had tried to give him space. In the days since the blowup, she'd walked carefully around him, treated him with exaggerated care, but the price to her was high. She simply couldn't stand being on the outs with her children. Last night, she'd hardly slept at all for worrying about it. Instead she'd lain in bed, staring up at the ceiling, envisioning one conversation after another. In her imaginings, she and Zach always ended up laughing about their differences . . . and he rededicated himself to USC and his sister. Sometimes he even finished with, *I know how young we are, Madre, don't worry so much, it's cool, thanks . . .*

Now, she stood at her bedroom window, staring out at her backyard as evening fell across the water.

Tonight was the last big high school party of the year—the grad barbeque. Truth be told, she didn't want to let them go. There was so much unresolved between them, so many things to discuss, but she knew nothing would be solved tonight. And if she denied them this party, they'd never speak to her again. But tomorrow. Tomorrow they were going to work through all this drama and get back on track. This was their last year together; she'd be damned if they'd spend it like strangers.

"Mom?" Mia said, knocking at her bedroom door and opening it wide. "Can I talk to you?"

That was fast becoming a dangerous sentence. Jude turned, forced a smile. "Of course, honey."

Mia looked beautiful in the bright late-afternoon light. She was dressed for the party in a pair of ragged, cutoff jeans with carefully placed holes, a tight white T-shirt, and a vintage men's paisley vest that hung off her slim shoulders. Her hair had been drawn back from her face in a loose ponytail; several red metallic baby barrettes held the tiny wisps out of her eyes. "You look sad."

"I'm fine."

Mia came up beside Jude, put an arm around her waist, and leaned against her. Side by side, supported by each other, they stared out the window. "He loves her, Mom."

"What does that—"

Mia turned, tilted her face up. "He *loves* her."

Jude fell silent. For the first time, the words actually resonated. Love. All this time she'd minimized it, trimmed its sails because of their age.

She'd told herself they were too young to understand their own lives. But it was true, their love; it might not last, but it was real.

"I'm breaking them up, making him go to school with me, and you know what the worst part is? They've stuck with me."

Jude touched her daughter's cheek, seeing the pain in Mia's eyes. This daughter of hers was so sensitive. "Of course they have. They'll always be there for you."

"I need to be there for them, too. That's the point."

"You are."

"I'm not going to USC, Mom. The three of us can go to community college and get an apartment."

"Mia—"

"If you and Dad won't pay for it, we'll get jobs. It's the right thing to do, Madre. You always said nothing mattered more than love and family. Did you mean it?"

"Mia, we've paid deposits, made commitments. It's not this simple. You can't just—"

The sound of footsteps in the hallway interrupted them. Zach came into the room. "There you are, Mia. It's time to go."

"Mom and I are talking," Mia said.

Zach rolled his eyes. "Just tell her you'll do what she wants. That's the A answer for team Farraday."

"That's not fair, Zach," Jude said. She felt unsettled, as if everything was unspooling around her, falling free, rolling away, and she couldn't find anything to hold onto.

"Fair?" Zach said. "Is that what matters now? You used to say you wanted us to be happy, but that's only true when we do what you want us to do." He looked at Mia. "Let's go. We have to pick up Lexi, and I don't want to be late to the party." On that, he turned his back on them and strode out of the room.

"Gotta go, Madre." Mia gave Jude a last, sad smile, and followed her brother.

"Wait," Jude called out, hurrying after her daughter, following her to the front door. Outside, she could see the Mustang, hear its engine roar to life.

"We'll talk tomorrow," Jude said to Mia. "This decision about USC is not made."

"Yes, it is." Mia gave her a bright smile. "Forgive me?"

"No. I do not forgive you," Jude said. "And sweet talking won't work this time. This isn't over. You have to think about your futures."

"I'm sorry, Mom, but it kinda is. Love you," Mia gave Jude a kiss on the cheek and then ran out to the car.

"I want you home by one o'clock," Jude said, following her daughter. It was too small, not really what she wanted to say at all, but it was all she had now. Tomorrow they would have a serious talk, all three of them. "At one-o-two, I'm calling the police or driving over."

At the car, Mia hugged her mother fiercely. "We'll be home," she promised.

"And no drinking," Jude said. She leaned down to see her son through the car window. "Zach, you're the designated driver. No matter what. That's our deal."

"I know," he said tightly.

She had to add: "If anything happens—"

"Yeah, yeah," Zach said. "We'll call home for a ride. Come on, Mia. Lexi's waiting."

"Be home by one," Jude said again, stepping back, watching them drive off. "I mean it," she said, but there was no one beside her to hear the words.

❧

Driving too fast, music blaring through the car, Zach turned onto Night Road. Lexi slid into the car door at every hairpin turn.

"Slow down," Mia yelled from the backseat, but Zach just cranked up the music. "Yeah," by Usher was at the edge of pain. . . . *got so caught up I forgot . . .*

When they got to the party, there were already more than a dozen cars parked in the clearing.

Zach pulled the key out of the ignition and dropped it in the well between the seats. "I need something to drink," he said, getting out of the car.

Lexi got out of the car and went to him. "But you're the d.d."

"I know that. And I know my limits. You're not my mom." He pulled away from her and strode toward the party.

Lexi didn't know what to do.

Mia came up beside her. "He's pissed."

"At me?"

Mia shrugged. "At you, me, my parents, himself. Everyone. He doesn't know what he wants and it's killing him. He's always been like that. When things come easily, Zach's cool. But when he's confused or hurting, he loses it. Sometimes he yells and sometimes he shuts up. This time he's yelling. He's especially mad at Mom and me."

"You guys would be crazy to give up USC for a crappy apartment and classes at a community college. He'll see that," Lexi said.

Mia took her by the hand, and they headed down the driveway. Deep in the woods, they found the small log cabin that was one of the island's original homesteads. A big bonfire danced in front of the beach. Beside it stood a pair of silver kegs. Over to the left, someone was grilling hot dogs.

Mia and Lexi stood at the perimeter of the party, talking. All around them kids were laughing and dancing and drinking. Out on the water, a pair of Jet Skis buzzed and raced. Music blared out from a boom box on the porch. The air smelled of pine trees and wood smoke and marijuana.

As they stood there, Tyler walked past them. Alaina Smith was draped all over him, hanging on him. He had his hand on her ass.

Mia drew in a sharp breath. Wiping her eyes, she walked over to the keg and got herself a beer, downing it as fast as she could.

"Are you okay?" Lexi asked.

"Just stay with me," Mia said shakily. "Don't let me be alone . . . I might make a fool of myself."

"I'd never let you be alone," Lexi promised. She got a beer, and even though she hated the taste, it softened her somehow, and Mia, too, and in no time they were smiling again and making jokes.

When she finished her second beer, Mia said, "We need Zach. I have a surprise for you two. Something to tell you. Meet me on the beach." She headed into the crowd before Lexi could stop her, and that was cool, because Lexi didn't want to stop her. As much as she loved being with her best friend, she wanted Zach here, too. This was their graduation party, the last one before the big day, and the three of them should be together.

Lexi headed down to the beach and sat in the sand, waiting.

"There you are," Zach said a few minutes later, sitting down beside her. "I've been looking all over for you."

"Where's Mia? She went looking for you."

Zach shrugged and handed her a bottle of rum. "Here."

"Hey, you're not supposed to be drinking," Lexi said.

"Last one, I promise. Here."

She hated to drink like this, without mixers or anything, but she didn't want to upset him, so she took a sip.

"She doesn't give a shit about what I want," he said and lifted the bottle to his mouth again.

Lexi didn't know if he was talking about his mother or his sister, but it didn't really matter either way. "Yes, she does."

He took another long drink, handed it to her. "Maybe I don't give a shit what she wants."

Lexi sighed. "Yes, you do."

He looked at her, his eyes wild. "I love you so much."

She knew exactly what he was feeling: it was the universe of her own emotions. She was afraid of watching him go; he was afraid of letting her stay. "I know," was all she could say. She believed him now, believed in his love, and that was everything.

They needed to be strong for each other, and she would be the one to start. "I'll never stop loving you, Zach."

In a taut voice, he said, "Come here," and took her hand and led her deep into the woods.

There, they kissed and undressed and made love in a way that was new; sad, maybe, and a little rough, with their bodies communicating all the difficult words they couldn't say. When it was over and they lay there, spent, staring up at the starlit sky, Lexi reached for the rum bottle and drank until their future didn't seem so sharp and a nice fuzziness blurred the edges.

Finally, unsteady on their feet, they left the copse of trees and returned to the party, which was now completely out of control. There were more than one hundred kids there, talking, laughing, dancing. Boys were tossing a football back and forth; a bunch of people were gathered around the kegs; more stood around the huge bonfire. On the cabin, a sign read: *Class of 2004—Good Bye and Good Luck.*

Mia shrieked when she saw them and stumbled toward them. "Where *were* you guys?" she said, handing Lexi a half-empty bottle of rum. "This is *our* night. The three of us. Okay?"

They stood there, a little drunk, staring at one another, an island in a sea of seniors. Mia reached out for Zach's hand, then for Lexi's, and, with that touch, the connection returned. They were *them* again.

"Let's party," Zach said, smiling at his sister.

Lexi could *see* the love between these two, and as much as it hurt to know that they would leave her, she was glad the fight was over. They needed this last summer together.

They merged into the party and became a part of it, laughing, drinking, dancing until the moon rose in a dark sky and the air turned cold. By two o'clock in the morning, the party was winding down. Kids lay sprawled on the ground, on the grass, on the porch.

Mia started to say something and stopped. "Wha was I saying?"

Zach laughed drunkenly. "You said you had a surprise for us. You've been saying it all night. What is it?"

"Ha, thass right," Mia said and fell sideways. Her head smacked on a rock and she moaned, "Shit. Tha hurt . . ."

Lexi helped Mia sit back up. "She's bleeding, Zach."

They all burst into laughter at that.

Lexi tried to use her sleeve to wipe the blood off Mia's forehead, but her balance was off and she kept poking Mia in the eye instead, and Mia just laughed harder.

Mia lurched up suddenly and stood there, swaying. "Oh man . . ." She clamped a hand over her mouth for a second and then stumbled sideways, falling to her knees in the sand and vomiting. The wretching sound and the smell made Lexi almost sick, too, but she went to Mia anyway, held her hair back.

"I am so hammered," Mia finally said, wiping her mouth with her sleeve and sitting back on her heels.

Zach lurched toward them. He was so unsteady he tripped over a stone and fell down. "Is she okay?"

"Iss time to go," Mia said. "Mom'll kill us if we're late. Wha time is it?"

"Two ten," Lexi said, squinting at her watch. She thought that was right. The numbers were dancing and blurring.

"Oh SHIT." Zach staggered to his feet. "We gotta go."

They made their weaving, unsteady way up the bank and across the grassy lawn, stepping around the bodies of their passed-out classmates. Mia stepped on someone's arm and laughed, yelled, "Oops! Sorry."

As they staggered to the car, it hit Lexi: Zach was drunk. She turned to him.

He stood there, swaying like a palm tree in the trade winds, his eyes closed.

Then she looked at Mia, who was puking again. Blood was dripping down the side of her face.

"You can't drive," Lexi said to Zach.

Mia got closer to the car and bent forward like a rag doll, pressing her cheek against the hood. "Call Mom," she said. She dug in her pocket for her phone, dropped it on the ground.

Lexi picked up the phone.

"No way," Zach said. "Lass time she practically grounded us."

"Hesh right," Mia said. "Less jus go."

Lexi tried to concentrate, but she couldn't. All she could really think about was that they should call Jude, but what would Jude think of Lexi then? What if Eva found out about this? Lexi had promised to be good, and here she was at a party again.

Mia shivered violently. "I'm freezing, Zach 'tack. Where's my coat? An my head hurts. Why does my head hurt?"

"We should sleep here," Lexi said.

"Mom would kill us," Zach said, stumbling forward, slamming into his car. He wrenched the driver's door open and fell into the seat. The keys were in the well; he searched around, swearing, and then laughed, "Got 'em."

"Get out of there, Zach," Lexi said. "You're too drunk to drive." She walked around the driver's side of the car, trying not to stumble or fall. "Mia, help me," Lexi said. "Tell Zach he's too drunk to drive."

"Iss only a mile . . ." Mia said. "An Mom did flip out lass time we called."

"I can do it," Zach said, smiling sloppily.

"Come on," Mia moaned, wiping more blood from her forehead. She opened the car door and fell into the backseat. "Ouch," she said, laughing, and then curled up into a fetal position on the seat.

Zach slipped the key into the ignition and started the engine, which roared to life in the quiet darkness. "Come on, Lex. Iss no big deal. Less go."

"I don't know," Lexi said, shaking her head. The movement pushed her off-balance and made her fall forward; she hit the side of the car. "Wait. I gotta *think*. This isn't a good idea . . ."

Eleven

Beep.
   Beep.
   Beep.

Jude sat up, bleary-eyed.

She was on the sectional in the living room. Her cell phone lay on the cushion beside her, chirping. An infomercial flitted silently across the TV screen.

She struggled to focus on the small face of her watch. 3:37. Then she flipped open her cell phone. There was a text from Mia.

Sry wr late. On our way. Luv U. The text had come in at 2:11.

Oh, they *would* be sorry. They'd come home late, not checked in with Jude, and forgotten to turn off the exterior lights. This would be their last party for a while. She got up, turned off the TV and the outside lights, and locked the front door. As she climbed the stairs, she tried to decide whether to wake them up or yell at them tomorrow.

She opened Mia's door and turned on the light. The bed was empty.

She felt a ping of fear, like a drop of acid on bare skin, and went to Zach's room.

It was empty, too.

Take a breath, Jude. They missed their curfew; that was all. They'd started to leave the party and then been caught up somehow.

She called Mia's cell. It rang and rang, then went to voice mail.

It was the same with Zach's phone.

She ran downstairs to her room. Miles lay sleeping in bed, a book open on his chest, the television on.

"It's late, Miles, and they're not home."

"Call them," he mumbled.

"I did. No one answered."

Miles sat up, frowning, and glanced at the clock. "It's almost four o'clock."

"They're never this late," she said.

Miles ran a hand through his hair. "We don't want to panic. They probably lost track of time."

"We could drive over there," Jude said.

Miles nodded. "I think—"

The doorbell rang.

"Thank *God.*" Jude felt a rush of relief, then a burst of anger. "They are *so* grounded," she muttered, leaving the room.

She stepped out into the long, dark hallway. It was black . . . and then red . . . yellow. Lights cut through the darkness, blinking, blaring.

Police lights.

She stumbled, almost fell. Then Miles was beside her, steadying her.

She felt herself moving forward but she wasn't really walking. She was a piece of flotsam caught up in her husband's motion.

Two policemen stood outside their door. It was raining, hard; why did she notice that? She knew these men, knew them and their wives and their children, but they shouldn't be here now, at her house, in the middle of the night, their images flashing red and yellow.

Officer Avery stepped forward, his hat in his hand.

She saw everything in pieces, out of focus, as if she were looking through binoculars set for someone else's eyes; staccato bursts of color, a macabre night, rain that looked like bits of ash falling from the sky.

I'm sorry. There's been an accident.

Words. Sounds. Lips that moved and the sound of heavy breathing. Falling rain.

Mia . . . Zach . . . Alexa Baill . . .

She couldn't process it, couldn't make sense of it. *My babies . . . you're talking about my children.*

"They've been airlifted to Harborview, all three of them."

"They're okay?" she heard her husband ask, and it shocked her so badly she almost pulled away from him. How could he find a voice now? Ask anything?

Did the policeman answer? What had he said? Jude couldn't hear anything over the rain, or the beating of her heart. Was she crying? Is that why she couldn't see?

Miles looked at her, and in his eyes she saw how breakable they both were, how fragile. It had happened in an instant, this new frailty; in the time it took them to walk from their bedroom to the front door, they had been pared down, their bones weakened. She thought his touch would bruise her now, leave a mark.

"Let's get dressed," he said, taking her by the arm. "We need to go."

The drive to the hospital seemed to take forever. There were no ferries running at this hour, so they had to take the bridge to Kitsap County and drive around to Seattle.

In the car, they didn't speak. Silence felt manageable; words did not. It took concentration just to draw in each breath and exhale without crying.

She wished she were a religious woman. All that spirituality she'd cultivated didn't help her now; she needed faith, an antidote to this escalating fear. When they parked, Jude turned to her husband. He looked drawn and gaunt and the look in his eyes was harrowing.

She wanted to comfort him, as she did so often when he came home from work still mired in loss. She wanted to tell him not to think of the worst, but she was too brittle to even offer an arm.

Inside the bright white hospital, Jude straightened her shoulders and forged ahead, trying to manage her fear by controlling everything around her. But her questions went unanswered, her calls for help unheeded.

"Stop," Miles finally said, taking her aside in the crowded hallway. "Just let them do their jobs. All we can do is wait."

She didn't want to do nothing, but she had no choice. So she stood there, overwhelmed by helplessness, trying not to cry. Waiting.

Finally, at just past six in the morning, they got an answer. It felt as if they'd been here for decades, but in truth, it had been less than an hour.

"Mia is in surgery," the man in front of her said. He was a big black man with tattooed biceps and the kindest, molasses-colored eyes she'd ever seen. His orange scrubs looked more like prison clothes than hospital wear. "She suffered some pretty severe internal injuries. That's all I know," he added when Miles began to question him.

"She'll be okay, though," Jude said. Everything felt scrambled in her head, sounds seemed to be muffled. Why could she hear her own heartbeat in all this noise?

"The surgeon will come out to talk to you when he's done, but it will be a while. They just went in," the nurse said.

"And Zach?" Miles asked.

"I'll take you to see him," the nurse said. "He sustained some chemical burns to his face and eyes, so he's bandaged. Before you ask, Dr. Farraday, that's all I know. He also cracked a couple of ribs. The girl, Alexa, is in with a doctor right now, but I think her injuries are less severe. A broken arm, a forehead laceration."

"Burns?" Jude said. "How bad is it? Has he seen a specialist? There's that doctor from the UW—what's his name, Miles?"

Miles took her hand. "Later, Jude," he said firmly, and she felt that helplessness rise up in her again.

They followed the nurse into a private room, where her son, the boy she'd thought only last week was looking so much like a man, lay in a metal-railed bed all alone, surrounded by machines. The right side of his face was bruised and swollen, misshapen somehow. Bandages wrapped his head, mushrooming out above his ears. A rectangular gauze pad covered the lower part of his right cheek and jawline.

Miles squeezed her hand, and this time she clung to him.

"We're here," Miles said.

"I'm holding your hand, Zach," Jude said, trying not to cry as she stared down at her son's bruised, burned face and bandaged eyes. His other hand was bandaged up past his wrist. "Just like I used to, remember? I used to hold your hand all the way into the classroom in kindergarten. You got cool in eighth grade—after that, I could only hold your hand in the car, and only for a few minutes. I used to reach back into the backseat, remember? And you'd hold my hand for a few minutes, just so—"

"Mom?"

For a moment she thought she'd imagined his voice. "Thank God," she whispered, squeezing his hand.

Zach tried to sit up. "Where am I?"

"Lie still, son. You're in a hospital," Miles said.

"I . . . can't see . . . What happened?"

"There was a car crash," Miles said.

"Am I blind?"

Of course not, Jude wanted to say. It couldn't be true, not to her son who had been afraid of the dark. "Your eyes are bandaged, that's all."

"We don't know the extent of your injuries yet," Miles said evenly. "Just rest, Zach. The important thing is that you're alive."

"How's Mia?" Zach asked quietly, still sitting up. He looked around, blind behind all that gauze. "And Lex?"

"Mia's in surgery right now. We're waiting to hear," Jude answered. "I'm sure she'll be fine. This is a wonderful hospital."

"And Lexi?" Zach asked.

"The nurse thought she was going to be fine. We'll know more soon," Miles said.

"Just rest, baby," Jude said, using her voice to soothe him as she had so often when he was little. "We'll be right here."

She sat by his bed, as she'd done so many times in his life. A few moments later, Miles left again to check on Mia's status. Waiting for answers was terrible, but Jude had to bear it. What choice did she have? And she believed in the deepest part of her soul that Mia would be fine. She had to believe that.

Behind her, the door opened again. "No news yet," Miles said.

Jude looked down at Zach again, trying to think of what to say to him. Words felt heavy and unwieldy and she couldn't tame her fear enough to *think*, so she dug deep into the past, went back to the days when she'd had two babies who tangled up together like puppies in her lap, and she told him his favorite story. She didn't remember it word for word, but she remembered enough to start. "The night Max wore his wolf suit to make mischief, his mother called him Wild Thing and sent him to bed without dinner . . ."

As she remembered the words—something about the gnashing of his terrible teeth—she tried to distance herself from the memories they evoked. But how could she? The story reminded her of a boy who'd cried when she turned the lights out in his room, a boy who'd been terrified of monsters in the closet and under the bed. Only his sister's presence could really calm him. Jude had ignored all the good parenting manuals and let the twins climb into bed with her and Miles.

And now his eyes were wrapped; he was deep in the dark.

"Mom?"

She wiped her eyes. "What, baby?"

"Have you seen Lexi?"

"Not yet."

"Go see her. Tell her . . . tell her I'm fine, okay?"

She squeezed his hand and let go. "Of course." She stood up, shaky on her feet, and turned to Miles. "You'll hold his hand while I'm gone?"

"Of course."

She pretended not to notice that they couldn't look at each other anymore. "Okay, then."

She stayed a second longer, unable somehow to leave her son; then she left the room and went out into the brightly lit hallway. Pausing to get her bearings, she walked up to the busy nurses' station.

"Can I get information on Alexa Baill?" she asked.

"Are you a relative?"

"No."

"She is in Room 613 west. That's all I can tell you."

Jude nodded and left the nurse's station.

At 613 west, she paused a moment, then opened the door.

The room held two beds. The one by the window was unoccupied. In the other lay Lexi. Although her bed was angled up, she was asleep. Her pretty, heart-shaped face was bruised, her left eye had a bandage above it, probably from a laceration, and her left arm was in a cast. Beside her, Eva Lange sat in a plastic chair. The woman looked older than Jude remembered, and smaller. She had her hands clasped tightly in her lap.

Jude had heard so many stories about this woman over the years, how she'd picked up Lexi sight unseen and offered her a home. Eva had had hardly any money, and only a rented trailer and a secondhand car to her name, but she'd welcomed Lexi in. "Hello, Eva," Jude said. "May I come in?"

Eva looked up. Her dark eyes swam with tears and the wrinkles on her cheeks were accordion-deep. "Sure."

"How is she?" Jude asked.

"How should I know? Getting a doctor to talk to you is like finding a winning lotto ticket."

"I'll have Miles get you some information. It's hard, though. We're waiting to hear about . . . Mia, too." Jude looked at Eva, and though they had almost nothing in common, they had this moment, this mother's worry strung between them.

"I don't get it," Eva said softly, her eyes moist. "She told me she was spending the night at your house. With Mia."

"Yes. That was the plan."

"But they weren't home at 3:30?"

It occurred to Jude suddenly, sharply, that her children were responsible in this, that they'd driven . . . and that she had let them go. "They ignored their curfew."

"Oh."

Jude moved closer to the bed, stared down at this girl her son loved. It all seemed so unimportant now, the fight they'd had because of that love. The question of colleges. Jude would do things differently from now on. *Honest, God. I'll be better. Just make Mia and Zach and Lexi okay.* "She's like a part of our family."

"I know how much she loves you all."

"We love her, too. Well. I better go back now," she said at last, stepping back. "We might get word on Mia."

"I'm praying for all of them," Eva said.

Jude nodded, wishing she knew how to pray.

Twelve

"Jude, honey, there's news."

Jude awoke with a start. She was slumped in a chair at Zach's bedside. Somehow she'd managed to fall asleep. She blinked and rubbed her eyes. It made no sense that sunlight was streaming through the window. She could tell that her son was asleep by the even strains of his breathing.

Miles helped her to her feet and led her out into the hallway, where a man in blue scrubs stood waiting for them.

She clung to Miles's hand.

"I'm Dr. Adams," the surgeon said, pulling the multicolored cap off his head. He had a shock of gray white hair and a pleated, basset hound face. "I'm so sorry—"

Jude's knees buckled. She held on to Miles's strong arm, but suddenly he was shaking, too.

"Injuries too severe . . . no seatbelt . . . thrown from the car . . ." The surgeon kept talking, but Jude couldn't hear him.

A hospital chaplain moved into her field of vision, dressed in black, a crow coming to pick at bones.

She heard someone screaming, and the sound blocked out everything. She pushed at the chaplain.

It was *her*. She was the one screaming *no*, crying.

When people tried to hold her—maybe Miles, maybe the chaplain, she didn't know who was reaching for her—she pushed free and stumbled aside, crying out her daughter's name.

She heard Miles behind her, firing questions at the surgeon, getting answers, something about cerebral blood flow and pentobarbital. When she heard him say *brain death* she threw up and sank to her knees in her own vomit.

Then Miles was beside her, handling her with the kind of gentleness that he usually reserved for his elderly patients. He put an arm around her, hoisted her to her feet and steadied her; she kept collapsing inward.

There were people gathered around, staring at her. *Take it back,* she thought, looking around at them.

Please, God.

Please.

She was making a scene, humiliating herself.

Miles took her into an empty room, where she collapsed onto a plastic chair, bowing forward. *It isn't real. It can't be.* "I was just with her," she said to Miles, looking up at him through scalding tears.

He sank to his knees in front of her and said nothing. She felt her insides draining away, emptying. Then there was a knock at the door.

How long had they been in here? A minute? An hour?

The chaplain stepped into the room. Beside him, a woman in a cheap blue suit held a clipboard.

"Would you like to see Mia?" the chaplain said.

Jude looked in his blue eyes and saw tears; this stranger was crying for her, and the cold truth settled deep, deep inside her.

"Yes," Miles said, and it was the first time she even thought of him, of his pain. When she looked at him, she saw that he was crying, too.

They were so fragile. Who had known that? Not her, surely. Until just now, as she reached for her husband's hand, she'd thought she was a strong woman. Powerful, even. Lucky.

They stood up together and walked down one corridor and then another until they came to the last door on their right. Far from other patients. Of course.

Miles had the strength to open the door, although how, Jude would never know.

The room was brightly lit, which surprised Jude; almost everything in it was stainless steel. And there was noise in here, machines whooshing, thunking. A computer screen showed a heartbeat spiking and falling across a field of black.

"Thank God," Jude whispered. She'd been wrong. In the roar of *I'm sorry,* she'd misunderstood. Mia wasn't gone. She was right here, looking as beautiful as always, her chest rising and falling. "She's okay."

Clipboard woman stepped forward. "Actually, she's not. I'm sorry. It's called brain death, and I can—"

"Don't," Miles said, so harshly the poor woman went pale. "I know why you're here and how long we have. I've spoken with Dr. Adams. We'll consent. Just leave us alone."

The woman nodded.

"Consent to what?" Jude looked at Miles. "She looks perfect. A little bruised, but . . . look how she's breathing. And her color is good."

Miles's eyes filled with tears. "It's the machines," he said gently. "Her body is being kept alive, but her mind . . . our Mia . . . isn't in there anymore."

"She looks—"

"Trust me, Jude. You know how much I'd fight for her if . . . our girl were still here to fight for."

She didn't know how to believe him. Everything inside of her was screaming that this wasn't fair, that it wasn't right, that a mistake had been made. She started to pull back, shaking her head, but Miles wouldn't let her go. He pulled her hard against his chest, held her so tightly she couldn't move.

"She's gone," he whispered into her ear.

She screamed out loud, struggling in his arms, saying *no no no,* and still he held her against him. She cried until her whole body felt limp and empty, and finally he let her go.

She moved woodenly to her daughter's bedside.

Mia was surrounded by machines and wires and needles and IVs. She looked healthy enough to wake up any second and say *Hola, Madre.*

"Hey, Poppet," Jude said, hating the way her brittle voice cracked on the familiar nickname. "She needs her Daisy Doggy. Why didn't we bring him?"

Miles came up beside her. "Hey, baby girl," he said, and he broke.

Jude wanted to comfort him, but she couldn't.

"The last thing I said to her was that I didn't forgive her. Oh my God, Miles—"

"Don't," he said simply.

If Miles hadn't been beside her, holding her up, she would have collapsed beside this girl who seemed to be sleeping so peacefully. Jude remembered how it had felt to carry her, to imagine and love her before she'd ever even seen her, how she used to talk to them, her unborn twins, swimming in her swollen belly like a pair of tiny fish, coiled together, always together . . .

Zach would be alone now. An only child.

How would they tell him this?

The world felt Bubble Wrapped and far away. Jude didn't focus on anything except her daughter. In the next hour, calls were made to friends and family. Miles did all the talking. Words came at Jude, words that had had no meaning before. *Organs. Heart. Corneas. Skin. Save people's lives.* She nodded and signed and looked at no one and said nothing. People pushed at her, jostled her as they ran tests on Mia. More than once Jude snapped at someone and told them to be careful with her daughter. It was all she could do now. She reminded them that Mia was ticklish, that she sang off-key and hummed all the time, that she hated to be cold.

No one seemed to listen. They looked impossibly sad and lowered their voices to whispers. At some point the chaplain sidled up to her, pulled her away from the bed, and tried to comfort her with rote words. She elbowed him hard and rushed back to Mia. "I'm here, Poppet," she said. "You're not alone."

She stood there as long as they let her, perfectly still, whispering words of love and telling stories and trying to remember every single thing about Mia.

Finally—and she had no idea when it was, or how long she'd been there—Miles came up to her.

"Jude?" he said, and she had the idea that he'd said it more than once, maybe even yelled it.

She tore her gaze away from Mia and turned to her husband.

Behind Mia stood a team of people in surgical scrubs. She caught sight of someone holding a red and white cooler.

"They have to take her now, Jude," he said, peeling her fingers from the bed rail.

She stared at him through hot tears. "I'm not ready."

He said nothing. What was there to say? Who could ever be ready for a thing like this?

"You're going with her?" she said, pressing a hand over his heart, feeling it beat.

"I'll be in the viewing area." His voice broke. "She won't be alone."

"I want to sit outside the OR," she said, even though she really wanted to run away.

"Okay."

She turned again, leaned down and kissed her daughter's plump pink lips. "I love you, Poppet." She pulled the blanket up to Mia's neck. It was an instinctive gesture, a mother's caress. Finally, she drew back, shaking, and let Miles pull her away from the bed. In a moment, Mia would be really gone . . .

They were wheeling her daughter out of the room when Jude remembered what they'd forgotten. How had they forgotten?

"Wait!" she screamed.

Miles looked at her. "What?"

"Zach," was all she could say.

❧

Lexi can hear Mia talking, laughing . . . saying something about part of your world . . .

She mumbled, "Huh?" to her best friend and reached over for Mia, but there was no one beside her. Lexi woke slowly, blinking. Something was wrong. Where was she?

She tried to sit up and felt a sharp pain in her chest. It hurt so badly she cried out.

"Alexa?" Eva got up. She'd been in a chair by the window, reading.

"Where am I?" Lexi asked, frowning.

Eva moved closer. "The hospital."

The two words stopped time. Lexi remembered everything in a rush of images: the car's white hood hurtling forward; the tree, burned white by the headlights; Mia's screaming; smoke; the sound of shattering glass . . .

"We crashed," she whispered, turning to look at her aunt. One look in Eva's sorrow-filled eyes and she knew it was bad. Lexi threw back the covers and started to get out of bed.

Eva grabbed her good wrist and held firm. "Don't, Lexi. You've got a broken rib and a fractured arm. Just be still."

"I need to see Zach and Mia—"

"She's gone, Lexi."

Lexi sagged with relief. "Thank God. When did she leave? And how's Zach?"

"Mia died, Lexi. I'm sorry."

Died.

Gone.

Lexi couldn't seem to comprehend the words. How could it be? She felt Mia beside her, leaning close, whispering, *don't let me be alone. I might do something stupid.* It had been a moment ago, a second. *Can I sit with you?* "No," she whispered. "Don't say that . . ."

Eva shook her head, and there it was, wrapped in the silence like some sleeping snake that had just been poked. The truth lashed out.

The car. The crash. Dead.

No. *No.*

"That can't be true," Lexi whispered. Mia was part of her; how could only one of them survive? "I'd *feel* it, wouldn't I? It can't be true."

"I'm sorry."

Lexi slumped back. She glanced over at the door and expected to see Mia there, dressed in some weird getup, her arms crossed, her hair braided unevenly, smiling that smile of hers and saying, *hola amiga, what should we do?*

Then she sat up. "Zach?"

"I don't know," Eva said. "He was burned. That's all I know."

Burned.

"Oh my God," she said. "I don't remember any fire."

Burned.

"Tell me what happened," Eva asked gently, holding Lexi's hand.

Lexi lay back, feeling as if her soul had been scooped out of her body with a ragged blade. If she could have willed herself into nonexistence, she would have. *Please God, let him be okay.* How could she live otherwise?

How could she live without Mia?

Jude stood beside the gurney, holding Mia's hand. She knew there was commotion going on all around her: people coming and going, the team members talking about "the harvest" as if Jude were deaf. There was a boy that desperately needed Mia's strong, loving heart, only a year younger than her daughter, and another boy who dreamed of playing baseball . . . a mother of four who was dying of kidney failure and just wanted to be strong enough to walk to school with her children.

The stories were heartbreaking and should have comforted Jude. She'd always cared about things like that. But not now.

Let Miles find peace in these donations. She did not. Neither did they upset or offend her. She just didn't care.

There was nothing inside of her but pain; she kept it trapped inside, behind pursed lips. God help her if she started screaming.

At her back, she heard a door open and she knew who it was. Miles had brought Zach to say good-bye to his twin sister. The door closed quietly behind them.

It was the four of them now, just the family. All those doctors and specialists were outside, waiting.

"Something's wrong with Mia," Zach said. "I can't feel her."

Miles went pale at that. "Yeah," he said. "Mia . . . didn't survive, Zach," Miles said at last.

Jude knew she should go to her son, be there for him, but she couldn't make herself let go of Mia's hand, couldn't move. If she let go, Mia would be gone, and the idea of that loss was overwhelming, so she held it away.

"She d-died?" Zach said.

"They did everything they could. Her injuries were too extensive."

Zach started ripping the bandages off his eyes. "I need to see her—"

Miles pulled their son into an embrace. "Don't do that," he said, and by the end of his breath, they were both crying. "She's right here. We knew you'd want to say good-bye." He led their burned, bandaged son to the gurney, where his sister lay strapped down, her body covered in white and kept alive by wheeled machines.

Zach felt for his sister's hand and held it. As always, they came together like puzzle pieces. He bowed forward, let his bandaged head rest on his sister's chest. He whispered the nickname from their babyhood, "Me-my . . . ," and said something Jude didn't understand; probably it was a word from long ago, forgotten until now, a word from the twin language that was theirs alone. It had always been Zach chattering back then, talking for his sister . . . and it was that way again.

Behind them, someone knocked on the door.

Miles took his son by the shoulders, eased him back from the gurney. "They have to take her now, son."

"Don't put her in the dark," Zach said in a hoarse voice. "I'm not really the one who was afraid. It was her." His voice cracked. "She didn't want anyone to know."

At that little reminder of who they were, who they'd been—the twins—Jude felt the last tiny bit of courage crumble away.

Don't put her in the dark.

Jude squeezed Mia's hand tightly, clinging to her daughter for as long as she possibly could.

Miles and Zach came up around her, reached out. They held one another upright, the three of them, the family that was left.

The knock at the door came again.

"Jude," Miles said, his face wet with tears. "It's time. She's gone."

Jude knew what she had to do, what they all were waiting for. She'd rather cut out her own heart. But she had no choice.

She let go of her daughter's hand and stepped back.

Thirteen

Jude crouched in the hallway near the OR door. At some point, she'd lost her footing and fallen to the cold linoleum floor, and she stayed there, her face pressed to the wall. She could hear people coming and going around her, rushing from one trauma to the next. Sometimes they stopped and talked to her. She looked up into their faces—frowning and compassionate and a little distracted—and she tried to understand whatever it was they were saying, but she couldn't. She just couldn't. Her whole body shook with cold and her vision was cloudy and she couldn't hear anything except the reluctant beating of her heart.

No. I do not forgive you.

We'll talk tomorrow.

These were the words that ran in an endless loop through her mind.

"Judith?"

She turned slightly, saw her mother standing there, tall and straight, her white hair perfectly styled, her clothes ironed. She knew her mother had been here for hours; she'd tried repeatedly to speak to Jude, but what good were words now between strangers?

"Let me help you, Judith," her mother said. "You can't sit here in the hallway. Let me get you some coffee. Food will help."

"Food will not help."

"There's no need to yell, Judith." Mother glanced up and down the hallway, to see who might have heard the outburst. "Come with me." She reached down.

Jude wrenched sideways, scurrying tighter into the corner. "I'm fine, Mother. Just let me be, okay? Find Miles. Or go see Zach. I'm fine."

"You most certainly are not fine. I think you should eat something. You've been here seven hours."

Already Jude was sick of people saying this to her. As if food in her stomach would remedy the hole in her heart. "Go away, Mother. I appreciate you coming here, okay? But I need to be alone. You wouldn't understand."

"Wouldn't I?" Her mother made a quiet sound, and then said, "Fine." She lowered herself to her knees beside Jude.

"What are you doing?"

Her mother collapsed the last inch to the cold linoleum floor. "I'm sitting with my daughter."

Jude felt a stirring of guilt—no doubt this was one of her mother's self-interested gestures, a way to force Jude into bending to her will. At any other time, it would have worked, Jude would have sighed in defeat and gotten to her feet, doing as her mother asked. Now, she didn't care. She wasn't going to leave this spot until Miles came to get her. "You shouldn't sit here, Mother. It's cold."

Her mother looked at her, and for a split second, there was an unbearable sadness in her gaze. "I've been cold before, Judith Anne. I'm staying."

Jude shrugged. It was all too much for her. She couldn't think about anything right now, and certainly not her mother. "Whatever," she said tiredly, and the minute the word was out of her mouth, she regretted it. How could one word bring back an era, a child, in such exquisite detail?

She saw Mia at thirteen, braces and acne and insecurity, saying "whatever" in answer to every question . . .

She closed her eyes and remembered . . .

❧

"Jude?"

She looked up, confused by the sound of her own name. How long had she been here? She glanced sideways; her mother was asleep beside her.

Miles stood outside the OR.

"It's over," he said, reaching down for her.

Jude started to get up and fell back down. He was beside her in an instant, steadying her. When Jude was standing on her own, he helped Caroline to her feet.

"Thank you," Caroline said stiffly, smoothing her hair back from her face, although no strands had fallen free. "I'll go to the waiting room," she said. Glancing at Jude for a moment, she almost said something more; then she turned and walked away.

Jude clung to her husband's arm and let him lead her into the operating room, where Mia lay on the table, draped in white. Her silvery-blond hair was covered in a pale blue cap. Jude took it off, let her daughter's hair fall free. She stroked it as she'd done so many times before.

Mia still looked beautiful, but her cheeks were pale as chalk, her lips were colorless.

Jude held Mia's hand and Miles held Jude's. The three of them stayed connected, no one saying much of anything, just crying, until a nurse finally came in.

"Dr. Farraday? Mrs. Farraday? I'm sorry to bother you, but we need to take your daughter."

Jude tightened her hold on Mia's cold hand. "I'm not ready."

Miles turned to her and tucked her hair behind one ear. "We have to be with Zach now."

"She'll be gone when we're done."

"She's gone now, Jude."

Jude started to feel pain and pushed it away, letting numbness return. She couldn't allow herself to feel anything. She leaned down and kissed Mia's cheek, noticing how cold it, too, was, and whispering, "I love you, Poppet." Then she drew back and watched Miles do the same thing. She didn't know what he said; all she could hear was her own blood, rushing into and out of her heart. At first she was dizzy, but as she walked down the busy hallway and stepped into the elevator and rode down to the sixth floor, she lost even that slim sensation.

"Mrs. Farraday?"

"Jude?"

From somewhere in the fog, she heard Miles say her name. The impatient tone told her that he'd said it more than once.

"This is Dr. Lyman," Miles said.

They were in another hallway, outside Zach's room. Jude didn't even remember getting here.

"I'm sorry for your loss," Dr. Lyman said.

She nodded and said nothing.

Dr. Lyman led them into her son's room. Zach sat slumped in bed, his arms crossed.

"Who's there?" he said.

"It's us, Zach," Jude said, trying to sound strong for her son.

Dr. Lyman cleared his throat and moved to Zach's bedside. "How are you feeling?"

Zach shrugged, as if it didn't matter. "My face hurts like hell."

"It's a burn," Dr. Lyman said.

"I'm *burned*?" Zach said quietly. "On my face? How?"

"It's rare," Dr. Lyman said. "Most people don't even know it's possible, but car airbags have something like jet fuel in them, a propellant. Normally they deploy just fine, but sometimes, and this is what happened to you, Zachary, it can go wrong and cause chemical burns. That's what happened to your eyes, too."

"What do I look like?"

"The burns aren't bad," the doctor said. "There's a small patch along your jaw that we're going to watch carefully, but there should be little or no real scarring. We don't anticipate needing any skin grafts. May I remove the bandages now?"

Zach nodded.

Dr. Lyman went over to the sink and washed his hands and then carefully unwound Zach's bandages. Zach's hair had been shaved on one side and left long on the other, and it gave him a lopsided, off-balance look.

As the bandages came off, Jude saw the whole blistered, oozing burn, the way it swept down along his hairline, across his cheek and jaw.

Slowly, Dr. Lyman removed the bandages on Zach's eyes, and the metal, honeycombed cups over each eye. He tilted Zach's head and put some drops in his eyes. "Okay," he finally said, "open your eyes."

Zach's lashes were crusty and spiked looking. He wet his lips and bit down on his lower lip.

"You can do it, Zach," Miles said, leaning toward him.

Zach's eyelashes fluttered like a baby bird's first lifting of wings, and then slowly, slowly, he opened his eyes.

"What can you see?" Dr. Lyman asked.

Zach took his time, turned his head. "It's blurry, but I can see. Mom. Dad. New guy with white hair."

Miles sagged forward. "Thank God."

Dr. Lyman said, "The blurriness is temporary. Your vision should clear up in no time. You're a lucky young man."

"Yeah. Lucky."

❧

Jude could hear Zach crying, and it brought her fresh pain, both because it was happening and because she couldn't think of how to make him feel better. There was nothing she could do to help him or herself or Mia.

"It's okay, Zach," Miles said when the doctor left them.

"It's my fault, Dad," Zach said. "How am I supposed to live with that?"

"Mia wouldn't blame you," Miles said, and though his words were reasonable, his voice betrayed the depth of his pain. Jude could tell how hard her husband was trying to grieve for one child while comforting the other. She could tell because her struggle was the same.

"I wish I *were* blind," Zach said, and for the first time, he sounded like a man. Certain. "I don't want to go home and see Mia's room. Or her picture."

Just then, Officer Avery walked into the room. He was holding a crumpled-up paper bag in his hands, worrying the rolled crease with his blunt-tipped fingers. "Dr. Farraday? Jude?" he said, clearing his throat. "I'm so sorry to bother you at this difficult time." He cleared his throat again. "But I need to ask Zach some questions."

"Of course," Miles asked, stepping closer to the bed. "Zach? Can you answer a few questions?"

"Whatever," Zach said.

The officer cleared his throat and then stepped awkwardly toward Jude, offering her the paper bag. "Here," he said. "I'm sorry."

She felt as if she were underwater, reaching for something that looked close but was really far away. She was faintly surprised when she felt the rough brown paper. Opening it, she saw a blur of quilted pink— Mia's purse—and she closed the bag quickly, clutching it in shaking hands.

The policeman stepped back a respectful distance, opened a small notebook. "You are Zachary Farraday?"

"You know I am. You were Officer Friendly in fourth grade."

Officer Avery smiled briefly at that. "And it was your white Mustang that was totaled on Night Road last night?"

"It was my car."

"And you attended a party at the Kastner house on Saturday night, with your sister and Alexa Baill?"

"And about a hundred other people."

"And you were drinking alcohol," the officer said, consulting a piece of paper. "I have test reports here that show your blood alcohol level at point twenty-eight," the officer said. "That's almost four times the legal limit."

"Yeah," Zach said quietly.

I won't drink and drive, Madre . . . you know you can trust me? How many times had Jude heard him make that promise?

She closed her eyes, as if darkness offered any refuge from this.

The officer flipped a page. "Do you remember leaving the party?"

"Yeah. It was about two o'clock. Mia was having a cow about us being late."

"So you all decided to get in the car and drive," the officer said. The words were like a battering ram. Jude felt each one hit her spine and reverberate up.

"Lexi wanted to call home," Zach said quietly. "I told her not to be stupid. We did that once and Mom flipped out. I didn't want to miss another party."

"Oh, Zach," Miles said, shaking his head.

Jude thought she might be sick again.

She'd forgotten all about that other time, when they'd believed her words and called her for help. And what had she done—made them pay for it by forcing them to skip several events that weekend.

Oh, God.

"You were fine until you came to Night Road," Officer Avery went on.

"There was no one on the road. Mia was . . . Mia was in the backseat, singing along to the radio. That Kelly Clarkson song. I told her to shut up, and she hit me in the back of the head and then . . ." Zach drew in a deep breath. "We weren't even going that fast, but it was dark and the turn just came up, you know? That hairpin just past the Smithsons' mailbox. Like out of nowhere. I heard Mia scream, and I yelled at Lexi to hit the brakes and tried to grab the wheel . . . and then . . ."

Jude's head snapped up. "You told *Lexi* to hit the brakes?"

"She was driving," Zach said. "She didn't want to. *I* was supposed to. I was the designated driver. It's my fault."

"Ms. Baill's blood alcohol level was point zero nine. The legal limit is point zero eight. Of course, she's under twenty-one, so she can't legally drink at all," the officer said.

Lexi was driving, not Zach.

Zach hadn't killed his sister.

Lexi had.

"I need to see Zach."

"Oh, Lexi," her aunt said, her face slackening with sorrow. "Surely—"

"I *need* to see him, Aunt Eva."

Her aunt started to say no, but Lexi wouldn't listen. Before she knew it, she was crying and pushing past her aunt, limping down the hall.

She saw him through the open door at the end of the hallway.

He was alone in his room.

"Zach," she said at the doorway, moving toward him.

"She's gone," he said, barely moving his lips.

Lexi felt those two words crash into her again. She stumbled. "I know . . ."

"I used to *feel* her, you know. She was always humming inside my head. Now . . . now . . ." He looked up. When he saw her, his eyes filled with tears. "It's quiet."

She limped over to the bed and took him in her arms as best she could with one arm and a broken rib. Every breath hurt, but she deserved it. "I'm so sorry, Zach."

He turned away from her, as if he couldn't bear to look at her face anymore. "Go away, Lexi."

"I'm sorry, Zach," she said again, hearing the smallness of those words. She'd held them in her hands like a fragile flower, thinking they would bloom somehow when she offered them to him; how naïve she'd been.

Jude came into the room, carrying Mia's purse and a can of Coke.

"I'm sorry," Lexi stammered, trying to stop her stupid, useless tears. Failing.

Then her aunt was beside her, taking hold of her hand. "Come away, Alexa. This is not the time."

"Sorry?" Jude said dully, as if she'd just processed Lexi's apology. "You killed my Mia." Her voice broke on that. "What is sorry supposed to mean to me?"

Lexi felt her aunt stiffen, straighten. "This from the woman who knew her children were going to drink and gave them car keys. I'm sorry, but Lexi is not the only one responsible here."

Jude drew back as if she'd been slapped.

"I'm sorry," Lexi said again, letting her aunt pull her away. When she finally dared to turn back around, Jude was still there, standing beside Zach's bed, clinging to her daughter's purse.

"Oh, no," Eva said, coming to a stop.

Lexi was crying so hard, she could hardly tell what was going on around her. She felt Eva's grip on her wrist tighten. "What's wrong?" she whispered, not really caring. She glanced down the hallway. His door was closed now.

"Look," Eva said.

Lexi turned, wiped her eyes.

A police officer was standing outside her room.

Eva held Lexi's hand as they walked down the hallway. At their approach, the officer straightened. He pulled a small notepad out of his shirt pocket. "Are you Alexa Baill?"

"I am," Lexi said.

"I have a few questions for you. About the accident," he said, uncapping his pen.

Eva looked up at him. "I may work at Walmart, sir, but I watch *Law and Order* every week. Alexa will be getting an attorney. He'll tell her what questions she can answer."

❧

Jude shut the door. She was shaking so hard it took a real effort to hold on to the knob and pull.

"Mom?"

She heard her son's voice, heard the pain in it, and she moved automatically to his bedside.

It was where she was supposed to be, where she belonged. So she stood there, holding Mia's purse and pretending to be whole. But every time she looked down at the quilted pink leather in her hands, she thought of the stuffed puppy Mia had loved, Daisy Doggy, and the footed jammies she'd worn as a child and the color her daughter's cheeks had been yesterday . . .

"It's my fault, not Lexi's," Zach said miserably.

"No, it's . . ." Jude's voice broke like an old twig, snapped into quiet. She wondered dully if she'd ever be able to look at Zach again without wanting to cry. It was all so tangled up—her memories of Mia were inextricably bound with images of Zach. Her babies. Her twins. But now there was only the one, and when she looked at him, all she saw was the empty space beside him where Mia should have been.

She wanted to say the right thing to him, but she didn't know what that was anymore, and she was so exhausted. She couldn't put her words through a mill and crank out smaller, prettier versions. It took every scrap of courage she had just to stand here, to stand by him and pretend he'd done nothing terrible and pretend they would all be fine.

"How?" he said, looking at her through green eyes swimming in tears.

Mia's eyes.

"How what?"

"I was the designated driver but I drank. It's *my* fault. How do I get through this?"

Jude had no answer for him.

"Tell me," he cried. "You always tell me what to do."

"But you don't always listen, do you?" The words were out before she could stop them. She should have taken them back, at least wished them back, but she was too broken right now to care.

"No," he said miserably. He took her hand, squeezed it. She felt his touch like a shimmer of heat on the road: distant, fleeting.

"She would forgive you, Zach," Jude said. It was the truth, and all she could think of.

Jude stared dully out the window. *I do not forgive you.* The last words she'd said to Mia.

"Why didn't I just tell her I wanted to go to USC?"

Jude thought about telling him about Mia's last decision to go to SCC with Lexi and Zach, but what was the point? It would only hurt him more to learn how much Mia loved him.

"Mom? Maybe I'll go anyway. For both of us."

Jude saw how desperate Zach was for her approval, and it broke her heart. As if a college choice could undo all of this tragedy somehow and return their family to them. It was her fault he felt this way. She'd made college so damned important, and he wanted her love as much as he needed Mia. She knew she should talk to him about this, tell him it was a bad idea; her voice was gone, though. All she could think about was the woman she'd been before. The mother to whom USC had been so important.

I do not forgive you.

She flinched at the memory of those last terrible words. "None of this matters now, Zach. Just sleep."

She knew she should say something more, help him with his grief, but what good were words to them now? She looked away from her son's sad, sad eyes and stared out the window at a bright and shiny day.

Fourteen

I t felt like they'd been at the hospital for days, but it had been less than thirteen hours. While Jude sat at Zach's bedside, news of the accident spread through Pine Island. By early evening, the phone calls had begun. Jude answered the first few, eager to have something to do, to think about beside her loss, but within seconds she knew it had been a terrible mistake. Even as she listened to murmurs of support, she heard the relief in other people's voices, the immense gratitude that it wasn't their child who had died. She heard *I'm so sorry* until she despised those words as she had never despised anything in her life, and she discovered an anger in her soul that was new. Toxic.

Finally, she turned off her phone and buried it in her purse and let Miles handle the condolences. She drank so much coffee she felt jittery, a racehorse at the gate with no race to run. A mother of twins who only had one child.

She paced the hallways, walked up and down the bright corridors, seeing nothing. She couldn't sit by Zach anymore, couldn't talk to Miles, couldn't go see Mia. Her existence was defined by that which she couldn't do or have. So she kept moving, sobbing on and off, clutching wads of Kleenex that turned into soggy gray lumps in her hand.

"Jude?" She heard her name as if from a distance and looked up, disoriented. Where was she?

Molly was in front of her, holding an overnight bag clutched to her stomach. Without makeup on, dressed in pink Juicy sweatpants and a white cardigan, with her white hair a spiky mess, she looked as ruined as Jude felt inside.

Molly moved toward her awkwardly, let the bag thump to the floor between them. She kicked it aside and took Jude in her arms. When Molly began to cry, Jude felt as if she were floating away, disappearing, only her friend's embrace kept her in this corridor at all.

"I'm so—"

"Don't say it," Jude said, easing out of Molly's arms. "Please." Her eyes felt painfully dry, sandpapery, and yet her vision was blurred. She saw now where she was—near the entrance to the waiting room.

Molly tried gamely to smile, but it didn't work. "I brought you some clothes. Toothbrush. Whatever I could think of."

Jude nodded. The last thing in the world she wanted was to stand here, pretending she wasn't shattered inside, but she couldn't make herself move, either.

Just down the hall, in the waiting room, she saw the crowd of women sitting together, watching Jude from a safe distance. They were women she knew from the island, women with whom she'd chaired committees, played tennis, had lunch. Women with whom she'd shared both motherhood and friendship. Neighbors, friends, acquaintances. They'd heard about the accident and come to help in whatever way they could, the modern equivalent of a quilting bee. In hard times, these women came together to help one another. Jude knew all of this because she was one of them. If someone else's child had been killed, Jude would have put everything else aside and come to offer help.

They *needed* to support her. Jude could see that, but she couldn't seem to care about it.

How could she make them understand that the woman they knew was gone? She wasn't the woman who'd befriended them anymore.

She wasn't the durable woman she'd always imagined herself to be. She wasn't courageous. If she'd been a soldier in wartime, there would be no hill charge led by her. She wouldn't throw her body on a grenade.

Rather, she froze.

There was no better word for it. All the strength she had—and it was a slippery thing, her strength, as small as a guppy and as hard to hold—she used to control her emotions. She didn't see how she could accept sympathy or make other people feel included. It took everything she had inside to pretend to be "handling" this.

"They're here for you, Jude," Molly said. "We all are. What can we do to help?"

Help. It was what women did for one another, even when there was no way to accomplish it.

She took a deep breath and tried to straighten her shoulders. The attempt was a dismal failure, and she ended up rounded again, a woman curling up inside like a thin strip of wood. Still, she clutched Molly's hand and moved forward, one step at a time.

The women in the waiting room rose as one, an audience getting to its feet.

Jude moved into their midst, let them surround her, hold her. She wished they wouldn't cry, but they did, and their tears kept hers at bay.

Jude stayed as long as she could, engulfed by the women who'd defined her for years, feeling desperately alone. As soon as possible, she got back to her feet, shaky now, more vulnerable than before, and ran back to the quiet in Zach's room.

For the next twenty hours, she rarely ventured into the hallway again. She knew people were out there, hovering and drifting and whispering—Molly and her husband, Tim, and several of their island neighbors, and her mother, but Jude didn't care.

She and Zach sat together, both staring dully at the TV hanging from the ceiling, saying little. Mia's absence filled the antiseptic-scented air, and her loss was all either wanted to talk about, but neither had the strength to form such painful words, so they sat in silence. The only time they turned the channel was when the news came on. The media had picked up the story of the accident, and neither Jude nor Zach could stand to watch the coverage. Miles, thankfully, handled the influx of calls with a calm "no comment."

Finally, on Tuesday morning, the hospital discharged Zach.

On the drive home, Miles kept up a steady stream of conversation. He was trying to "go on," to merge into the lane of their new existence, but neither Jude nor Zach could go there with him. Each of Miles's attempts landed in the big empty backseat of the Escalade, and he eventually gave up, turning on the radio instead.

". . . Pine Island teen killed—"

Jude snapped it off and the silence returned. She slumped in her leather seat, with the heat cranked high enough to warm her frozen core, staring dully out the window as the ferry pulled into port. She was so mired in grief that she hardly saw the familiar island landscape until all at once she recognized her surroundings.

Miles had turned onto Night Road.

She gave a gasp of recognition. "Miles."

"Shit," he said. "Habit."

The trees on either side of them were giants that blocked out the struggling mid-June sun. Deep shadows lay banked on either side. High in one of the branches, a lone eagle perched proudly, watching something far below.

They turned a hairpin corner, and there it was: the scene of the accident. Twin skid marks scarred the gray asphalt. A tree was cracked, half of it fallen aside. At its base, a memorial had sprung up.

"Oh, man," Zach said from the backseat.

Jude wanted to look away but she couldn't. The ravine between the road and the broken tree was strewn with bouquets of flowers, stuffed animals, high school pennants, and photos of Mia. Parked along the side of the road was a van with a satellite disk perched on top: a local news vans. Jude knew what she'd see on the evening news tonight: images of teenagers, kids she'd known since they had gaps in their teeth, looking haggard and drawn now, older, crying about Mia's death, laying mementos of her short life on the ground, holding lit votives in small glass jars.

And what would happen to all those stuffed animals that had been put here? Fall would come and rain would pound the color out of everything, and this place would become another ragged reminder of their loss.

Less than a mile, she thought as Miles turned onto their gravel driveway.

Mia had died less than a mile from home. They could have walked . . .

At the front door was another shrine. Friends and neighbors had layered the entrance with flowers. When Jude got out of the car, she smelled the sweet, heady fragrance, but already some were fading, their petals beginning to curl and turn brown.

"Get rid of it," she said to Miles.

He looked at her. "They're beautiful, Jude. It means—"

"I *know* what it means," she said tightly. "People loved our daughter—a girl who is never coming home again." Her voice caught, and she hated how overwhelmed she felt when she looked at these flowers. She would have done the same thing for a neighbor's child, and she would have cried as she bought the flowers and placed them here. She would have felt an incredible sense of loss, and the sharp, sweet relief of knowing that *her* kids were okay. "They'll just die," she finally said.

Miles pulled her into his arms.

Zach came up beside them, leaned into Jude. She wanted to put her arm around him, but she felt paralyzed. It took concentration just to breathe with the cloying scent of all these flowers.

"She liked white roses," Zach said.

At that, the grief came at Jude again. How had she not known that about Mia? All those hours she'd spent in her garden and never had she planted a single creamy white rose. She looked down at the flowers by her front door. There were dahlias, zinnias, and roses of every color except white.

In a burst of anger, she scooped up all the flowers and carried them over to the woods behind the garage and threw them into the trees.

She was just about to turn away when something white caught her eye.

An unopened rosebud lay on the top of the flowery heap, its petals as rich in color as fresh cream.

Jude scrambled through the brush, feeling stinging nettles lash across her face and hands, burning her skin, but she didn't care. She picked up the lone rosebud, clutching it in one shaking hand, feeling the prick of thorns.

"Jude?"

She heard Miles's voice coming at her. Clutching the single stem, she looked back at him.

In the harsh sunlight, he looked slight suddenly, fragile. She saw the hollows of his cheeks and the spidery look of his fingers as he reached out. He took her hand and helped her to her feet. She stared up into the gray eyes that had been her only real home and all she saw now was emptiness.

They walked into their home, which was bright with lights and sweltering hot.

The first thing Jude saw was a shamrock-green sweater hanging from the antique hall tree by the door. How many times had she asked Mia to take it up to her room?

I will, Madre. Honest. Tomorrow . . .

She let go of her husband's arm. She was about to reach for the sweater when she heard her mother's voice.

"Judith?"

Her mother stood in the entryway, dressed in an elegant steel-gray fitted blouse and black pants. She reached out, pulled Jude into her arms. Jude wished there was comfort in this embrace, but it was as cold and rote as everything else between them.

She drew back as quickly as she could, crossing her arms. She was freezing cold suddenly, even though the house was warm.

"I've put the food away," Mother said. "Your friends have been so supportive. I've never seen so many foil-wrapped casseroles in my life. I've put everything in the freezer, marked and dated. I've also made all the funeral arrangements."

Jude looked up sharply. "How *dare* you?"

Her mother looked worriedly at her. "I was trying to help."

"We are not having a funeral," Jude said.

"No funeral?" Miles said.

"Remember your parents' funerals? And I remember my father's. No way I'm going through that for Mia. We're not religious. I'm not going to—"

"You don't need to be religious to have a funeral, Judith," her mother said. "God will be ther—"

"Don't you *dare* mention God to me. He let her die."

She saw her mother pale, draw back, and, just like that, Jude lost her hold on anger. Without it, she felt so exhausted she could hardly stand.

"I need to sleep," she said. Clutching Mia's purse and the single white rose, she turned her back on her family and stumbled down the hallway to her bedroom, collapsing on her bed.

Mia's purse spilled out; the contents lay scattered across the expensive sheets.

Jude lay on her side, snuggled up to her pillow, staring down at Mia's things.

The pink Juicy Couture wallet that had been last year's Christmas gift. A tube of lip gloss, a bent and mangled tampon, a crumpled-up twenty-dollar bill, a half-empty pack of gum, and a used movie ticket. Inside the wallet was a picture of Zach, Mia, and Lexi taken at senior prom.

Forgive me?

If only she'd hugged Mia right then, told her that she loved her. Or if she'd said no to the party. Or taught her children that alcohol was dangerous even though parties were fun. Or insisted on driving them. Or not bought the kids a car or . . .

The list of her regrets grew too heavy, weighed her down; she closed her eyes.

Behind her, she heard her bedroom door open and close.

Miles came toward the bed—she could sense that it was him, but she couldn't turn toward him or open her eyes. He slipped into bed, pulled her against him. She felt him stroke her hair, and she shivered at his touch, freezing again.

"Your mother left. She said something about knowing when she wasn't welcome, which of course is completely untrue."

"And Zach?"

"That's the first time you've asked about him."

"Don't tell me how to grieve, Miles. I'm doing the best I can."

"I know."

"I never planted a white rose," she said quietly. "Why didn't I ask Mia what flower she liked? Why didn't I know?"

He stroked her hair. "We can't do this," he said. "Going through our whole lives, tilling it up, looking for mistakes. It'll kill us."

She nodded, feeling tears start again.

God, she was already tired of crying, and it hadn't even started. She'd been without her daughter for less than three days. The rest of her life stretched out before her like the Gobi Desert.

"We have to have a funeral," Miles said softly.

"Because it's the thing to do?"

"Because Zach and I need it."

Jude pressed her face into the pillow, blotting her tears. "Okay," she said, overcome again by all of it. "I'm going to sleep now," she said, closing her eyes.

Miles left the room and closed the door behind him.

SEATTLE TIMES

Local Teen Killed in Drunk Driving Accident

An eighteen-year-old Pine Island girl was killed early yesterday morning in a single car crash on Night Road.

Mia Farraday, a Pine Island High School senior, was thrown out of a Ford Mustang when it hit a tree, authorities said.

The driver, eighteen-year-old Alexa Baill, of Port George, was reportedly intoxicated at the time. Another passenger, Zachary Farraday, was also injured in the incident.

Pine Island Police Officer Roy Avery is "tired of delivering bad news to parents of local teens." He pointed out that before this most recent fatal crash, an accident in another part of the county killed a sixteen-year-old Woodside girl.

"Both wrecks happened on dark, twisty, two-lane roads, and both young drivers had been drinking," Officer Avery said.

"We have to stop these teens from partying. That's all there is to it. The consequences are tragic. Every year, there's a grad-party accident. This year, someone was killed."

The local chapter of MADD has taken a strong interest in this incident. President Norma Alice Davidson demanded publicly that charges be brought against this young driver. "Only stiffer penalties will make teens take notice of the danger," she said.

Prosecuting attorney Uslan declined to comment about whether Ms. Baill would be charged with DUI vehicular homicide. A memorial service for Mia Farraday will take place Wednesday at Grace Church on Pine Island at 4:00 P.M.

৯৫৫

All over Pine Island, there were reminders of Mia's death: on the high school reader board, *WE MISS YOU, MIA*; on the movie marquee, *IN MEMORY OF MIA*. There were signs in store fronts and taped to car windows.

But those reminders weren't the worst of it. Now, as Lexi walked up Main Street, she was bombarded by memories. She and Mia had painted ceramic platters together there, at the Dancing Brush . . . they'd bought designer jelly beans at the candy store and books at the bookstores.

Books.

That was what had brought them together in the first place, two lonely girls who, before each other, experienced the world from afar, through words.

Can I sit here?

Social suicide.

Eva handed Lexi a wad of toilet paper. "You're crying."

"Am I?" She wiped her eyes, surprised to find how hard she was crying.

Eva touched her arm gently. "Here we are."

The lawyer's office was just off Main Street, tucked back in a tree-lined quad that housed a yarn shop, an antique shop, and an art gallery.

The small, squat brick building had big windows and a bright blue door that read: *Scot Jacobs, Attorney at Law.*

Lexi followed Eva into the office. The main room held a big oak desk, three plastic chairs, and a framed black-and-white photograph of driftwood on a beach. A tired-looking older woman with black horn-rimmed glasses sat behind the desk.

"You must be Alexa," the receptionist said. "I'm Bea."

"Hi, Bea. This is my Aunt Eva."

"You both can go in now."

"You ready for this?" Eva whispered to Lexi.

Lexi shook her head.

"Me either." They walked down a narrow hallway, past a conference-type room.

At the back office, a youngish man sat behind a big glass desk. At their approach, he rose. In a crumpled blue suit and overwashed pink shirt, he looked like the kind of attorney they could afford, and of course they couldn't really afford him. His hair was unstylishly long, a little tousled, and he needed a shave, but his brown eyes were kind and compassionate.

"Hello," Lexi said, moving forward to shake his plump, slightly damp hand.

Lexi sat down in one of the two upholstered chairs that faced the desk. Beside her, Eva put her purse on the floor and sat down in the other chair. "Thank you for agreeing to see us," her aunt said.

Mr. Jacobs steepled his pale fingers and studied Lexi. "You're in a bad spot, Miss Baill. Your accident has sparked a firestorm around here. The regional MADD organization is fired up. They want an example made of you."

"What does that mean?" Lexi asked.

"They think that if you go to prison, kids will get the message. And a lot of people want to see this message go out to kids."

"Prison? *Prison?*" Lexi said, feeling the floor drop out from under her.

"But she's a kid," Eva said.

"Actually, she's eighteen. That makes her an adult, and she was legally intoxicated at the time of the accident. Of course, at her age, point zero is the legal limit."

"They send girls to *prison* for an accident like this?" Eva asked.

"When alcohol is involved, they can. They can also go for probation and community service. There are a lot of potential outcomes here, and a lot of choices along the way. That's what I'm for: to help guide and defend Lexi."

"So what should I do?" Lexi said quietly. She was shaken to her core by the whole idea of this. She'd seen what happened as an accident. It was a crime, though. Now she saw how much more she had to face, and it terrified her.

"We fight."

"Fight? But I did it. I drove drunk."

"It wasn't your car, and you were the least intoxicated of the three," Scot said. "It doesn't take a brain surgeon to figure out what happened. You thought you were the safest among you to drive. And jurors tend to drink. They'll know a thing like this can happen to anyone. I'll need to hire an investigator, but you'll definitely plead not guilty. Last year I defended a man who killed two people in a similar situation, and I got him acquitted. It's not over till it's over."

Acquitted. Not guilty. How could Lexi ever face Zach in court and say she wasn't guilty? How could she face anyone on the island and say that? "But she's *dead*. I can't pretend I didn't do anything wrong."

"Prison isn't the answer, Lexi. Believe me." He collated some papers on his desk, thumped them into a packet. "Here's the plan. You're going to speak to high school kids and share your story. I'll set something up for you. It'll look good if you take responsibility for your actions. Show the community and the media that you can send a message to other teens without going to prison." He gave her a sad smile. "I know your whole story, Lexi. People will respond to what you've been through."

"What do you mean?"

He opened a file and looked at it. "Your mother, Lorena Baill, was first arrested in 1986, when you were three months old. You lived with seven foster families in your first fourteen years. Every time your mom got out of rehab or jail, she came back for you. The courts kept giving her chances." He looked up. "You've had a hard life, Lexi. And you were with your mom when she overdosed."

Lexi swallowed hard. It was a memory she tried never to remember. "Yes."

"Jurors will have sympathy for you. Trust me to take care of you. Okay?"

"How much do you cost?" Aunt Eva asked.

"I'm a one-man shop, Eva. I can't afford to take this case pro bono, and I won't lie to you. It'll be expensive. But I'll save you money wherever I can."

Lexi felt sick at that. Her aunt already worked fifty hours a week to pay the ordinary bills. How was she going to pay for this, too?

"I have some savings," Eva said. "My husband's life insurance."

"No," Lexi said. "That's your retirement."

"Don't argue with me, Alexa," Eva said. "It's my money; I'll spend it my way."

Scot reached for a couple of business cards and handed them across the desk. "If the police or the prosecuting attorney's office or another attorney contact you, say nothing and give them my number. *Nothing*. I can't stress that enough. I will tell them that I'm representing you and find out what I can. If we're lucky, they'll decide not to charge you. If we're not . . ." He shrugged.

Eva stood up. "Thank you, Mr. Jacobs."

"Call me Scot. Please. And don't you worry, Lexi. We'll keep you out of prison."

ॐ

"Are you sure about going today?" Eva said.

Lexi stood at the window, staring outside. "How can I not go to my best friend's funeral?"

"It won't be easy."

"I killed her," Lexi said quietly. "I don't expect it to be easy." She didn't think anything would ever be easy again. But she had to do this. She had to stand there, ashamed, and let her friends see what came from drinking and driving. And she had to see Zach one more time—and his parents—and tell them how sorry she was.

She went into the bathroom and sat on the beige fiberglass rim of the bathtub. She closed her eyes and felt Mia beside her. *Do you want to come to my house after school? I'll meet you at the flagpole . . . she just came right up to me, Madre, and asked if she could sit down . . . move over, Zach Attack, you're hogging my best friend . . .*

Lexi cried until there was nothing left inside of her. Then, drawing in a deep breath, she exhaled slowly and got to her feet.

Feeling hollow and shaky, she dressed in a pair of plain black pants, black flats, and a short-sleeved blue angora sweater that Mia had bought for her.

In the living room, she found Eva standing by the kitchen table, dressed all in black, looking worried. She was gulping coffee—it was what she did when she was nervous; that was one of the things Lexi knew about Eva now. Whenever Eva missed smoking, she drank black coffee until the craving passed. "This is a bad idea. What if there are reporters there?"

"I have to face them sooner or later."

Eva gave her one last worried look, started to say something, and changed her mind. Lips thinned by those unspoken words, she walked out of the double-wide and led the way to the old Ford Fairlane.

They drove onto the island in silence.

As they passed the high school, Lexi noticed the reader board. Now it read: *Mia Farraday Memorial. Grace Church. 4:00 P.M. today / GRAD SATURDAY @ 1:00.*

The parking lot in front of the church was full.

Lexi let out her breath.

Eva pulled into an empty spot and parked.

Lexi got out of the car. As she moved forward, her broken arm started to ache and nerves fluttered in the pit of her stomach.

"You can do it," Eva said, taking hold of Lexi's good arm.

Inside, the church was full of teenagers and parents and teachers. Up by the altar was a poster of Mia in her costume from *Once upon a Mattress*. In the beaded blue bodice, with stage makeup emphasizing her green eyes, she looked radiant and beautiful, a young woman with a bright future.

Lexi stumbled; Eva kept her going.

Lexi heard people whisper as she passed.

". . . Lexi Baill . . . surprise . . ."

". . . if she'd been a better friend . . ."

". . . poor thing . . ."

". . . some nerve . . ."

"Hey, Lexi, you want to sit here? *Lexi*."

She turned slowly, saw Zach's ex-girlfriend, Amanda Martin, sitting in the pew to her right.

Amanda scooted sideways, made her mom and dad scrunch together to make room.

Lexi sat down by Amanda. She looked into the girl's sad eyes, and suddenly they were both crying. They hadn't been friends in high school, but it didn't matter now; all that stuff just fell away. "It totally wasn't your fault," Amanda said. "I don't care what people say."

Lexi was surprised by how much that meant to her. "Thanks."

Before Amanda could say anything else, the service began.

The priest said Mia's name, and every high school girl in the church burst into tears, and more than a few boys joined in. The priest's words painted a picture of a happy eighteen-year-old girl who was almost Mia and yet not quite. He didn't say that she snored when she lay on her back or that she moved her lips when she read or that she liked to hold her best friend's hand while they walked through the mall.

His words she could withstand. It was the slideshow of Mia's life that devastated her. Mia in a pink tutu, her arms circled above her head . . . Mia holding a Captain Hook action figure, grinning . . . holding Zach's hand as they stood in the cold ocean water, grimacing. The last picture was of Mia alone, wearing a crazy tie-dyed T-shirt and cutoffs, smiling for the camera, giving the world a thumbs-up.

Lexi closed her eyes, sobbing now. Music began to play: it was not the right music. Mia wouldn't have liked the droning, solemn chords. And somehow that hurt most of all. Whoever had picked the music hadn't thought of Mia. It should have been a Disney song, something that would have gotten Mia on her feet and made her sing along with her hairbrush as a microphone . . .

Sing with me, Lexster. We could be in a band . . . and Zach, laughing, saying, *no more, Mia, dogs are starting to howl . . .*

Lexi wanted to clamp her hands over her ears, but the words came from inside of her, memories blooming up and spilling over.

"Time to go, Lexi," Amanda said gently.

Lexi opened her eyes. "Thanks, for letting me sit with you."

"You coming to graduation?"

Lexi shrugged. Had it only been six days ago she and Mia and Zach had been together in the gym, practicing for graduation? "I don't know . . ."

People moved into the aisle, streamed toward the double doors. Lexi felt their gazes on her. Faces frowned in recognition as they passed her. Parents looked judgmental; kids looked sad and sympathetic.

Finally she saw the family. They sat in the front pew, still and stiff and dressed in black. People paused to offer condolences as they passed.

Lexi moved toward them, unable to stop herself. She was going against the flow; mourners stared at her, frowned, moved out of her way.

In the front row, the Farradays rose in unison and turned.

Neither Jude nor Zach acknowledged her. They just stared, dull-eyed, their faces streaked with tears.

Lexi had practiced what she would say to them a hundred times, but now, faced with the magnitude of their loss and her guilt, she couldn't even open her mouth. The whole family turned away from her and walked to the church's side door.

Lexi felt Eva come up beside her. She sagged into her aunt, giving up the strength it had taken to come here.

"No one blames him," Eva said bitterly. "It's not right."

"He wasn't driving."

"He should have been," Eva said. "What good is it to make a promise and then ignore it? He should be blamed, too."

Lexi remembered how he'd looked at her in the hospital; the green eyes she loved so much had been darkened by more than grief. She'd seen guilt there, too, as deep as her own. "He blames himself."

"That's not enough," Eva said firmly. "Let's go."

She took Lexi by the arm and led her out of the church. Lexi could hear people whispering about her, blaming her. If she'd been less culpable, she might have agreed with Eva, maybe been pissed at Zach, but any other blame was less than hers. That was all there was. Zach had failed to live up to a promise. She'd made the deadly decision herself. Guilt and remorse filled her to the brim; there was no room for anger, too. Zach had screwed up; Lexi had done far, far worse.

"Someone should have told me it was a bad idea to go to the funeral," Lexi said as they drove out of the parking lot.

"If someone had," Eva said, "I'm sure you would have listened."

Lexi wiped her eyes. "Of course."

❧

Jude sat huddled in the limousine's dark interior. Outside, it began to rain; drops landed on the roof like infant heartbeats.

She was so deep in grief that when the car door opened, letting in a blast of gray and yellow light, it stung her tear-burned eyes and she looked around, disoriented.

"We're here," the driver said, standing by the open door. He was a slash of more black in the rain, a slanted shadow beneath an umbrella. Behind him, Molly and Tim stood huddled with their grown children.

"Come along, Zachary," her mother said, herding him out of the limousine.

Miles slid past Jude and got out of the car. Then he held out his hand for her. "Jude."

"Go on," she said, glad that he couldn't see her eyes behind the dark sunglasses she wore.

"I'll catch up with you," Miles said to Caroline, who no doubt nodded and walked briskly away, making sure Zach stood up straight and didn't cry. That was what Jude remembered about her father's funeral: not crying. No one had cried for him. Her mother simply hadn't allowed it. She'd treated grief like a malignancy of some kind—a few snips, a few stitches, and you were good as new.

"You can't not go," Miles said, squatting beside the car. Rain pelted his face, straightened his hair.

"Watch me."

"Jude." He sighed.

It was their family sound now; before it had been laughter. Now it was the sigh. "Don't you think I want to be strong enough for this?" she said. "I'm ashamed of myself, and I *want* to be there. I just . . . can't. I'm not ready to watch them lower her into the ground. And I'm sure as hell not ready to stand next to you while you let go of pink balloons." Her voice broke on that. "Like she's up in some heaven waiting to catch them."

"Jude," he said tiredly, and she understood.

He wanted her to believe that Mia was in a better place, but Jude couldn't do it.

She knew what it was costing her, this inability of hers to be strong, but she couldn't do it. There was simply nothing of her left. Try as hard as she might (and honestly, it exhausted her to even try), she couldn't seem to be *present,* not even as a mother.

Zach knew she wasn't herself anymore. He treated her as if she were made of spun sugar. He approached her warily, making sure never to say anything about Mia. But sometimes, when she said good night to him, she saw the need in his eyes, the naked pain, and it hurt her to her bones. She'd reach for him in those moments, but he wasn't fooled. He knew it wasn't *her* touch, that somehow she wasn't there, and when she walked away, she saw that he looked more broken after she'd soothed him than before.

"You're breaking Zach's heart," Miles said. "I know you know that. He needs you today."

Jude swallowed hard. "I know. And I can't do it. I can't stand there. Did you see how they all looked at us at the funeral? All I could think was that I hated them all, with their healthy kids. I look at people who aren't us and I hate them. And I look at Zach, and all I see is the emptiness beside him. He's half a person, and we all know it . . . and sometimes I can't help blaming him. If he hadn't gotten drunk . . ." She drew in a sharp breath. "Or if I hadn't let him go that night . . ."

"You can't keep this up . . ."

"It's been less than a week," she snapped. "And if you tell me time will heal this, I swear to God, I'll kill you in your sleep."

Miles stared at her a long time and then pulled her into his arms. "I love you, Jude," he whispered into her ear, and against her best intentions she started to cry.

She loved him, too. And she loved Zach. It was inside her somewhere. She just couldn't reach it.

"I'll tell her good-bye for you."

She heard the car door click shut, and she was alone again. Thankfully. For a long while, she sat there in the darkness, listening to the rain on the roof, trying not to think about anything, but her daughter's presence was everywhere, in every breath, every sigh, every blink of the eye. Finally, furtively, she reached into her small black purse and pulled out Mia's cell phone. With a quick glance around, she flipped it open and listened to Mia's outgoing message.

Hi! You've reached Mia. I'm way too busy to talk now, but if you'll leave me a message, I'll totally get back to you.

Jude listened to it over and over again, sometimes talking to her daughter, sometimes crying, sometimes just listening. She was so caught up in *reaching* Mia that she gasped when the door opened. She snapped the phone shut and shoved it in her purse as Zach climbed into the limousine. His eyes were red and swollen.

Jude slid over to him and took his hand. She hated the way he looked at her—surprised by her touch—and she wanted to offer words of comfort, but she had none.

She and Zach and Miles slumped together on the long ride home.

Her mother sat opposite them, her hands clasped in her lap, her beautiful eyes glistening with tears that never fell. Jude was surprised by that sign of emotion, of loss. Only a week ago the sight of her mother's improbable tears would have amazed Jude, made her want to reach out. Now, she didn't care. Her own pain crowded out everyone else's. It was a pathetic, humiliating truth, but a truth nonetheless.

At the house, Jude got out of the car and walked to the front door alone. All she wanted to do now was sleep. She must have said it out loud because she heard her mother say, "That's a good idea. Sleep will help."

Jude seemed to awaken at that. "Will it, Mother? Really?"

Her mother patted Jude's wrist. It was a light touch, barely there before it was gone. "God doesn't give us more than we can bear. You're stronger than this, Judith."

Anger blindsided Jude. It was one of her new emotions. She had never been angry before, not really, but it was always with her now, as much a part of her as the shape of her face and the color of her skin. It took tremendous effort not to show it all the time. She spun away from her mother before she said something she would regret and headed into the house.

In the entryway, she came to a halt. "Where's Mia's sweater?"

"What?" Zach said, coming up behind her.

"Mia's green sweater. It was hanging right here." Jude's anger mutated into panic.

"It's in the laundry," her mother said. "I was going to wash it along with—"

Jude ran to the laundry room and pawed through the pile of dirty clothes until she found Mia's sweater. Bringing it to her face, she pressed the soft wool to her nose, inhaling Mia's scent. Her tears dampened the fabric, but she didn't care. Ignoring her family's stares, she stumbled into her bedroom and slammed the door shut behind her, collapsing on the bed.

Finally, after what felt like hours, she heard her bedroom door open.

"Hey," Molly said from the doorway. She stood there, looking sad and uncertain in a chic black dress with a cinch belt, wringing her hands together. Her white hair was a mess, pulled back from her face in a thin headband; a black grow-out line spread along her forehead. "Can I come in?"

"Could I stop you?"

"No."

Jude crawled to a sit, leaned back against her silk upholstered headboard.

Molly got up onto the big bed and took Jude into her arms, holding her as if she were a child. Jude didn't mean to cry again, but she couldn't help it.

"I used to think I was strong," Jude whispered.

"You *are* strong," Molly said, tucking a damp strand of hair behind Jude's ear.

"No," she said, pulling back. "I have no idea who I am anymore." It was true. All of this had shown her the truth of her soul: she was weak, fragile. Not the woman she'd imagined herself to be at all.

Or maybe that wasn't true. Maybe she knew now what she hadn't known before: she wasn't kind and caring and compassionate and even-tempered. She was angry and weak and even a little vindictive. Most of all, she was a bad mother.

Everything lately pissed her off. Sunshine. Healthy children. Parents who complained about their kids. Lexi.

Jude suddenly didn't want to be touched. She pulled out of Molly's arms and slumped back against the headboard. "She wasn't wearing her seatbelt." She said it quietly, afraid; it had only been a few days, and already Jude had learned that people didn't want to hear about Mia. How was she supposed to stop talking about her daughter? But just the mention of her name could send people running for the door.

"Tell me," Molly said, holding her hand, settling in beside her.

"Thanks," Jude said. "No one wants to hear about her."

"I'll listen to anything you want to say."

Jude turned to her. "She *always* wore her seatbelt." She drew in a shaking breath and reached over into the nightstand for tissues.

A mistake; she saw that instantly.

Inside the drawer, she saw a small blue velvet ring box sitting beside a pair of Costco reading glasses. Knowing she shouldn't touch it, she took it out, flipped it open.

"What's that?" Molly asked.

"Mia's graduation present."

Molly was silent for a moment. "It's beautiful."

"I was going to take her shopping with me for the stone. A girls' day. Maybe a mani-pedi when we were done." On that, Jude's resolve cracked, and she started to cry.

"Oh, Jude," Molly said, hugging her again.

Jude should have felt enveloped by her friend's love, but she couldn't feel anything at all. Not then, as she stared down at this beautiful, unfinished ring with gaping, empty prongs . . .

Fifteen

The high school parking lot was full of cars on this sunny Saturday afternoon.

Lexi sat in the passenger seat of her aunt's Ford Fairlane, staring through the grimy windshield at the crowd gathered around the flagpole.

"You belong here, Alexa," her aunt said. "You've worked as hard for this day as anyone else."

"I'm afraid," she said quietly.

"I know," her aunt said. "That's why I'm here."

Lexi took a deep breath and reached for the door handle. The old door creaked open, popping at the end of its arc.

She and Eva walked through the chattering crowd of family and friends who had come to see the class of 2004 graduate. Lexi kept her head down, not making eye contact with the reporters at the flagpole. As she passed them, she heard one of them say, "Two hundred and seventy-two seniors, Phil. It should have been two hundred and seventy-three."

At the edge of the football field, Lexi paused.

"You better hurry," Eva said. "We're late."

Lexi nodded, but as she looked at the rows of folding chairs set up on the green football field, she felt sick to her stomach.

"I'm proud of you, Alexa," her aunt said. "You're a good girl. And don't you dare think otherwise."

Eva gave her a bright smile and then disappeared into the crowd of proud parents streaming up into the bleachers.

Lexi saw the Farradays up there. Jude and Miles were seated in the second row, with Molly and Tim and Grandmother Caroline. Even from here, Lexi could see how pale and thin Jude looked. The black sunglasses she wore accentuated the pallor of her skin and the sharpness of her cheekbones. She had no lipstick on, and she was carrying Mia's pink purse.

Lexi knew then she couldn't do it. She couldn't walk through this crowd and go into the gymnasium, where all her friends were dressed in caps and gowns, waiting to walk triumphantly to the seats on the field. She couldn't see Zach, not on this day, when Mia's absence would be so keenly felt.

She pulled off her cap and unzipped her gown, stuffing them both in her big patchwork purse. She was about to leave when the class of 2004 filed onto the field, a stream of royal blue and marigold yellow robes against a cloudless sky.

She moved into one of the empty aisles beneath the bleachers. On the field below, her classmates moved into their assigned seats.

Zach was walking alone. In sunglasses (probably to protect his burned eyes in this bright sunlight), with his shaved head and burned jawline, he hardly looked like himself. Like Jude, there was a new hollowness to his face, and he wasn't smiling.

When the last of the seniors had taken their seats, the audience burst into applause.

Amid the noise, Principal Yates walked onto the stage and stood at the podium. He spoke eloquently about Pine Island and what it was like to grow up on land that was surrounded by water, how it strengthened the sense of community. At the end of his speech, he said, "This is a class that has been touched by a sudden, terrible tragedy, and these students who were on their way to adulthood have grown up in the past week. We hope as they move forward and are faced with choices in their lives, both big and small, they will remember what they learned about consequences in the year 2004." He gave the class a sad, knowing smile. "And now, Amanda Martin is going to sing a song in memory of a very special girl, who should have been with us today."

Lexi tried to steel herself, but when the music began, she felt a terrible ache in her chest. And then Amanda's voice, pure and sweet, rang out: *I can show you the world . . . shining, shimmering, splendid . . ."*

The song brought Mia bursting back to life, twirling on the dance floor, singing off-key. She'd loved the Disney movies so much. *I'm Ariel,* she used to say all the time. *You're Belle. No Snow White or Cinderella, not for us; we're the new-school Disney girls . . . we go for what we want . . .*

Lexi wasn't the only one sobbing when Amanda finished her song. At least half of the senior class was crying.

The applause was thunderous, and when it faded once again, the commencement began. One by one, her friends' names were called, and blue-robed girls and boys bounded onto the stage to take their diplomas and wave to the crowd.

"Alexa Baill."

The audience stilled. People looked around.

Onstage, the principal cleared his throat and went on. "Andrew Clark . . ."

Lexi's heart pounded. She was sure someone would point to her, yell, "There she is; there's the girl who killed Mia."

"Zachary Farraday."

Zach walked woodenly up the aisle and onto the stage. He took his diploma from the principal and faced the bleachers. Slowly, he upheld a framed photograph of Mia and then leaned closer to the microphone. "She wanted to do a cartwheel today . . ."

A cartwheel, Lexster . . . that would get their attention.

Lexi sagged back against the sun-warmed concrete wall, closing her eyes. The ceremony went on, calling names and handing out diplomas, but she hardly noticed. All she could hear were memories, things Mia had said to her over the years . . .

"Lex?"

She drew in a sharp breath and opened her eyes to see Zach standing in front of her. Behind them, down on the field, there was sound and color and movement, but here it was quiet and still. They were alone in an alcove beneath the bleachers. "H-how did you find me?"

"I knew you'd be here."

She'd hoped for this moment, dreamed of it, thought of ways to make him understand how sorry she was, but she could see that he knew, that he understood. "I love you," she said softly. It was the only thing that hadn't changed.

"I love you, too, but . . ."

"But what?"

He shook his head, shrugged. She understood the gesture perfectly: it meant that nothing mattered anymore, their love least of all. His look was the saddest thing she'd ever seen.

"You'll never forgive me, will you?" she said.

"It's me I can't forgive," he said, and on that, his voice broke and he turned away from her. "I gotta go."

"Wait." She reached into her purse, burrowed past the polyester of her gown, and pulled out her worn, dog-eared copy of *Jane Eyre*. It was a stupid gift for a girl to give a boy, but it was all she had that mattered to her. "I want you to have this," she said.

"It's your favorite book. I can't take—"

"Please. It has a happy ending."

He reached out; for a second, they were both touching the book. "I gotta go."

"I know. Good-bye, Zach," she whispered, watching him walk away from her.

She pulled away from the wall and walked out beneath the bleachers. She didn't bother to hunch her shoulders or avert her eyes. She didn't care if people stared at her.

In the parking lot, she climbed into Eva's old car and waited.

"Couldn't do it, huh?" Eva said later, when she got behind the wheel.

Lexi shrugged. "Who cares? It's just a dumb ceremony."

"You cared."

"Before," Lexi said, realizing as she said it that her whole life would now be divided into two parts: before she'd killed her best friend, and after.

※

Graduation was more than Jude could handle. The day had been full of ghosts, missing faces, the wrong girls . . .

By the time the ceremony finally ended, she felt like crumbling into a heap. She'd tried to convince Zach to go to the grad-night party with his friends. *You'll always remember it,* she'd said tiredly, although they both knew it was a lie. Intellectually, she knew she should make him go, pretend that his life was still going forward on the same old track, but she couldn't really *feel* that.

So they'd driven home in silence. She sat slumped against the car window, cold to the bone even though the seat's heater was set on high. In the seat behind her, Zach drummed his fingers on the seat rest, and when they got home, he bolted out of the car and ran up the stairs. No doubt he wanted to lose himself in video games.

"Lexi was there," Miles said later, when he and Jude were alone in the kitchen.

Jude felt a rush of anger. Whole, healthy Lexi, with just a white arm cast to mark her place in the car that night.

"That takes nerve. I hope Zach didn't see her."

"He did," Miles said, looking at her. "Don't do that, Jude. You'll make it worse."

"Worse? Are you *kidding* me? How could this possibly get worse?"

"Don't make Zach choose between you and Lexi. He loves you; you know that. He's always done everything he could to make you proud of him. Don't use that against him now. He and Lexi have things to work out."

Jude sighed heavily and headed to her bedroom, closing the door behind her.

For the next forty-eight hours all she did was lie in bed, sometimes sleeping, sometimes crying. She lay there with her eyes closed for hours, thinking *come to me, Mia,* talking to her daughter, but nothing happened. Not a breeze across her face that felt like a breath, not a flickering of the bedside lamp. Nothing. And she didn't really believe that Mia could hear her.

By the time she finally crawled out of bed, she looked like a ninety-year-old homeless woman who had found a designer dress on the street and worn it for weeks. She knew Miles didn't understand. Last night he'd made that sound—that sigh of desperation or despair—when she couldn't change into a nightgown. He didn't understand how fragile she felt. If she lifted her arms, they might break off.

She changed into an old pair of sweats. Not bothering to shower or brush her teeth, she made her way out of the bedroom, drawn forward by the scent of Starbucks coffee.

Miles was in the kitchen, sitting at the granite counter, sipping coffee. At her entrance, he sat up straighter, gave her a smile of relief that should have warmed her broken heart.

The television was on. Before Jude could say anything, she heard the newscaster say, ". . . killed her best friend in a drunk-driving incident only a week before graduation."

Jude shouldn't have looked at the screen, but she did. The twisted, ruined Mustang with the windshield shattered made her almost violently ill. She hadn't seen that image before . . . and then Lexi's face was on-screen, smiling brightly. "Local MADD president Norma—"

Miles hit the remote, and the screen went black.

Jude felt that new anger rising in her again; it drowned out everything else. She heard Miles talking to her, but she couldn't hear anything except this roaring white noise in her head. She poured herself a cup of coffee and walked out of the kitchen.

How would she survive this? How could she see Lexi again on the street someday and not just fall to her knees?

Lexi, who could go on with her life . . .

Jude stood in the great room, trembling, wondering what to do. Should she go back to bed?

She closed her eyes, trying to clear her mind of the image she'd just seen of Zach's car . . .

At first, she thought she heard her heart beating, and she thought: *that's odd*, and then she realized someone was knocking on the front door. Wiping her eyes, she went to the door, expecting to see a friend with a casserole, saying, *I'm so sorry*, but it was a stranger who stood there, a tall, elegant-looking, gray-haired man in a pinstriped blue suit.

"Hello, Mrs. Farraday. I don't know if you remember me. I'm Dennis Uslan. I'm the prosecuting attorney assigned to your case. My niece, Helen, graduated with Zachary."

Jude's breath released in a rush. She hadn't even realized she'd been holding it. "Yes, Dennis. Of course I remember you. You helped with construction of the new ball field at Rotary Park."

"Yes, that's right. I'm sorry to simply stop by, but your phone seems to be off the hook."

"Reporters," she said, stepping back. "They call constantly asking for a 'comment on our tragedy.' Come in." She led him into the great room, where sunlight shone through the giant windows. The view over the Sound was spectacular on this crystalline day.

Dennis had just taken a seat when Miles walked into the room, dressed in shorts for running.

"Miles," Jude said. "This is Dennis Uslan. He's the prosecuting attorney for our case."

Miles looked at Dennis. "I wasn't aware we had a case."

Dennis rose from his seat. "That's what I wanted to speak to you about. I'm getting a lot of pressure from MADD and the community to charge Alexa Baill with DUI vehicular homicide. Obviously a trial can be a lengthy and heartbreaking undertaking, and I wanted to know where you stand on the idea."

"What would happen to Lexi?" Miles asked.

"If convicted, she could face more than fifteen years in prison, although, admittedly, that outcome is extreme. She could also be found not guilty or plea bargain to something lesser. Any way you go, though, it's tough on the victim's family."

Jude flinched at the word *victim*.

"I don't think it will help anyone if Lexi goes to prison," Miles said. "We need to forgive her, not punish her. Maybe other kids could learn from her mistake? She could—"

"Forgive her?" Jude couldn't believe what her husband had just said.

"Mrs. Farraday," Dennis asked, "what do you want?"

Jude knew the right answer, knew what she would have said before all of this, what she would have believed: that Miles was right. Only forgiveness could ease Jude's pain.

But she wasn't that woman anymore. "Justice," she said at last, seeing Miles's disappointment in her. "What mother wouldn't want that?"

❧

In the nine days since high school graduation, Lexi had become a lost soul. On Monday morning, she'd shown up bright and early for work at the ice cream shop, only to be told (kindly, but told just the same) that she'd been fired. *Try and understand,* Mrs. Solter had said, *there's a lot of anger against you in town right now. It would be bad for business to have you working here.*

After that Lexi had stayed home, reading one book after another. For the first time in years, she turned to *Jane Eyre* for comfort. She was reading it again when someone knocked on her door.

"Lexi?"

"Yeah?"

"Your lawyer is here."

Lexi put down her book and went out to the living room.

"They filed charges against you," Scot said before Lexi even sat down. "DUI vehicular homicide and assault. Your arraignment is Wednesday. We'll plead not guilty and get a court date."

"Not guilty?" Lexi said, trying to process it all. She didn't even know what she felt anymore.

"The question is not whether you were driving or whether Mia died. It's about legal responsibility. You had an accident. You didn't commit a crime. So our plan is . . ."

Lexi didn't hear anything past "responsibility." Suddenly, she was her own mother, trying to run away from what she'd done. "No," she said sharply.

Scot looked at her. "No, what, Lexi?"

"I'm going to plead guilty," she said.

"You most certainly will not," Eva said.

Lexi loved her aunt for that. "Come on, Eva. Am I supposed to get away with killing my best friend? I did it, and we can't afford—"

"You will not plead guilty," Eva said again. "I have the money in my retirement fund."

"You're letting your emotions run wild," Scot said. "I can see that you're a good person, and you want to do the right thing, but pleading guilty isn't it. DUI vehicular homicide is a class-A felony, punishable by up to life in prison. Believe me, prison is not where you want to be, Lexi. And with the sentiment out there . . . we have to fight for your freedom."

Could she stand up in court and say she wasn't guilty when everyone knew she was? "We all know what's right here. Don't you want me to do the right thing, Aunt Eva?"

"You are too young to know what's right here, Lexi. You did a terrible thing. I admit it. But is prison the answer? No. You were there; you visited your mother." Eva moved closer. She cupped Lexi's face in her chapped, dry hands. "I know you're worried about me, but don't be. We can afford whatever we have to."

"Even if you pled guilty and we got a plea bargain," Scot said, "the judge wouldn't have to follow it. He can impose any sentence he wants, within the guidelines. And with the media out there, he may want to make an example of you. You could spend your life behind bars, Lexi."

"I *am* an example," Lexi said quietly. "I am the worst thing that can happen, and kids should know that. How can I stand in that courtroom and say I'm not guilty?"

"Hasn't enough bad come from that night?" Eva asked.

"This discussion is over. You're paying me for my advice, and this is it: you're pleading not guilty," Scot said firmly.

Lexi sighed. They were talking about the law and her future. That wasn't really the point at all, but they were trying so hard to save her. She didn't want to disappoint them, too. Especially not Eva. "Okay."

Jude sat in the courtroom between her husband and her son. Zach sat perfectly upright, as she'd often begged him to do. Gone was the slouching, playful kid he'd been. Now he pulled his pants up and wore a belt and cleaned his room without being asked. She knew why, too: he was trying so hard to make her happy. He lived in fear of saying or doing the wrong thing around her, of making her cry. Especially here, in front of everyone they knew.

The benches in the courtroom filled up quickly. As soon as word had gotten out about Lexi's arrest and arraignment, admittance to this courtroom had become the hottest ticket in town. People had lined up before dawn in the hopes that they would get a seat. Everyone had an opinion on the case: some thought Lexi was a victim; others deemed her a danger to society. Some blamed Jude and Miles for lackluster supervision and bad parenting; these were the parents who swore their own children didn't drink. A few whack jobs even blamed the drinking age, saying that if it were eighteen, things like this wouldn't happen.

Local reporters, and perhaps one or two national journalists, milled through the hallway outside. Jude didn't look around, didn't want to see the friends she'd made over her years here on Pine Island, the women she'd talked to during class parties or in the carpool lane or in the checkout line at Safeway. Many of them called her regularly, and she took the calls, but they rarely lasted long. Jude simply couldn't think of what to say anymore. Neither did she care about representatives of MADD, who had conducted a press conference just this morning and were demanding prison time for Lexi.

Lexi.

Just the name was enough to send Jude spiraling into anger or despair. She did her best never to think about the girl who'd caused all of this, who'd killed her daughter. The girl her son had loved. The girl *she'd* loved.

"I'm sorry I'm late," her mother said, taking a seat on Zach's other side.

The judge cracked his gravel down and called for order.

The gallery quieted.

"Ms. Baill," the judge said, "you are aware of the crimes with which you have been charged?"

At the defendant's table, Lexi and her lawyer stood. She looked incredibly fragile and small standing there. Her hair was unkempt and frizzy, out of control. Her cheap black pants needed ironing and were a little too short.

"I am, Your Honor," Lexi said.

"And on the charge of DUI vehicular homicide, how do you plead?"

Lexi paused. "Guilty, Your Honor."

There was a moment of stunned surprise in the courtroom and then pandemonium broke out. Both attorneys jumped to their feet, yelling over each other to be heard.

"In my chambers," the judge said harshly. "Now. You, too, Ms. Baill."

Lexi followed her attorney out of the courtroom. In their wake, the gallery started whispering furiously among themselves.

Zach turned to Jude. "I don't get it. What's she doing?"

Jude sat very still, breathing as best she could, trying to feel nothing. This was some kind of ruse, a way to garner sympathy. She couldn't have answered Zach if she had known what to say. Finally, the lawyers filed back into the courtroom. The crowd quieted.

The judge sat down and looked at Lexi. "And on the charge of vehicular assault?"

"Guilty, Your Honor," Lexi said.

The judge nodded. "Ms. Baill, it is my duty to remind you that you have the right to a trial in this case, to have your actions judged by a jury of your peers. You understand that by pleading guilty, you are relinquishing this right?"

"I do, Your Honor."

"And you understand that a guilty plea means that you will be convicted of this crime without a trial and that you may be subject to immediate sentencing?"

"I do, Your Honor," she said again, stronger this time.

"Although it is unusual, given the terrible consequences of this case on the community, this court is prepared to put this matter to rest. Ms. Baill, do you have a statement you'd like to make?"

Lexi nodded briefly and rose. "I do, Your Honor."

"You may go to the podium," he directed.

Lexi walked over to the podium and looked out over the gallery. Her gaze went to Zach. "I drank, and I drove, and I killed my best friend. My lawyer tells me that guilt or innocence is a question of law, but he's wrong. How can I atone? That's the real question. I can't. I *can't*. I can only pay for it and say how deeply, deeply sorry I am. I love . . . Zach and the Farradays and Mia. I will always love them, and I pray that someday they will hear those words from me and not be hurt by them. Thank you." She returned to her place at the defendant's table and sat down.

The judge looked down at some papers spread in front of him. "I have an amicus brief from Mothers Against Drunk Drivers, asking for a sentence that will make an example of Ms. Baill and let other teens know what they could face in similar circumstances. And now, to the family." He looked up and smiled gently. "I know it's unexpected, but would any of you like to make a statement to this court?"

Miles looked at Jude. The prosecuting attorney had told them they'd be allowed to speak after the trial, so they'd thought about what they'd say, but it wasn't supposed to happen until weeks from now.

Jude shrugged, uncertain.

Miles rose to his feet and stood for a moment. Only the slightest tightening of his jaw betrayed the depth of his emotion. Looking at him now, no one in this room would imagine that he had begun to cry in his sleep.

He smoothed the pale pink tie at his throat and went to the podium at the front of the room, looking out at their friends and neighbors. "As I'm sure everyone in this room knows, it has been an incredibly difficult time for my family. There are no words to express the depth of our loss. Still, I'm surprised by Lexi's plea. I'm sure she was advised not to do so by her counsel.

"I know Lexi. She's been like a member of our family for the past few years. I know she would undo all of this if she could, and I am not so naïve as to believe that she is purely at fault and my own children are blameless. I should have forbidden my children to drink instead of remembering my own high school years. I should have been harder on them, perhaps taught them better lessons about alcohol. There is plenty of tragedy to go around here, and plenty of blame. It doesn't fall on Lexi alone."

He looked at Lexi. "I forgive you, Lexi, for what that's worth, and I admire your decision to plead guilty. I'm not sure I could have advised one of my children to do the same.

"Thank you, Your Honor, for this opportunity to speak," Miles said at last, looking at the judge. "I ask only that you treat Lexi as a girl who made a terrible mistake and owned up to it, not as a cold-blooded killer. Prison is no answer. It is just another tragedy, and there's been enough of that." He turned away from the podium and went back to his seat.

Jude didn't make a conscious decision to speak. She stood like some kind of marionette on someone's strings. Jerkily, awkward. She didn't even know what she would say until she stood at the podium, staring out at the people she'd known for years. She'd watched their children grow alongside hers, gone to their birthday parties. Some of them had younger kids who had yet to face the upcoming high school drinking parties.

"I wish to God I hadn't let my children go to the party that night," she said quietly, feeling something inside of her break. "I wish they hadn't gotten drunk. I wish Mia had put on her seatbelt. I wish they had called me to come and get them." She paused. "I will never hold my daughter again. I won't do her hair on her wedding day or hold her first baby." She reached into her pocket and pulled out the ring she'd bought for Mia's graduation. The gold shone brightly beneath the fluorescent lighting, the empty prongs like fingers reaching. "This is the ring I was going to give Mia for graduation. I thought a pink pearl would be nice here, but I was going to let her decide." Her voice weakened on that, and her strength evaporated. She looked at Lexi, sitting there, crying. Those tears should have meant something to Jude; she knew that, but they didn't. Regret wouldn't bring Mia back. "I can't forgive Lexi Baill. I wish I could. Maybe justice will help me. At the very least, maybe it will send a message to the next kid who thinks it's okay to drive home from a party." She walked back to her seat and sat down, trying not to notice Miles's obvious disappointment in her.

"Ms. Lange?" the judge said.

Lexi's aunt walked slowly to the podium. Instead of looking at the gallery, she looked at the bench. "I am not an educated woman, Your Honor, but I know that justice and revenge are two different things. Lexi is a good girl who made a bad choice. I am proud of her for standing here and admitting that. I beg you to be merciful in sentencing. She has a lot of good she can do in this life. And I am afraid of what prison will do to her." Eva composed herself and then returned to her seat.

The judge looked up. "Anyone else?"

Jude felt Zach shift in his seat, and then, slowly, he stood.

A gasp moved through the gallery. Jude knew what they saw when they looked at Zach: his burns, the newly shaved head, the discolored skin around his eyes, but mostly those who knew him saw his sadness. The boy who used to smile was gone. In his place stood this paler, injured version of her son.

"Zachary?" the judge said.

"It's not all her fault," he said without going to the podium. "I was the designated driver that night. I was the one who'd said I wouldn't drink. But I did anyway. I did. If she hadn't driven, I would have. I should go to prison instead of her."

He sat back down.

"Please stand, Ms. Baill," the judge said. "Teen drinking and driving is an epidemic in this country. Toxicology reports confirm that you were intoxicated when you decided to get behind the wheel of a car. At the end of the night, a girl was dead and a community and a family are left to grieve." He looked at Zach. "Others might share moral responsibility for this tragedy, but the legal responsibility for this crime is yours alone. Obviously, no amount of prison time can make up for Mia's bright light or bring solace to the Farraday family. But I can make sure that other teens see this case and understand the risk they take when they drink and drive. I sentence you to sixty-five months in the women's correctional facility in Purdy."

And the gavel fell.

❦

Lexi heard her aunt cry out.

Guards moved toward Lexi; one pulled her arms behind her and clamped handcuffs around her wrists. She felt her aunt's arms come around her. Lexi couldn't hug her back, and, after all that had happened in the last weeks, that was when it really sunk in.

For the first time, she was really, truly afraid. All she'd thought about was her soul and atonement, but what about her body? How would it be to spend more than five years behind bars?

"Oh, Lexi," Eva said, tearing up. "Why?"

"You took me in," Lexi said. Even now, with all that was happening, that sentence meant so much. Lexi found it hard to say more. "I couldn't let you waste your savings on me."

"Waste?"

"I'll never forget what you did for me."

Eva started to cry in earnest. "Be strong," she said. "I'll visit as often as I can. I'll write to you."

"That's enough," the guard said, and Lexi felt herself being pulled away, led out of the courtroom and down a long hallway and up two sets of stairs. Finally, they put her in a room that was about ten by ten, with cement walls; no window; a metal, seatless toilet; and a metal bench. The place smelled of urine and sweat and dried vomit.

She didn't want to sit down, so she stood there, waiting.

She didn't wait long. Soon, the guards came back for her, talking to one another about something that had happened at lunch as they led her out of the back of the courthouse to a waiting police car.

"We're taking you directly to Purdy," one of the guards said.

Purdy. The Washington Corrections Center for Women.

Lexi nodded and said nothing.

The guard shackled her ankles and snapped her handcuffed wrists to the chain around her waist.

"Let's go."

She hobbled along behind him, her head hung low. In the police car, she was buckled into the backseat. The chains around her waist bit into her back, so that she had to sit forward, with her nose almost pressed against the grill that protected the officers in the front seat. As they drove to the corner, they came to a stoplight.

In front of them, the Farradays were crossing the street; they looked like paper-doll versions of themselves, thin and fragile and bent. Zach was in the back, alone, his shoulders slumped downward, his chin dropped. From this side, his shaved head and burned jaw turned him into someone she hardly recognized.

Then the light changed, and they drove away.

Purdy prison was a monolithic slab of gray concrete set behind a wall of razor-wire fencing. All around it were green trees and blue skies. The surrounding beauty only served to make the prison look darker and more menacing.

As she moved toward this life she'd never imagined, Lexi wished suddenly, fervently, that she had pled not guilty as her lawyer had suggested.

Inside the prison, they put her in a big cage. Crouched inside like an animal, she could see some of the prison. Bars of steel and walls of Plexiglas and women in khaki gathered in groups.

Lexi closed her eyes and tried to make it all go away.

Finally, a guard came to get her, unlocked the cage, and herded her forward. She stood numbly beside him as he pressed her fingers onto an inked pad and rolled her prints onto paper. They positioned her in front of a camera, snapped a picture. Then someone yelled *next!* and she was moving again, shuffling forward into the loud, pulsing, clanging heart of the prison.

The guard led her into a room. "She's all yours."

Two female guards came forward. "Strip," one said, resting a plump hand on the walkie-talkie on her belt.

"H-here?"

"We can do it for you—"

"I'll do it." Lexi's hands were shaking as she unhooked her belt and pulled it free from the loops.

The guard took the belt from her, coiling it in her hands as if it were a weapon.

Swallowing hard, Lexi unbuttoned her pants and stepped out of them. Then she kicked off her black flats and unbuttoned her white shirt. It took every scrap of bravery she possessed to reach behind her back to unhook her bra.

When she was naked, the heavier of the two guards came forward. "Open your mouth."

Lexi followed one humiliating instruction after another. She opened her mouth, stuck out her tongue, lifted her breasts, coughed, wiggled her fingers, turned around and bent over.

"Open your cheeks."

She reached back and held her butt cheeks open.

"Okay, Inmate Baill," the guard said.

Lexi straightened slowly and turned to the guard again. She couldn't look the woman in the eyes, so she stared at the dirty floor.

The guard handed her a stack of clothes: a pair of scuffed white tennis shoes, khaki pants and shirt, a used white bra, and two pairs of discolored underwear.

Lexi dressed as quickly as possible. The bra didn't fit right and the underwear itched and she needed socks, but of course she said nothing.

"Be careful who you hang around with, Baill," the guard said in a voice that didn't match her gruff exterior.

Lexi had no idea what to say to that.

"Let's go," the guard said, indicating the door.

Lexi followed the woman out of the reception area and into the prison again, where the noise and the pounding and the catcalls seemed deafening. She kept her eyes downcast and followed, feeling the floor literally shaking beneath her feet from the hundreds of women stomping on the cell block before her.

Finally, they came to her cell, an eight-by-ten block of space hemmed on three sides by concrete walls and on the fourth by a solid metal door that had a small window, probably so the guards could look inside. The cell had two bunks with thin mattresses, a toilet, a sink, and a small desk. On the lower bunk sat a scrawny white girl with a cross tattooed on her throat. At Lexi's entrance, she looked up from her magazine.

The door clanged shut behind Lexi, but she could still hear the stomping and the catcalling going on in the cell block. She crossed her arms across her chest and stood there, shaking.

"I got the bottom bunk," the girl said; her teeth were brown and ruined.

"Okay."

"I'm Cassandra."

Lexi saw now how young her cellmate was. The lines in her face and the circles under her eyes aged her, but Cassandra probably wasn't much past twenty-three. "I'm Lexi."

"This is receiving. We won't be cellmates for long. You know that, right?"

Lexi didn't know anything. She stood there a minute longer, then she climbed up onto her rickety bunk that smelled of other women's sweat. Lying on the coarse gray blanket, staring at the dirty gray ceiling, she couldn't help thinking of her mother, of that one terrible prison visit.

Here I am, Mom. Just like you after all.

Sixteen

Before the accident, Jude would have said she could handle anything, but grief had overwhelmed her. Intellectually, she knew it had to be dealt with somehow, and yet she couldn't imagine how to accomplish such a thing. She was like a swimmer in deep water who saw a great white approaching. Her mind screamed *swim,* but her body just hung there, paralyzed.

To everyone else, the so-called trial had been the end of the story. *Justice was served; now go back to your regularly scheduled program.* Jude had felt pressure from everywhere to heal now.

Instead, she'd gone gray. It was the only way to describe her life. A depression unlike anything she'd ever known or imagined descended. She could find nothing to look forward to, nothing to do.

One by one, in the past six weeks, people had given up on her. She knew she'd disappointed her friends and family, but she couldn't *care* about it. Her feelings were either gone or buried in such a dense fog that they eluded her. Oh, sometimes she was normal—she might go to the store or drop something off at the post office, but she was always at risk of finding herself standing somewhere, in front of a row of plump purple eggplants or holding a letter, with no memory of how she'd gotten there or what she needed. She'd gone to the store twice in her pajamas, and once she'd worn shoes that didn't match. The simplest tasks loomed like Mount Everest. Making dinner was beyond her.

She cried at the drop of a hat and screamed out for her daughter in her sleep.

Miles had gone back to work, as if it were completely normal to live with a frozen heart. She knew how much he was still hurting, and she ached for him, but he was already growing impatient with her. Zach hardly came out of his room. He'd spent the summer in his new gaming chair, with his headphones on, killing animated enemies.

They were doing their best, Zach and Miles, and they didn't understand why Jude couldn't pretend, why she couldn't go out for lunch with her friends or work in her garden. Something. She saw how Miles looked at her in the evenings, over a dinner he'd brought home in Styrofoam containers. He would say things like, "How are you today, honey?" What he really meant was, "When are you going to get over this and come back to me?"

He thought that was the endgame. For him, the memory of their daughter was already becoming a treasured family heirloom that you put on a high shelf, behind a case of glass, and took down once or twice a year, at birthdays or Christmas. You couldn't handle it too roughly or too often for fear it would break.

It wasn't like that for her. She saw blank spaces everywhere—in an unused chair at the dinner table, in teen magazines that came addressed to Mia Farraday, in clothes left in a hamper. Mostly, she saw Mia in Zach, and it was unbearable. On good days, she could smile at her son, but there were so few good days; and on black days, when she couldn't get out of bed, she lay there thinking what a shitty mother she'd become.

By the middle of August, she'd stopped doing almost everything. She had to remind herself to shower and wash her hair. The only time she even got out of bed was to welcome her husband home, and she saw the sadness in Miles's eyes when he looked at her then.

She knew she was depressed. Miles kept asking her to "see someone." He didn't understand how deep this new darkness in her ran and how afraid she was to let go of it. She didn't want to get better. Really, she just wanted to be left alone. On the rare day when she even thought about *trying,* she told herself that Zach needed her, that Miles needed her, that she'd always thought of herself as a strong woman, but the words were like snapshots found in a drawer that showed a stranger's life. Impossible to care about.

Now, she and Miles were out on the back patio, pretending to be the couple they'd been before.

Miles was in the lounge chair beside her, with his feet stretched out. In his lap lay an open newspaper, but she knew he wasn't really reading it. They all tended to avoid the news these days; there was always a story about drunk driving somewhere within the pages. She felt him looking at her, but she didn't meet his gaze.

Instead, she counted the minutes until she could make some excuse and go back to bed. She was holding Mia's unset, unfinished ring in her hand. She did that a lot lately, just held it.

"You should put that away," Miles said. There was a taint of irritation in his voice that had become familiar.

"And go on," Jude said. "Yeah. I know."

"This can't continue," he said, raising his voice.

She was startled by the volume. "Save your surgeon voice for people who work for you."

"You're letting it drown you. Us."

"It." She finally turned to him. "Our daughter's *death.* So what, I'm overreacting? How disappointing for you."

Miles tightened his jaw. "Enough. I'm not going to let you turn me into the bad guy who didn't love Mia enough because I can still some-how love my son and my wife. You need help. You need to start."

"Start what? Forgetting her?"

"Letting go. It's not healthy to keep hanging on to her. Zach needs you. *I* need you."

"And there it is. The real point. You miss your wife, so I better toe the line."

"Damn it, Jude, you know that's not what I'm saying. I'm afraid we're going to lose us."

Somewhere deep inside, she felt the sting of that, and the truth of it. She experienced a rare desire to explain, to try to make him understand. "I went to Safeway last night. At midnight. I thought no one would be there. And I was right. I wandered around the aisles, just looking at stuff. When I ended up at the check stand, I had four tomatoes and ten boxes of Lucky Charms. The cashier said, 'Wow, you must have a lot of kids.' I stared at her and thought, *How many kids do I have? What do I say to people? One, two. One now?* I ran out without paying. You're right. I need help. How about if I get some of it from you and you just back off?"

"I don't know how to back off. I'm scared as hell you're going to fill up your pockets with rocks and walk out into the water one day, like that stupid movie we saw."

"I wish."

"See? See?" He got to his feet. "All right, Jude. You want my help? I'm going to give it to you. I'm going to get us started." He walked toward the sliding pocket doors and went into the house.

She let out a relieved sigh and sank back into the chair. That was how all of their conversations seemed to go lately. Miles storming off or walking away or trying to cure her with a hug. None of it meant much to her.

She stared down at Mia's stoneless ring, seeing the way the sunlight glanced off the prongs.

Then it hit her.

She knew what Miles was going to do to "help" her. It was something he'd mentioned often. *You can't keep putting it off,* he'd say. As if grief were a train that needed to stay on schedule.

With a cry, she flew out of her chair and ran up the stairs.

Mia's door was open.

She stumbled to a stop, frozen. She hadn't been able to touch the doorknob since that terrible night. She'd kept the door closed, as if not seeing the pink room would diminish her pain somehow.

But now Miles was in there, probably starting to box up her things.

To give to other kids, Jude. Children in need. Mia would want that.

She shrieked his name and ran for the open door, ready to scream at him, grab at him, claw at him.

He was kneeling on the wheat-colored carpet, his head bowed, clutching the soft pink stuffed puppy that had once been their daughter's second-best friend in the world, next to her brother. "Daisy Doggy," he said thickly.

Jude remembered with a stunning clarity how much she loved this man and how much she needed him. She tried to think of what to say to him now, but before she found her voice, Zach came up beside her.

"What's all the—" He saw his dad, holding Daisy Doggy, crying, and Zach started to back up.

"Zach," Miles said, wiping his eyes, but Zach was already gone. Down the hall, a door slammed shut.

"We're losing him," Miles said quietly. Slowly, as if his arm didn't quite work right, he put down the stuffed puppy.

Jude heard the censure that had crept back into his voice, the blame he placed on her, and she felt weighed down by it. "We're all lost, Miles," she said. "You're the only one who doesn't get that."

Before he could answer that, she went back downstairs and crawled into bed.

❧

Lexi knew now why her lawyer had wanted her to plead not guilty. Prison was a place where women beat one another up for a hand-rolled cigarette. You had to be careful every second. The wrong look at the wrong woman could literally get you killed.

She was afraid all of the time, and when she wasn't afraid, she was irritated. Her temporary cellmate, Cassandra, had turned out to be a crystal-meth addict who would do anything for drugs and moaned all night in her sleep. Lexi had spent the first four weeks dodging the big mean women who ran the drug trades. She spoke to no one.

Today, though, she had something to look forward to.

It was visiting day. Lexi knew it was wrong to make Eva come up all this way, and she wished she were strong enough to tell her not to come, but she couldn't. It was so damned lonely here. Eva's visits were the only good thing left in her life, the only hour all week to which she looked forward.

She spent all morning counting the minutes, listening to Cassandra puke in their lidless steel toilet. When the guard showed up to take Lexi to the visitors' room, she practically leaped up. Following instructions precisely, she made her way through the various doors, past the inspections, and into the big, windowed room where family and friends came to visit.

There, she found an empty table and sat down, tapping her foot nervously on the floor. Guards were stationed around the room, watching everything, but other than that, it almost looked like a school cafeteria.

Finally, Eva came through the door. She looked smaller and older, with her gray hair frizzing out around her pleated face. As always, she looked uncomfortable in here, out of place.

"Over here, Aunt Eva!" Lexi said, raising her hand as if she were a high school girl again.

Eva shuffled forward. At the table, she stopped suddenly and kind of collapsed into the chair. "Lord, help me," she said, pressing a hand to her chest. "You'd think *I* was the criminal."

"What do you mean?"

"Oh. I didn't mean that. It was just an ordeal, getting in today. Something must be up. That's all. How are you?" She reached across the table and patted Lexi's hand, smiling brightly. "How are you this week?"

Lexi didn't mean to grab her aunt's hands, but she couldn't help herself. It felt so good to touch someone. The depth of her need surprised her. She was so hungry for conversation, for connection, that she launched into a review of the book she'd read this week, and she told Eva all about her job in the laundry. In turn, Eva told her about the summer sale at Walmart and the weather in Port George.

It wasn't until Lexi had run out of news that she really looked at her aunt, and that was when she saw the changes. It had only been two months since Lexi's incarceration, but these visits had already left marks on Eva's face. Her wrinkles were deeper, her lips thinner. She had to keep clearing her throat, as if it hurt to speak.

Once Lexi saw all of that, she couldn't unsee it. She understood all at once how selfish she'd been to this woman who had never been anything but kind.

"Have you started taking college courses yet?" Eva asked, pushing the fuzzy hair out of her eyes.

"No."

"You can get a degree in here. Just like you planned."

"I think ex-cons have a hard time getting into law school." Lexi slumped back in her chair, feeling defeated now, alone. She'd been through this kind of thing before, back when she'd been in the care of strangers. She'd waited and waited to see her mom, only to be heartbroken again and again. Sometimes the only way to survive was to stop hoping. Stop waiting.

Eva had been there for Lexi in a way that no one else ever had. *We're family,* Eva had said to her on that day, so long ago now, when they'd first come together, and it had become the truth.

Now it was Lexi's turn. If she didn't release Eva now, her aunt would stay here, connected to this terrible place by a string of uncomfortable visiting days. "You should go to Florida," she said quietly.

Eva stopped. Had she been saying something? "What do you mean? I can't leave you."

Lexi leaned forward, grasped Eva's hands across the table. "I'm going to be in here for more than five years. And I know how much you want to live with Barbara—this rainy weather is so hard on your knees. You deserve to be happy, Eva. Really."

"Don't say that, Lexi."

Lexi swallowed hard. She knew what she had to do. Eva would have to be forced to let go. "I won't see you again, Eva. It won't do you any good to come back."

"Oh, Alexa . . ."

It was all in that softly spoken name—the regret, the disappointment, the loss—and it hurt to hear it; mostly it hurt to know that she was pushing away the only person in the world who loved her. But it was for Eva's own good.

And wasn't that what love was supposed to be?

"When I get out, I'll come to Florida," Lexi said.

"I won't let you do this," Eva said, her eyes filling with tears.

"No. I won't let you do this," Lexi said. "Give me this, Eva. Please. Let me do this for you. It's all I can do."

Eva sat there a long time. Then, finally, she wiped her eyes. "I'll write every week."

Lexi could only nod.

"And I'll send pictures."

They kept talking, both of them trying to say everything that was needed, building up a store of words that would keep them warm come winter. But finally, the time was over, and Eva got to her feet. She looked even older now, more tired. And Lexi knew she'd done the right thing.

"Good-bye, Alexa," Eva said.

Lexi stood there, nodding. "Thanks for . . ." Her voice broke.

Eva pulled her into a hug and held on to her tightly. "I love you, Alexa," she said.

Lexi was shaking when she drew back. "I love you, too, Eva."

Eva looked at her through shiny eyes. "And you remember this: I knew your mama. You are *nothing* like her, you hear me? And don't you let this place change that."

And then she left.

Lexi stood there for as long as she could see her aunt. Finally, she left the visitors' room and returned to her cell. She hadn't been there for more than forty minutes when a guard came and stood in the open doorway.

"Baill. Get your things."

Lexi scooped up her few belongings—toiletries, letters, photographs—and put them in a dented shoe box, then she followed the guard into the main section of the prison.

All around her, women were stomping their feet and calling out to her. In the steel and concrete prison, the noise was thunderous. Lexi didn't look up, just kept her belongings pressed to her chest and her eyes downcast.

The guard stopped suddenly.

The cell door in front of them buzzed loudly, clicked, and opened.

The guard stepped aside. "Inside, Baill. This is your permanent cell."

Lexi stepped around the guard's bulky body and peered into the cell that would probably be her home for the next sixty-three months.

The cement walls were plastered with photographs and drawings and magazine ads. A heavyset woman sat on the lower bunk, her broad shoulders slumped forward, her thick, heavily tattooed arms resting on her bent knees. She had long, ropey strands of gray-black hair and dark skin. Moles dotted her cheeks, and tattoos curled around her throat.

The door clanged shut behind her. "I'm Lexi," she said, having to clear her throat before she had enough confidence to add, "Baill."

"Tamica," the woman said, and Lexi was surprised by the pretty sound of her voice. "Hernandez."

"Oh."

"My kid's about your age," Tamica said, heaving her considerable bulk off the narrow bed. It was concrete and steel; no springs pinged at the movement. She moved forward, pointed to a tattered, worn photograph taped to the concrete-block wall. "Rosie. I was pregnant with her when I got in here. Didn't know it, though." Tamica crouched down by the toilet and rolled a cigarette. As she smoked, she exhaled into the vent on the wall. "You got any pictures?"

Lexi put down her box of belongings and sat next to Tamica on the cold floor. She picked up a few photographs from the pile. "This is my Aunt Eva. And this is Zach." She stared down at his senior picture. She touched it all the time. Already it felt as if she were starting to forget him, and that terrified her. "And this is Mia. The girl I . . . killed."

Tamica took the picture of Mia, studied it. "Pretty girl. Rich?"

Lexi frowned. "How'd you know that?"

"You're here, ain't you?"

Lexi wasn't quite sure how to answer that. The question seemed to imply facts that weren't quite true, or that she hadn't really seen before.

"I killed my husband," Tamica said, indicating a picture on the wall.

"Self-defense," Lexi said. It was something you heard about a lot in here. She seemed to be the only guilty person in prison.

"Nah. Killed the fucker in his sleep."

"Oh."

"I been here so long now I can hardly remember the bad shit I done." Tamica put out the cigarette and hid the unsmoked half inside of her mattress. "Well, I guess we might as well talk. Get to know each other." She looked at Lexi, and in those dark eyes, there was a sadness that made Lexi uncomfortable. "We got time, you and me. And I could use a friend."

"When will you get out?"

"Me?" Tamica smiled slightly. "Never."

On a Wednesday in late August, Zach emerged from his bedroom looking disheveled and a little disoriented. His short hair was dirty and spiky; his T-shirt had a big stain across the front.

Jude and Miles were in the great room, staring at the TV, though neither was watching. They hadn't spoken in more than an hour. When Zach walked into the room, Jude's heart ached at the sight of him. If she weren't so exhausted, she would have gone to him, maybe asked how he was, but she hadn't slept in weeks, and even the merest movements were beyond her. She'd lost fifteen pounds this summer, and the loss left her looking skeletal and wan.

"I'm going to USC," he said without preamble.

Miles rose slowly. "We've talked about this, Zach. I don't think that's a good idea. It's too soon."

"It's what she would want," Zach said, and with that, the air seemed to get sucked out of the room, leaving them all breathless.

Miles sank back to the sofa. "Are you sure?"

"Sure?" Zach said, his voice dull. "It's what I'm doing, okay?"

Jude stared at her son, seeing the salmony patch of new skin along his jaw. Blue veins in his cheeks looked like cracked lines in aged porcelain. He was this big, broad-shouldered kid who'd been whittled down by grief. How could she tell him to stay here, in this airless, dead place? "Okay," she said at last.

❧

For the next few days, Jude made a herculean effort to act like her old self. She wasn't that woman, of course, but she wanted—this one time—to think about her son instead of her daughter. In the old days— only months ago now, a lifetime—she would have thrown a huge "good luck in college / going away" party for her kids. Now, it took everything inside of her to invite a few friends over to say good-bye to Zach. Honestly, she didn't want to do even that, but Miles insisted.

On the big day, she took a shower and washed and dried her hair. When she looked in the mirror, she was surprised by the thin, fragile-looking face that stared back at her. Too many sleepless nights had left dark circles under her eyes, and even in this final week of August, after a long, hot summer, she was as pale as chalk.

She brought out her makeup kit and went to work, and by three o'clock, when the doorbell rang, she looked almost like her old self.

"They're here," Miles said, coming up behind her. He slipped his arms around her waist and kissed the side of her neck. "Are you ready?"

"Sure," she said, forcing a smile. In truth, she felt a fluttering of panic. The thought of people around her, of having to pretend she was *okay, getting over it, moving on,* made her hyperventilate.

Miles took her by the hand and led her down the hall to the front door.

Molly and Tim stood on the front porch; both were smiling just a little too brightly. They had come bearing food, with their kids in a group behind them. The freezer was already full of foil-wrapped food that people had brought after the accident. Jude couldn't look at any of it, couldn't eat a bite of it. Just the sight of foil made her queasy.

"Hey, guys," Miles said, stepping aside to let them in. "It's good to see you."

Instead of welcoming them, Jude crossed her arms and glanced out at her garden.

Prickly, ugly weeds grew everywhere. Her once-beloved plants seemed to be climbing over one another in a rush to leave their confinement.

"Jude?"

Jude blinked and saw Molly standing beside her. Had she been talking? "I'm sorry," she said. "Senior moment. What did you say?"

Molly and Miles exchanged worried glances.

"Come on, honey," Molly said, putting an arm around her.

Jude let her friend sweep her up like a warm tide and carry her into the front room, where a *Good luck, Zach* banner hung across the mantel. Miles put music on the stereo, but at the first song—Sheryl Crow singing "The First Cut Is the Deepest"—he snapped it off and turned on the television instead. The Seahawks were playing football.

One by one, Zach's friends filed into the house. They took up space, these boys and girls she'd known for so long. She'd been with most of them since kindergarten. She'd fed them and driven them to and from events and even occasionally advised them. Now, like Zach, they were getting ready to leave the safety of the island and go off to college.

Minus one.

Miles came up beside Jude, touched her arm. "Is he going to come down?"

She looked up at him, and in his eyes she saw the same thought that dogged her: the old Zach would never have been late to his own party. "He said he would. I'll go get him," she said.

She nodded and left, realizing too late that she'd just walked away from Molly. She should have excused herself.

Honestly, it was hard to remember things like that these days.

At Zach's closed door, she reached into her pocket—always full now of aspirin—and she chewed one. The terrible taste actually helped.

Then she knocked on the door.

There was no answer, so she knocked again, harder, and said, "I'm coming in."

He was slumped in his gaming chair, wearing headphones and wielding a controller like a fighter pilot. On the TV screen in front of him, a remarkably realistic tank rolled down a barren hillside, gun blazing.

She touched his head, gave it a little scratch.

He leaned into her hand, and she wondered how long it had been since she'd touched him. With that thought came the loss again, the grief and the guilt. "What you doing?"

"Trying to beat this level."

"Your friends are here . . . to say good-bye," she finally said.

"Yeah," he said, sighing.

"Come on," she said.

They went downstairs together, saying nothing.

In the living room, there was a moment of silence as they entered, awkward and uncomfortable. How could this ever be a celebration, really? Then Zach's friends came up him, smiling uncertainly, talking quietly.

Jude stood back. She was trying like hell to stay *present*, to stay in this moment that mattered to her son, but it hurt so much. She should have expected it, should have known she couldn't celebrate Zach's journey to college—to *USC*—without also mourning the fact that he was going alone.

She stayed as long as she could, smiled more than she would have thought possible; she even cut the cake and asked Miles to make a toast, but long before the day turned to early evening, she slipped down the hallway and hid in her dark office.

How could she go to USC, say good-bye to her son and not be overwhelmed with grief? USC was Mia's school—everyone knew that. Her bedroom walls were studded now with red and gold USC paraphernalia. The worst part (which she would never admit to anyone) was that she *wanted* him gone. Every time she looked at him, she broke all over again. Without him, she could just do nothing. Be nothing.

Feeling shaky, she went to the sofa and sat down. Suddenly she couldn't breathe.

"You can run, but you can't hide," someone said, and the lights came on.

Molly stood there, holding a plate of lemon bars. She took one look at Jude and rushed to the couch, sitting down beside her. "Breathe, honey. In and out. In and out."

"Thanks," Jude said when the panic subsided.

"I don't want to set you off again, but your mother's looking for you."

"Reason enough to hide out."

"I don't know what to say to you anymore, Jude. But I'm here. You know that, right?"

"I know it."

Molly's gaze was steady, worried. "You can call me anytime . . . I know how hard it will be on you when Zach is gone."

"Gone." The word was like the flick of a knife. Zach was leaving. Mia was *gone*.

She forced a smile. The only way to stop a conversation like this was to pretend she was okay. "Yes. Well. I better go see my mother before she decides to redecorate." She reached for a lemon bar, which she had no intention of eating, but it was the polite thing to do. The normal thing.

The next day, she and Miles and Zach set off for the airport.

It should have been a joyous occasion. Each of them tried to pretend. Miles made inane conversation and stupid jokes all the way to Sea-Tac.

On the airplane, they pretended not to notice the empty seat across from Miles. Before, they'd always sat two and two. Now they filled up a row themselves. The three of them.

At the college, they walked around in the hot California sunshine, remarking on the beauty and elegance of the campus.

Throughout the weekend, grief, always elastic, stretched out and snapped back, surprising them with its force at the oddest times. Seeing a blond girl in a black vest . . . seeing a girl in a pink sweater do a cartwheel on the grass, hearing Zach's roommate ask about sisters or brothers . . .

But they made it through. On Sunday night, they had a last family dinner at Mastro's Steakhouse in Beverly Hills and then took Zach back to his dorm room. There, Jude saw the decorations on Zach's roommate's side—posters and family pictures and a quilt made by the kid's mom. It occurred to her then, too late, that she should have shopped for Zach, filled this room with everything he would need to succeed at school. The old Jude would have moved him in with boxes and boxes . . .

"We'll miss you," Jude said, trying not to cry.

"Call your mother," Miles said gruffly. "Keep in touch."

Zach nodded and hugged his dad. When he drew back and looked at Jude, she saw the uncertainty and shame in his eyes. "I'll do well, Mom. You don't have to worry about me."

Jude pulled him into her arms and held him as tightly as she could. Her shame and guilt were almost unbearable. She wanted to tell him how much she loved him, but the words that had once come so easily were impossible to form now.

He held her for a long time, and then slowly they drew apart.

"Good-bye," Zach said quietly.

It all came down to that one word. Good-bye. Once you said it out loud, it was real.

"Bye, Zach," Jude said softly. She and Miles walked out of his dorm room, into the busy hallway. Behind them, his door quietly clicked shut.

$\mathscr{S}$ even teen

That fall, time seemed alternately to fly forward and to crawl. With Zach gone, the house was as quiet as a tomb. Miles worked longer hours than ever. Jude knew he was afraid to come home to her. He hated how far she'd fallen into the gray.

But now it was November, Thanksgiving weekend, and Zach was home. She'd promised Miles, and herself, that she would make a real effort for her son. She *wanted* that. At least her mind wanted it, and she was determined for once to act like a mother.

And so she had come up here, to the attic above the garage. She stood in front of the red and green boxes that contained their Christmas decorations.

What had she been thinking?

How could she hang three stockings on the mantel? Or hold the Life-Savers-and-white-yarn ornament Mia had made in kindergarten? How?

She turned her back on all of it and headed for the door. By the time she got back into the house, her hands were shaking and she was cold.

She never should have told Miles she'd decorate, but the sadness in Zach's eyes had filled her with guilt. She'd thought that decorating for Christmas might cheer him up. He'd been so depressed all week. He claimed that school was going well, that he had great grades—and even swore that med school was still his future, but he was so quiet that sometimes she forgot he was even home. He never answered his cell phone, and after a while it had stopped ringing.

She moved into the living room. Sunlight shone through the tall windows, gilding the wooden floors. Zach and Miles sat next to each other on the big, overstuffed sofa, both wielding controllers, while two ninjas kickboxed each other on the big flat-screen TV.

"You find the ornaments?" Miles said, without looking up.

"No."

Miles sighed; lately he was always sighing. So was she, for that matter.

Their whole relationship seemed to be made of air, filled with nothing. She wanted to make him happy, but she couldn't find any way to say what he needed to hear.

The doorbell rang, and she was relieved. She hated guests, but anything was better than this retread conversation about who she used to be. "Are we expecting anyone?"

"Hardly. People don't drop by anymore," Miles said.

"Maybe it's Drew or Greg," Jude said, steeling herself to see one of Zach's friends.

She went to the door and opened it.

A stranger stood there, holding a manila envelope.

No. Not a stranger, but she couldn't place his face. "Hello?"

"I'm Scot Jacobs. Alexa—Lexi—Baill's defense attorney."

"Come in, Mr. Jacobs," Miles said, appearing beside Jude.

She felt herself being pushed aside. She heard the door shut. Feeling light-headed, she followed the men into the living room.

"I came to speak to Zachary," the lawyer said, and, at his name, Zach put down the controller and stood. "I have these papers from Lexi. She asked me to deliver them to you personally. She thought you would be home this weekend." He didn't look at Jude—just Zach—and offered the envelope. "She's pregnant," he said quietly.

※

How long did she stand there, staring? She could feel the blood moving in her veins, pounding on the walls of her heart. A high-pitched scream filled her head.

No. She was *making* that sound. Was that really her? The anger she'd spent months suppressing came roaring back. Zach was talking, saying something, but Jude didn't hear the words; she didn't care anyway.

"Get out of this house," she said suddenly. Yelled.

"I'm sorry . . ." Scot said.

"Sorry? *Sorry?* Your client kills my daughter, but that's not enough for her, is it? She's not done with us. Now she has to ruin my son's life, too. How do we even know Zach is the father? How far along is she?"

"Mom!" Zach said sharply.

Miles looked shaken and pale, but the anger Jude felt was nowhere to be seen in his eyes. That pissed her off even more. She was always alone in her feelings lately, always wrong.

"She's five and a half months pregnant," Scot answered.

"How convenient. What is in the envelope? What does she want from Zach?"

"These are adoption papers, Mrs. Farraday, and I can tell you that Lexi did not come to this decision easily. If . . . Zach doesn't want the baby, she's prepared to undergo the adoption process alone. She'll find a good family. She doesn't want her baby to be in foster care."

"If Zach doesn't want the baby?" Jude said, incredulous. "He's eighteen years old, for God's sake. He can't remember to wash his clothes."

"She hated foster care," Zach said quietly.

Scot nodded. "She doesn't want that for her baby."

Jude couldn't make sense of all of this; there seemed to be some undercurrent pulling at her, swirling around her, but she couldn't see a ripple. "Where's a pen?" Jude said tightly.

"Judith," Miles said, using his reasonable voice, the one that meant she was being a bitch or a shrew or whatever. She couldn't care less. She was sick to death of his reasonableness. The pain in her heart was all consuming, unbearable. It took every scrap of control she possessed not to howl in agony. "This is our grandchild we're talking about. We can't be cavalier."

"You think I'm being cavalier?" Jude stared at her husband, hating him as much as she'd ever hated anyone. "You think it's not tearing me up inside? You think I haven't dreamed of my first grandchild? But not like this, Miles. A child by the girl who killed our Mia? No, I won't—"

"Stop," Zach said loudly.

Jude had forgotten he was even there. "I'm sorry, Zach. I know this is terrible, tragic, but you need to listen to me."

"When have I ever done anything *but* listen to you?" he said.

She heard the anger in his voice and stepped back from it. "W-what are you saying, Zach?"

"It's my baby," Zach said firmly. "Mine and Lexi's. I can't just turn my back on that. How can you want me to?"

Jude felt the floor beneath her open up, and suddenly she was falling. She saw his whole sad future in a flash: no college degree, no decent job, no falling in love with the right girl and starting fresh in life. At that, her last, desperate hope that he would someday climb out of this pit and learn to be happy again disappeared.

"I'll be a dad," Zach said. "I'll quit school and come home."

Jude couldn't breathe. How could this be happening? "Zach," she pleaded. "Think about your future—"

"It's done, Mom," he said. "Will you guys help me?"

"Of course we'll help," Miles said. "You can stay in school. We'll find a way."

Scot cleared his throat, and the three of them looked at him. "Lexi thought Zach would feel this way . . . or maybe she hoped. Anyway, she has also had me draft custody papers. She's prepared to give Zach full custody. She's asked for only two things from you. She doesn't want her child to know that she's in prison. Ever. She actually suggested that you tell the baby she . . . died." He paused, looked at Zach. "And she wants to hand you the baby herself, Zach. Only to you. So you'll need to be at the hospital when she gives birth."

Jude turned sharply on her heels and walked away. In her bedroom, she took three—no, four—sleeping pills and crawled into bed. As she lay there, trembling, praying for the pills to work, she tried to think about a baby, this baby, her grandchild; she tried to picture a tiny version of Mia, with hair like corn silk and eyes like green marbles.

How could she look at a baby like that and ever feel anything but her own loss?

❧

Lexi was in the prison cafeteria when the first labor pain hit. She grabbed Tamica's wrist, squeezing hard.

"Oh my God," Lexi said when it was over. "Is that what it's going to be like?"

"Worse." Tamica led her across the crowded cafeteria to one of the guards positioned by the door. "The kid's going into labor."

The guard nodded, radioed the news to someone else, and then told them to go back to their cell. "Someone will come for you, Baill."

Lexi let herself be led down to her cell. There, she curled up on Tamica's lower bunk and made it through the rising pain. Tamica stroked her hair and told her silly stories about her life. Lexi tried to listen and be polite, but the pains were sharper and coming faster now.

"I . . . can't . . . take . . . it. How do women take it?"

"Baill?"

She heard her name through this fog of pain; when the cramp ended, she looked up groggily.

Miriam Yungoh, the prison doctor, was there. "I hear there's a baby who wants to come out and play."

"Drugs," Lexi said. "Give me drugs."

Dr. Yungoh smiled. "How about if I examine you first?"

"Yeah," Lexi said. "Whatever."

Lexi hardly paid attention to all the things that happened next. It was probably just as well. There was the pelvic exam that any prisoner walking past the cell could see, the strip search in receiving (to make sure that she wasn't trying to sneak something out of the prison in her vagina—ha!), and the reshackling of her wrists and ankles.

She didn't relax until she was lying in the gurney in the back of an ambulance, shackled to the bed's metal rails. "Can Tamica come with me? Please? I want her at the hospital," Lexi said between pains.

No one answered her, and when the next pain hit, she forgot everything else. By the time she got to the hospital, her pains were coming so fast it was like being in the ring with a prizefighter. She was in a private hospital room, with guards stationed both inside and outside the room. She wanted to roll over or walk or even just sit up, but she couldn't do any of that. She was shackled to the guardrails of the bed on the left side. One ankle and one wrist. And they wouldn't give her drugs because it was too late for that. Whatever the hell *that* meant.

Another pain hit. The worst one yet. She screamed out, her belly tightening so hard she thought she was going to die.

When the pain abated, she tried to sit up and then spoke to the guard. "Get a nurse or doctor in here, please. Something's wrong. I can tell. It hurts too much. Please." She was panting now, trying not to cry.

"My job isn't—"

"Please," Lexi begged. "Please."

The guard looked at Lexi; her eyes narrowed. Lexi wondered what the woman saw: a murderer chained to a bed, or an eighteen-year-old girl, giving birth to a baby she'd probably never know.

"I'll check," the guard said and left the room.

Lexi fell back into the pillows. She tried to be strong, but she had never felt so alone. She needed Aunt Eva here, or Tamica, or Zach or Mia.

Another pain ripped through Lexi; she strained against the restraints, felt the cold metal bite into her wrist and ankle. Then it was over.

Sagging back into the pillows, she exhaled. Her whole body felt wrung out.

She touched her belly. She could feel her baby in there, wriggling, probably trying to find her way out of this pain. "It's okay, little girl. We'll be okay."

She squeezed her eyes shut, trying to imagine the baby inside of her. For months now, as she'd lain in her lonely prison bed, she'd dreamed of this baby, and in her dreams it was always a girl.

When the pain came again, she cried out, certain this time that her stomach was going to split open like that scene in *Alien*. She was still screaming when the doctor came into the room, with a nurse beside him.

"Chained to the bed? Where are we, medieval France? Uncuff her. Now."

"I'm sorry, Doctor, but I can't do that," the guard said. To her credit, she actually *looked* sorry.

"Hello, Lexi. I'm Dr. Farst," he said, coming to her bedside.

"H-hi," she said. "I think I'm dying. Do they ever rip you in half?"

He smiled. "It just feels that way. I'm going to examine you now."

"Okay."

He pushed her gown aside and positioned himself between her legs.

"Can you see her yet? Aagh—" Lexi arched up in pain again.

"Okay, Alexa, it looks like someone is ready to be born. When I say push, you bear down as hard as you can."

Lexi was so tired, she could hardly move. "What does that mean, bear down?"

"Like you're constipated and trying to go."

"Oh."

"Okay, Alexa. Push."

Lexi strained and pushed and screamed. She lost track of how many times the doctor told her to stop and start and stop again. She hurt so badly she could hardly stand it, and she wished someone were beside her, telling her she was okay, that she was doing great. That was how it happened in the movies.

And then a baby cried. "It's a girl," the doctor said with a smile.

Lexi had never known before that a heart could take flight, but that was how she felt suddenly; the pain was gone—already forgotten—and angels were lifting her up. She saw the doctor hand the baby—her baby—to the nurse, and she couldn't help reaching out to hold her. One arm lifted; the other clanged against the restraint.

"Uncuff her wrist," the doctor said to the guard, pulling off his blue surgical cap. "Now."

"But—"

Dr. Farst turned to the guard. "In this room, I'm God. Take off the cuff. Leave the ankle if you have to. That should keep society safe from this teenager." He walked over to the bed. "You're young," he said.

It meant he thought she had lots of time ahead of her, that someday she'd be in a room like this, giving birth to a child that she would bring home and love. That someday she would nurse her own child.

She could have told him that he was wrong, that she wasn't young anymore and that dreams were ephemeral things, like balloons that, once loosed, disappeared into the sky above you. But he was so nice, and she was tired, and she didn't want to look truth in the face right now.

The nurse came up beside her, handed Lexi a tiny bundle wrapped in pink.

Her daughter.

"I'll leave you two alone for a minute. I know . . . there are people waiting."

There was an awkward moment when truth muscled its way into the room, and then the nurse and doctor left.

Lexi stared down at her baby in awe, mesmerized by her little pink face and her bow-shaped lips, by her muddy blue eyes that seemed to know secrets that Lexi hadn't yet learned. Lexi reached down and touched a grape-sized fist. "I have so much to say to you, little girl, but you won't remember it. You won't remember me. But I'll remember you."

Lexi held her daughter close, gave her all the love she had inside of her, hoping to imprint her in a way that would last. "Like geese," she whispered into the tiny, shell-pink ear, "their babies imprint on the mama in the first sighting and never forget."

There was a knock at the door. The guard answered, spoke to someone in the hallway outside, and then opened the door. Scot walked in. He was as rumpled as always, in a cheap wool suit and an out-of-date tie, but the look in his eyes was so caring and compassionate that she felt the start of panic. She instinctively tightened her hold on her baby.

"Hey, Lexi," he said. At the red mark on her wrist, he frowned. "They shackled you? Motherfu—"

"It's okay," she said. "Look."

Scot leaned down. "She's beautiful, Lexi." At the words, his face seemed to kind of fall. "It's time," he said gently.

"He's here?" she asked, and even with all the pain that she knew was coming, her heart skipped a beat.

"He's right outside."

"Help me sit up, would you, Scot?"

He helped her get positioned, then drew back. "You sure you want to do this?"

"What choice do I have?"

"You don't have to give up full custody, that's for sure. When you get out—"

"Look at her," Lexi said, staring down at this beautiful girl. "She'll be loved by them. She'll *feel* loved. She'll feel safe. She'll have all the things I can't give her. Believe me, Scot, she doesn't need a mother like me."

"I don't agree, but it's your choice," Scot said. "I'll send him in."

Lexi sat up straighter, and then *he* was there, in the doorway.

It hurt more than she'd expected, more than the labor she'd just suffered through. He stood tall, bigger than she remembered, his shoulders broader. Wheat-blond hair fell across his eyes, and she remembered how much he used to hate that, how she'd laugh when she pushed it aside to see his eyes as he leaned down to kiss her.

She loved him so much. It wasn't only in her blood, the way she loved him; it *was* her blood. She didn't know if everyone else was right and her love for him would someday begin to fade like an old photograph; how could she know that? She only knew that her love for him was the very best of her and without it her heart would be empty.

He moved closer, looking uncertain.

She was glad her daughter was in her arms, because she would have touched him. She wouldn't have been able to stop herself.

Up close, she saw the scar along his jawline; the wrinkled skin was the same pink as their baby's face. Soon, maybe, it would be gone altogether or become too fine to see, but it was there now, a visible reminder of her crime.

"Hi, Zach," she said, hearing the tremble in her voice.

He drew in a breath, saying her name quietly, and there finally was the heartache. His voice reminded her of nights on the beach, of kisses that went on all night. Of dreams and futures.

"She looks just like Mia," he said, and, with that, the past was here with them again, crouched alongside this bundled-up bit of the future.

Lexi wanted to apologize, but she held back. There was no point anymore; those days were over. This was about something else. Someone else. "I would name her Grace," Lexi said, wiping her eyes. "If it was up to me."

"You're her mother," Zach said.

Her mother. Lexi didn't know what to say to that, so she said nothing.

"I thought you wanted to name . . . I thought you liked Katya."

She drew in a breath at that: so, he remembered. It felt like a lifetime ago, that conversation of hope between two kids who thought that love was easy. They'd been on their beach, spinning diaphanous dreams of the future. "My friend . . . Tamica is a Catholic. She says when God forgives you, he grants you grace." She looked down at her daughter. "Gracie? Is that you?"

The baby made a mewling sound, and Lexi started to cry. "Don't cry, baby," she said, kissing the tiny pink lips.

Then she looked up at Zach. "Tell her I loved her enough to do what was best for her."

"I'll bring her to visit—"

"No." She kissed her daughter one last time, and then slowly, slowly handed her to Zach. "I don't want her to grow up like I did. Keep her away from me."

He took the small bundle in his arms. "Grace," he said. "Grace Mia Farraday."

Lexi felt the pain of that. "I love you, Gracie," she whispered, wishing she'd kissed her daughter one more time before she handed her over. "And Zach, I—"

There was a knock at the door. It was so loud it startled her.

"That will be my mom," Zach said. "What were you going to say?"

Lexi shook her head. "It doesn't matter."

He paused, moved his gaze from the baby to Lexi. "I ruined everything," he said softly.

She couldn't find her voice, not even to say good-bye to her daughter or the boy she loved.

❧

Jude had tried to prepare for this day. She told herself *this would be it,* the start of a new Jude, and so when Zach came out of Lexi's hospital room, holding a pink-wrapped newborn, his eyes glazed with emotion, Jude felt hope rising within her, standing tall.

"Grace Mia Farraday," Zach said.

"She's gorgeous," Miles said, coming up beside his son, cupping the baby's small head in his long surgeon's hand.

Jude looked down into her granddaughter's small face, and time seemed to fall away.

For a second, she was a young mother herself, with a baby in each arm and Miles beside her.

Grace looked exactly like Mia.

The same bow-shaped lips and muddy blue eyes that would turn green, the same pointed chin and white-blond eyelashes. Jude drew back instinctively.

"Mom?" Zach said, looking up at her. "Do you want to hold her?"

Jude started to shake. The cold in her heart radiated out to her fingers, and she wished she'd brought a coat. "Of course." She made herself smile and reach out, taking Mia—*no, Grace*—in her arms, holding her close.

Love her, she thought desperately, beginning to panic. *Feel something.*

But there was nothing. She stared down at her own granddaughter, this baby who looked enough like Mia to fool anyone, and Jude felt nothing at all.

❧

Physically, Lexi healed quickly. Her boobs shrank back to their normal size, and her milk dried up. Within a month, a few pale silvery lines on her lower belly were the only evidence that she'd ever had a child.

She felt as faded as those marks. Pregnancy had changed her. A girl named Alexa Baill had gone into that hospital, chained to a bed, and given birth to the most beautiful baby in the world. She'd seen the boy she loved one last time. And then it was all gone, and an older, wiser Lexi had come back to Purdy.

Before, she'd been fragile, even hopeful; she saw that now, the way you saw a missing fence post. The lack stood out. She'd been damaged, broken by the terrible thing she'd done, but she'd believed in redemption, in the power of justice. She'd thought that going to prison would be an atonement and that with atonement she could be forgiven.

What a crock.

Her lawyer had been right. She should have fought the charges, said she was sorry and young and stupid.

Instead, she'd done the right thing and been crushed. She'd lost everything that mattered to her, but nothing hurt more than the loss of her child.

In the two months since Grace's birth, Lexi had tried to hold on to who she was, but the best parts of her were draining away. Day after day, she attempted to write letters to her daughter, and each new failure stripped away a piece of her, until now there was so little left she felt transparent. Especially today.

She was in the yard, sitting on a bench beneath a pale denim sky. Over to her left, some khaki-clad women were playing basketball. The trees outside the prison were in full, vibrant bloom. Every now and then a pink blossom floated over the skeletal mountain of razor wire and landed on the ground like an impossibly kept promise.

"You look like someone who could use a boost."

Lexi looked up. The woman standing there had a carrot-colored crew cut and a blue kerchief tied around her shorn head. A snake tattoo peeked out from her collar. She was a stocky woman with powerful hands and skin that looked like someone had scrubbed at her cheeks with steel wool.

Lexi knew who this woman was. Everyone did. Her nickname, Smack, said it all.

Lexi got slowly to her feet. In all the time she'd been here, she'd never spoken to Smack. There was only one reason women befriended Smack, and once you started talking to her, you never stopped.

"I can make your pain go away," Smack said.

Lexi knew it was wrong, dangerous to listen to that promise, but she couldn't help herself. This pain of hers was unbearable, especially today. "How much?"

Smack smiled slowly, revealing black, ugly teeth. Meth. Mouths like that were a dime a dozen in here. "For the first time? A sweet thing like you? I think—"

"You get the hell away from her, Smack."

Lexi saw Tamica barreling this way like a mama grizzly bear. She put a paw-sized hand on Lexi's chest and pushed her aside hard. Lexi stumbled, almost fell. She regained her balance quickly and surged forward. "This is *my* business, Tamica. You can't tell me what to do."

Tamica went toe-to-toe with Smack. "Back off or I'll take you apart like cheap-ass furniture."

Lexi pushed in between the women. "I *need* it," she said to Tamica, almost pleading. "I can't stand it anymore. I don't want to feel anything."

"Hold out your hand," Smack whispered.

"No," Tamica said. "I won't let you do this, *hermana*."

Lexi made a roaring, wailing sound of pure unadulterated pain and punched Tamica in the nose.

A whistle blew.

Smack slipped two pills into Lexi's hand and then ran so fast it was as if she'd never been there.

"You crazy?" Tamica said, stumbling back. "I don't know why I care about you."

"I don't either. I never asked you to."

"*Hermana*," Tamica said, sighing. "I know how much it hurts."

"Do you? A year ago today I killed my best friend."

Two guards stepped in between them and pushed Lexi away from Tamica. "Back up, Baill."

"I fell," Tamica said.

"Nice try, Hernandez," one of the guards said. "I saw the whole thing. Come on, Baill."

Lexi knew where they were taking her, knew and didn't care. Yesterday she would have said that nothing scared her more than going to The Hole, but now, on the anniversary of Mia's death, in a world where Lexi had had a child and lost her, it barely warranted a sigh.

They led her down one hallway after another, finally coming to a small, windowless room. When the door opened, Lexi got a whiff of urine and filth and she started to panic, to turn away.

"Too late," the guard nearest her said, giving her a shove inside. There was a rough steel-gray blanket on a metal bed. The mattress and pillow were made of old, misshapen rubber. The only opening in the door was the size of a TV remote. Food probably came through that slot three times a day.

Lexi stood in the darkness, shivering suddenly, although it wasn't cold. The stench of the cell was making her eyes water.

"You're here," one of the guards said. "Learn something."

The door clanged shut, and she was in the dark.

Lexi stood there, freezing already. She opened her palm. It was too dark to see the pills, but she felt them. She put them in her mouth and swallowed them without water. It took a while for them to take effect, but finally a calm settled over her. She closed her eyes and forgot all about Mia's off-key singing and Zach's promise of love and Grace's mewling baby sounds. She sat on the cell's rubber mattress staring at nothing, thinking nothing, feeling nothing, just passing through time that felt interminable.

Part Two

Though nothing can bring back the hour
of splendor in the grass, of glory in the flower;
We will grieve not; rather find
strength in what remains behind.

—WILLIAM WORDSWORTH, *ODE:*
INTIMATIONS OF IMMORTALITY
FROM RECOLLECTIONS OF EARLY CHILDHOOD

Eighteen

2010

From a distance, the Farraday family appeared to have healed.
Miles, the renowned surgeon, was back to doing what he did
best, and if he spent too many hours in the OR, it seemed right
that he should save as many lives as he could. Zach had surprised everyone who knew him by blistering through both junior college and the
University of Washington; he'd graduated in three years and started
medical school a year early. Now he was in his second year, and his
grades were stellar. He had moved into a rental house on the island, and
he did two things in his life: school and fatherhood. He seemed not to
care that he had no time for a social life. Islanders spoke of him with
pride, saying how tragedy had shaped him, and how well he'd risen to
the challenge of fatherhood.

And then there was Jude.

For years, she had tried to reclaim the woman she'd been before her
daughter's death. She'd done what was asked of her, what was expected.

She'd gone to support groups and therapists. She'd taken Xanax and Zoloft and Prozac at various times. She'd slept too much and then too little. She'd lost too much weight. Mostly, she'd learned that some pain simply could neither be cured nor ignored nor healed.

Time hadn't healed her wounds. What a crock of shit *that* little cliché was. The kind of thing lucky people said to those who were less fortunate. Those same lucky people thought that talking about grief helped, and they thought nothing of telling you to "try to get on with your life."

Finally, she'd stopped expecting to feel better, and that was when she found a way to live. She couldn't control her grief or her life or much of anything, really (that was what she knew now), but she could control her emotions.

She was careful. Deliberate.

Brittle.

That most of all. She was like an antique porcelain vase that had been broken and painstakingly repaired. Every scar was visible up close, and only the gentlest touch could be used in handling the piece, but from a distance, from across the room, in the right light, it looked whole.

She followed a rigid routine; she'd learned that a schedule could save her. A to-do list could be the framework for a life. Wake up. Shower. Make coffee. Pay bills. Go to the grocery store . . . the post office . . . the dry cleaners. Put gas in the car.

This was how she moved through the hours of every day. She cut and styled her hair even though she didn't care how she looked; she wore makeup; she dressed carefully. Otherwise, people would frown at her, lean closer, and say, "How are you, *really*?"

Better to look healthy and keep moving. On most days, that worked for her. She woke up and made it through the interminable daylight. On weekdays, she fed her granddaughter breakfast and drove her to kindergarten. A few hours later, she picked Grace up from the elementary school and dropped her off at the afternoon day care program that allowed Zach to spend his days in medical school.

Jude had learned that if she focused on the minutiae of life, she could keep her grief at bay.

Most days, anyway. Today, though, no amount of pretending could protect her.

Tomorrow was the sixth anniversary of Mia's death.

Jude stood in her designer kitchen, staring at the six-burner stove. Late-afternoon sunlight slanted through the window, made the tiny bronze flecks in the granite countertop sparkle.

Miles came up beside her and kissed her cheek. He had stayed close to Jude all day. "Zach and Grace will be here for dinner," he reminded her.

She nodded. It occurred to her a moment too late that she could have turned into his arms and kissed him back, but as with so many things, her timing was off. She watched him move away from her, saw the distance between them expanding. It was a skill she'd acquired; she actually saw empty space now.

She knew he was disappointed in her, in their marriage, just as she knew that he still loved her. At least he wanted to, and for Miles desire and reality were the same thing because he made it so. He still believed in them. He woke every day and thought *today*: today would be the day she'd remember how to love him again.

She went to the fridge for ground beef and pork and set about the comforting task of making meatballs. For the the next hour, she lost herself in routine: dicing vegetables, forming meatballs, frying them up. By the time her sauce was made, the house smelled of red-wine-based tomato sauce and savory thyme-rich meatballs. A humid sweetness hung in the air as water boiled on the stove. She turned the sauce down to simmer and made a salad. She was just closing the refrigerator door when she heard a car drive up.

She tucked the hair behind her ear, feeling the coarse new strands of gray that threaded through the blond—tactile reminders of her loss. As she neared the living room, Miles saw her coming and met her halfway, putting an arm around her waist.

Grace walked into the sunlit entry. In her butterfly-print capri pants and smocked pink blouse, with her corn-silk blond hair fighting its way out of a lopsided ponytail, she looked like a little wood sprite. It wasn't until you studied her small, heart-shaped face, with its pointed chin and sharp nose, that you saw that there was nothing truly elfin about the serious child in front of you. Like the rest of them, she rarely smiled and laughed quietly, covering her mouth with her hand as if the sound were unpleasant.

Miles released his hold on Jude and went to his granddaughter, scooping her up in his arms and twirling her around. "And how's my little Poppet today?"

Jude flinched at the endearment. She'd tried to stop her husband from using it, but he said he couldn't do it, that he looked at Grace and saw Mia, and the nickname slipped out.

Jude saw Mia in Grace, too. That was the problem. Every time Jude looked at this child, the wound reopened.

"I'm good, Papa," she said. "I found an arrowhead on the beach at recess."

"No, you didn't," Zach said, kicking the door shut behind him.

"I *could* have," Grace said.

"But you didn't. Jacob Moore found it, and you punched him in the nose when he wouldn't give it to you."

"Jacob Moore?" Miles said, peering down at his granddaughter through the rimless glasses he now wore. "Isn't he the kid who looks like Bigfoot?"

Grace giggled and covered her mouth, nodding. "He's *seven,*" she whispered solemnly. "And in kindergarten."

"Don't encourage her, Dad," Zach said, tossing his keys on the table by the door. "She's already looking at cage fighting as her only career option." He hung up his backpack, pausing for a second at the green sweater still hanging on the hall tree. His long fingers brushed the fabric. They all did that, touched the sweater like a talisman every time they came into the house. Then he turned away and headed toward the great room.

Jude was so removed from her own life that she saw her son from a distance even when he was right in front of her. His blond hair had grown out again; it was too long, messy and unkempt. His jawline was stubbly—his beard grew in some places and not others because of the burn; his shirt was on inside out, and probably had been all day; and when he took off his sneakers, his socks didn't match. Worse than all of that was the exhaustion in his eyes. No doubt he'd spent last night studying and still gotten up bright and early to make Grace breakfast. One day he was just going to drop where he stood.

"You want a beer?" Miles said to his son as he kissed Grace's pink cheek.

"I'm not allowed to drink beer," she said brightly.

"Very funny, young lady. I was asking your daddy."

"Sure," Zach said.

Jude grabbed two beers from the fridge and poured herself a white wine; then she followed her men out to the patio.

She sat down in the lounge chair by the barbeque. Miles was to her left, and Zach sat at the outdoor table, slumped in an armchair, with his stockinged feet planted up on the table. Grace walked past them and sat alone at the edge of the grass, where she started to talk to her own wrist.

"She's still got her invisible friend, I see," Miles said.

"Ordinary kids have invisible friends," Zach said. "Grace has an invisible *alien* friend who is a princess trapped in a jar on her planet. And that's the least of our problems." He took a sip of beer and set the bottle aside. "Her teacher says she has trouble making friends. She lies about everything, and she's . . . started asking about her mother. She wants to know why she doesn't live with us and where she is."

Jude straightened in her chair.

"She needs us more," Miles said.

"Maybe I should quit med school for a while," Zach said, and it was obvious from his voice and his body language that he'd been considering this for some time. "Third year is supposed to be wicked hard, and, honestly, I'm jammed as it is. Every second of my life I'm either studying or rushing to be with Grace. When I'm with her, I'm so tired I'm useless. You know what she said to me last night? 'Daddy, I can take care of myself if you're too tired to make dinner.'" He ran a hand through his hair. "She's five years old, for God's sake. And she's worried about me."

"And you're twenty-four," Miles said. "You're doing a hell of a job, Zach. We're proud of you, aren't we, Jude? You can't quit med school now. You're almost there."

"Tomorrow I have study group at night. If I don't go, I'll blow the final. I know it."

"I'll pick her up and feed her dinner," Jude said. It was expected of her; she knew it. "You study as long as you need to."

Zach glanced over at her.

He didn't trust her with Grace; of course he didn't. He still remembered the early days when Jude had tried to be a grandparent and failed. Her grief had been knife sharp then: it stabbed at the strangest times and left her for dead. Because of it, she used to oversleep and forget to pick Grace up. Once—the worst of times—Miles had come home at night to find Grace lying forgotten in Mia's bedroom, in a dirty diaper, while Jude lay curled in the fetal position on her own bed, sobbing, holding Mia's photo.

They all knew that Jude couldn't look at Grace without feeling an overwhelming grief. Everything Grace did reminded Jude of her loss, and so she kept her distance from her granddaughter. It shamed Jude and embarrassed her, this weakness, but there was no way she could fix it. She'd tried. But in the past two years, she'd gotten better. She picked Grace up regularly from both kindergarten and the day care she went to after school. It was only on the worst of days, when Jude fell into that gray world, that she crawled into bed and forgot everything she had to do and everyone around her. Especially her granddaughter.

"I'm better now," she said to Zach. "You can trust me."

"Tomorrow is—"

"I know what tomorrow is," Jude cut him off before he could say what they all already knew: tomorrow would be a bad day for all of them. "But you can trust me this time."

※

It should have been raining. The landscape beyond her window should have been ominous and black, like ink spreading, with swollen charcoal skies and cobwebbed black leaves skidding across dirty sidewalks and crows gathered on telephone lines. A scene out of *The Stand*. Instead, the sixth anniversary of her daughter's death dawned bright and sunny, with the kind of cornflower-blue sky that turned Seattle into the prettiest city in the world. The Sound sparkled; Mount Rainier came out to play, its vivid white peak resplendent over the city's shoulder.

Still, Jude felt cold. Freezing. All around her, tourists walked through the Pike Place Market, dressed in shorts and T-shirts, carrying cameras and eating food off sticks or out of greasy white bags. Long-haired musicians staked out the primo street corner locations, hammering away at their accordions or guitars or bongo drums. One even had a piano.

Jude wrapped the heavy cashmere scarf around her neck and resettled the purse on her shoulder. At the end of the market, a triangular patch of grass provided a resting spot for the homeless. A giant totem pole looked down on them.

She crossed the busy street and walked up a steep hill to a swizzle stick of a building that poked high into the clear blue sky.

"Ms. Farraday," the doorman said, tipping his ridiculous hat at her.

Unable today to smile, she nodded and walked past him. Waiting for the elevator, she tapped her foot on the tile floor and bit her lip. She took off her scarf and put it back on. By the time she reached Dr. Bloom's austere glass-walled office, she was so cold she expected to see her own breath.

"You can go in, Ms. Farraday," the receptionist said at her entrance.

Jude couldn't respond. She passed through the waiting area and went into Dr. Bloom's elegantly decorated office. "Turn on the heat," she said without preamble, collapsing onto the plush chair beside her.

"There's a throw beside you," her doctor said.

Jude reached down for the camel-colored mohair blanket and covered herself with it, shivering. "What?" she said, realizing the doctor was staring at her.

Dr. Harriet Bloom took a seat opposite Jude. She was as austere as her office—steel-gray hair, an angular face, and dark eyes that noticed everything. Today she was wearing a houndstooth sheath with black hose and fashionable black pumps.

When Jude had first folded under Miles's relentless pressure to "get help" and "see someone," she'd visited a string of psychiatrists and therapists and counselors. At first her sole criterion had been their ability to dispense prescription drugs. In time, she'd weeded out the touchy-feely purveyors of hope and the idiots who told her boldly that someday she would smile again. The minute someone told her that time healed all wounds, she got up and left.

By 2005, only Harriet Bloom remained—Harriet, who rarely smiled and whose demeanor hinted at a personal understanding of tragedy. And she could prescribe drugs.

"What?" Jude said again, shivering.

"We both know what day it is."

Jude wanted to make a smart comeback, but she couldn't. All she could do was nod.

"Did you sleep last night?"

She shook her head. "Miles held me, but I pushed him away."

"You didn't want comfort."

"What good is it?"

"Are you going to do anything to mark the anniversary?"

The question made Jude angry, and anger was good, better than this free-falling despair. "Like send balloons up to her? Or sit by that granite stone in the grass where her body is? Or maybe I should invite guests over and celebrate her life . . . which is over."

"Sometimes people find comfort in such things."

"Yeah. Well. I don't."

"As I've said before, you don't want comfort." Harriet wrote something on her notepad. "Why do you keep coming to me? You control your feelings so tightly we can hardly make progress."

"I come to you for drugs. You know that."

"How are you doing, really?"

"Tonight will be . . . bad. I'll start remembering her, and I won't be able to stop. I'll think that Miles was wrong. That she could have gotten better, or that if I'd kissed her she could have woken up like a Disney princess. I'll imagine that I should have tried mouth-to-mouth or pounded on her heart. Crazy things." Jude looked up. Tears blurred Dr. Bloom's sharp face, softened it. "I'll take some sleeping pills, and then it will be tomorrow, and I'll be okay until Thanksgiving, and then Christmas, and then . . . her birthday."

"Zach's birthday."

She flinched at that. "Yeah. Not that he celebrates it anymore, either."

"When was the last time your family celebrated anything?"

"You know the answer to that. We're pod people like in that body-snatcher movie. We only pretend to be real. But why are we rehashing all of this? I just want you to tell me how to get through today."

"You never ask me about tomorrow. Why is that?"

"What do you mean?"

"Most patients want to learn how to *live*. They want me to make a map that they can follow to get them to a healthy future. You simply just want to survive each day."

"He-*llo*. I'm not bipolar or schizophrenic or borderline. I'm sad. My daughter died, and I'm devastated. There's no getting better."

"Is that what you want to believe?"

"It's the way it is." Jude crossed her arms. "Look, you've helped me, if that's what this is about. Maybe you think I should be doing better by now, maybe you think six years is a long time. But it's not, not when your child died. And I am doing better. I grocery shop. I cook dinner. I go out with girlfriends. I make love to my husband. I vote."

"You didn't mention either your son or your granddaughter."

"It wasn't meant to be an exhaustive list," Jude said.

"Are you still stalking Grace?"

Jude pulled her scarf off. She was hot now, sweating, in fact, and the scarf was choking her. "I don't stalk her."

"You stand in the trees and watch her at that after-school program, but you won't hold her or play with her. What would you call it?"

Jude started to unbutton her coat. "Man, it's hot."

"When was the last time you held Grace? Or kissed her?"

"Really. It's an oven in here . . ."

"It's not hot."

"Damn menopause."

"Jude," Harriet said with an irritating patience. "You refuse to love your granddaughter."

"No," Jude said, finally looking up. "I *can't* love her. There's a difference. I've tried. Do you really think I haven't tried? But when I look at her, I feel . . . nothing."

"That's not true, Jude."

"Look," Jude sighed. "I get what you're doing. We've done this dance for years. I tell you I can't feel, and you toss back that I don't want to. My brain is the boss. I get it. I do. The old me would have been certain you were right."

"And the new you?"

"The new me is living. That's enough. I don't burst into tears when I see pink anymore; I can start my car without crying; I can look at my son and not be angry at him. Sometimes I can look into his eyes without even thinking about Mia. I can pick my granddaughter up from school and give her a bath and read her a bedtime story, all without crying. You know how much progress this is. So can we just, for now, forget the next step and let me get through this day?"

"We could talk about Mia."

"No," Jude said sharply. She'd learned a long time ago that talking about Mia only sharpened the pain.

"You need to talk about her. You need to remember her and grieve."

"I do nothing but grieve."

"No. Your grief is an artery that's been clamped off. If you don't take that clamp off and let it flow, you'll never heal."

"So I won't heal," Jude said tiredly, leaning back into the sofa. "Big surprise. How about if we talk about Miles? We made love last week. That's a good sign, don't you think?"

Harriet sighed and made a notation on her pad. "Yes, Jude. That's a good sign."

❧

Every day after kindergarten was over, Grace went to the Silly Bear Day Care until Daddy got home from big-boy school.

On good days, like today, they all got to play outside, but Mrs. Skitter made them walk from the day care to the beach holding a scratchy yellow rope. Like they were babies.

As usual, Grace was at the very front of the line, right behind the teacher. She could hear the other kids laughing and talking and horsing around. She didn't join in; she just followed along behind, staring at the big pillows of her teacher's butt.

When they reached the beach park, Mrs. Skitter gathered the ten of them in a circle in front of her. "You know the rules. No going in the water. No fighting. Today we're going to play hopscotch in the sand. Who wants to help me make the squares?"

Hands went up, kids started yelling, "Me, me, me!" and bouncing up and down. It reminded Grace of the baby birds she'd seen at the newborns exhibit her dad had taken her to. *Chirp, chirp.*

She walked over to her usual spot. Everyone knew she liked it here. She sat on a log in the sand, way out of the waves' reach. Sometimes, if she was lucky, she saw a crab or a sand dollar. Mostly, she just talked to her best friend.

She stared down at the pink band she wore on her wrist. On its center, where there used to be a Minnie Mouse watch, her daddy had placed a small round mirror, about the size of her palm. It was the best present she'd ever gotten. It had allowed her to leave her bedroom. Before the wrist mirror, she'd spent hours standing in front of her bedroom mirror, talking to her friend, Ariel, who was a princess on another planet.

Grace wasn't stupid. She knew that some of the other kids made fun of her for having an invisible friend, but she didn't care. The kids in her class were stupid anyway.

None of them knew how quiet this planet could be, so they hadn't learned to listen like she had. She was used to quiet. Her grandparents' house was like a library sometimes.

There was something wrong with Grace. She'd known that her whole life, even if she didn't know what it was. People didn't like her, not even her grandma. Grace tried to be likable and nice and quiet, she really did, but none of it ever worked, and things just went wrong for her, no matter how hard she tried. She broke things and tripped over stuff and couldn't seem to learn her letters.

Hey, Gracerina, Ariel said.

Grace looked down at the circle of glass. She couldn't really *see* Ariel. It wasn't like that. She just knew her friend was there now, and she could hear the voice in her head.

Grown-ups always asked Grace how she knew when Ariel was around or what her best friend looked like. Grace told them Ariel looked exactly like Cinderella.

It was sort of true.

She couldn't actually *see* Ariel, but she knew when her best friend was in the mirror and when she was gone. And she *did* look like Cinderella. Grace would swear it.

She still remembered the first time Ariel had shown up.

Grace had been a baby, still in diapers. She'd been home with Nana, who used to babysit sometimes when Daddy was busy with school. All Grace remembered about those days was the sound of Nana crying. Everything made Nana sad: the music on the radio, the color pink, the dumb old green sweater hanging in the entry, the closed door upstairs. And Grace.

Just looking at Grace made Nana cry.

One day, Grace had done something wrong. She didn't know what it was. All she knew was that one minute she was standing there with a stuffed pink puppy that she'd found in her grandparents' room, and the next minute Nana was yanking the puppy out of her hands so hard Grace stumbled sideways and plopped onto her butt.

Nana burst into tears and so did Grace. She waited for her daddy, but no one came to get her, and finally she just sat there alone, sucking her thumb.

Then she'd heard someone say her name.

Gracie, come here . . . follow me . . .

She'd wiped her slimy nose and stood up. Holding her yellow blanket, she followed the voice up the stairs to the door that was always shut. No one ever played in this room.

Inside, it was like something out of a fairy tale, all pink and yellow and perfect.

Over by the dresser was a big mirror that was shaped sort of like a football, with a red and gold flag stuck into the hinge. A bunch of glittery gold stuff framed the oval mirror—bracelets and metal flowers and sparkly rainbows.

Gracerina?

She remembered peering into the mirror, seeing a flash of yellow and smear of pink.

You okay?

Grace frowned, looked harder, seeing . . . something. A girl, maybe, a little older than her. *Are you okay?* the girl asked.

"I'm bad," Grace said, feeling tears start again. "Grace bad."

You're not bad.

"Who are you?"

I'm Ariel. I'll be your friend as long as you need me. Here, Gracerina. Lie down on the carpet, go to sleep. I could tell you a story.

Grace had been so tired. She'd curled up on the soft carpet and pulled her blanket around her. Sucking her thumb, she'd fallen asleep to the pretty sound of her new friend's voice. Since then, Ariel had been her bestest—her only—friend.

Why don't you go play with the other kids?

Grace looked down at her wrist. "They're stupid." She poked a stick into the sand at her feet.

Boy alert.

Grace sat up straighter and looked around. Sure enough, Austin Klimes was coming this way. His face was big and fat, like someone had konked him in the head with a pan. "Uh, you wanna come play hopscotch with us?" he said, breathing heavily. His cheeks were flushed, too.

The teacher had made him come over here. Grace could see the other kids huddled together across the beach, watching her and giggling. They thought it was funny that no one liked her.

"Ariel isn't allowed to hopscotch."

Austin frowned. "Everyone's allowed to play hopscotch."

"Not a princess."

"Your fake friend isn't a princess."

"Shows what *you* know."

"You're a big fat liar."

"Am not."

"Are too." He crossed his big arms across his chest.

Calm down, Gracerina. He's just a bully.

"Your *only* friend is invisible," Austin laughed.

Grace was on her feet before she could stop herself. "You take that back, lardo."

"Who's gonna make me, you? Or your invisible friend?"

Grace punched him right in his piggy nose. He screamed like a baby and ran for the teacher.

Oh, boy.

Grace watched the kids huddle around Austin. They turned to point at her and then huddled again. Mrs. Skitter led Austin over to the ice chest, where she kept all her teacher stuff. In no time at all, Austin must have been fine, because he ran off to play hopscotch.

Here she comes.

Grace didn't need Ariel to tell her she was in trouble. She leaned forward and rested her arms on her thighs.

"Grace?"

She cocked her head up. Fine blond hair fell across her face. "Yeah?"

"May I sit down?"

Grace shrugged. "I guess."

"You know you shouldn't have punched Austin in the nose."

"I know. And you're gonna have to tell his parents."

"And your dad."

Grace sighed. "Yeah."

"I shouldn't have sent him over."

"They don't wanna play with me. And I don't care."

"Everyone wants friends."

"I have Ariel."

"She's been a good friend to you."

"*She* never makes fun of me."

Mrs. Skitter nodded. "I've lived on this island a long time, Grace, and I've seen a lot of kids come and go. I used to know your daddy, did I ever tell you that? I worked in the lunch room when he was in high school. Anyway, the point is, everyone makes friends sooner or later."

Grace shook her head. "Not me. No one likes me. And I don't care."

"Things change, Gracie. You'll see." Mrs. Skitter sighed, put her hands on her thighs. "Well, I was going to collect some beach stones. The pretty kind. You want to help?"

"I might not find any."

"Or you might."

Mrs. Skitter stood up, put her hand out.

Grace stared at her teacher's white hand. A simple gold band on one finger meant she was married.

"My daddy's not married," she said impulsively.

"I know."

"That's cuz my mom is a super spy."

Mrs. Skitter frowned seriously. "Really? How exciting. You must miss her."

"I do. But I'm not s'posed to."

For the next two hours, she followed Mrs. Skitter around, bent over, peering down at the rocks at her feet. One by one, the other kids went home, until finally it was only Grace and her teacher on the beach. Mrs.

Skitter kept looking at her watch and making a tsking sound. Grace knew what that meant.

It was getting dark when Papa showed up.

"Hey, Gracie," her grandfather said, smiling down at her.

"Grandma forgot me again," Grace said, letting the fistful of rocks tumble from her hand.

"She's not feeling well. But I'm here, and I thought I'd take my best girl for ice cream." He bent down and scooped Grace into his arms. She clung to him, wrapping her legs around him like a little monkey.

He carried her over to Mrs. Skitter, and they said good-bye. Then he put her into the car seat in the back of Grandma's big black car.

"You have something to tell me," he said, starting the engine.

"I do?" She looked up, saw her grandpa looking at her in the rear-view mirror.

"The fight with Austin Klimes."

"Oh," Grace said, sighing. "That."

"You know you're not supposed to hit other kids, Gracie."

"He started it."

"He did? How?"

"He kicked sand in my face. And he said I was stupid."

"Really?"

"And he said a bad word."

"Still, Grace, you shouldn't be hitting kids."

"I thought you only said I couldn't hit girls."

"You don't think that."

"Okay," she said, slumping in her seat. "I won't hit Austin Klimes anymore, even if he's a butt."

"You said that about Jacob Moore, too."

"But I didn't hit Jake."

She could tell that Papa was trying not to smile. "We are not going through the kids in day care one by one. You can't hit *any* of them. And before you look for a loophole, no hitting kids in kindergarten, either. Okay?"

"What's a loophole? Is that like a hula hoop?"

"Gracie?"

"Okay. Are you gonna tell my daddy?"

"I have to."

For the first time, Grace felt truly bad about what she'd done. Now her daddy would give her that disappointed look, and she'd get scared and snuggle up to him and hope he wouldn't leave her. She didn't have a mommy. What would she do without a daddy?

Nineteen

S cared? What do you mean, you're scared?"

Lexi leaned against the gray wall of her cell. After seventy-one and a half months in prison, she was finally getting out. She'd served her whole sentence—and then some, thanks to bad choices—so there would be no parole for her, no probation. She had a community service advocate who was prepared to help her "transition," but the truth was that in a few minutes, she'd be just another citizen, free to go where she pleased. All she knew was that she was going to Florida to be with Eva; after that, her life stretched out like a desert highway with no end or turns in sight.

Strangely, now that the day was upon her, she was afraid to leave. This ten-foot square cell had become her world, and there was a safety in the familiarity of it. There were eight steps from the bed to the toilet; two from the sink to the wall; three from the bed to the door. The walls were covered with Tamica's family photos—pictures of people that had become like family to Lexi. Her own pictures, of Aunt Eva and Zach and Mia, had been taken down years ago. Looking back was too painful, and a waste of time on top of it. She could never forget Mia's smile, with or without a reminder.

"Lexi?" Tamica put down the tabloid magazine she was reading. "What do you mean, you're scared?"

"I know who I am in here."

"You don't want to focus on whoever you became in here, *hermana*. Especially not you. You got so much life ahead of you."

Lexi looked down at her few belongings. On the end of the bed were her prized possessions, all that she'd hoarded and collected in the past years: a shoe box full of letters—from Aunt Eva and to Grace; Mia and Zach's senior pictures and a photograph of the three of them at a school dance; and a worn, often-read paperback copy of *Wuthering Heights*. No more *Jane Eyre* for her; why read about someone else's happy ending?

A guard appeared at the door. "Time to go, Baill."

Tamica moved slowly off the bed. In the past few years, as Lexi had whittled her own body down to a runner's leanness, Tamica had packed on the pounds. She claimed menopause was the culprit, but prison food didn't help.

Lexi stared at the sad, dark face of the woman who had saved her in here, had been a friend when she desperately needed one; if Lexi still knew how to cry, she would have. "I'll miss you," Lexi said, wrapping her arms around Tamica's broad, rounded back.

"I'll write to you," Lexi promised.

"Send me a picture of you and Grace."

"Tamica . . . I gave up that right," she said. "You *know* that."

Tamica grabbed her by the shoulders, shook her. "You know what I would give to be walking outta here with you? Don't you dare be JELL-O. You made a mistake and you paid for it. Period." She pulled Lexi into another hard embrace. "See your daughter, at least."

"Come on, Baill," the guard said.

Lexi let go of Tamica and walked over to the bed, where she gathered up her few belongings. She intended just to walk out, be as cool as possible, but she couldn't. At the door, she paused and turned back.

Tamica was crying. "Don't you come back," she said, "or I'll whoop your white ass."

"I won't," Lexi promised.

As she carried her pathetic shoe box through the prison, women catcalled and yelled to her. She remembered how they had scared her at first, these women. She was one of them now, and she knew that no matter how long she lived or how much she changed, a part of her would be here, behind bars. Maybe a part of her always had been. A girl without a mother was a prisoner of a different kind.

At the desk, another uniformed guard handed her some paperwork and a bag with her own clothes in it, as well as a small manila envelope.

"You can change in there," the guard said, pointing to a door down the hall.

Lexi went inside the room and shut the door. Alone, she stripped out of her faded, worn prison khakis and secondhand underwear.

Inside the bag, she found the wrinkled black pants and white blouse she'd worn to the courthouse so long ago, along with her own beige bra and black panties and a flattened patchwork denim purse. Black kneesocks and cheap black flats completed the old Lexi look. Or the young Lexi.

She dressed carefully, enjoying the feel of the soft cotton against her dry skin. The pants were too big for her now; they hung off her protruding hip bones. So was the bra. In her zeal to keep busy and get strong, she'd spent long hours in the gym, and her body had turned almost freakishly sinewy. Her boobs had all but checked out.

She buttoned up the black pants and tucked her shirt into the baggy waistband before turning to the mirror. For years, she'd imagined joy on this day, pictured it. But now, when she stared at her reflection, all she saw was a tired, stringy version of who she'd been.

She looked like an adult. More than that even, she looked at least ten years older than she was, with her pale skin, her prominent cheekbones and colorless lips. Her black hair had been cut off a few years ago by the prison barber, who had taken all of seven minutes to chop off twelve inches of hair. The pixie cut had grown out into soft curls that framed her angular face.

She opened the yellow envelope and found an expired driver's license with a young girl's face on it, a half-empty package of gum, a cheap drugstore watch, and her promise ring from Zach.

A knock on the door roused her.

"Baill. You okay?"

She put everything, including the ring, in her purse, threw the bag and envelope in the wastebasket, and left the room.

At the prison office, she signed one document after another and took the two hundred dollars that was her exit money from the state. How a person was supposed to start a new life with two hundred bucks and no valid ID was beyond her.

She followed instructions and did as she was told, until she heard a door clang shut behind her and she was standing in the open air, beneath a bright late-afternoon sky.

Free air.

She tilted her face to the sky, felt the day's warmth on her cheeks. She knew the van was waiting for her—it would take her to the nearest bus station—but she couldn't seem to make herself move. It felt amazingly good to just stand here, with no bars or razor wire defining her space and no women getting in her face. No—

"Lexi?"

Scot Jacobs walked up to her, smiling. He was older—his hair was short now, conservative looking, and he wore glasses—but other than that, he looked the same. He might even be wearing the same suit. "I wanted someone to be waiting for you."

She didn't know how to process the gratitude she felt. After so many years of bottling emotions, it wasn't easy to open them. "Thank you."

He stared at her for a moment, and she stared back, then he said, "Well, let's go," and started walking toward his car.

She automatically fell into step behind him.

He stopped, waited for her to catch up.

"Sorry," she mumbled. She wasn't a prisoner anymore. "Old habits, I guess."

This time she walked next to him to the blue minivan parked in the lot.

"Don't mind the junk in the car," he said, opening the passenger door. "It's my wife's car, and she says she never knows what she's going to need, so she never takes anything out."

Lexi climbed up into the passenger seat and stared at the imposing gray of the prison.

She snapped her seatbelt into place. "It's really nice of you to pick me up, Mr. Jacobs."

"Call me Scot. Please," he said, pulling out onto the road and away from the prison.

She opened the window and stuck her head out, breathing in the sweet, clean air. The landscape was exactly as she remembered: towering trees, summer blue sky, distant mountains. Out here, life had gone on without her.

"I was sure bummed to hear they added time on to your sentence for bad behavior. I expected to pick you up a while ago."

"Yeah. Well. 2005 was a bad year. After I lost Gracie . . ." She couldn't even finish the sentence. All of that was behind her now, anyway.

"You're better now?"

"As good as an ex-con can be. I don't do drugs or drink, if that's what you're asking."

"I hear you got your degree. Your aunt was so proud."

"Sociology," Lexi said, turning her head to stare out the window.

"Still dreaming of law school?"

"Nope."

"You're still young, Lexi," he said.

"So I hear." She leaned more deeply into the comfortable seat, watching the miles fly past. Soon, they were in Port George, driving through the Native-owned land, past the fireworks stands that lined the road in early summer. And then they were on the bridge, crossing over Shallow Pass.

Welcome to Pine Island, pop. 7,120.

She felt her chest tighten. There was the entrance to LaRiviere Park . . . the high school . . . Night Road. By the time Scot pulled up in front of his office, Lexi's jaw ached.

"Are you okay?" Scot asked, opening her door.

Get out, Lexi. Smile. If there's one thing you know how to do now, it's fake a smile.

She managed it. "Thanks, Scot."

He handed her one hundred dollars. "This is from your aunt. And here's a bus ticket to Pompano Beach. The bus leaves tomorrow afternoon at 3:30."

"Tomorrow?"

How was she supposed to keep her distance when she was *here,* at the scene of her crime and the only place that had ever felt like home?

"Jenny invited you to spend the night and have dinner with us if you'd like," Scot said.

"No." She said it too quickly and realized her mistake. "Sorry. I don't mean to be rude, it's just that I haven't been around people for a long time. Two thousand one hundred forty-four and a half days." She smiled tiredly and looked around, anxious to be on her own.

"Aren't you going to ask me?" Scot said.

Lexi wanted to shake her head, maybe even say *hell, no,* but she just stood there.

"She lives with her dad in the old Tamarind cabin on Cove Road. I see her every now and then in town with her dad."

Lexi didn't react. In prison, she'd learned to hide everything, especially pain. "Does she look happy?"

"She looks healthy."

Lexi nodded. "That's good. Well, Scot—"

"We could fight for her, Lexi. Partial custody or at least visitation rights."

Lexi remembered "visitations" with her mom: the two of them in a room while a social worker looked on. What Lexi remembered about those rare days was how scared she was of the woman who'd borne her.

"I'm a twenty-four-year-old ex-con whose last real job was part-time at an ice cream shop. I have no place to live, and I doubt like hell I'll be hired at any decent job. But I should swoop in and see my daughter, wedge myself into the Farraday family again, and bring up all that pain . . . so that I can feel happier. Is that it?"

"Lexi—"

"I won't be like my mother. I won't make any decision that isn't in my daughter's best interest. That's why I'm going to Florida tomorrow. Grace deserves better than me, and if I'm around she'll love me anyway. That's what kids do: they love loser parents, and it breaks their hearts."

"You're not a loser. And what's wrong with her loving you?"

"Don't."

Scot pursed his lips. Reaching into his pocket, he pulled out a set of keys and extracted one. "This is the key to my office. There's a sofa bed in the conference room and a bike by the front door. The combination is 1321. We closed up early today, so the place is all yours."

She took the key and pocketed it. "Thank you, Scot."

"No problem. I believe in you, Lexi."

She should have walked away then, said nothing more. That was what she meant to do; instead, she found herself looking up at him, saying, "Did Zach get married?"

"No. He's still in school, I think. No wife. He lived with his parents for a few years and then moved into that cabin on the cove."

"Oh."

"He never wrote?"

"A few times. I sent all the letters back unopened."

"Oh, Lexi," Scot said, sighing. "Why?"

She crossed her arms, trying not to remember the feel of those letters in her fingers, the sight of them on the rough gray wool of her blanket. But she'd been so angry then, so wounded. She'd acted out in all kinds of terrible ways. By the time she was past all of that, stronger, it was too late. He never wrote again, and she hadn't had the courage to write to him.

"I should have taken your advice," Lexi finally said, unable to look at Scot as she said it.

"Yes."

"Well. Thanks again. I think I'll go for a bike ride. It's a beautiful day."

Scot went over to the front door of his office, got the bike, and guided it back to her.

She wanted to tell him how much it had meant to her, his being there today. For years she'd prepared to be all alone when she got out of prison, and she saw now how painful that would have been.

"You're welcome," he said quietly.

She nodded one last time and took the bike from him and rode away.

Soon she was smiling in spite of herself. It felt so good to be *free,* to turn when she felt like it and go where she wanted. She would never take this for granted.

She spun by the theater—saw that they'd added on to it—and the bank and the beauty salon where Aunt Eva had gotten her hair cut. There, she saw a pay phone. After a quick signal, she turned into the parking lot and called Eva, collect.

There was no answer.

Disappointed, she climbed back onto the bike and started pedaling.

The ice cream shop was still there; beside it was a new coffee shop and a computer repair place.

When she came to the high school, she slowed down. A big new gymnasium dominated the campus. It looked nothing like she remembered, except that the flagpole was still there and that was enough.

Meet me at the flagpole, by the admin building . . .

She pedaled harder, down the bumpy asphalt road and up Raspberry Hill. Out here, there were occasional dirt roads and the odd mailbox, but mostly it was uninhabited. Sunset was nearing, and the sky was a deep midnight color, and before she knew it she was on Night Road. She hadn't even meant to turn here.

But here she was, at the hairpin turn. The skid marks were long gone, but the broken tree remained, its pinkish flesh almost black now. Dying.

She came to a stop and half stumbled off the bike, hearing it clatter to the pavement behind her. On either side of her, trees blocked out the sun.

The memorial to Mia was tattered now, only visible if you knew what to look for. The small white cross had been grayed by the changing seasons and stood drunkenly to the left. Here and there empty vases lay in the bushes. An old, airless balloon hung limply on a high branch.

She released her breath in a long, shaky sigh.

In prison, she'd spent years in group therapy, talking about the pain, the remorse. Her counselor had told her often that time and hard work would heal her. That she would be whole when she could forgive herself.

As if.

Even if she could forgive herself, which was inconceivable, it wouldn't bring Mia back. That was what all those positive thinkers didn't get: some things could never be made right. If Lexi became Mother Teresa, Mia would still be dead and it would still be Lexi's fault. It had been six years, and still Lexi prayed to Mia every night. Every morning she woke to a split second of joy and then the pulverizing reality. It was that sense of loss that had caused her to turn to Valium for a few years, but ultimately she'd discovered that you could run from your pain, but you couldn't hide. It was something she should have known already, a lesson she should have learned from her mother. When she realized the ugly truth—that she was becoming her mother—she quit taking the Valium. She was so clean now she hardly even took aspirin. The only real answer lay in the courage to see a thing clearly and try to do better. Be better.

She knelt there a long time, on the cold, hard roadside, knowing it was dangerous to be stopped on this curve and not caring. If anyone saw her here . . .

Finally, she got back on the bike and started to ride. She almost sped right past the Farraday house, but at the last minute she stopped. Even in the falling darkness, she could see how different the place looked. The garden was untended, the planter boxes were empty.

She saw the mailbox: their name was still on it.

When a pair of headlights shone at her, she jumped on the bike and rode away. From a safe distance, she watched a silver Porsche turn into the driveway behind her.

Miles.

Sighing, she rode back into town and bought dinner at a fast-food place. At Scot's office, she locked up the bike and went inside through the back door. In the conference room, she found a red floral sofa bed with a neat pile of white sheets set on the cushion. Beside the sheets lay a manila envelope.

She picked up the envelope. Below it, stuck to the cushion, was a pink Post-it note.

Lexi—She's in kindergarten. Morning class.
F.Y.I.
S

She opened the manila folder and found a single photograph. There, smiling up at her, was an elfin blond-haired girl in a pink blouse.

Her daughter.

Man plans. God laughs.

Lexi understood that sentence for the first time.

She had planned her release from prison down to the smallest detail. She'd talked about her plans in Group and told Tamica everything. She had intended to go to Florida and move in with Eva and Barbara and start looking for a job. She'd even dreamed of graduate school. She would make a good social worker; maybe she could help girls in trouble. It hadn't occurred to her that once she left the razor wire behind, she would be back in a world where unexpected things happened.

Who would have thought she'd end up here, on Pine Island? The only place in the world she didn't want to be.

She made up the sofa bed and then crawled between the softest sheets she'd ever felt. Pale light from an outside street lamp fell through the window, lighting the dark room. She closed her eyes and tried to will herself to sleep, but it was so quiet, and she could have sworn that the picture of Grace was breathing.

For years, she'd ruthlessly suppressed all thoughts of her daughter. She walked away when Tamica mentioned Grace and turned away when the TV screen showed images of little girls running into their mothers' arms. She'd told herself that Grace deserved the kind of life Lexi could never offer.

But now, in the dark, with the photograph beside her, she felt that resolve weaken.

She slept fitfully, dreaming dreams that were best forgotten. Finally, at six o'clock, she threw the covers back. Padding barefooted to the bathroom, she was surprised to find a shower. She took her first private shower in years and dried off with a soft white towel.

Her reflection afterward showed a face that was pointed and thin, like a drowned rat, framed by wispy black curls. Towel drying her hair, she dressed in the courtroom clothes that were all she had and went in search of breakfast, which she found at a local diner.

Still, the photograph in her purse kept breathing. Sometimes she heard a giggle, and, irrationally, she thought it came from the bag.

After breakfast, she walked up Main Street and found a local thrift shop that was just opening for the day. She used seven dollars to buy a pair of secondhand Bermuda shorts, a blue T-shirt that had a dragonfly stenciled on the front, and an aqua cotton hoodie. She traded her black flats for a pair of flip-flops and threw the kneesocks away.

Walking out of the store, she smiled, feeling really free for the first time. She had a bus ticket to Florida in her pocket. In no time at all— just seven and a half hours—she'd be on her way out of here . . .

A yellow smear moved in a gust of black exhaust. A school bus. Small faces peered out from the windows.

Lexi didn't make a conscious decision to follow the bus; rather, she just kept walking. On Turnagin Way, she angled left and walked up the hill. By the time she reached the four-way stop, there were kids all around, laughing and talking and dragging ridiculously big backpacks on the sidewalk beside them. There were mothers everywhere, too, monitoring crosswalks and conversations and movement.

A line of buses was parked in front of the elementary school. The carpool lane ran through a row of parked cars, parents dropping their kids off.

A black SUV pulled past her and stopped.

Lexi's breath caught. From her place by the tree, she saw Jude get out of the SUV and go to the back passenger door, opening it wide.

And there, sitting in a big car seat, was a miniature version of Mia, with buoyant corn-silk blond hair and a heart-shaped face.

Lexi inched sideways for a better view, making sure she was partially hidden within the crowd of schoolchildren.

Jude helped Grace out of the car and stepped back.

Grace didn't smile, and Jude didn't give her a kiss, and then Grace walked away alone.

Lexi frowned. She couldn't help remembering how it had been before, when Jude had driven Mia and Lexi to school. The kisses, the hugs, the game-show contestant waves good-bye.

Maybe Jude was having a bad day. Or Grace had just said a bad word or gotten in trouble. Or maybe Grace had asked not to be kissed in public and Jude snuggled with her before they got in the car.

Lexi hardly noticed when the SUV started to move again. By the time she reached the crosswalk, it was in the line of cars exiting the school grounds, but Lexi wasn't looking there. All of her attention was focused on the little girl in the yellow T-shirt wearing a ridiculously big Hannah Montana backpack. Her shoulders were slumped, and she moved reluctantly toward the school, dragging her feet.

No one talked to Grace as she walked into the school.

Moments later, the bell rang, and the few remaining students ran for the school doors.

Lexi stood on the patch of grass between the bus lane and the carpool lane, staring at the now-quiet brick grade school. *She's in kindergarten. Morning class.*

She had walked alone into too many schools herself, with no one waving good-bye, no one coming to pick her up. She remembered how alone she'd felt at lunchtime.

Alone.

That was what Lexi remembered most about her early childhood. She had always felt alone, a stranger in someone else's family, an outsider in some new school. Even after Eva, Lexi had never quite felt *enfolded* in a family . . . until she'd met the Farradays. From that first day of ninth grade, when she'd met Mia and come home with her, Lexi had felt welcomed into their midst.

That was why she'd given them custody of Grace, so her daughter would know how it felt to be loved.

Lexi looked down at her watch. It was not quite nine o'clock. How long did morning kindergarten last? Two hours? Three?

The bus for Florida didn't leave until 3:30. That gave her several hours with nothing to do.

She could ride her bike around town or get something to eat or go to the library and read. But even as she ran through the list of things she could do, she knew there was only one thing she wanted to do.

Don't do it. You made your choice. Think of Grace.

The arguments rifled through her thoughts, but she paid them no mind. She couldn't, not this time. For every day of her daughter's life, Lexi had pictured Grace happy and well adjusted. Loved and adored. *That* Grace she could make herself walk away from.

But this little girl, with her draggy feet and slumped shoulders . . . this little girl didn't look happy.

"She is though," Lexi said aloud. "Anyone can have a bad day."

Still, she walked around the school, up past the portables, to the big playground out back. Here, confined within a chain-link fence was the elementary school play yard: basketball hoops and paved pads and grassy areas and a baseball diamond. She found a giant evergreen shadowing a patch of grass. There, she sat down and waited.

As the minutes passed, she told herself she'd misinterpreted what she'd seen, imposed her own sad school history on Grace. Her daughter was a happy girl—she had to be—the Farradays were the Bradys for a new generation. No one lived in the Brady house and felt lonely or unloved. She'd prove it to herself and then be on her way.

Around ten-thirty, a bell rang. The big double doors banged open and a herd of small kids ran out onto the playground.

Kindergarten recess. It was obvious. There were only about thirty kids, and they were so *small*. A pretty brunette woman in jeans and a red blouse supervised their play.

Lexi got to her feet, moving along the fence line.

Grace was the last one to come out of the school. She stood off to the side, alone. She seemed to be talking to herself. To the back of her hand, actually. The other kids laughed and played and ran around. Grace just stood there, talking to her watch.

Smile, Lexi thought. *Please.*

But Grace never smiled, not once, during that ten-minute recess. None of the kids talked to her, and she didn't join into any of the games.

No one likes her, Lexi thought, with a stab in her chest. "Gracie," she whispered, shaking her head.

Across the playground, Grace looked up, although she couldn't possibly have heard her name spoken aloud. Lexi felt that look pierce her. Unable to help herself, she waved.

Grace looked behind her. Seeing no one there, she turned back to Lexi. Slowly, she smiled and waved back. Then the bell rang and she ran into the school.

Lexi could have lied to herself then, could have made up stories or tried harder not to care, but she didn't bother with any of that. She didn't want to rush to judgment, didn't want to make a terrible mistake—again—but neither could she ignore what she'd seen.

Grace wasn't happy.

No.

Grace *might be* unhappy, and that changed everything.

There would be an empty seat on the Florida-bound bus today.

Twenty

G race sat in the backseat of the car, feeling very small.
"How was school today?" Nana asked without looking in the rearview mirror.

"Okay, I guess."

"Did you make any new friends?"

Grace hated that question. Her grandmother asked it all the time. "I am queen of the kindergarten. Allison Shunt is making me a crown."

"Really? That's wonderful."

"I guess." Grace sighed. It *was* wonderful, for Stephanie, who really was the queen of the kindergarten. She stared down into the little magic mirror on her wrist, wishing Ariel would come to visit her, but the circle was blank.

Ariel, she mouthed. *I'm lonely.*

Nothing.

Grace rested her head on the car seat's fluffy side and stared out the window, watching the big green trees blur past. They drove up one street and down another and around a big corner, and then they were home.

Nana drove carefully down the dirt driveway to the cabin.

Grace waited patiently to be let out of her car seat, and, once freed, she grabbed her backpack and followed Nana up the gravel path to their front door.

Inside, she heard Nana mutter something under her breath as she start picking up stuff. Nana didn't like Daddy to leave clothes lying around, and she hated Gracie's toys.

Grace turned on the TV and climbed up onto the sofa to wait for her daddy. When Nana wasn't looking, she sucked her thumb. She knew it was a babyish thing to do, but Nana made her nervous and sucking her thumb helped.

"Grace?" Nana said.

Grace pulled the thumb out of her mouth. "I wasn't sucking my thumb. I was biting my fingernail. Is that bad, too?"

Nana frowned, and Grace felt her heart beat faster again, a sick feeling settled in her tummy.

Nana came closer. "There's nothing wrong with sucking your thumb, Grace."

Her voice was sweet and silky, like honey, and Grace felt herself starting to smile. "Really?"

"Maybe I should try it."

Grace giggled. "It makes me feel better."

"God knows that's a good thing."

"You said there was no God. That's what you told Daddy when he wanted to go to the cemetery."

Nana's smile faded. "I'm going to make dinner now."

Grace knew immediately that she'd done something bad again. She wanted to suck her thumb, but instead she dragged her blanket into her lap and sat there, watching Nana cook. No one said anything for the longest time. Grace kept looking down at her wrist mirror, whispering Ariel's name, but her friend was gone.

For the next two hours it was just Grace and her grandmother, together in this small house, hardly ever talking.

Then, finally, Daddy was home. Grace heard his car drive up, saw the headlights flash light into the house. She jumped down from the sofa and ran for the front door.

"Daddy!" she yelled when he came into the house. He dropped his big backpack and scooped her into his arms. Just like that, her world righted itself.

He kissed her cheek. "How's my girl?"

"I'm good, Daddy."

He smiled at that, but she could see how tired he was. His eyelids were kind of saggy, and he'd forgotten to comb his hair again today.

"Hey, Mom," he said. "Something smells good."

Nana came into the room. She was wiping her hands on a towel, but that was stupid because she never made a mess or got dirty. "Meatloaf and au gratin potatoes. The salad is in the fridge."

"You didn't have to do that," he said, starting to loosen his hold on Grace.

She clung to him like a cobweb. "I love you, Daddy," she said.

"I love you, too, Princess."

Nana came closer. She peered at Daddy, her pretty face turning into another frown. "You aren't sleeping."

"Finals," he said.

Grace didn't understand. Of course he wasn't sleeping. He just got home. "Are we gonna play rodeo tonight, Daddy?" That was her favorite. She got to ride on his back while he bucked her high into the air.

"Maybe Grace should stay with us tonight," Nana said.

Grace tightened her hold on her daddy. "I won't bother you, Daddy. I promise. I'll let you study."

"Thanks, Mom," Daddy said, "but we're good."

Nana gave him a long steady look, and then shrugged. "Okay. I'll be here before eight to pick her up. Don't stay up too late."

Grace felt a rush of relief when Nana was gone. She didn't quite know why, but her grandmother scared her. It was like playing with someone's extraspecial toy, you were always afraid you were going to accidentally break it.

She looked at her daddy and saw how tired he was. She hated when he got quiet. "They made me the queen of kindergarten," she said, hoping to make him proud.

"Even after you punched Austin?"

"No one likes him, Daddy. They were glad I punched him."

"What is it, the *Lord of the Flies* day care?"

"Huh?"

He carried her over to the sofa and sat down. She snuggled up to him, resting against his chest. This was her favorite place in the whole world. The only time she ever felt safe was when he was holding her.

"Why did they make you queen?"

She scrunched her face in thought. Then she remembered *Charlie and the Chocolate Factory*. Charlie got to be the winner cuz he was the nicest boy. "I saved Brittany from drowning. She went in too deep so I saved her."

"Saved Brittany from drowning," he said, staring down at her.

She felt her cheeks grow hot. How come lies just popped out of her mouth like little soap bubbles? She couldn't help it. No wonder no one liked her.

Daddy touched her cheek. "You know, Grace, when I was a kid, I thought I had to do everything right. Go to the right school, get the right grades, follow the rules. I wanted to make my mom . . . and my sister . . . proud of me." He looked away. For a long time, he was quiet, and the silence made her heart hurt. Had she said the wrong thing again? Finally he cleared his throat and said, "The point is: I'm proud of you just the way you are. I love you no matter what, Gracie. You can take that to the bank."

She didn't know what he meant. She hated the bank, except for the strawberry candies they gave out, and she knew the rest of it wasn't true. Once, she'd heard Daddy tell Papa that Grace was having trouble in school. *Behavioral problems* and *no friends* were the words she'd heard through the door. Her daddy had said a really bad word and asked Papa when they all just got to be happy again.

He *wanted* her to have friends. It was important to him. "I'm pop'lar, Daddy. I can't hardly finish my lunch cuz everyone is talking to me so much."

He leaned down and kissed her cheek. "Okay, Princess," he said with a sigh. "Okay. Now let's have something to eat before I pass out."

"I made the meatloaf," Grace said, smiling proudly at him. Her dad's smile was sad, and that scared her so much she added, "And the 'tatoes."

He kissed her again and got up. "Come on, Gracie, let's eat."

She hurried along behind him, trying to keep up.

❧

Once again, Jude had awakened too early. There was no light bleeding through the louvered blinds in her bedroom, but she could feel dawn gathering on the horizon like an army before a charge.

Beside her, she felt Miles move in his sleep; he turned toward her, took her in his arms, his breath a warm caress against the back of her neck.

She rolled over and snuggled close to him, slid her bare leg between his. His eyes opened slowly, lazily, and he smiled.

He leaned closer, kissed her lightly at first, then more passionately. His hands slid down her silky nightgown and found the lacy hem, then bunched it, dragged it up, up, until she was naked. He took off his boxer shorts and threw them aside.

She followed the lead of his desire, touched him the way he liked, arching into his hand until she had to have him inside of her. When she came, it was an explosion of feeling from somewhere deep inside of her. She cried out so loudly it embarrassed her, and when she collapsed beside him, she was trembling.

They never spoke about this new passion of theirs; she knew that he, like she, was afraid that words would jinx it. For so many years after their loss, sex had simply been gone, like smiles and laughter. Its return had surprised both of them. Somehow, they'd learned to connect by touch, to communicate their love almost solely without words. It wasn't the A answer, wasn't enough for Miles, whom she still caught looking at her with infinite sadness most of the time, but it was what they had now, and she knew how lucky they were to have it.

She kissed him lightly and drew back. Reaching down for her nightgown, she slipped it back on and got out of bed. At the windows, she stopped and twisted the shades' rod, letting the light stream in. To her left was the garden she'd given up on. It was a riotous mess of flowers and branches and leaves, without order or care. Ugly.

Miles came up beside her, kissed her shoulder. "We're still watching Grace today?"

Jude nodded. "Zach has a finals study group this morning. He seems stressed out."

"I was stressed out second year and I wasn't a twenty-four-year-old single dad." He squeezed her upper arm. "Why don't we bring Gracie over here? Zach can come over whenever he gets done. We can play a game. We still have that Candy Land around somewhere, don't we?"

Jude saw their reflections in the window: watery, pencil-drawing-like shapes. At the words *Candy Land,* time fell away; she was a young mother again, hunkered down on the floor with her twins, reaching for a card, laughing . . .

She slipped out of Miles's arms and went into the bathroom. She was out of her nightgown and into the shower before he could get to her.

"I forgot," he said, standing in the doorway, giving her that disappointed look again. "I shouldn't have said that."

"Don't be silly. It's just a game." Her voice barely cracked, but she knew it betrayed her.

There was a pause before he said, "I'll go for a run and meet you at Zach's."

"You run too much," she said.

He shrugged. It was his way of dealing with the loss. He ran; he worked.

"See you later," she said finally. She stayed in the shower until she heard him leave, and then she got out and began drying her hair. By the time she'd dressed in a pair of pale beige capris and a soft cotton T-shirt, she was in control of her emotions again.

Grief was like that these days: a stealth bomber. She could be going along just fine, moving forward, and then something would blow up unexpectedly. Years ago, when it had all been fresh, she could spend days off the path, in a gray world where nothing was stable. Now, she could right herself most of the time.

That was progress.

She started to leave the bathroom and remembered halfway to the door that she hadn't brushed her teeth or put on makeup.

She went back and brushed her teeth but decided to forgo the makeup. She'd only have to remove it tonight, and nothing left her more wrung out than a day with Grace and Zach. It took so much effort to be present in their lives without really being *present* that she came home exhausted.

She went to her car, a black hybrid SUV, smaller than the old Escalade, and started the engine. Backing out of the garage, she executed a tight three-point turn and drove up the gravel driveway, noticing the wildness of their land. Everything had grown in the past few years; blackberry bushes climbed like bullies over everything.

She turned onto the main road and drove to Zach's house.

As always, walking into this cabin was a little like going back in time for Jude. The blue sofa was the one she and Miles had gotten for their first apartment; the chairs were from the year they'd had the twins. They'd stored all of their old furniture and outdated trinkets for their kids. They used to say jokingly, *with two moving out, we'll need to save it all.*

Zach was raising his daughter and going to med school in a house that mirrored the one in which she and Miles had done all the same things.

"Anyone here?" she called out.

Zach came around the corner from the kitchen, holding a cup of coffee and carrying Grace, who clung sleepily to him.

"Don't say it," Zach said, rubbing Grace's back. "I know I look like shit. I was up until four. Can you guys still watch Gracie today? I have study group."

"Of course."

"Thanks. I can be home by seven."

Jude nodded and went into the kitchen, where she started cooking breakfast. Because she kept Zach's house stocked with food, she knew she'd find everything she needed for waffles, scrambled eggs, and a fruit plate.

When Miles got there, hair still wet from his shower and smiling in the way that only he among them still could, Jude felt a weight slide off her shoulders. Miles was the glue that held their lives together. Around him, Jude and Zach breathed easier.

"There's my girl," Miles said, opening his arms wide.

Zach put Grace down and she ran for her grandfather, hurled her little pink polka-dot flanneled body at him.

Miles scooped her up and whispered something in her ear, and she giggled.

Jude felt a spasm in her chest. There were times, like this, when all that she'd lost hit her so hard she had trouble standing.

"Let's eat while it's hot," she said tightly.

"Yummy!" Grace said, scampering out of Miles's arms and running for the table. As always she sat next to a blank spot and an extra place setting. That was the place for her "invisible friend."

The alien princess trapped in a jar.

"So, how's the clinical stuff going?" Miles asked Zach when he sat down.

"I love the clinical. Diagnosing is awesome, but pharmacokinetics? That stuff is kicking my ass," Zach answered, scooping eggs onto his daughter's plate.

Miles reached over to stab a waffle with his fork. "Pathology was my downfall second year. I don't know why. You just have to get through it all with the knowledge. Third year is when you really get into it."

Jude watched the way her son buttered Grace's waffle while he talked to his father, how he cut it up into small pieces for her and put her napkin in her lap, and she was so proud of him that she thought, *we're all going to be okay. Someday we'll be laughing again.*

She found herself smiling at the unexpected idea of happiness, of a future together. She listened to one of Zach's stories about diagnosing some terrible disease, and how he'd screwed up, and she laughed along with her husband and son.

After breakfast was over, the unanticipated sense of lightness remained. Jude sent Zach off to the UW with a kiss on the cheek and a hug that was so fierce he actually frowned at her.

"Go on. We'll have fun today," she said.

"Thanks, Mom," Zach said.

"No problema," she answered without thinking. At the silly reminder of who they'd been, she fell silent.

And then he was grabbing his backpack and heading out the door.

"Papa, can I go to my playhouse?" Grace asked when her dad was gone.

"Put on your clothes and brush your teeth first," Miles said distractedly. He was looking for the TV remote. When he found it, the screen thumped to life and a baseball game filled the screen. Miles flopped onto their old sofa and put his feet up on the coffee table.

While Jude washed the dishes, she saw a yellow flash blur past her. "Stay away from the water, Gracie."

"Ariel and me are just gonna play Barbies in the playhouse," Grace answered, grunting to open the sliding glass door.

"Ariel and I," Jude said automatically. "Miles, do the ordinary rules of grammar apply to imaginary friends?"

He said, "Huh? What was that, babe?"

Jude went back to washing the dishes. She heard the sliding door thump shut and she glanced to the left.

Outside, Grace ran nimbly across the yard, toward the pink and yellow Princess Playhouse Santa had brought her last year. It was positioned just beyond the deck, on a patch of grass that looked out over the gray sandy beach.

"Come on, hurry," Grace was yelling to her imaginary friend.

Jude dried the dishes and put them away. When she was finished, she glanced out at Grace again. She could see her granddaughter through the plastic castle's open window. She was talking to the air while she made Barbie dance.

"You going out to the magic kingdom?" Jude asked Miles.

"In a sec. I just want to see this play."

"Okay. I'm going to make them a chicken casserole for dinner," Jude decided on the spot. She didn't want Zach to be hungry when he got home from studying.

She moved through the familiar family recipe with almost no effort. Every few minutes she looked up to make sure that Grace was okay, and then she went back to work.

When the casserole was in the fridge, along with a note about cooking it, she cleaned up the kitchen again and then headed into the living room. She was about to say something to Miles when a flash of movement caught her eye.

She opened the sliding glass door and stepped out onto the weathered deck. It was a beautiful June day, with sharp blue skies and no clouds. To the right of the property was a thick stand of evergreens that blocked the view of the neighboring house.

Grace was standing by the trees.

Beside her stood a girl dressed in faded shorts and a blue T-shirt. Was it Mildred's daughter, from next door? Was she home from college?

Then the girl turned and Jude saw her face.

Jude reached out to the sliding glass door to steady herself and was about to call for her husband when pain exploded in her chest. It hurt so much she couldn't think, couldn't move, couldn't do anything except plaster her hand over her heart and fall to her knees.

Lexi rode down to LaRiviere Park.

As she got off the bike and looked out over the gray sandy beach, with its mounds of silvered driftwood tangled along the shore, she was assailed by memories.

She locked her bike into the rack and then moved past the driftwood, remembering the first time Zach had told her he loved her. They'd been right there . . .

She walked down to the pebbled beach. Here, the stones were polished to glassy perfection by the waves. Counting the houses, she knew when she reached her destination.

There it was: the old Tamarind cabin. There had been a party here once, back in her junior year of high school. Jude had never found out about that one.

Tall cedar trees ran in a thick line along one side of the property. To their right, on the lot next door, she saw a colorful plastic castle/playhouse, complete with a pointed gray turret and bright pink pennant. Beside it, perched like a baby bird at the end of the grayed deck, sat a little girl dressed in yellow. She was talking to her wrist again.

Lexi approached her daughter slowly, taking care to stay hidden by the trees. The last thing she wanted was for Zach to come storming out of the house like a Nazgul, telling her to get the hell away from his daughter.

Really, all Lexi wanted was to make sure that Grace was happy. Everything could go on as planned as long as Grace was happy.

She started to say, "Hey," but her voice caught. She cleared her throat and tried again. "Hey, Grace."

"I'm not s'posed to talk to strangers."

"I'm not a stranger, Gracie. I've known you all your life."

"Oh." Grace cocked her face to the right, studying Lexi. Her lips pursed. "I saw you at school."

"Yes." It took everything Lexi had inside of her just to stand there. She wanted to fling herself at Grace and hold her in her arms and beg for forgiveness. Still, she took care to stand in the shade of the trees, out of the house's view.

"You waved. How come?"

Lexi took a step closer. Her heart was taking flight. "I knew you when you were a baby."

"Do you know my daddy?"

She nodded.

Grace's face scrunched up. "Prove it."

"Does he still like chocolate-chip-mint ice cream and hate anything that looks like a comb?"

Grace giggled and immediately covered her mouth to stifle the sound. "Nana says his hair looks like a beetle, which is funny cuz beetles are gross. Especially the ones who live on poop."

Lexi battled a smile. "Can I stand by you?"

"Sure."

Lexi moved closer, stood beside a huge tree. "How come you're out here all alone?"

Grace's little face drooped. "My daddy is gone. *Again*. Nana's in the kitchen."

"Does your grandma still dance while she cooks?"

Grace frowned up at her. "She hates me."

"Your Grandma Jude hates you?"

"I look like *her*."

A chill crept down Lexi's spine. "Her?"

"Daddy's dead sister. That's why Nana never looks at me. I'm not s'posed to know that, but I do."

"Really?"

"She was murdered by pirates. That's why no one talks about it." Grace sighed. "My daddy sometimes cries when he looks at me, too."

"You do look like Mia," Lexi said quietly.

"You knew Daddy's sister?"

"I did," Lexi said quietly. "She was—"

"Hey, do you have a dog?"

Lexi was startled by the change in subject. "No. I've never had one."

"I want a dog. Or maybe a chipmunk."

"Have you asked your dad for a pet?"

"We had rattlesnake for dinner last night. With peanuts."

Something was going on here; Grace was throwing stuff at her, but why? Had the talk of Zach's emotions scared her? Lexi said the only thing she could think of. "I ate ostrich once."

"Wow."

"So, your daddy's not here?"

"Nope. I'm a big girl. I get to stay home alone all the time. I can take my own bath and everything. Last night I made dinner all by myself."

"Does he go out a lot?"

Grace nodded.

Lexi studied her daughter's gorgeous face, with its sad green eyes and pale skin, and wondered if she'd left any mark on this girl at all. "Do you have any friends at school?"

"F-friends?" Grace said, then grinned. "Tons. I'm the most pop'lar girl in the class."

"You're lucky. I was lonely sometimes in school," Lexi said, watching her daughter closely. She couldn't help herself; she took a step closer.

Grace's lips trembled a little. "I really don't have—"

"Grace!" someone yelled sharply. "Get in here. *Now.*"

Lexi jumped back into the trees. Peering around a shaggy green branch, she saw the cabin. The sliding glass door was open, and Miles stood there, frowning. He hadn't seen Lexi, she was sure of it. So why did he sound so pissed?

"Grace, damn it," he yelled again. "Get in here. *Now.*"

"Gotta go." Grace popped to her feet.

"Does he always yell at you like that?"

Grace started to turn away, but Lexi dared to reach out and take hold of her girl's hand. "I'd like to be your friend," she said softly. It was hard to stop there. Suddenly there was so much more she had to say. She'd been a fool for thinking she could walk away from her daughter.

A smile broke over Grace's face, its brightness warming Lexi. "Okay. Bye," Grace said, waving. Then she turned and ran back for the house.

Lexi got up slowly. She understood at last how it felt to stop running.

She walked back to her bike, climbed aboard, and pedaled up the hill toward town.

An ambulance passed her, lights flashing, siren blaring, but she hardly noticed.

She was on her way to see Scot Jacobs.

Twenty-one

Jude was in the emergency ward of Seattle Hope. She lay in a narrow bed, connected to all kinds of monitors and machines and alarms, but it was all unnecessary. She hadn't had a heart attack.

She looked up at her husband, feeling foolishly fragile. She'd broken so easily, again. "I thought all of that was behind me."

He stroked the sweat-dampened hair away from her face. "So did I."

"A panic attack." She practically spit the words out.

Grace climbed up the metal bed rails. She slipped and plopped back to the floor, then climbed up again. The rattling *clang* reverberated through Jude's tense body, made a headache blossom at the base of her skull. "What's panic?" Grace asked, banging her chin against the bed rail.

"It means you're scared," Miles said.

"I saw a beach rat once. It was scary," Grace said. "And those big hairy black spiders are scary. Did one crawl up your leg?"

"Nana's really tired, Gracie," Miles said. "Why don't you read that book over there for a minute?"

"But I wanna know what scared Nana."

"Not now, Gracie. Okay?" he said gently.

"Is it like when I had chicken pox and I just wanted sleep?"

"Exactly."

"Okay, Papa." Grace slid down the side of the bed and shuffled over to the chair in the corner and sat down. She opened a tattered copy of *The Cat in the Hat* and tried to sound out the words.

Jude felt bad—shaky, headachy, sick to her stomach. "I'm losing it, Miles."

"What do you mean?"

She loved the strong, steady movement of his hand through her hair. It calmed her more than any medication could. "I thought I saw her."

"Mia?" he whispered.

"No." Jude couldn't help feeling disappointed by the question. She'd *tried* to see Mia. Neither psychics nor prayers had worked. And certainly, seeing Mia wouldn't cause Jude to think she was having heart failure. The opposite would be true: such a vision would restart her heart.

She glanced sideways, saw that Grace was absorbed by the challenge of reading. "Lexi," Jude whispered. It was the first time she'd said the name aloud in years. "She was talking to Gracie."

Miles took her hand in his. He didn't look at all ruffled by her admission, and his calm soothed her. "It's common to experience dream-like sensations or perceptual distortions during a panic attack. You know that. Remember the time you thought a car was going to hit Grace? If I hadn't been there, you would have killed yourself running into traffic."

"This wasn't like that," Jude said, but even as she said it, she questioned herself. So many weird things had happened to her since Mia's death. "Her hair was short and curly. And she was really thin."

"It wasn't Lexi," Miles said evenly. She loved how certain he sounded. Sometimes Miles's certainty made Jude want to gouge his eyes out, but now she wanted to share his calm.

"How can you be so sure?"

"Her sentence was up in November. Remember how tense we all were, waiting to see if she would show up here?"

Tense was an understatement. Jude had spent the end of last year strung tighter than a trip wire. It wasn't until mid-January that she had begun to relax. Miles had wanted to call the state and track Lexi's movements, but Jude had been adamant about no contact whatsoever. She hadn't wanted anyone in their family to even say Lexi's name aloud, let alone find out where she'd gone.

"She didn't show. Didn't call or send a note. And she sent Zach's letters back unopened," Miles said reassuringly. "Lexi made her decision. She thinks G-R-A-C-E is better off without her."

"You sound as if you disagree."

"I've always disagreed. You know that."

Grace looked up. "Did you just spell my name, Papa?"

Miles smiled tightly at his granddaughter. "I was testing you. Good job, Poppet."

Grace beamed at him. "I'm the best speller in my class. I'm getting a trophy for it."

"She's not coming back, Jude," Miles said softly, leaning down to kiss her forehead. "All of that is behind us."

※

Grace loved hospitals. They were grownup places, and because her Papa was a surgun—or something like that—people brought her books and juice boxes and gave her paper and crayons. Sometimes, when a doctor wanted to be alone with Nana and Papa, one of the nurses would even take her for a walk through the busy hallways. Her favorite was seeing the newborn babies in the see-through plastic boxes. She loved their tiny pink and blue caps.

Even so, after a few hours, she was bored. Ariel was hiding; she hadn't come to Grace's wrist mirror since the playhouse, and Grace's hand was hurting from coloring so many pictures.

She was about to whine—again—when the door to Nana's room

burst open. Dad rushed in, carrying a huge stack of books under one arm. "How is she?" he asked Papa.

"I'm fine," Nana said. She smiled, but it looked sorta flat. Like she was tired. "You two don't need to go into doc speak. I had a panic attack that felt a hell of a lot like a heart attack. They're discharging me now. It's embarrassing, really."

Dad put his books down on the chair beside Grace. Ruffling her hair, he moved past her and went to the bedside. "Panic attack? You haven't had one of those in years. Not since—"

Nana held up a shaking hand. "We all know the history."

"She thought she saw Lexi," Papa said.

Daddy drew in a sharp breath.

This was news. Nana had a reason, and the reason had a name. Grace scrambled up the metal bed rails again and hung on. "Who's Lexi?"

No one answered her. They just looked at one another.

"A delusion?" Daddy asked quietly.

"Your dad thinks so," Nana said. "Hopefully."

"She's made her feelings pretty clear," Daddy said. "Lexi, I mean. She's probably in Florida with Eva."

Grace reached over and put her hand in his back pocket. It made her feel connected to him, even if he hardly noticed. "Who's Lexi?" she asked again.

"Mildred's niece is back from school," Daddy said. "She has dark brown hair."

"I'm sure that's who it was," Nana said.

Grace bounced a little on the bed rail. The metal clanged. It bugged her that no one was paying attention to her. "I saw a baby with four arms," she said. "He's in the nursery."

"Why don't you take Gracie home, Zach?" Nana said. "She's been really good."

Grace slithered down from her perch and went to the desk, where she gathered up all her pictures and crayons. Taking one drawing of a butterfly on a flower, she handed it to her Nana. "This is for you."

Nana stared at the picture. "Thanks, Gracie. I feel better already."

"They're magic crayons. They make anyone better. That's why the hospital has 'em," Grace said earnestly. "The yellow ones can fly."

"Come on, Grace," Daddy said. He gathered all their things together and took her out to the car.

She climbed into the car seat in the back, and he strapped her in.

All the way home, Grace talked to her daddy.

She'd been quiet for *hours,* and she had so much to say. She told him about the new game Ariel had taught her and the sand dollar she'd found by the playhouse and about the new friend she'd made today and the seagull that had landed right in front of her.

"Look, Daddy," Grace said, sitting up straighter as they drove through town. "There she is. There's my new friend. Hi!" Grace yelled at the closed window, waving furiously. "Did you see her, Daddy? That's a cool bike she has. It's magic. I think she's a movie star. She said she ate an ostrich once."

Daddy kept driving. A few minutes later, he turned into their driveway and parked.

"You believe me about the ostrich lady, don't you? She says she—"

"Enough, Gracie. No pretending tonight, okay? Daddy's had a tough day."

"I wasn't pretending," Grace said, stung by the accusation. She dragged her blanket off the seat beside her and wrapped it around her neck. Her daddy was in one of those moods where he wasn't listening to her; even when he looked at her, she got the feeling he wasn't paying attention. Like he was seeing someone else in his head. And he looked sad.

Grace had grown up around sad. She knew it was best to stay quiet and cuddle when he was like this. But she'd been quiet all day, and she was desperate to talk to someone. To him.

In the house, Grace went right to the fridge and pulled out the heavy casserole Nana had made. She worked really hard not to drop it. "This goes in the oven, Daddy," she said, holding it out proudly.

He took it from her and put it in the oven. "I'm going to go take a shower. I'll put a DVD in for you."

She started to say she didn't want to watch a movie, but he was already turning away, going into the living room.

She climbed up onto the sofa with her blanket and sucked her thumb. No one was paying any attention to her, anyway. It seemed like Daddy took the longest shower in the world, and, when he was done and walking around in his baggy sweat pants, with his wet hair dripping onto the red USC T-shirt, she followed him around, talking about anything she could think of.

"On the way to the hospital, I got to sit in the front of Papa's car. We followed the am'blance. And he let me drive . . . just onto the ferry. I went really slow. I'm a good driver. I saw a killer whale eat a seal. It was gross."

Nothing made him pay attention. He hardly even looked at her, and his face just got sadder and sadder, so much that Grace started to feel sad herself. Lonely.

By the time he put her into her jammies and tucked her into bed, she felt like crying.

Dad curled up alongside her. "I'm sorry if I've been weird tonight, Princess. Being in the hospital reminded me of my sister."

"Mia," she said solemnly, showing off that she remembered the name they hardly ever said aloud. "I bet you *hate* hospitals."

"I wouldn't be much of a doctor if that were true." He smiled down at her. "Besides, I got you in a hospital."

Grace snuggled against him. This was one of her favorite stories. "What did I look like?"

"You were a perfect little princess. Your eyes were sort of brownish-blue then. You hardly even cried."

"And my mommy was there?"

"She named you Grace."

"And you named me after your sister. Then you took me home."

"I loved you from the very first second."

"I know, but how come—"

"Enough, Gracie," he said, reaching over for the book on the nightstand. "Daddy's had a hard day. How about if I read more of *The Secret Garden* to you?"

"But don't you want to hear about my new friend?"

"The movie star who ate an ostrich and rides a magic bike?"

"She might not *really* be a movie star. Maybe she's a spy who—"

"Enough, Gracie," he said, opening the book. "Now, where were we?"

He knew, though; he always knew. Grace smiled sleepily and murmured, "Colin is better."

"Oh. Yeah," Daddy said, turning to the right page and starting to read. "One of the strange things about living in the world is that it is only now and then one is quite sure one is going to live forever and ever . . ."

Grace popped her thumb into her mouth and listened to the music of her daddy's voice.

❧

"They yell at her, Scot. And she's always alone. No one bothers to come out and play with her. Her only friend seems to be invisible."

"My son's imaginary friend is a duck. What does that say about him, I wonder?"

"This is serious," Lexi said. She had spent endless hours wrestling with her own emotions, and no matter how often or how forcefully she told herself that Grace was better off without an ex-con for a mother, she couldn't trample the new feeling that she'd been wrong to abandon her daughter. It was like opening the door on a tornado—there was no stopping the damage that would be done inside, and no closing the door again.

Abandon. The word ate through Lexi's best intentions and stripped her bare. In all her attempts to be unlike her own mother, had she done the same thing? And how was it that she'd never asked herself this question before?

"You're right," Scot said, pushing back his chair. The metal wheels screeched on the Pergo flooring. "It's *very* serious. Why don't you sit down? You're moving like an egg beater."

She did as he asked and sat down.

"Talk to me, Lexi."

She took a deep breath. "Giving Grace up was the hardest thing I've ever done." Her voice dropped; it was difficult to say the words, even after all her therapy. "The only thing that kept me going was this image of what her life would be like. I saw pink dresses and birthday parties with ponies and bedtime stories and family Christmas dinners. I saw a little girl who grew up knowing she was loved, knowing where she belonged."

She looked up. "I *trusted* them, Scot," she said, anger surging up. "All of them. Miles. Jude. Zach. I trusted them to give her the childhood I never had. And you know what I found? A lonely little girl whose daddy is too busy to be with her . . . a girl who gets yelled at for nothing . . . who plays all alone. A girl with no friends . . ."

"What do you want to do?"

She got up again and began pacing. "I'm a felon. An ex-con. I'm twenty-four years old with almost no job experience. Gee, I worked in the prison library and an ice cream shop, and I picked raspberries in the summer. I'm broke. What *can* I do?"

"Did your Aunt Eva have money when she took you in?"

Lexi stopped moving and stared out of the office window. Outside, a young mother was helping her red-haired daughter up to a silver drinking fountain. "She had a job and a place to live."

"You have a college degree and you're a hard worker. On top of that, you're one of the most honorable people I know. You know more about love—and its lack—than most people. So I'll ask you again: what do you want to do? It's a simple question. Either you stay or you go."

"And if I choose to stay?"

"We would petition the court to modify the parenting plan. We'd seek joint custody. Or, failing that, visitation rights."

"Supervised, I suppose. Me being an ex-con."

"You aren't a violent offender, Lexi," he said. "You aren't your mother. But yes, they might impose supervision at the start. I didn't say it would be easy, but you *will* get visitation rights at least, and you'll quite possibly get joint custody. We wouldn't get full custody, but you're her *mother,* Lexi. The court knows how important you are to her. And you're welcome to stay at my office until you find someplace else."

You're her mother.

For years, even before Gracie was born, Lexi barred that thought from her consciousness. The words were simply too painful to consider, but now, hearing them spoken aloud, she heard their sweetness, and longing swelled inside of her.

She could hold Gracie, hug her and kiss her and take her to the park . . .

"It won't be easy," Scot said into the building silence. "I imagine the Farradays will fight you."

It was too late to worry about that now. She'd loosened the idea of motherhood, and it had uprooted her, swept her skyward. "Let's file the papers," Lexi said.

"You're sure?"

She finally turned to face him. "I'm sure."

Jude gave up trying to sleep at about four o'clock. She left the warmth of her bedroom and made her way into the dark living room. There, standing in front of the tall black windows, she stared at her own tarnished reflection.

She knew what the doctors wanted her to believe: that panic had caused her delusion rather than the other way around.

She wanted to believe it, too.

But she didn't believe it and that was that. Sometime during the night, she'd become convinced. So much so that hours later, when Miles shuffled through the great room in search of coffee, she said. "I saw her. Lexi. I saw her."

Miles looked confused. "Wait." Walking past her, he went into the kitchen and came out with a cup of coffee. "None for you. You look ready to blast off as it is. Now, say it again."

"I saw her. I wasn't mistaken." She tapped her foot nervously, stared up at him.

"I always wanted to keep track of her."

She nodded curtly. "I know. I didn't. Out of sight, out of mind."

"Yeah. That's how it works." He stood there, naked except for his blue boxers, staring out the window. "Okay," he finally said and handed her his coffee. "Let's find out."

He went to his laptop, pulled up a phone number, and then made a call.

"Hey, Bill, sorry to call so early, but we have a situation here. Can you find out when Alexa Baill was released? . . . yes, I'm aware we asked not to know. Something has changed. Yes. Thank you. I'll be right here."

He hung up and took his coffee back. "Are you okay?" he asked gently, touching her hair.

"I've been better."

They stood there together, staring out at the backyard, saying nothing as the sky turned bright and blue. Time passed like the beats of their hearts, quiet and steady. The phone startled Jude so much she let out a little scream.

Miles answered. "Hello?"

Jude tapped her foot again and crossed her arms, digging her fingernails into her own arms so tightly she almost drew blood.

"Really?" Miles said, frowning. "Why is that? Oh. Okay, thanks. Again, sorry to bother you." He hung up.

"Well?" Jude said, wishing she'd downed a Xanax.

"She was released two days ago. Time was added onto her sentence for bad behavior."

Jude's foot tapped so fast she was practically dancing. "She came straight here."

"You don't know that."

"We have to *do* something. Get an injunction or something. Maybe we should move."

"We are not going to move." Miles took her by the shoulders and made her look at him. "Calm down, Jude."

"Are you *insane*?" Jude felt hysterical laughter bubbling up inside of her. She knew it was inappropriate to laugh now, but her emotions were all cross-wired these days. Sometimes she cried when she was happy and laughed when she was scared and screamed when she was tired.

She pulled free of Miles and ran to her bedroom, where she found her Xanax and fumbled to open the bottle. "Damn child-proof caps."

Miles took it from her and opened it, handing her a pill, which she downed with his hot coffee. "You better get me an appointment with Dr. Bloom."

She survived the next two hours in a medicated haze. She washed and dried her hair and dressed in a pale beige summer-weight sheath. It wasn't until she was in Dr. Bloom's chair, squirming under the psychiatrist's sharp gaze, that she realized she was still in her slippers. "Thank you for making time for me," Jude said, trying to hide her slippered feet.

"A panic attack. You haven't had one in more than eighteen months. What happened?"

She couldn't meet Harriet's penetrating gaze. It made her feel weak and delusional. So she glanced to her left. "I was at Zach's house on Saturday morning, making breakfast for everyone. Zach is studying for finals. School is going late this year. All those damn snow days add up."

"And?" Harriet prompted.

"I saw Gracie outside . . . talking to . . . Lexi."

"Lexi is the girl who was driving the car that night."

"Yes."

"We haven't talked much about her. In fact, I believe you said you'd never come back if I mentioned her again."

"Out of sight, out of mind," Jude answered by rote, tapping her foot again.

"So you saw her again, after all these years, and you had a panic attack."

"She was talking to Gracie!"

"Her daughter," Dr. Bloom said.

Jude snapped to her feet and started pacing. She was having trouble breathing. "She gave up that right when she went to prison. She signed documents."

"Is that when you think she gave up the right to be a mother? When she went to prison? Or when she killed your daughter?"

"Both," Jude said, breathing hard now. Her chest hurt. "What's the difference? She can't waltz back in and act as if it never happened. Zach finally has his life back on track. I won't let him see her again."

"Sit down, Jude," Dr. Bloom said in a reasonable voice.

"What if she wants . . . what if—oh, God." Jude drew in a great gulping breath and started to panic. Dr. Bloom was beside her almost instantly, touching her back, rubbing it in a soothing way.

"You're all right, Jude. Just breathe. Here, sit down."

Jude got her breathing under control and the pain in her chest receded. With a shaking hand, she pushed the sweat-dampened hair out of her face and tried to smile. "I'm falling apart."

"Would that really be so terrible?"

Jude wrenched away from the doctor. "Are you sure you went to med school?"

"Jude. You can't control this situation."

"Thanks for that pearl." She looked longingly at the door. This wasn't helping. "I should have swallowed a handful of pills when . . ." She couldn't say the words out loud. She'd never been able to.

"You thought about it," Dr. Bloom reminded her. "But even in the darkest times, you had hope."

"You think hope is what stopped me?"

"What stopped you?"

She was not going to answer that. She hated the answer, anyway. "I'm worried about Zach, damn it. He's fragile, like me. He's never gotten over his guilt . . . or his grief. To see Lexi again . . . and what if she wants to be Grace's mother? I won't let her be a part of our family again. Oh, God . . ."

"She's already a part of your family," Harriet said.

"Shut up."

"Excellent retort. By the way, you don't sound like a woman who feels nothing for her granddaughter."

Jude reached for her purse, snagged it. "I need to see a lawyer, not a shrink."

"What makes you think you need a lawyer?"

"I need to protect Grace and Zach. Maybe we need a restraining order . . ."

"You think keeping Lexi away will protect them?"

"Of course. Have you even been listening to me?"

"Lexi is your granddaughter's mother," Dr. Bloom said gently. "You tell me you used to put a lot of store in motherhood."

Jude reeled back. "I need to get out of here." Without waiting for a response, she headed for the door. As she wrenched it open, she heard Dr. Bloom say, "She was eighteen years old, Jude. Think about that."

Jude slammed the door behind her.

Twenty-two

Jude called Miles and asked him to meet her at Zach's; then she drove straight down to the ferry dock. Her timing was impeccable. They were loading the boat when she got there.

The thirty-minute Sound crossing seemed to take forever. She tapped her fingers nervously on the steering wheel.

She wasn't sure about anything except this: she had to get to Grace. All she wanted to do right now was gather her family together, as if her arms were the safe place they'd once been. What was left of her family, anyway, what Lexi had left of her family.

Off the ferry, she drove through town slowly, her eyes peeled for a dark-haired girl in Bermuda shorts and a drugstore T-shirt. She thought she saw Lexi a dozen times, and she stomped on the brakes so often that horns honked behind her.

She veered onto Turnagin Way and drove past the elementary school to the day care. There, she got out of the car and strode up to the pretty little

A-frame house that was the Silly Bear Day Care. Inside, she found an empty playroom full of brightly colored plastic tables and bean bag chairs.

She went out to the backyard, where a dozen kids were playing on Lincoln Logs–type swing sets, in sandboxes, and in a playhouse. She took it all in at once, and then began looking for Grace, who she knew would be alone.

"Hi, Jude," said the day care's owner, Leigh Skitter. They had known each other for years. Leigh's youngest son had played soccer with Zach. "You're here early."

"I don't see Grace," Jude said, realizing too late that she hadn't said hello and that her voice was sharp.

"She's with Lexi," Leigh said. "She sure looks different, doesn't she?"

Jude felt a chill go through her. "You let her see Grace?"

Leigh seemed surprised by the question, or maybe it was Jude's raised voice. "She said you'd agreed to it. And there's no restraining order in place, is there? I mean, I know she doesn't have custody, but we all knew she'd come back someday . . ."

Why hadn't Jude thought of this scenario? Leigh Skitter had known Zach and Lexi in their high school days. She'd said on several occasions how much she liked Lexi. No doubt she even felt a little sorry for her. So many people did—when *Dateline* did their segment on the show, plenty of people piped up to say that Lexi's punishment had been too harsh. Yeah. Poor Lexi.

Jude felt the start of panic. Why hadn't they gotten a restraining order against Lexi, just in case? At the very least, she should have told Leigh and the school that Lexi was not to be allowed near her daughter. Didn't full custody give them that right?

"Jude? Is something wrong? Zach never asked me to keep Grace away from her mother."

Jude pushed past Leigh and ran across the sawdust-strewn backyard. At the childproof gate, she manipulated the latch and kept going, racing through the trees toward the beach. There, she shuddered to a halt.

There were kids everywhere, laughing and playing. The day care's other supervisor was over by the driftwood, watching the kids.

Calm down, Judith.

She scanned the shoreline.

There she was—a little blond girl alongside a dark-haired young woman.

Lexi.

Jude ran forward, almost falling in her sudden fury. She grabbed Lexi by the arm, spun her around.

Lexi paled. "J-Jude."

"Hey, Nana," Grace said. "This is my new friend."

"Grace. Go over to Tami," Jude said tightly.

"But—"

"*Now,*" Jude yelled.

Grace flinched at the harshness of the command. Her little shoulders hunched forward and she shuffled away, her head hung low.

"You have no right to be here," Jude said.

As Lexi looked up, Jude noticed several things at once: Lexi was hard looking, almost stringy, but she was still very young. And when she noticed the girl's frizzy, curly, untamed hair, she thought of Mia saying, *she's like me Madre, is that coolio or what?* Jude stumbled back at the memory. She shouldn't have come here, shouldn't have approached Lexi. She wasn't strong enough. "Go," Jude said weakly. "Please . . ."

"I needed to see her."

"And you have." Jude felt frail enough to drop to her knees. It took concentration just to keep standing.

"She's lonely," Lexi said, looking toward Grace, who stood apart from the other kids and stared back at them.

"What do you expect?" Jude said bitterly. "She's grown up in a broken family."

"I told myself I'd see that she was happy and I'd leave. But she's not happy."

Jude opened her purse, reached in for her wallet with shaking hands. "I'll pay you to go. How much? Twenty thousand dollars? Fifty? Just tell me how much you want." Lexi's face changed at that, but Jude was shaking too hard to focus clearly. A dull thudding squeezed her chest and she had the terrible thought that she might pass out. "A hundred thousand. How about that?"

"I gave her to Zach," Lexi said. "*Gave* her. Do you know how hard that was? Can you imagine?"

"Losing a child?" Jude said. "Yes, Lexi. I know how it feels."

"I did it because I loved her. And because I trusted you and Zach and Miles to be her family."

Jude saw the censure in Lexi's eyes, and she knew it was warranted, and that only made it hurt more. "We are her family."

"No. She's afraid of you, did you know that? She says you never hold her or kiss her. She wonders why you don't love her."

Jude felt exposed suddenly; fear bled up inside her, bubbled out until she was shaking so hard she dropped her purse. "How dare you?" But the words had no bite, no venom.

"I trusted all of you." Lexi's voice broke. It was the first evidence of real emotion, and Jude seized it.

"Zach has given up everything for Grace. Everything."

"You mean USC, don't you? Your Holy Grail. You never cared that he was happy, just that he did what you wanted him to."

"That's not true."

"He *loved* me. But that meant nothing to you."

"You killed his sister," Jude said.

"Yes," Lexi said, her mouth trembling. "And I have to live with that every day of my life. I did everything I could to make it up to you and Zach and Grace, but there is no making it up. I gave you my freedom and my daughter—and still you want more. Well, fuck you, Jude. You don't get any more. Grace is my daughter. My Mia. And I want her back. My lawyer filed the petition today."

As Lexi walked away, Jude just stood there, eyes stinging, throat tight, hearing Lexi's voice say over and over again, *my Mia.*

Once Lexi started walking down the beach, she couldn't stop. She was going in the wrong direction; her bike was parked in the public area at the end of the dead-end road. But she couldn't turn around, couldn't watch Jude bundle Grace up and take her away, as if it were dangerous for Grace to know her own mother.

A cool summer breeze plucked at her hair. Her eyes watered in the wind. Still, she put her hands in her pockets and kept walking. She turned and looked back down the beach. Jude was still there.

Lexi wanted to be tough and hard, to feel that she was justified in coming here and wanting her daughter back, and she did feel it—justified, for all the reasons she'd given Jude. Mostly because the Farradays had had a chance to make Grace happy and they'd failed.

But Lexi's guilt and remorse, always floating inside of her, were rising now. She had destroyed the Farradays. In the beginning, she'd hoped that her years in prison would heal them somehow, but she knew better than anyone that time and distance didn't heal you. It had been naïve to assume that Grace could be raised as Mia and Zach had, in the bosom of love and happiness. So in a way, it was Lexi's fault that her daughter was unhappy now.

All of that was true, and all of it weighed heavily on Lexi, but there was something else too, a lightness that she hadn't felt in years. It was hope—a bright beam in the blackness of her guilt.

She could lift Grace up. She could be the kind of mother she'd dreamed of having. Maybe they wouldn't have money or a big house or a new car, but Lexi knew better than most that love could be enough. Eva had proved that. She hated to hurt the Farradays—and Zach—again, hated it to her marrow, but she'd paid enough for her mistake.

The decision anchored her. Wiping her eyes, she looked around, surprised to see how far she'd walked. Behind her, the public beach was a gray comma of sand tucked tightly against dark woods. She couldn't tell if people were still there or not.

She started to turn back when a flash of hot pink plastic caught her eye. She paused, looked up the beach.

It was the playhouse, with its fluttery pink pennant and mock stone turret.

She didn't really make a decision to go that way. Rather, she just found herself moving toward it, walking, walking, and suddenly she was standing there, on the sandy beach, in the shade of a giant tree, looking at a little girl's playhouse.

But in her mind, she was on another beach, years ago, standing under a different tree, in the glow of distant house lights, with her best friend and the boy she thought she'd love forever.

We'll bury it.

A pact.

We'll never say good-bye.

How shiny their naïveté had been, like polished silver, glinting in the darkness. She had never believed in anything as much as she'd believed in the three of them at that moment.

She bent down, peered through the small, plastic-shuttered window to the castle's interior. Several Barbies lay in plastic beds, their clothes scattered around. An open Dr. Seuss book lay beside an empty juice box.

Here was where Grace played alone.

Lexi let her fingers trail atop the flat, mock stone roof as she moved into the yard. The grass was lush and green—summer hadn't sapped its color yet or turned it crisp. A worn deck jutted out from the log cabin, clearly a construction afterthought. In one corner was an old picnic table with two benches; beside it a plastic-tarped barbeque. Along the split-rail fence line, roses grew wild, their leggy green branches climbing over one another like adolescent boys offering bright pink flowers to a girl.

The house—Zach's house—was a rustic log cabin with a roof that sprouted moss along its seams. Gray stone chimneys bookended the place, seemed to hold it together. She remembered again the party they'd come to here, as juniors. That was before alcohol had taken over their class. Back then, only a few of the kids had been drinking. Mia and Lexi had spent most of the night on the beach, just the two of them, listening to music coming from behind them. Zach had been dating Emily Adamson then, and Lexi remembered how sharp her longing for him had been.

The sliding glass door rattled open, and there he was.

"Lexi."

How many times had she dreamed of seeing him again, of hearing him say her name that way?

He stepped out of the cabin and moved closer. She had thought of him so often, pored over his senior picture until every inch of his face was imprinted on her memory, so she saw instantly how much he had changed. He was taller, and his shoulders were broader, even as he'd lost weight. He had on a ripped gray T-shirt that said USC and a pair of khaki shorts that hung low on his narrow hips. His face was sculpted and lean. He wasn't as heart-stoppingly handsome as he'd been before; he had a hard, tired look to him, and his eyes were sad.

"Aren't you going to say anything?" he said.

"I didn't think you'd be here."

"I didn't think *you'd* be here."

Was there accusation in his voice? She reminded herself that he'd let her down, that their daughter was unhappy living with him, but it couldn't quite grab hold, that emotion. As always, when she saw him, a part of her melted. It was her great weakness—*he* was her weakness and had been from the moment she'd first seen him. But she knew better now. He'd let her go to prison and let her give up custody of their daughter. "I needed to see Grace . . . needed to know that she was happy."

The gravity that had always connected them exerted its force, and before she knew it, she was moving toward him. It wasn't until she was close enough to be held by him that she realized he hadn't moved toward her. He had stayed where he was and let her come to him. Of course.

"Why are you here?" he said.

"I had to see my daughter."

"Our daughter."

"Yes." Lexi swallowed hard. She'd imagined this reunion a thousand times, a million, and never had it been so awkward, so seething with loss and distance. She wanted to ask him about Grace, ask if her daughter was like her at all, but she couldn't do it, couldn't hand him her heart in those few words. It was a mistake she'd made before.

He stared down at her. She could feel the heat from his body, and the soft exhalations of his every breath. "She makes a little whistling noise when she sleeps—just like you do. Used to, I mean."

Lexi didn't know how to respond. Of course he knew what was on her mind; he'd always known what she was thinking. She was breathing faster now; so was he, she noticed. She stared at his mouth and remembered how he'd looked when he smiled, and how much they used to laugh, and she felt the loss all over again.

"You never answered my letters."

"What would have been the point?" she said to him. "I thought we'd be better off if we just forgot each other. And those first two years in prison were . . . hard."

"I used to think about you all the time."

Used to. She swallowed hard, shrugged.

He touched her upper arm in a tentative, careful way, as if he were afraid she would either break or scream, or maybe he thought she wouldn't want him so close. She stood there, staring up at him, realizing with a start that she wanted him to kiss her.

Fool.

She stumbled back from him, needing distance between them. She'd been an idiot to get this close. From the moment they'd met, she'd given him her heart. How could she not have learned anything after all that had happened? "You let me go to prison," she said to remind herself who he really was.

"I had no choice."

"Believe me, Zach, you've always had choices. I'm the one who didn't." She took a deep breath and looked up at this boy—man—she'd loved from the first time she saw him, and the pain of their past was overwhelming. "I want Grace," she said evenly. "I filed the papers today."

"I know you hate me," he said. "But don't do that to Grace. She won't understand. I'm all she has."

"No," Lexi said. "That's not true anymore." She heard a car drive up, tires spin on gravel, and she had no doubt about who had arrived.

Jude. Sweeping in to save her son and granddaughter from terrible Lexi.

"Good-bye, Zach," Lexi said, turning away.

"Lexi, wait."

"No, Zach," she said without looking at him. "I've waited long enough."

⁂

Jude was shaking as she strapped Grace into her car seat.

"Ow, Nana!"

"Sorry," Jude mumbled. A headache had spiked behind her eyes, and she could hardly see. She texted Miles to get home ASAP and then climbed into the driver's seat. But she couldn't go home. Lexi knew where they lived.

"How come I'm goin' home early, Nana?" Grace said from the back-seat. "Was I bad again?"

Home. That was it.

She drove—too fast—to Zach's cabin and parked beside his truck. Once there, she took Grace in her arms and hurried inside, slamming the door shut behind her.

The sliding glass door was open. The whole place smelled of the beach at low tide. Zach stood on the deck, looking out at the Sound.

Jude carried Grace into her bedroom and put her down on her bed. Handing her a well-worn copy of *Green Eggs and Ham,* she said, "Read this for just a minute, okay? I have to tell your daddy something, and I'll be right back."

Jude left the room and closed the door behind her. Then she went out to the deck and approached her son. She could tell by his stance—his shoulders rounded in defeat, his hands plunged deep in his pockets—what had happened. She hadn't gotten here in time. "Lexi was here," she said bitterly.

"Yes."

"She wants another chance, but we don't get one. Mia will always be gone. I can't look at the girl who killed her every day."

Zach looked at her. "Grace is her daughter, Mom."

The simplicity of that made Jude catch her breath. She felt suddenly as if she were hurtling toward a precipice, as if they all were. It scared her to her bones; in the past years, they'd healed just enough to survive. They couldn't go through it again.

She'd watched from a distance as her immature, coltish boy had become a man. Grief had shattered him; fatherhood had put him back together.

She flipped open her cell phone and called the friend who had been their lawyer for years. "Bill. Jude Farraday. The girl who killed Mia is out of prison, and she's filed a petition to get custody of Grace . . . tomorrow? Great. See you then." Jude hung up the phone.

"Grace is unhappy," Zach said, and the heartbreak in his voice was terrible.

"Lexi isn't the answer, Zach. She's the cause. Remember that." Jude touched his arm. He needed her to be strong now. Maybe he'd needed that for years and not had it, but she would be there for him now; this time she would protect him.

Twenty-three

T he next morning, Jude woke up early and dressed carefully.

"It's not a funeral," Miles said when he saw her in the kitchen.

"Really? It feels like one. I'll meet you in the car," she said, hurrying away from him. The last thing she wanted to hear right now was his moral superiority or more endless questions about what they were doing. Of course, the Zen Master wanted to explore the idea that bringing Lexi into their lives could heal them. Last night, when they'd gotten home from Zach's, she'd actually told him to shut up for the first time in their marriage.

He'd learned his lesson, apparently, because he said nothing as they picked up Grace at kindergarten, dropped her off at the Silly Bear, and drove into Seattle.

At one o'clock, Zach joined them in the lobby of the Smith Tower, and by ten past, they were seated in a corner office that overlooked Elliott Bay and Pine Island. From this vantage point, the island was a mound of thick green forests floating on a steel blue sea; it looked uninhabited.

"Scot had the petition delivered to my office," Bill said when they'd finished with the pleasantries. "Alexa Baill is seeking to modify the parenting plan in which Zach has full custody."

"She wants to take Grace away from me?" Zach asked, sitting very still. "She thinks I've been a bad father?"

"No, actually. She is seeking joint custody," Bill answered.

"How can she do that?" Jude asked. "She gave up custody when Grace was born."

"Parenting plans are rarely set in stone, Jude. In this case, Alexa will need to show a substantial change in circumstances—which getting out of prison certainly provides."

"So what will happen?" Zach asked.

"First, we'll have what's called an adequate-cause hearing, which establishes only that her circumstances have changed enough to move forward. Next comes the motion for a temporary order. This will establish the custody or visitation rights pending trial. Realistically, it will be at least a year before we actually go to trial. A guardian *ad litem* will be appointed by the court to determine what the best interests of the child are and to represent Grace's interests."

"It sounds expensive," Miles said. "How can she afford that?"

"Probably a Legal Aid lawyer. Or someone might handle the case pro bono," Bill said.

"At best she'll get visitation rights; at worst, joint custody. Know this, though: the court will be pushing for reunification with the mother unless she's clearly unfit or poses a danger to Grace."

"You're saying she'll be a part of our lives forever," Jude said.

"She already is," Miles answered. "She's Grace's—"

"I wasn't speaking to you," Jude hissed at her husband. To their lawyer, she said, "But she *is* unfit. She abandoned Grace at birth and never even sent her a birthday card. She has no job, no family around here. Her own mother was a felon and a drug addict. Who's to say what friends she made in prison? We wouldn't want Grace exposed to people like that."

"Mom," Zach said, straightening. "Come on. That's not even fair. Lexi is nothing like her mother."

"You have to fight her on this," Bill said, giving Zach a steely look. "You're a father now. Not a high school kid. Your job is to protect Grace; to do that, you need to preserve your rights. If Alexa got custody, even partial, who is to say she wouldn't take off with Grace? And she made a choice, as I understand it. She's never communicated with Grace. Not once. That doesn't exactly give me a warm and fuzzy feeling about her parenting. We have to do what's in your daughter's best interest. At least for now, we have to keep her away from Grace."

"Absolutely," Jude said.

"How is that in Grace's best interests?" Zach said. "Lexi is her mother."

Bill opened a file. "I'll tell you how it's in her best interests. I've read Alexa's prison record, Zach, and it's not pretty. There are reasons she served an extra six months. Fighting. Not following the rules. She was found buying drugs in prison more than once. Valium, I believe, among others. You know who she was, Zach, but prison changes people, and it looks like your Alexa made some bad choices there. You don't know her anymore. Do you really think Grace is safe around a person like that?"

"Drugs?" Zach said, frowning.

"And with her family history. I don't think she's the girl you remember, Zach. She spent a lot of time in solitary confinement. She broke a woman's nose," Bill said. "She could actually be dangerous."

Zach sat back in his chair, sighing heavily. "Drugs," he said again, shaking his head.

"We'll fight her," Jude said. "We have no choice."

Bill nodded. "Good. I'll file our response and let you know when the adequate-cause hearing is scheduled."

❧

"I'm hurting them again, Scot," Lexi said, pacing her lawyer's office.

"Yeah," Scot said. "I imagine they don't want to be reminded of . . . what happened."

"What I did."

"What you did isn't the sum total of who you are, Lexi. We're not even talking about you here. This is about your daughter. You love her, and she needs you. That's what you have to focus on now. That's what you can control. The Farradays' grief is their problem."

She had been ruined again by just seeing Zach. Wanting him made her want to run away again, to hide. How long would she love him?

"I saw how much Zach loves her," Lexi said softly.

"It's not about him. Or them. Or what you did. It's about Grace. What does it feel like, Lexi, when a mother turns her back on you?"

Lexi stopped pacing and looked at her lawyer. "Thank you. That puts it in perspective."

His intercom buzzed. Scot reached forward and picked up his phone. "Hey Bea . . . Bill Brein, huh? Okay, thanks." Hanging up, he opened his desk calendar and wrote something down. Then he looked up at Lexi. "You're going to need to be strong, Lexi."

"I'm trying."

"Really strong," he said. "They're fighting back."

☙

Two days later, Lexi was back in a courtroom. Just stepping through the doorway brought a flood of painful memories. So much so that when Scot asked Lexi to dress in black, she said no. She would not re-create that day. Instead, the day before the hearing, she went to the thrift store again and purchased a flared, ankle-length sea-green skirt, a barely worn V-neck sweater that was only a shade or two lighter, and a pair of bronze sandals.

In her new, feminine clothes, Lexi tried to feel unlike the girl in black who'd once been taken out of a room like this in chains.

She felt Scot come up beside her. He touched her arm gently.

"They're here," he said.

She felt herself straightening; the hair on the back of her neck stood up. She tried not to turn, but how could she stop herself? That gravitational pull toward Zach was too strong.

Lexi's heart leaped a little at the sight of him. The suit he was wearing was the same one he'd worn to the homecoming dance; now it pulled across his chest.

Can I kiss you, Lexi? . . .

She looked away from him, tried to forget. She and Scot walked up to the table on the left side of the courtroom; Zach joined his lawyer at the table across the aisle from them.

The commissioner was the last to enter. He was a portly man with a shiny bald head and rimless bifocals that rested over a veiny, bulbous nose. His bailiff, an elegant Asian man in uniform, smiled brightly as he took his place near the bench.

The commissioner smoothed his robes and sat down. "We're here for adequate cause," he said, rifling through the paperwork on his desk, finally finding what he needed. "Modification of a parenting plan. Mr. Jacobs?"

Scot stood up, whispering for Lexi to do the same. "Ms. Baill is petitioning this court for a modification of the parenting plan. In 2004, Ms. Baill was an ordinary high school senior, in love for the first time, and looking forward to college. Her exemplary grades and academic record earned her a scholarship at the University of Washington. At eighteen, she had dreams of becoming a lawyer.

"One bad decision on a summer night changed everything for both my client and the Farradays. Although Zachary Farraday had promised to be the designated driver at a high school drinking party, he failed to keep his word and became inebriated. His twin sister, Mia, also drank all night. And so, tragically, Alexa offered to drive the Farradays home. It was less than a mile away.

"In the crash, Mia was killed. At the time, I counseled Alexa to plead not guilty and fight for her freedom, but Alexa is a deeply moral young woman with a profound sense of right and wrong. So she pled guilty and went to prison, hoping her incarceration would help atone for her mistake.

"She didn't know then that she was pregnant. Originally she planned to give the baby up for adoption, but Zach surprised her by offering to raise their daughter. She was so grateful and so guilt ridden over Mia's death that she agreed to give Zachary full custody.

"In prison, Alexa earned a bachelor's degree in sociology, and she hopes now to get a master's degree in social work, so that she can help other teenagers who face difficulties in their lives.

"She is a wonderful young woman, and I have no doubt that she will be an exemplary mother to her daughter. The state has a strong interest in reunification of mothers and their children. In this case, it is absolutely clear that my client has substantially changed her situation and deserves to be reunited with her daughter." Scot touched Lexi's arm, said, "Thank you," and they both sat down.

Across the aisle, Bill stood up. In the small courtroom, with its dull walls and scuffed floor, he was an imposing figure, with his expensive gray suit and stern profile.

"There can be no adequate cause to modify the parenting plan here. Ms. Baill went to Purdy for DUI vehicular homicide. A class-A felony." He paused, looked meaningfully at Lexi. "Purdy, Your Honor. That's less than an hour's drive from Pine Island. She did not have to be cut off from her daughter's life. She *chose* not to be a mother. When Zachary Farraday wrote her letters about their daughter—even sent pictures—Ms. Baill sent the envelopes back unopened. She wrote no letters to her daughter and made no phone calls. Throughout the entire duration of her incarceration, she never once attempted to communicate in any way. A former cellmate of Ms. Baill's—a Cassandra Wojocheski—will testify that Ms. Baill told her point-blank that she never intended to see her daughter.

"It's hardly surprising, this lack of a mothering instinct in Ms. Baill. Her own mother was a felon and a drug addict. For all we know, Ms. Baill has a drug problem herself.

"In conclusion, we ask that the custody agreement remain in place. Ms. Baill is not a fit parent, and her circumstances are not significantly changed from the time when she voluntarily relinquished custody of her child." Bill nodded once and sat down.

The commissioner tapped a pen on the desk.

Lexi could hardly breathe for anticipation. Bill's words had loosened a poison in her bloodstream. She could feel it burning through her veins.

"We have adequate cause to move forward here," the commissioner said. He opened the laptop on his desk and made a few keystrokes as he peered at the screen. "We'll set a trial date of April 19, 2011. Does that work for counsel?"

Both attorneys agreed.

"A year?" Lexi whispered. "That can't be—"

"Hush," Scot said sharply.

The commissioner went on. "Until then, let's move on to the motion for temporary order to begin reunification. I'll appoint a guardian *ad litem* to investigate the issues and interests herein and to report the finding to this court." He flipped through some pages. "I'll appoint Helen Adams. If she has a scheduling conflict, I'll let the parties know. And now, to the temporary plan. Mr. Jacobs?"

Scot stood up again. "Ms. Baill is seeking immediate reunification with her daughter and asks that a temporary order of joint custody be entered."

Bill stood up. "That's patently ridiculous. Ms. Baill has no job and no money and nowhere to live. How can she possibly take the responsibility of joint custody for the minor child? Additionally, Ms. Baill has no parenting skills. As I pointed out previously, her own mother was an addict who abandoned her, so Ms. Baill knows nothing about positive parenting. Perhaps after some parenting classes she would be ready to assume some limited custodial care, but not now. Also, we should overlook neither Ms. Baill's bad behavior in prison—she was repeatedly sent to solitary confinement in 2005 for fighting and drug use—nor the flight risk she poses. Her only family is in Florida. Who is to say she won't try to take Grace away with her? She's already shown a disregard for the laws. We submit that there should be no visitation and no attempt at reunification until the parenting plan is modified next year. That will allow Ms. Baill time to show her true desires with regard to parenting."

"Your Honor!" Scot said, rising. "That's punitive on its face. Ms. Baill does not have a drug problem. It's—"

The commissioner held up his big hand. "I am going to allow supervised visitation between your client and her daughter. Because of the severity of this situation and the extreme separation that has occurred, a professional reunification specialist will supervise every visit unless one of the child's relatives agrees to be present. Between now and the trial date, this court will receive regular reports from the GAL." He hit his gavel on the desk. "Next case."

Lexi felt that little gavel strike reverberate up her spine. Turning to Scot, she tried to keep a smile on her face for his benefit. He had tried so hard. She didn't want him to know how the words *supervised visitation* sickened her. She'd been in that room before, under the watchful eyes of some dispassionate professional; only she'd been the little girl. Now she'd be the untrustworthy mother. "I get to spend time with her, that's what matters, right?"

Scot took her by the elbow and steered her toward the side door. Once in the hallway, he led her down to a quiet corner. "I'm sorry, Lexi."

"Don't be sorry. I know you did your best. And I get to see her. Get to *know* her. I'll prove to all of them that I deserve another chance. A year is a long time. Maybe by then—"

"It's not that simple," he said.

"What do you mean?"

"The court wants a professional social worker to accompany your visits, someone who specializes in difficult reunifications."

"I heard that."

"People like that are really, really expensive."

An unfamiliar bitterness welled up in Lexi, left a sour taste in her mouth. "Of course it comes down to money."

"I'll get started on research. There must be a way around this, but all I can see on its face is to ask one of the Farradays to supervise."

"Yeah. *That's* going to happen."

"Don't give up, Lexi. I'll keep trying."

"Sure," she said, slinging her purse over her shoulder. She couldn't wait to get out of these ridiculously girly clothes. She should have known better. The whole legal system was set up to give people like the Farradays what they wanted. "I'm outta here, Scot. Thanks." She started to walk away.

He grabbed her by the arm. "Don't do anything stupid, Lexi."

"Like what? Love my daughter?" Her voice broke on that and she turned away, walking fast.

Twenty-four

Lexi sat on a park bench outside Scot's office.

She knew about giving up. Back when she'd been neglected by her mother, and, later, when one foster family after another let her go, she had tried to stop hoping for more. As a young girl, sitting in a series of crowded government offices, waiting for new parents, she'd stared at the clock on the wall, watching the minutes tick past, thinking with every tiny *click* that this time she wouldn't care, this time she would give up her hope, and, without it, she would be invulnerable.

But it had never worked. For some reason she'd never quite understood, hope was hardwired into her. Even in prison, when she'd stood in lines of women who wore blank, hopeless expressions, she had been unable to become one of them. Even Valium hadn't helped to dim that small bright part of her. The problem was that she *believed*. She wasn't sure what she believed in—was it God? goodness? herself? She had no answer to the question; she knew only that she owned this belief that if she did the right thing, if she always did her best and took responsibility for her mistakes and lived a moral life, she would succeed. She would not become like her mother.

But she'd done all of that. She'd gone to prison to atone for her mistake. She'd given up her daughter because she loved Grace so, so much. She had tried to do the right things, and yet still she was being thwarted.

She had the right to see Grace, but not the money.

How could she take a whole year of living in this community, seeing her daughter, but never being able to be with her? And how could she get a job—as an ex-con with practically no work history or recommendations—that would pay her rent and living expenses and give her enough left over for legal fees and social worker bills? And if she did somehow accomplish all of that, she would spend weekends with her daughter always being judged and scrutinized. How could a real relationship bloom under such dark skies?

It would be easier to give up. She could hop on a bus to Florida, where apparently the sun always shone. Once there, she could write letters to Grace—no one could deny her that now—and she and her daughter could get to know each other the old-fashioned way. Maybe in a few years, a visit could be arranged.

All she had to do was give up. Just concede defeat and get on the next bus.

Abandon her daughter a second time.

Just the thought of it made her ill. She remembered all the hours she'd spent in solitary confinement, feeling as if she were draining away in that fetid darkness, wanting to disappear. It had been Grace that pulled her out of all that, Grace who had convinced Lexi to quit tranquilizing herself with Valium and acting out with her fists. Grace who had made her come back to herself. At least, it had been the idea of Grace.

She got up and went into Scot's office. Waving at the receptionist, she walked into his office without knocking. "I'm sorry to bother you."

"You're no bother, Lexi," he said, pushing out from behind his desk.

She pulled out the one hundred dollar bill Aunt Eva had sent her. "How much time with Grace will this get me?"

"Not much," he said sadly.

Lexi bit her lip. She knew what to say next, but she was afraid. "There's really only one way for me to see my daughter, isn't there?"

Scot nodded slowly.

Another minute passed. She waited for him to talk her out of it.

"Okay, then," she said after a long silence. Resettling her purse over her shoulder, she left the office. Outside, she unlocked the bike and climbed aboard, riding out of town. Although it would have saved her three miles, she avoided Night Road and went the long way. She didn't allow herself to think about where she was going or what she was going to do until she reached her destination.

At the top of the long gravel driveway, she got off her bike.

The house still looked beautiful against the blue Sound and even bluer sky. The garden was an absolute mess, but only someone who'd seen it before would know that. To the first-time observer, it was simply a riot of color.

Lexi held on to the handlebars and guided the bike down the bumpy road. At the garage, she laid the bike gently on its side in the shorn grass and then she walked up to the front door and rang the bell.

It was funny how that one little action—ringing the doorbell—thrust her back in time. For a split second, she was innocent again, an eighteen-year-old girl, wearing her boyfriend's ring, coming to her best friend's house.

The door opened and Jude stood there. In a black T-shirt and leggings, she looked dangerously thin; her pale hands and feet seemed too big, and bony, with blue veins just beneath the skin. Lavender shadows beneath her eyes aged her, and a line of gray hair ran along her part.

"You have a lot of nerve coming here," Jude finally said. Her voice was shaking a little, and that vibration helped Lexi gain control of her own runaway nerves.

"You've got some nerve, yourself. She's my daughter."

"Grace isn't here. And the day care won't let you see her again."

"I didn't come here to see Grace," Lexi said. "I came here to see you."

"Me?" Jude was growing paler by the second. "Why?"

"May I come in?"

Jude hesitated, and then backed up, whether to let Lexi in or put distance between them, she wasn't sure; still, Lexi walked inside and closed the door behind her.

The first thing she saw was Mia's shamrock green button-up sweater hanging from the hall tree. She drew in a sharp breath and reached for it.

"Don't touch that," Jude said sharply.

Lexi drew her hand back.

"What do you want?"

Lexi couldn't stand here next to this sweater she could neither touch nor turn away from, so she walked past Jude and went into the glass-walled great room. Through the floor-to-ceiling windows, she saw the beach. Just over there, Zach had told her he loved her . . . and there, they'd buried their time capsule. Their proof. Their pact.

She turned her back on the view. Jude was standing by the massive fireplace now, with its roaring fire on this summer day, and still she looked cold.

Lexi remembered how beautiful and confident Jude used to be, how much Lexi had ached for a mother like her. "You remember the first time we met?" Lexi said quietly, not moving closer. "It was the first day of freshman year. I just went up to Mia and asked if I could sit with her. She told me it was social suicide, and I said—"

"Don't . . ."

"You don't want to remember. I get it. Do you think *I* do? I can feel her sitting here; I can hear her laughing, saying, 'Madre, can you make us something to eat?' and you laughing, saying, 'I live to serve you, Mia.' I was so jealous of the kind of family you were. The kind of mother you were. I used to dream that I could belong here, but you know that. It's why you wanted Zach to go to USC. You wanted him away from me." Lexi sighed. "Maybe you were right. What would I do if Grace fell in love at seventeen? Who knows? It's so young. I see that now. Too young." She moved toward Jude, who flinched at her approach. "You used to be the best mother in the world."

"So?" Jude said dully.

"So . . . you should know how I feel about Grace. Why I need to see her. You, of all people, should understand."

Jude drew in a sharp breath and crossed her arms in front of her chest. "Go, Lexi. Now."

"I can't afford a social worker to supervise my visits with Grace. But I could see her if *you* would supervise me."

"Get out of my house."

Lexi closed the distance between them. She could feel the animosity in Jude, but there was also sadness in her, and it was to the sadness that Lexi spoke. "You love Grace. I know you do. You're like me—you don't know how to go forward or backward, maybe, but you remember how love feels. I'm her mother. Regardless of what I've done, she needs to know I love her. If she doesn't know that . . ." Lexi's voice finally broke. "I won't hurt Grace. I swear it. And I'll stay away from Zach. Just let me get to know my daughter. I'm begging you."

Lexi tried to think of more to say, but nothing came to her. The silence between them grew heavy, and finally Lexi shrugged and walked to the front door, where the green sweater was a sharp reminder of her best friend. Pausing, she glanced back at the great room. Jude hadn't moved.

"Mia would have been on my side in this," Lexi said.

Jude finally looked at her. "Thanks to you, we'll never know, will we?"

Jude stood there, freezing cold, staring at the closed door, at the blur of green beside it, trying not to feel anything at all. At some point, she became aware that the phone was ringing. Walking woodenly into the kitchen, she picked up the cordless handset and answered. "Hello?"

"The phone rang and rang," her mother said.

Jude sighed. "Did it?"

"Are you having another one of your bad days? I could—"

"Lexi was just here," she said, surprised to hear the words spoken aloud. She didn't really want to talk about this with her mother—hell, she didn't want to talk about anything with her mother—but right now, she couldn't hold back. Her nerves felt as if they were poking out of her body.

"The girl who was driving the car that night?"

"Yes."

"Oh. My. That takes some nerve."

"That's what I told her." Jude sagged against the wall, feeling depleted by the whole thing. "She wants me to supervise visitations so she can see Grace."

"You told her no, of course. That's what I would do."

It took a moment for her mother's words to sink in. When they did, Jude straightened. "That's what you would do?"

"Of course."

Jude pulled away from the wall and walked over to the window. Looking out, she saw her mangled, untended garden. It was a heady mix of bright color and dying black leaves. *That's what I would do.*

"You can't let that girl hurt you again," her mother said.

Mia would be on my side in this.

Her mother was still talking, saying something about grief, maybe, as if she knew what Jude were feeling right now, but Jude wasn't really listening. She started moving toward the stairs, drifting like a woman caught in a rip current. Before she knew it, she was at Mia's bedroom door, reaching for the knob, opening it for the first time in years. She went to the closet, opened it, and stepped inside. A light came on automatically, and there it was, just as she'd left it. The box marked *Mia*.

A fine layer of dust attested to how long she'd been away. It had taken her years to find the strength to pack up these belongings. And once she'd done it, there had been no strength left to remember them.

"Good-bye, Mother," she said, and hung up the phone, dropping it to the carpeted floor. She sank to her knees and opened the flaps. The mementos of Mia's short life lay carefully arranged within. Yearbooks. Trophies for soccer and volleyball. An old pink tutu that had once fit a six-year-old. USC sweats. Barbie dolls with no clothes and a pair of scuffed white baby shoes. Everything except the journal, which she'd never found.

She pulled each item out, smelling them, holding them to her face. Although she'd cried for years and years, it felt as if these tears were new somehow, hotter; they burned her eyes and her cheeks. At the bottom of the box lay a framed picture of Mia and Zach and Lexi, their arms hung negligently around one another. The smiles on their faces were bright and shiny.

She could almost hear them laughing . . .

Mia would have been on my side in this.

Strangely, that sentence brought back Mia as brightly as if she'd just sailed through the door, saying, *hey Madre,* and laughing. And not the Mia of static memories, but Mia herself, with her megawatt smile and crazy fashion sense and her insecurities.

Mia *would* be on Lexi's side in this. The thought of her daughter's opinion shamed Jude to the depths of her soul. Mother had appealed to the worst in Jude—*you told her no, of course.* Lexi had appealed to the best in her.

You used to be the best mother in the world.

The words brought memories surging forward, and Jude was too exhausted, too depleted to hold them at bay any longer. She thought of Mia as she'd been in senior year—a quiet, thoughtful eighteen-year-old girl who had no idea how beautiful she'd become, who'd fallen in love for the first time and had her heart broken by a boy. A girl who loved without boundaries and found joy in simple things—an old stuffed rabbit, a Disney movie, a hug from her mother.

At that, Jude felt something break inside of her, like muscle tearing away from bone.

Hola, Madre, how was your day?

They'd thought they were fluent, both of her kids, after a year of Spanish. It used to crack Jude up, and they'd known it.

She sat there a long time, remembering Mia for the first time in years—really remembering her—and in finding the memories of her

daughter, she reclaimed a lost piece of herself. And she was ashamed of
who she had let herself become.

Jude had no idea how long she sat there.

Finally she looked down at her watch, surprised to see that it was time
to pick up Grace from day care. In the old days, she would have forgotten
her granddaughter on a day like this. She would have spent hours in the
closet, perhaps even fallen asleep. Now she went downstairs, found her
car keys, and drove over to the Silly Bear, where she parked out front,
right on time.

"Hey, Nana," Grace said wanly when Jude showed up, and it struck
Jude suddenly, sharply, what Lexi had said: she's afraid of you.

On the short drive to Zach's house, Jude watched Grace in the rearview mirror.

She looked so much like Mia, but for once, it wasn't the physical simi-
larities that hurt Jude; it was the differences. Mia and Zach had laughed
and chattered constantly, exploring their world like a pair of miniature
Magellans, confident and happy . . . and secure in the knowledge that
they were loved.

Jude parked the car and helped her granddaughter out of her car seat.
Grace scrambled out of the car and bounded up to the house.

"You want to play a game?" Jude said, coming up beside her.

Grace looked up at her in obvious surprise. "*You* wanna play with me?"

"Sure."

"Goody!" Grace ran into the house and back to her bedroom. She
emerged a few moments later, holding a brightly colored Chutes and
Ladders box. "You ready?"

Jude followed Grace to the table.

"You seemed quiet today at day care," Jude said, moving her game
piece forward.

Grace shrugged.

"How come?"

Grace shrugged again. "Jake's mom brought treats."

"And you didn't get any?"

"I got some." Grace stared down at the board.

"Oh." Jude said, getting it. "His *mom* brought treats."

"Everyone's mom brings stuff sometimes."

Jude sat back in her chair. How could this possibly surprise her? For eighteen years, she'd been the mom who brought treats. She'd been the party mom, the field trip mom, the constant presence. But she'd never done any of that for her granddaughter. "I could bring cupcakes sometime."

"Okay," Grace said, not looking up.

Again, Jude understood. "It's not the same as a mom, is it?"

"Are you gonna play?"

"Sure," Jude said. For the next hour, she concentrated on moving through the multicolored squares. She kept up a steady stream of conversation, and by the second game Grace had started to talk to her.

But she knew Lexi was right: Grace was not a happy little girl. Most of her talk was directed to the small mirror on her wrist, her imaginary friend. And why did children create imaginary playmates? You didn't need to be a shrink to answer that question. It was because they felt too alone and had no real friends.

Jude was watching Grace so closely she didn't hear the front door open.

Zach walked into the cabin, tossing his heavy backpack onto the coffee table.

"Daddy!" Grace's face lit up as she ran into Zach's arms. He scooped her up and kissed her all over her face, until she giggled and told him to stop.

Miles came in behind him, smiling.

Jude stared at the two of them—the husband she'd loved for so long and practically abandoned and the boy she'd nurtured like a rare flower for so much of his life and then turned away from. She saw the marks that grief had left on their skin, in their eyes, even in their posture, and she knew the part she had played in all of this. She had been the mud that kept them mired in grief. On their own, they might have healed.

You used to be the best mother in the world.

Jude stood up. "I need to talk to you two."

Zach frowned. "Gracie, why don't you get your coloring book and crayons? I love watching you color."

"Okay, Daddy." She slid out of his arms and scampered off.

Jude clasped her hands together. She had their full attention now, but she was afraid to say the words out loud. "Lexi came to see me today."

Zach went very still. "What did she want?"

Jude looked at her son. He was a man; young, but a man, and she was so proud of him she could hardly bear it. When in the last few years had she told him that? "She asked me to supervise her visits with Grace. She can't afford the court-ordered social worker."

"What did you say?" Miles asked, moving to stand by his son.

"She can't get to know . . . her daughter unless I agree," Jude said, stalling now.

"What did you say?" Zach asked the question again.

Jude felt the rapid beating of her heart. "I'm scared," she said softly. It was perhaps the most vulnerable she'd felt in years. She was out of control and uncertain and afraid. Usually she hid those emotions away from Zach and Miles, boxed them up; now she didn't have that kind of strength.

She moved toward Zach, who had never been afraid when his sister was alive, and never lonely, but now she saw both of those emotions in his eyes. "I don't want to do it," Jude said, "but I will."

"You will?" Zach said quietly.

"For Grace and Mia," Jude said, gazing up at her son. "And for you."

Twenty-five

Something weird was happening.

Grace and Ariel were on the sofa, curled up in Grace's favorite fuzzy yellow blanket. The cabin lights were low and it was dark outside, so she couldn't really see her wrist mirror, but she knew Ariel was there because she was humming. Ariel loved to hum.

Grace couldn't tell time, but she knew it was late. She never got to stay up this long after dinner, and the movie on the TV had all kinds of bad words in it, and no one cared that she was hearing it. Or that she saw some guy shoot a bad guy in the head.

No one was paying attention to Grace at all. Daddy and Nana and Papa had been whispering together all night. They'd made a bunch of phone calls and looked at Daddy's school calendar about twenty times. Grace didn't know what they were talking about, but Nana kept snapping at Papa, saying things like, *I know what you think, Miles,* and, *What will I say to her? Maybe I've made a mistake . . .*

Papa said it was _too late_ for that because _Lexi knows_ and the loud whispering had begun again.

"Who's Lexi?" Grace asked, looking up from the sofa.

The three grownups stopped talking and looked at her.

"It's time for bed, Princess," Daddy said, and Grace wished she'd kept her big fat mouth shut. Whining, she shuffled over to her Papa and opened her arms for a hug. He scooped her up and twirled her around, kissing her neck. She clung to him still, giggling as he let her go, and she slipped back down to the floor.

Grace went to Nana, who stood by the sliding glass door, chewing on her thumbnail. It took a lot of nerve, but Grace said, "Nana? Thanks for playing Chutes and Ladders with me."

Nana stopped biting her thumbnail and looked down.

Grace tried to smile, but it wasn't very good.

Then Nana did the most amazing thing: she bent down and picked Grace up.

Grace was so surprised she gasped. She would have hugged her Nana, but it was over so fast Grace barely had time to blink before Nana was whispering, "Night, Gracie. Don't let the bed bugs bite."

It was so _weird_. Grace sidled close to her daddy and slipped her hand in his back pocket, just so she could be close to him. He plucked her up and carried her down to the bathroom they both used. He helped her brush her teeth and get ready for bed. When she had on her jammies, he put her in her bed and sat down beside her.

Her room was messy, with toys everywhere, and her Wall-E comforter in a bunch at the end of the bed. Daddy pulled it up carefully, tucking Grace in.

"Are we gonna read more of _The Secret Garden_ tonight, Daddy?"

"Not tonight, Princess."

Ask him.

"What?" Grace whispered furiously to her wrist.

"How come you're talking to Ariel when I'm right here?" Daddy said, frowning at her.

"Ariel thinks something weird is happening."

"She does, does she? And what does she think it is?"

"What is it?" Grace whispered to her wristband, but Ariel had vanished. "I guess she went to sleep."

Daddy reached over and unhooked Grace's wristband.

"Can't she sleep with me tonight?" Grace mumbled. It was an old fight, and she didn't expect to win, but she had to ask.

"You know the rules. She sleeps on the nightstand."

Her daddy stretched out on the narrow bed, with her big stuffed panda bear as a pillow behind him. Grace snuggled against him and looked up. "Daddy?"

He stroked her hair. "What, Gracie?"

"Who's Lexi?"

He stopped stroking her hair. "Lexi is your mother."

Grace scrambled to sit up. This was news. "What?"

"Lexi is your mother, Grace."

"Wow," Grace said. "Is she a spy?"

"No, honey, she's not."

"An astronaut?"

"No."

Grace felt bad, but she wasn't sure why. "Where has she been?"

"She's been . . . busy. I guess those are questions you'll have to ask her."

"I get to ask her questions?"

"She wants to see you, Gracie."

"She does?" Grace felt a brand-new emotion unfold with her. It was shiny, like tinfoil, and sparkly as a birthday crown. "Did she miss me?"

"I think she did," he answered.

"Wow," Grace said again. She tried to imagine what it would be like to have a mommy, someone who would know everything about her and love her anyway. Now Grace would finally be like all of the other kids.

But why had her mommy left her in the first place? And how long was she gonna stay? What if she didn't like Grace? What if—

"Daddy?" Grace said, frowning. "How come you look sad?"

"I'm not sad, honey."

"Don't you want me to see my mommy?"

"Of course I do," he said, but she could tell that he was lying. She'd seen him look sad lots of times, but this time he looked worse than sad.

"What if she doesn't like me?"

"It's me she doesn't like, Princess."

"If she doesn't like you, I don't like her," Grace said, crossing her arms. She could tell that her daddy was hardly listening to her. He was just staring at the picture on the nightstand—the picture of him and his sister sitting on a gray beach log.

He didn't want her to see her mommy. Why?

And suddenly Grace was scared. She remembered what happened to Allyson in her class last year when her parents got divorced. One day Ally was in class and the next day she was gone to live with her mommy, who moved away. "I'm gonna see her, but I'm staying with you, right, Daddy? Right?"

Her daddy said, "Right, Gracie. Of course," but for the first time in her life, she didn't believe her dad.

"I'm staying with you," she said stubbornly.

Lexi had spent the last twenty-four hours on an emotional roller coaster, rising with hope and plunging with fear. Through it all, she planned and organized. She gathered up the shoe box full of letters she'd written to Grace in prison and tied a ribbon around it. Her gift to her daughter. It was all she had.

And then, she waited impatiently.

Finally, though, it was time. She climbed onto her borrowed bike and pedaled out of town.

At the Farradays' driveway, she slowed and rode cautiously down the gravel road. After parking the bike near the garage, she slung her ragged, out-of-style purse over her shoulder and went to the front door. There, she took one deep breath and rang the bell.

Jude opened the door almost immediately. Her face was pale, her eyes icy. No makeup added false vibrancy to her face, and without it she looked both younger and older. Her blond hair—in need of a dye job—

was pulled back into a severe ponytail, and she was dressed in soft white knit pants and a watery gray sweater. All in all, she looked colorless, a woman made of clouds. "Please knock in the future. I don't like the bell. Come in."

Lexi stood there, reminded of what she'd done by the look in Jude Farraday's eyes.

Jude stepped back to allow Lexi into the house.

The green sweater caught her eye.

"One hour," Jude said. "And you'll stay in the great room."

Lexi nodded. Unable to look at the pain on Jude's face any longer, she moved past her and went into the great room. Sunlight streamed through the windows and seemed to set the exotic wood ablaze. A fire burned in the giant fireplace and sent waves of unnecessary heat into the room.

At Lexi's entrance, Grace stood up. The little girl was dressed in a pretty yellow blouse and pale blue overalls. A pair of blond pigtails stuck out above each ear like apostrophe marks.

"Hi," Grace said brightly. "I'm waiting for my mommy."

"I'm Lexi," Lexi said nervously.

"*You're* Lexi?" Grace said.

"I am."

Grace looked at her suspiciously. "You're my mommy?"

Lexi had to clear her throat. "I am."

Grace made a squealing sound and ran for Lexi.

Lexi picked up her daughter for the second time in her life, holding her so tightly that Grace started to squirm. Sliding down to her feet, Grace grabbed Lexi's hand and dragged her over to the sofa, where they sat down together.

Grace snuggled up to Lexi. "You wanna play a game?"

"Can we just sit here a minute? It feels so good to hold you again."

"What do you mean, again?"

"When you were born, the doctor put you in my arms for the first time. You were so little and pink. Your fist was the size of a grape."

"How come you didn't want me?"

"I did want you," Lexi said softly, seeing the confusion in her daughter's green eyes. "I wanted you like crazy." She offered Grace the shoe box full of letters. "I wrote these letters to you."

Grace frowned down at the wrinkled letters stacked in the dusty box, and Lexi couldn't help feeling ashamed, as if her love was as threadbare as her offering. "Oh."

"I know it isn't much of a present."

"My daddy loved me from the first second he saw me."

"Yes, he did."

Grace's lower lip trembled just a little. "He says you named me Grace and he named me Mia."

"He loved his sister more than anyone else in the world. Except you."

Grace peered up at Lexi. "Did you know her?"

Lexi heard Jude's sharp intake of breath. Lexi looked up. Across the room, Jude stared back at her.

"She was my best friend in the whole world," Lexi said. "Mia Eileen Farraday. You are so lucky to look like her. She loved practical jokes. Did anyone ever tell you that? She used to put Saran Wrap across your daddy's toilet seat. And she couldn't sing at all, but she thought she could, and when your dad told her to shut up, she laughed and sang louder." Lexi felt something open up inside of her when she talked about Mia. These memories had been trapped for so long, like a dragonfly in amber, but now they were softening. She looked at Jude. "I gave Mia that green sweater hanging in the entryway. It took all the money I made one month, but when I saw it, I knew it would be perfect—it would match her eyes—and I wanted her to know how much her friendship meant to me."

"Daddy never talks about her."

"Yeah," Lexi said, looking down at her daughter again. "It's easier that way, I guess. When you love someone . . . and you lose them, you can kind of lose yourself, too. But your daddy has had you to love all these years. I want that, too."

"What do you mean?"

"What would you think about living with me sometimes? We could get to know each other, and I could—"

"I *knew* it." Grace scrambled off the couch. "I am not gonna leave my daddy."

"I didn't mean that, Grace."

"You did. You said it." She ran over to where Jude sat and climbed into her lap, coiling around her like a baby monkey.

Lexi followed. She knelt on the hardwood at Jude's feet. "I'm sorry, Grace, I—"

Grace twisted around to look at Lexi. "You didn't want me."

"I did," Lexi said.

"Why'd you leave me?"

How could she answer that? As she knelt there, staring at her frightened daughter, she remembered *being* that little girl, confused by a mother who'd never wanted her but sometimes pretended to. The memories sickened her, made her feel pathetic and selfish. "I always loved you, Gracie."

Grace jutted out her pointed chin. "I don't believe you. Good mommies don't *leave*."

Lexi remembered saying the same thing to her own mother, who had burst into tears and sworn that her love was true.

She knew, better than anyone, that only time could prove the truth of her love. Grace would have to *learn* to believe her mother loved her.

"I wanna live with my daddy," Grace said stubbornly.

"Of course you do," Lexi said. "I was wrong to say anything. I've been . . . away for a long time, and I don't know much about little girls. But I want to learn."

"You're a mommy. You should already know," Grace said, clutching Jude's sleeve.

What could Lexi say to that? She got slowly to her feet and looked down at them. "Maybe I should go. Thank you, Jude," she said thickly. "I know you didn't do it for me, but thank you."

"You're leaving me *again*?" Grace asked.

"I'll come back," Lexi promised, backing away. In ten minutes with her daughter, she'd done everything wrong. She'd scared Gracie. "Next week, okay? Same day and time?"

"You left something on the couch," Jude said.

Lexi looked back at the stack of letters. They looked small from here, dirty and disheveled in this perfect room. She'd been a fool to think that letters would matter to a five-year-old. Another mistake. "They're for Grace," was all she could manage to say, and then she left her daughter again.

∗∖∗

"She doesn't even know I can't read," Grace said, her voice heavy with disappointment. She slithered out of Jude's grasp and got to her feet. "When does my daddy get home?"

Jude couldn't take her eyes away from the battered shoe box on her sofa. It looked absurdly small and out of place against the expensive fabric.

"Nana?" Grace said, stomping her foot for emphasis. "I want to go home."

Jude looked up, seeing Grace standing by the fireplace with a mutinous look in her eyes. Her granddaughter was scared, and so she lashed out. It was exactly what Zach would have done at that age. "Okay. But I don't know when your daddy will be home."

"I don't care," Grace said, but her voice wobbled a little.

"You want a hug?"

"I just wanna see my daddy."

Jude sighed. It was hardly surprising that Grace didn't want to be comforted by a grandmother who'd spent years ignoring her. "Get your things together and we'll go."

As Grace picked up her toys, Jude walked slowly into the living room. For a moment or two, she stared at the shoe box full of letters.

"I'm ready," Grace said, holding her yellow blanket against her cheek.

Jude picked up the box and carried it out to the car. She strapped Grace into her car seat and placed the letters in the passenger seat beside her, where now they seemed to take up a lot of room.

Jude could tell how upset her granddaughter was, and she wanted to soothe the little girl, but too many separate years had left them strangers.

Grace didn't even look to her grandmother for comfort. "It's okay to be upset, Gracie. Meeting your mom is confusing, I'll bet."

Grace ignored her, talking furiously to her wrist.

Jude stared down at her granddaughter for a long time, perhaps longer than ever before, and then slowly, she stepped back and closed the car door. On the way back to Zach's, Jude tried to start a few conversations, but Grace didn't answer. The little girl just kept saying, *come back, Ariel, I need you, really,* and the fervent whispers reminded Jude of years ago, when a little girl who looked just like Grace used to whisper to her brother constantly in a language only he could understand.

At the cabin, Jude parked and helped Grace out of her car seat.

She took hold of Grace's small hand. "How about if I read you a story?"

Grace looked suspicious. Finally, she said, "Okay," slowly, as if she expected Jude to rescind the offer and maybe start laughing.

They walked silently into the cabin and Grace headed straight for her bedroom. She grabbed the silvery white princess doll that was her favorite and climbed up onto the white spindle bed, wiggling under the colorful Wall-E comforter. "I'm sucking my thumb," she said defiantly.

Jude couldn't help smiling. "Maybe I will, too." She popped her thumb into her mouth.

Grace smiled. "You're too old."

Laughing at that, Jude went to the bookcase.

A thin white-jacketed book caught her eye. Slowly, she picked it out from among the others and sat next to Grace. Opening the book, she began to read: "The day Max wore his wolf suit and made mischief of one kind or another and his mother called him 'Wild Thing' . . ." The words took Jude back to a room that was full of action figures and plastic dinosaurs, to a little boy who laughed all the time and wouldn't listen to stories unless his sister was beside him. The memories were close enough to inhale. For a second, she was a young mother again, sitting in the middle of a big king-sized bed with a baby tucked under each arm and a book open in her lap . . .

"It's not sad, Nana. Why are you crying?"

"I forgot how much I loved this book. It reminds me of my . . . children." It was the first time in years she'd said the tender word aloud. Children. She'd had two.

"I like it, too," Grace said earnestly, moving closer to Jude, almost snuggling up against her. For a long time, they sat there, connected as Jude read the story. When she closed the book and looked down, Grace was asleep.

She kissed Grace's soft pink cheek and left the room, closing the door behind her.

In the living room, she found the letters waiting for her, sitting on the coffee table where she'd left them.

They weren't hers to open.

Still, she stared down at the accordionlike array of letters. The envelopes were unsealed; she could see that. Maybe Lexi had wanted to reread what she'd written over the years.

She finally picked up the whole box and sat down with them in her lap. She stared at them a long time, knowing it was wrong to read them.

Just one. To see if this will break Zach's heart . . .

She pulled out the first envelope in the box and opened it. The letter inside was written on cheap white paper. Gray splotches marred the surface. Tears.

This letter was dated November 2005. It had taken Lexi a long time to write this first letter.

With a tightening in her chest that felt a little like the start of a panic attack, Jude began to read. She had read only the first few paragraphs when the front door opened and Zach walked in. He looked nervous, upset.

"Hey, Mom," he said, tossing his backpack onto the floor. It skidded across the hardwood and thunked against the wall. He shoved the hair out of his eyes impatiently. "How did it go with Lexi today?"

Had it always been that way, she wondered suddenly? Had he always had Lexi on the forefront of his mind? And if so, how hard had it been to shut those feelings off?

"Listen to this," Jude said.

"Can I listen later? I want to know—"

"It's a letter Lexi wrote to Grace in prison."

"Oh, man . . ." Zach collapsed onto the La-Z-Boy chair by the fireplace.

Jude saw how afraid he was to hear these words, and she understood. It was easier to suppress heartache than to overcome it. At least that was the road they'd both chosen. She cleared her throat and began to read:

Dear Grace,

I was eighteen years old when I had you. It seems sort of dumb to say since I'm only nineteen now, but I figured it would be something you'd want to know about me.

I wish I could forget about you. That's a terrible thing to say, but if you were old enough to read this letter you'd already know where I am and what I did. Why I can't be your mother.

So, I wish I could forget you.

But I can't.

I wake up in this place and the first thing I think of is you. I wonder if your eyes turned green like your dad's or if they are blue like mine. I wonder if you sleep through the night yet. If I could, I'd sing you to sleep every night. Not that I know any lullabies.

I fell in love with you before I ever even saw you. How is that possible? But I did, and then I held you, and then I handed you to Zach.

What was I supposed to do? Have you visit me in this place, have you see me through bars? I know how bad that is.

I read somewhere that grief can be like breaking a bone. You have to set it right or it can ache forever. I pray that someday you'll understand that and forgive me.

I won't send you this letter, but maybe someday when you're grown up, you'll come looking for me and I'll have this box of letters and I'll give them to you. I'll say <u>See? I loved you.</u> Maybe you'll even believe me.

Until then, at least, I know you're safe. I used to dream I was a

Farraday. You're so lucky to have the family you do. If you're sad,
go to Miles. He can always make you laugh. Or ask Jude for a
hug—no one hugs better than your grandma.
   And then there's your dad. If you let him, he'll show you all the
stars in the sky and he'll make you feel like you can fly.
   So I won't worry about you, Gracie.
   I'm going to try to forget you. I'm sorry, but I have to.
   It hurts so much to love you.

Jude looked up at her son, whose eyes were bright with tears. He looked like her boy again, her golden Zach, and in that moment, she remembered the young Lexi, the girl who'd worn her heart on her sleeve and been the best friend Mia had ever had. She remembered the girl from the trailer park who had never known a mother's love and yet always had a smile on her face. "It didn't go well today with Lexi and Grace. Lexi screwed up."

"What do you mean?"

"She went too quickly, pushed Grace before she was ready."

"She doesn't know how to be a mom. How could she?"

"No one does," Jude said quietly. "I remember how overwhelmed I felt by you and . . . Mia."

"You were a great mom."

Jude couldn't look at him. "Once, maybe. Not anymore, though. I haven't acted like your mom in a long time, and we both know it. I . . . lost that. I thought . . ." She paused and forced herself to look at him again. "I blamed you. I did, even though I know I shouldn't. And I blamed Lexi. And myself."

"It wasn't your fault. We knew better . . . that night," he said.

Jude felt a searing pain in her heart at the reminder. It was the kind of pain that had always been a barrier before, something from which to retreat. Now she pushed through it.

"You're right," she said softly. "You shouldn't have drunk that night, but Lexi shouldn't have driven, and I shouldn't have let you go. I knew there was going to be drinking there. What was I thinking to trust drunk eighteen-year-olds to make wise decisions? Why did I just assume that we couldn't stop you from drinking? And . . . Mia should have had her seatbelt on. There's blame enough to go around."

"It's *my* fault," he said, and although Jude had heard him say it before, she felt the weight of his burden for the first time. It shamed her that she'd been so focused on her own grief that she'd let her son carry his alone.

She went to him, took him by the hand, and pulled him to his feet. "We *all* carry this, Zach. We've carried it for so long it's reshaped our spines, bent us. We have to stand up again. We have to forgive ourselves."

"How?" he asked simply. In his green eyes, she saw Mia, too. She'd forgotten that somehow, in her grief; her babies were twins, and Mia would always be alive in Zach. And now there was Grace, too.

She put a hand on his face, seeing the faint scar along his jawline. "She's there . . . in you," she said gently. "How did I forget that?"

Twenty-six

"Come on," Lexi-Mommy says, holding out her hand. "You want to live with me, don't you?"

The hand turns black and long yellow nails grow out from the fingers like hooks, and Grace screams—

"I'm right here, Princess."

She heard her daddy's voice and threw her arms around him. He smelled like he was supposed to, and the nightmare faded away until she remembered that she was in her own bed, in her own room, just where she belonged. There were no wild things here.

Her dad held her close and stroked her hair. "You okay?"

She felt like a baby. "Sorry, Daddy," she mumbled.

"Everyone has bad dreams sometimes."

She knew that was true, because when she was little, she used to hear him screaming in his sleep, and she'd go to him and climb into his bed.

He never woke up, but he stopped yelling when she was with him. In the morning, he'd smile tiredly at her and say something about how she really should be a big girl and learn to sleep in her own bed.

"Don't make me go away, Daddy. I won't lie anymore. I promise. And I won't sock Jacob in the nose, *ever.* I'll be good."

"Ah, Princess," he said, sighing. "I should have known your mom would come back for you. I should have prepared us both. It's just . . . I tried not to think about her."

"Cuz she's mean?"

"No," Daddy said, and it scared her, how sad he sounded. "She's the opposite of mean."

"Maybe she got mean when she was a spy."

"She's not a spy, Princess."

"How do you know?"

"I just know."

Grace bit her lower lip nervously. "What's she like?"

Daddy shook his head. For a long time, he was quiet. Grace was about to ask something else when he said, "I met your mom in high school." His voice was weird; it sounded like he had something stuck in his throat. "I would have asked her out on that first day, but she was already Mia's friend. So . . . I tried not to love her . . . until one night . . . she almost kissed me. That changed everything. I couldn't stay away from her after that."

"Girls aren't supposed to do that," Grace mumbled around her thumb.

"Your grandmother would tell you that girls can do anything. That's what she told my sister, anyway."

Grace frowned. Daddy seemed all . . . gooey, and his eyes were shiny. He was acting like he loved Mommy, but that was stupid because he said she didn't like him. None of this made sense. "But she didn't want me," Grace said. "She left me."

"Sometimes people don't have a choice about what they do."

"Is she gonna visit me again?"

Dad looked down at Grace. "Your mom is really special, Princess, and I know she loves you. That's what matters now. The reason she's been gone is . . . well, really it was my fault, too. I let her be the one who was wrong. But I was wrong, too."

"Wrong about what?"

He acted like he was going to say something, then he must have changed his mind. He kissed her forehead instead.

"Daddy?"

"You go to sleep, baby. This is all going to work out. You'll see. We're going to work all this out."

"But you'll stay with me, right, Daddy?"

"Of course, but she's your mom, Gracie, and you need her, no matter what you think."

❦

"I screwed up, Scot," Lexi said again. She was in his office, pacing back and forth in front of the window, chewing on her thumbnail.

"Lexi. *Lexi.*"

She stopped, faced him. "Did you say something?"

"Sit down. You're making me dizzy."

She went to his desk and stood there, looking down at Scot, who looked a little tired today. His hair was a mess and his tie was askew. "Are you okay?"

"Danny has colic. Jenny and I aren't sleeping much. But I'm fine."

Lexi reached down for the framed photograph on Scot's desk. In it, a pudgy bald baby boy held a plastic key. It made her sad, seeing this baby, thinking of Grace, wondering if she'd had colic or if she'd slept through the night like an angel. "I don't know anything about being a mom," she said quietly, feeling defeated again.

"No one does at the start," Scot said. "I kept looking for a manual with Danny, but all he came with was a blanket. And I'm pretty sure his grandma gave it to him. Sit down, Lexi."

She collapsed more than anything, realizing all of a sudden how exhausted she was. "I don't know what I was thinking."

Scot handed her a newspaper. "It won't do any good to dwell on your mistake. Now is the time for action, Lexi. We need to show the court, and the Farradays, that you're here to stay and that you're ready to parent Grace. The best way to do that is to find a job."

"A job. Of course."

"I've circled a few possibilities. I wish I had enough business to employ you here—"

"You've done enough. Thank you, Scot."

"Jenny has a navy blue suit that she thought you might want to borrow. It's hanging off the door in the conference room."

Lexi was once again filled by gratitude to this man, and his wife. She got slowly to her feet. "Danny is a lucky kid. You know that, right?"

He looked up. "So is Grace."

"I hope so," Lexi said quietly, feeling a thin resurgence of hope. Saying good-bye to Scot, she went into the conference room and put on Jenny's navy blue summer-weight suit. It didn't look great with Lexi's ice blue T-shirt and flip-flops, but it was the best she had.

In less than forty minutes, she was on her bike, heading to the local drugstore, which had advertised for a sales clerk. Full time, minimum wage.

Inside the bright store, with its array of colorful shelving, she paused and looked around. At the nearest cash register, a heavyset woman with a beehive-like gray pile of hair stood, talking on her cell phone.

Lexi went to the checkout line and stood there.

"You buying something, hon?" the woman said, lowering the phone just a little.

"I'm here for the job."

"Oh." The woman bent forward, pressed one scythelike red fingernail to the store intercom, and said, "Manager to register one, please." Then she smiled at Lexi, straightened, and went back to her phone conversation.

"Thank you," Lexi said, although the woman wasn't listening.

Lexi saw the manager approach register one. He was a tall, thin man, very Ichabod Crane–y, with a nose like an eagle's beak and spiny eyebrows that grew wild as blackberry bushes.

She moved toward him confidently, extended her hand. "Hello, sir. I'm Alexa Baill. I've come to apply for the clerk position."

He shook her hand. "Follow me."

She followed him back into a small, windowless office that was stacked high with cardboard boxes. He sat behind the metal desk and pointed to a stool in the corner.

She dragged the stool over to the desk and sat down, feeling a little conspicuous on the perch.

"Do you have a résumé?"

Lexi felt her cheeks heat up. "No. It's a sales clerk job, right? In high school, I worked at Amoré, the ice cream shop. I'm good with money and even better with people. I'm a good employee, and I can work any shift. I could get you some recommendations."

"When did you work at Amoré?"

"From 2002 to 2004. I . . . quit in June, after I graduated from high school."

He wrote something down on a piece of paper that looked like an application. "And you're home from college now? Is this a summer job for you?"

"No. I'm looking for full-time employment."

He looked up sharply. His thick eyebrows veed together. "You went to Pine Island High?"

"Yes."

"Most local kids don't work here full-time. Where have you worked since high school?"

Lexi swallowed hard. "Part-time in a library."

"What library?"

She let out a quiet breath and lost her good posture. "Purdy."

"You don't mean—"

"The prison. I've been in prison for a few years. But now I'm out, and I'll be a good employee. I guarantee you that." She was speaking, but it was useless. She saw the way his face shuttered at the word *prison,* the way he wouldn't meet her gaze now.

"All right, then," he said, giving her his first smile—and it was pure fiction. "I'll contact you when we've made our decision."

"That means no job," she said, sliding off the stool.

"It means I'll contact you if we want to hire you."

"Yeah." She tried to stay optimistic; it was only the first of many potential jobs. Maybe other employers would be more liberal minded. "So, do you want my phone number?"

He looked at her finally. "You can give it to me if you want."

She wanted to tell him *no way* and walk out with some stitch of dignity, but she had Grace to consider, so she wrote down her phone number and left the drugstore's bright interior. Outside, she opened her newspaper and found the next opening. A waitress position at Esmerelda's Mexican Kitchen.

For the rest of the afternoon, Lexi tried to believe in herself, even as one job after another evaporated in front of her. Most of the available positions were part-time, without benefits. She lost track of the times some employer had mentioned the economy as her enemy. Apparently she'd gone to prison in good times and come out in bad. Minimum wage was less than nine dollars an hour. That gave her maybe fifteen hundred dollars a month income, before taxes; well over half would go to rent.

But apparently none of that mattered because she couldn't get a job. She'd spoken to twelve employers today, and every conversation ended up the same way.

What have you been doing since high school?

College, really? Where?

Who was your last employer?

Oh (and the look)—*the prison library.*

I'm sorry, the position had been filled . . . You're too young . . . I'll let you know . . .

One excuse after another. The hell of it was, she couldn't blame them. Who wanted to hire a twenty-four-year-old ex-con?

And if that weren't bad enough, after her useless job interviews, she'd checked out housing on the island.

There were only three apartment complexes, and one thing was sure: she couldn't afford to live in any of them. The smallest of the available units rented for nine hundred fifty dollars per month. Plus, the landlord required first and last month's rent and a security deposit in advance. Twenty-four hundred dollars, due on the day she signed the lease agreement.

It might as well be a million dollars.

A few phone calls confirmed that Port George was no better.

There were more rentals available on the other side of the bridge, but they were still way too expensive.

The whole day defeated Lexi. By the time she gave up, it was seven o'clock at night and she just wanted to be alone. She rode her bike through the quiet summer night and parked outside Scot's office. Using her key, she walked inside. All she wanted to do was sleep. Or scream.

"Lexi? Is that you?"

She sighed and forced a smile. She owed Scot everything; it wasn't his fault she was such a pathetic loser. "Hey, Scot," she said, heading into his office. "You're working late."

"I was waiting for you. I have a surprise. Come here."

He took her by the hand and led her to the conference room. On the long wooden table, a laptop was open. "Here," he said, "sit down."

Lexi did as she was told.

Scot left the room for a few moments and then returned. "Okay, we're ready." He pushed a button on the laptop and Aunt Eva's worried face filled the screen. "I don't know, Babs. How can you tell if it's working?"

The sight of her aunt's face was like a tonic. Lexi felt a loosening in her chest. For the first time in hours, she smiled. She *wasn't* as alone as she'd thought. "Hey, Aunt Eva," she said, scooting forward.

"She's here, Barbara!" Eva's face broke into a bright smile. "Come look! This is my Lexi."

My Lexi.

A heavyset woman with a head of steel gray curls bent at the waist and peered into the camera, smiling. "Hello, Alexa. My sister never stops talking about you."

"Hey, Barbara," Lexi said softly, overcome with emotion.

Barbara's face moved out of view and Eva scooted closer to her computer. She looked different, older; her cheeks were deeply tanned and lined and her hair had gone completely white. "So, tell me everything, Lexi."

Scot left the room and shut the door behind him.

"I met Gracie," Lexi said. It was the first thing that came to mind.

"How is she?"

"Sad. Beautiful. Lonely."

"Oh. That must be hard to see."

"It's all hard, Aunt Eva. I didn't want to come here, because I knew it would be hard, but now I'm here and everything is a mess."

"I suppose you've seen your young man?"

"Yeah."

"And?"

Lexi shrugged. "It's been a long time."

"You look tired, Lexi."

"It's been a bad day. It's going to be hard for me to get a job and hard to afford a place to live. Impossible, maybe."

"You just got out, Lexi. Maybe you need to come home and get taken care of. Barb and me got a hide-a-bed just waiting for you. You could get a job down here and save up your money. Floyd at the Tilt-a-Curl says he'd be happy to hire you to answer phones and clean up. Without rent to pay, you'll have a nice little nest egg in no time."

Home.

Lexi had to admit, the ease of it appealed to her. She *needed* to be wanted somewhere. "But how can I leave Grace again? She'll never forgive me."

"You know how hard it can be on a kid to have a momma who isn't ready. Take some time for yourself. Get strong and happy and then go back to your daughter. You go back when you've got your life together. I think that's the responsible thing to do."

"The responsible thing," Lexi repeated, hating the idea, even as she recognized the truth of it. She would only confuse Grace now. How could she be a mother when her own life was in shambles? Grace deserved better; she deserved stability. Lexi knew about moms who were unreliable. It didn't make a child feel safe.

"Alexa?"

She smiled as brightly as she could. She didn't want to talk about this anymore. It was breaking her heart. "So, what's up with you? Did you ever take those knitting classes?"

"Lord, yes," Eva laughed. "Barbara and me got enough blankets to fill a motel. When you come down here . . ."

⁂

The view from the forty-second floor was dreary on this wet June day. The Space Needle hovered to her right, a black-and-white disc suspended against a dull gray sky.

Jude stood at the window, seeing her ghostly reflection in the glass. She was trying to stand still, appear calm, but it wasn't working. She felt jittery and uncomfortable in her own skin, as if she'd drunk ten cups of coffee on an empty stomach. She chewed on her thumbnail and went back to pacing. Panic lurked just outside her field of vision; she felt it stalking her, a shadow in the corner, waiting to pounce. But she couldn't pinpoint the source of her fear. She just knew that she was afraid, that she'd been afraid ever since she'd read that letter of Lexi's.

"I'm proud of you, Jude," Harriet said in that strangely even voice of hers. "It took a lot of courage to face Lexi again."

"I didn't face her. In fact I tried not to look at her."

"But you did look at her, didn't you?"

Jude nodded, gnawing on her thumbnail now, tapping her foot.

"What did you see?"

"I saw the girl who killed my daughter . . . and my granddaughter's mother and my son's first love. And . . . a girl I used to care about." Jude scratched nervously at the side of her face. Her skin was crawling suddenly. "What's wrong with me, Dr. Bloom? I feel like I'm going crazy."

"Not crazy. I think maybe you're ready to try a Compassionate Friends meeting. There's one today, you know. At two."

"That talk again?" Jude sighed and sat down, tapping her foot, fisting and unfisting her hands. "I am not going to go sit in a meeting with a bunch of other grieving parents. Should I *talk* about Mia? Will that bring her back?"

"In a way."

"Spoken like a person who hasn't lost a child. No, thanks."

"The only way to get clos—"

"So help me, God, if you say closure, I'll walk out. There's no closure. That's just a bunch of claptrap. I still can't listen to music—any music. I still cry almost every time I shower. Sometimes I scream in the car. I talk to my daughter and she can't hear me. None of that goes away."

"You used to say that you felt gray."

"I said I live in the gray. A thick ashy fog."

"And you thought the rain looked ashy the night Mia died?"

"Yeah, so?"

Harriet peered at her over the rims of her half lenses. Her point had been made. "So if you're still in the gray, I think maybe you should look around. Maybe you can see something now. Shapes. People."

Jude stopped chewing her nail. "What do you mean?"

"I know your pain won't end, Jude. I'm not a fool. But maybe you're finally getting ready to accept that there might be more than just pain. That's why you're acting like an overbred poodle right now. You're afraid of *feeling,* and it's happening anyway. You opened up enough to let Lexi Baill into your house. That's a huge step, Jude."

"I read Grace a story and played a board game with her," Jude said quietly.

"How did that make you feel?"

Jude looked up. "Like a grandmother." Tears filled her eyes. She hadn't realized that until right now. "I've been hard on Zach. I just . . . couldn't look at him without remembering . . ."

"Remembering is okay, Jude."

"Not the way I do it, Doc. It . . . breaks me."

"Maybe you need to be broken a little before you can put yourself back together."

"I'm afraid I won't be able to put myself back together."

"You will. You're on your way, Jude."

"What do I do next?"

"Follow your heart."

Jude shivered at the idea of that. She'd worked so hard to shut down her emotions; the idea of opening them up again was terrifying. She didn't know if she could do it. If she even wanted to.

For the rest of her scheduled hour, Jude tried to listen to Dr. Bloom, but that sense of panic was rising again, drowning out everything except the in-and-out strains of her own breathing. What if she opened herself up again and the pain simply engulfed her? What if she lost all the progress she'd made? It hadn't been that long ago that Jude had been practically useless, a crying gray form that couldn't get through the day without drugs.

At the end of her session, she said something to Dr. Bloom—she didn't remember what—and walked outside.

The weather now was both bright and gray. Clouds the color of beach sand hung low in the sky. Sunlight glowed through in places while rain fell in drops so small no local even noticed, but tourists in the market huddled beneath brightly colored umbrellas. She stood at the corner in front of Dr. Bloom's building, beneath this crying sky, and tried to remember which way to go. It felt suddenly as if any move could be wrong.

"Are you okay, Ma'am?" a kid said, appearing beside her. With shaggy hair and a skateboard clamped under his arm, he reminded her of long ago—or maybe a second ago—when Zach and Mia had been in middle school.

She would have given anything to run to her car right now, to drive down to the ferry terminal and go home. But she couldn't. It was Wednesday.

"I'm fine," she said to the kid. "Thanks." She moved forward, walking slowly. Rain tapped at her head, occasionally a drop landed in her eye, but she barely noticed.

In no time at all, she was standing in front of her mother's art gallery. In windows on either side of the closed door hung large canvases—one was a traditional landscape, the tulips in the Skagit Valley, done in golds and reds, beneath a shadowy, melancholy black sky; the other was a still life, a vase full of pink dahlias. Only on close examination could one see the hairline crack in the aged-looking porcelain.

Next door, she opened one of the huge glass doors and entered an elegant lobby. Saying hello to the doorman, she headed for the elevator and rode it to the top floor.

The elevator opened onto the penthouse: four thousand square feet of ivory marble flooring dotted with exquisite, uncomfortable French antique furniture. Floor-to-ceiling windows captured the Seattle skyline, Elliott Bay, and, on good days, Mount Rainier.

"Judith," her mother said, coming toward her. "You're early. Would you like a glass of wine?"

"Desperately." Jude followed her mother into the living room. The few solid walls in this space were painted a creamy white and supported giant works of art, none of which Jude liked. They were all dark and despairing somehow; sad. Just looking at the artwork in this room had always depressed Jude. Other than the paintings, there was no color anywhere. Jude sat down in a white chair by the fireplace.

Her mother brought her a glass of white wine. "Thanks, Mother."

Her mother sat down on the pale sofa opposite Jude. She looked ready to host an elegant party—her white hair was coiled with effortless chic into a French twist; her face was expertly made up to emphasize her green eyes and minimize the lines that fanned out around her thin lips.

"You look upset," Mother said, sipping her wine.

It was a strangely intimate observation for her mother to make. Normally, Jude would have smiled and made up a pretty excuse, but she had been undone by Lexi's return, by that damned letter, by the obvious pain her son was now in—all of it. She had no strength left, and she was afraid, even though she didn't know what scared her. Staying put? Letting go? Holding on? Nothing felt safe anymore. And she wanted someone to talk to, someone to help her find a way out. But her mother was hardly that person.

She wanted to smile and change the subject and pretend she had nothing pressing on her mind, but her whole life was falling apart, it seemed, and she had no strength left for pretense. "Why is it we never really talk?" she said slowly. "I don't even know you. And you certainly don't know me. Why is that?"

Her mother put down her wine glass. Backlit by the gray day, she looked ethereal. For the first time, Jude noticed how old her mother looked, how tired. Her shoulders were thin as bird bones and her spine had begun to curve forward. "You, of all people, should understand, Judith." Her mother's voice was sharp and thin, a razor blade, but the look in her eyes was perhaps the softest expression Jude had ever seen. There was sadness there. Had it always been there?

"Why should I understand?"

Her mother glanced out the window. "I loved your father," she said quietly, a crack in her voice. "After he passed, I knew I had you to care for, and I wanted to care for you, to love you . . . but there was nothing inside me. Even my ability to paint vanished. I thought it would last for a day or a week." She looked at Jude. "It just went on and on, and when it finally lifted enough that I could breathe, you were gone from me. I didn't even know how to get you back."

Jude stared at her mother in shock. How was it that she'd never made this connection? She'd known that her mother quit painting on the day of her father's funeral, that she'd walked out of the house and never returned, not really.

"I watched the kind of mother you became, and I was so proud of you. But I never said that. You wouldn't have heard me anyway, although perhaps I want to think that. Either way, I didn't say it. Then I saw you make the same mistake I did: I saw you stop loving Zach . . . and yourself. It broke my heart. I would have told you what you were doing wrong, but you were always so sure that I was weak and you were strong. So yes, Judith, you—of all people, you—should understand my mistakes. You should know why I treated you the way I did."

Jude didn't know what to say. It felt as if her whole life, her whole identity, had just cracked open.

Her mother got to her feet. For a second, Jude thought she was going to walk over here, cross the distance between them, and maybe even sit down beside her. "You're young," her mother said finally. "You can undo this mistake."

Jude felt herself starting to shake. Here it was, the thing she'd been afraid of. "How?"

"People think love is an act of faith," her mother said. "Sometimes it's an act of will. I didn't have the strength to love you, Jude—or to show that love, I guess. I don't know which it was, and in the end, what's the difference? You're stronger than I ever was."

In a way, it was the same thing Dr. Bloom had been saying for years. Jude glimpsed the regret in her mother's gaze, and it was like looking into her own future. She didn't want to someday be eighty years old and alone. "I'm not the only one who can undo a mistake, Mom."

"I'm not young anymore," her mother said. "I've missed my chance. I know that."

"That's what the lunches were about."

"Of course."

"And that's why you wanted me to take over the gallery. So we'd have something in common."

"Did you ever wonder where the gallery name came from? JACE. Your father named it for all of us: Judith Anne, Caroline, Edward. He thought we'd always be together in it." Mother sighed. "Another regret of mine."

Jude got to her feet. The trembling in her hands eased; suddenly she felt stronger than she had in months, maybe years. She didn't know how she would correct all the wrong paths she'd taken, but it was time to start undoing her mistakes. One at a time. "On Saturday, I'm going to take Gracie to the aquarium. Why don't you come with us?"

Mother gave her an uncertain smile. "Really? I could meet you at the ferry terminal. Say 11:00. We could have lunch at Ivar's after. You and your father used to love throwing french fries to the gulls."

Jude remembered it in a rush: standing by the railing with her parents, throwing fries to the gulls teeming overhead. *That's it, punkin . . . kid's got quite an arm, doesn't she, Caro?*

"He loved us both," Jude said.

Her mother nodded. "It's good to talk about him finally."

And just like that, Jude knew what she had to do. Maybe she'd known for years, but just now, this instant, in the sweet glow of this new start, she was ready to try. "I can't stay for lunch. I'm sorry. There's something I need to do."

"Of course," her mother said. If she was surprised by the sudden change, she didn't show it. She led the way to the elevator.

There, they stared at each other for a long time; in her mother's aged porcelain face, Jude saw the long-forgotten image of another woman, one who'd loved to paint.

"I've missed you, Judith," her mother said softly.

"Me, too. I'll see you Saturday."

Jude left the austere penthouse and returned to the underground parking structure on Virginia Street. From there, she drove out of the dark lot and into a rainy day. Driving carefully, she arrived at the Capitol Hill Community Center. There, she sat in her car for more than ninety minutes, waiting. Every moment she sat there was an act of courage; it would have been so much easier to drive away. That was what she'd done a dozen times before . . .

Finally, a car pulled up and parked in front of her, and then another. Within a few minutes, she could see people going in. Most of them were women, walking alone in the rain, without umbrellas.

Jude knew how dangerous and frightening this choice was, but she knew how dangerous the other choice was, too.

Love is an act of will.

For too long she'd been afraid of it.

Her hand was shaking as she opened her car door and stepped out into the rain. She fisted her hands and walked across the street.

A woman came up beside her. She was young, with flowing black hair and brown eyes that were full of tears.

Jude fell into step with the woman, although neither one said anything.

A sign beside the open door read: *Compassionate Friends. 2:00 P.M. Grief support group.*

Jude paused, maybe even stumbled. Fear opened up inside her so fast and sharp she couldn't breathe. It occurred to her to turn and run. She wasn't ready for this. She didn't want to do this. What if they wanted her to let go of Mia?

The woman beside her touched Jude's hand.

Jude gasped, turned. She looked at the woman with the dark hair, and now she saw more than tears. She saw understanding. Here was another woman who had empty eyes and a pinched mouth and had forgotten to color her hair. Jude knew this woman knew how it felt to be both filled with pain and achingly numb.

Is this what I look like? Jude thought suddenly. She did what she'd never done in her life: she reached out to a stranger and held on. Together, they walked through the open doors.

❦

In the end, it was exactly as it had been in the beginning. No one had a job for an ex-convict with a sociology degree and no real experience. As her prospects dwindled, so did her hope, until by late Thursday afternoon, she knew she was just going through the motions.

Now, as she sat on her driftwood log at LaRiviere Park, she understood.

She'd never had a chance, really.

Lexi closed her eyes at that.

She knew what she had to do. The hours down here had been a bandage, nothing more.

It was time. She'd put off the inevitable long enough.

She walked over to where she'd left her bike and climbed on, pedaling up the hill toward the main road. She bypassed Night Road and circled back to the Farraday house. Holding tightly to the grips, she made her bumping way down the gravel driveway and stopped at the garage. She was shaking so badly it was hard to position the bike near the side wall of the building, and finally she gave up and let the bike fall into the tall grass. She couldn't help noticing again the runaway garden and remembering how clipped and cared for it once had been.

Ripples, she thought. Grief had endless consequences. Pushing that thought aside, she went to the front door and knocked quickly—before she lost her nerve.

Jude opened the door. "Lexi," she said, obviously surprised.

"I want to give you something for Grace."

"She's up in Zach's old room, watching a movie."

"Oh. I didn't think she'd be here."

"Would you like to see her?"

Lexi knew she should say no, but how could she? She nodded. Unable to dredge up words to accompany the gesture, she turned away from Jude and went up the stairs to Zach's old room. At the door, she paused just long enough to draw a strengthening breath, then she knocked on the door, heard a chirpy *come in,* and opened the door.

"Hi, Mommy. What are you doing here?" Grace sat up in Zach's bed, frowning.

Lexi actually stumbled. She tried to cover her mistake with a smile, but realized that she'd done that badly, too.

It was a lot to handle all at once—Grace's beautiful face, her saying, *mommy* . . . and Zach's room.

Everywhere she looked, she saw reminders of the boy with whom she'd fallen in love—a tangle of plastic dinosaurs, a football, a colorful collection of Disney videotapes, green-spined video games. But it was the worn copy of *Jane Eyre* sitting on the dresser that killed her. She went to it, picked it up, felt its slick, crinkled cover . . . saw her name, scrawled in a lost penmanship on the inside cover. He'd kept it. All these years.

"You're not coming to take me away, are you?" Grace asked worriedly.

Lexi put the book down and turned to face her daughter. "No. May I sit next to you?"

"Okay."

Lexi climbed into the bed (Zach's bed, but she shouldn't think about things that didn't matter anymore) and scooted as close to Grace as she dared. "I scared you the other day."

"Nothin' scares me. I punched Jacob in the nose and he's way bigger'n me."

"I shouldn't have said I wanted you to live with me. That wasn't what I meant to say at all."

"Oh. That. You don't want me to live with you?"

Lexi flinched. "I don't know much about being a mom. And I can see how much you love being with your daddy."

Grace seemed to relax at that. "Do you know how to make cupcakes?"

"No. Why?"

"I dunno. Moms just make stuff."

Lexi leaned back against Zach's headboard. The bulletin board across the room, above the dresser, was still full of newspaper clippings and ribbons he'd won in high school. For what, she couldn't even remember. "So I guess you want the kind of mom who makes cupcakes and walks you to school."

Grace laughed and covered her mouth to stifle the sound. "I live *way* too far to walk. Samantha Green's mom makes everyone a cape for Halloween. Do you know how to sew?"

"Nope. I pretty much blow in the good-mother category." Lexi looked down at her daughter, feeling loss yawn inside of her.

"I wish I had a chipmunk," Grace said. "I'd let you play with it."

Lexi couldn't help laughing. "That would be cool."

"Daddy says chipmunks aren't pets, but I think they could be," Grace added, laughing. She immediately covered her mouth.

Lexi gently pulled Grace's hand away from her mouth. "Don't ever be afraid to laugh, Gracie."

Grace looked up at Lexi through hopeful eyes.

Lexi knew she would always remember this moment, and if she were lucky, and she didn't do anything to screw it up, maybe Grace would remember it, too.

She took the sapphire ring off her finger and offered it to Grace. "I'd like you to have this, Grace."

"It's a grownup ring."

"Maybe your dad can put it on a chain so you can wear it as a necklace until it fits you."

"It's really pretty."

"Not as pretty as you are, Princess."

"That's what my daddy calls me. Why are you giving me this? It's not my birthday."

Lexi swallowed hard. "I need to leave, Grace. I thought. It doesn't matter what I thought. I was wrong to come here. I'm not ready."

"Ready for what?"

Lexi couldn't say it out loud. "I'll be back as soon as I can, though. That's what I want you to remember. And I'll write every week and call as much as I can. Okay?"

Grace's lower lip trembled. "I was mean to you."

"You didn't do anything wrong," Lexi said. "I shouldn't have come here. I just . . . keep hurting the Farradays . . . and I . . . Can I have a hug?"

Grace scrambled over Lexi's lap and gave her a huge hug.

Lexi clung to her daughter, trying to physically imprint the memory of this embrace on both of them. "I love you, Grace," she whispered into her ear. "Don't you forget that, okay?" She heard Grace's little hiccup, and the sound pushed Lexi over the edge. She felt the start of tears, and this time there was no holding them back.

"Don't cry, Mommy."

Lexi wiped her eyes and pulled back just enough so that she was face-to-face with Grace. "Crying is a good thing sometimes. I've waited a long time for those tears. You can send me your school drawings, and I'll put them on my fridge." Lexi leaned closer and kissed her daughter's plump little mouth. "And I'll learn to make cupcakes."

"Okay," Grace said. She looked sad and confused and uncertain.

Lexi didn't know how to mend those emotions without making promises she couldn't keep. Some endings simply couldn't be what you dreamed. All she could do was make memories now, say good-bye, and hope for a better future. She'd save her money as fast as she could and come back to claim a life with her daughter.

She kissed Grace one last time and uncoiled herself from her daughter; then she got off the bed and stood there, looking down.

Grace was furiously whispering at her wrist mirror and trying not to cry.

"Don't cry, Gracie. It'll be okay," Lexi said, stroking her hair.

"That's what *she* says."

Lexi actually managed to smile at that. "You're lucky to have such a good friend, but I'll make you a deal: if you make friends with someone in your class, *really* make friends, I'll send some cupcakes in September for the first-grade party."

Grace wiped her eyes and looked up at Lexi. "How?"

"How what?"

"How do I make a friend? No one likes me."

Lexi sat down again. "Well, you can't keep punching boys and lying. If you want to make friends, you have to do friendly things. Who is the nicest girl in your class?"

"Samantha. But she never talks to me."

"Okay. Tomorrow, you just go up to Samantha and say something nice to her. And you don't cheat or lie one time. Tell her you like playing with her."

"What if I don't?"

"You will," Lexi promised. "I had a best friend once, and I could tell her anything. She always made me smile. I never felt alone when she was around."

She hugged her daughter one last time and forced herself to walk away from the bed, past the copy of *Jane Eyre,* touching it once more (it didn't mean anything that he'd kept it; don't think otherwise). In the hallway, she paused and looked back.

Grace sat huddled in the big bed, looking incredibly sad and small.

"I love you, Gracie."

"Bye, Mommy." Grace sniffled.

"Tell your daddy I said . . . hey." She closed the door behind her.

She should have run from this house as fast as she could. And she would have, if she hadn't looked down the hallway to Mia's room. She moved toward it almost instinctively, opened the door.

The room welcomed her as it always had, drew her in. She went to the dresser, where Mia's phone lay beside an English lit paper with an *A* written across the top. A row of plastic Breyer horses lined the windowsill. There were a dozen pictures of Mia—at play rehearsal, at dance class, sitting by the beach with Zach. There were no pictures of her and Mia in the room anymore. Once, though, they'd been everywhere.

"I haven't let myself come in here in . . . a while," Jude said behind her.

Lexi spun around, her face hot. "I'm sorry. I shouldn't have—"

Jude reached down for the stuffed puppy on the nightstand, picked it up. *Daisy Doggy.* "I used to sleep in here. It worried Miles and my therapist after a while, so I closed the door. Erica cleans it, but I don't come in."

"I can feel her in here," Lexi said quietly.

"Can you? You're lucky then."

Lexi moved closer. "She loved this room but hated that mirror. She always said it looked like an art project. But she knew how much you liked it."

Jude sat down on the bed. When she looked up, her eyes were glazed with tears and her mouth was an unsteady line. "Why did you drive that night?"

Lexi was actually grateful for the honesty of the question. "I've asked myself that a million times. Zach was hammered, and Mia wasn't much better. Neither one of them could stand up, really. They didn't want to call you. It was so late, and they were so drunk." She paused. "I didn't want to call you. I wanted you to love me so much . . . and then Zach got behind the wheel. I couldn't let him drive."

"Why did I let you go that night? I knew there would be drinking. And I gave him the keys."

Lexi moved toward the bed, feeling like a ninety-year-old woman with rickety joints and watery eyes and sat down beside Jude. "It's my fault, Jude. All mine."

Jude shook her head slowly. "I wanted to believe that, didn't I?"

"It's the truth."

"I'm trying to be a little more honest these days. I know you love Grace. Do you still love Zach?"

"I've tried to stop. I'll keep trying."

"You should talk to him."

"I wouldn't know what to say."

"He'll be back soon," Jude said quietly. "Talk to him. Tell him how you feel."

Lexi almost broke at that small kindness. It reminded her of all the conversations she'd had with Jude over the years, all the moments when they'd been like mother and daughter. It was because of Jude that Zach had taken Lexi to the dance, where everything between them had really begun. "They were so lucky to have you, Jude. And they knew it. Mia loved you so much."

"I miss her voice."

Lexi slipped off the bed and crawled under it, feeling beneath the slats until she found what she was looking for. Holding it, she crawled back out and sat back on her heels, offering Jude the small pink journal with an orange lily painted on the front.

"Oh my God," Jude breathed, reaching out. "Her journal."

Lexi placed it in Jude's hands and then got to her feet. "I'll go now. Tell . . . Zach that I'm going to call Grace once a week and I'll write even more often."

Jude stared down at the journal, running her palm over it as if it were a piece of expensive silk. "What? Why?"

"I have something important to do before I leave." Lexi wasn't even sure if Jude was listening. "A good-bye I should have said a long time ago. But Jude . . . love Grace better, okay? She needs you."

Twenty-seven

Mia's diary.

It had been here all this time, waiting. Jude ran her fingertips over the mottled brass lock, and then, slowly, she opened the book.

Property of Mia Farraday. Private. Keep out. And yes that means you, Zach Attack.

Dear Diary,

I'm scared. Is it okay to write that down? I know how lame it makes me look. But you won't care, right, Diary?

No one at high school is gonna talk to me. Mom says h.s. will be better than middle school, but she always says stuff like that. How would she know what it's like to be me? She was a cheerleader and probably Homecoming Queen. What would she have done if Maribeth Astor called <u>her</u> *pizza face?*

I wish I hadn't cried. That just made everything worse.

And now I'll probably have to sit by MB in class.

Crap.

It used to be easy for me. So, like, what happened? In grade school I had lots of friends. Well, so, okay, maybe they were Zach's friends, but we all played together and I didn't know there was something wrong with me. Now I know. Boy do I know.

Madre is calling us for breakfast. <u>*The most important meal of the day.*</u> *Yeah, right.*

Loser out.

Dear Diary,

You won't BELIEVE what happened today. Ok I'm gonna write it all down so I don't forget anything.

First of all, Mom was wrong about h.s. At least at first. I walked into school with Zach, and even though he was holding my hand, it was like I was invisible. Okay maybe I shouldn't have worn the pink tutu and high tops, but I'm not like those other girls. They know and I know it. The clothes help keep them away. And so what if they laugh?

Lunch was a horrorfest. I walked into the lunch room and almost puked. No one made eye contact with me. Zach was sitting with all his Barbie and Ken friends and he waved me over. No way I was gonna go there, so I took my book and went outside.

That's when it happened Diary!

I was sitting on the grass by this scrawny tree, chewing and reading (Wuthering Heights) when this girl just walked up and said can I sit with you.

I told her it was social suicide and she smiled. <u>*Smiled.*</u> *Then she sat down and we started talking and Diary, we have like EVERY-THING in common.*

I don't want to jinx it but I think she wants to be my friend . . .

How cool is that???

Dear Diary,

Lexi stayed the night at my house last night. We totally fooled Madre and pretended to go to sleep at 11 but then we snuck out and went down to the beach. We sat there for hours, talking, about EVERYTHING. She likes me, and she doesn't care that no one else does. We are gonna be Harry and Hermione. Friends forever.

Dear Diary,

Lexi made me try out for the school play, Once Upon a Mattress. And I GOT THE PART!

What would I do without her?

Tod Lymer asked Lexi to the dance. She tried to keep it a secret, but high school is such a soap opera. No one can really keep a secret. Besides, Haley wanted me to know. She laughed when she told me and called me a loser who couldn't get a date.

How does Mom always know when something is wrong? When I got home from school, she took one look at me and just walked over and hugged me. I tried to push her away, but she held on, and I burst into tears. Yes, Diary, that's how cool I am. When I was done telling her the story, she said I needed to remember that good friends wanted the best for each other, and I should remember that.

I do, Diary. I do want Lexi to be happy. Totally I don't care at all if she goes to the stupid dance.

Lexi didn't go to the dance. She said she'd WAY rather stay home with her best friend and watch movies, so that's what we did. We made popcorn and watched movies. Zach even stayed home with us. He said any dance without us was a total waste of

"Nana?"

Jude looked up and saw her granddaughter standing by the bed. In her pink terrycloth sweats, with her curly blond hair a mass of tangles, she looked exactly like Mia at that age, and it disoriented Jude just a little. For the first time in years, Mia felt close enough to touch. The diary had brought her back to Jude.

Grace burst into tears. "M-my m-mommy left."

Love Grace better. She needs you.

Jude got out of bed and scooped Grace into her arms. "It's okay, baby," she whispered, and then suddenly Jude was crying, too. She clung to Grace, crying against the child's soft, plump cheek, smelling the sweet baby shampoo scent of her hair, remembering . . .

"I tole her I wanted to st-stay with Daddy," Grace said sobbing. "An I *do* wanna be with Daddy, but . . . but I want my mommy, too. I shoulda told her that."

"Oh, Grace." Jude looked at her granddaughter through a blur of tears. In the soft focus, she saw not only Grace, but Zach and Mia, too. And the Lexi who had been a part of them. They were all in Grace's face, in her eyes, in the pink bow of her mouth. How had Jude forgotten that?

No, she hadn't forgotten it. She'd known it all along; she'd looked away from it purposely, afraid that the pain would kill her. But not feeling had taken away her joy, too, left her in that gray haze of numbness.

In a way, they were all together again in this moment, embraced in one another's arms just as they would have been if Mia were alive.

She carried Grace up onto Mia's big bed and snuggled with her there.

Grace slowly opened her small fist. Resting on her palm lay the promise ring Zach had given Lexi. "Look what Mommy gave me."

Jude picked up the fragile ring. *This* was what she'd been so upset by all those years ago, a little circle of white gold with a sapphire chip; she'd thought a ring like this could derail a young man's life. "He was so romantic," she sighed.

Grace popped her thumb in her mouth and mumbled, "Who?" around it.

"Your daddy. I should have known that Miles and I would raise a romantic."

Why hadn't she rejoiced that her son knew how to love deeply? And to dream of the future. Why was it that pebbles looked like boulders until they were in your rearview mirror? "He gave your mommy that ring for Christmas."

Jude unhooked the slim gold chain necklace she wore. Letting the diamond enhancer fall into her lap, she took the ring from Grace and threaded the chain through it and then clasped the necklace on Grace. "You look like a princess," Jude said, kissing her granddaughter's cheek. And once she'd begun kissing Grace, she couldn't stop. She kissed and nuzzled and snuggled until Gracie cried out for mercy, yelling *stop it, Nana—that tickles!* and giggling.

Finally Jude drew back and looked at Grace. "I love you. I should have told you that a million times a day."

"That's a *lot* of times." Grace giggled again and covered her mouth.

"Don't try to quiet your laughter, Gracie. It's a beautiful sound."

"That's what my mommy said."

Mommy.

How was it that an ordinary word, one she'd heard all of her life, could suddenly be so sharp? *You used to be the best mother in the world.*

Regret was all around Jude; she felt choked by it, but then she looked down at the girl in her arms, and she could breathe again. The regret melted slowly away, was replaced by a fragile shoot of hope. "Your mom has a heart as big as Alaska. I forgot that. And she made my Mia—and your dad—happy."

"What's that?" Grace asked, pointing at the book in Jude's other hand.

She hadn't even realized she was still holding it. "It's your Aunt Mia's diary."

"You aren't 'posed to read stuff like that. Hannah Montana says—"

"It's okay."

"Cuz she's dead?"

Jude drew in a sharp breath, waiting for a pain that didn't quite come. It was there, of course, in that one awful word, but it left quickly, and she was surprised to find that she could still smile. And maybe it was better to face a thing, to say it out loud, rather than to hide it away. "Yeah. Now it's something she left for us."

"What was she like, Nana?" Grace asked, and Jude wondered how long Grace had held that question back, afraid to ask it of anyone in her family.

"She was like . . . a beautiful, fragile flower. Until she met your mom, she was afraid of her own shadow and lonely . . . so lonely." She wiped her eyes. "She wanted to be an actress, and I think she could have made it. All those quiet years weren't wasted. Mia was always watching people, soaking up the world around her. When she got onstage, she was a different girl completely. Your mom helped her with that. It was Lexi who talked Mia into trying out for her first play."

Miles appeared in the doorway. "What's this? You two look like you're having a party without me."

"We are, Papa!" Grace said, scrambling to her feet. She ran across the bed and launched herself into Miles's open arms.

"Nana was telling me about Aunt Mia," Grace said. "An' look what my mommy gave me." She held out the promise ring on the chain.

"She was telling you about Mia?" Miles asked, looking at Jude. Over Grace's golden hair their eyes met, and a quiet understanding passed between them. They both knew what it meant to simply say Mia's name. He got up into his daughter's bed and eased close to them, putting an arm around Jude.

"How have you been so strong?" she asked him.

"Strong?" He sighed, and in the sound she heard the wellspring of his loss. "I'm not strong anymore," he said. "But, thank God, I'm patient."

"I'm sorry," she said quietly.

Grace wiggled around until she was wedged between them. Then she sat up. Her pointed chin jutted out. "Won't Daddy be mad that Mommy gave me this ring?"

And suddenly Jude got it: she knew why Lexi had given Grace the ring. *Something important to do before I leave.*

Lexi hadn't just left Grace for the day. The ring meant good-bye.

❧

Lexi pedaled up Main Street and parked her bike in front of Scot's office.

He was still at his desk, talking on the phone. At her entrance, he smiled and held up a finger. *Wait,* he mouthed. *Don't go.*

She sat down on the sofa in the office, waiting. As soon as he hung up, she got to her feet and headed toward the desk. "I made a mistake," she said, standing in front of him.

He paused in gathering his papers and looked up. "What do you mean?"

"You know what Grace said to me? I'm already a mom. I should know how to be one. But I don't. I have no idea how to be my daughter's mommy. I don't have a job or a place to live. Anything. I'm not ready. All I did by coming back was hurt them again. Hurt Grace."

"Lexi, you can't give up."

"I'm not going to give up. I still want to modify the custody agreement, and I want to be Grace's mom. I want that more than anything. But I have to do it the right way. I have to do what's best for *her.* Not what's best for me." Her voice fell away; all she could do was shrug. "I tried to find a job. Ha. Apparently a twenty-four-year-old ex-con can't even be a part-time janitor. And forget about housing. At best I can rent a room in someone's house. I'll have to work seventy hours a week just to *live.* How do I take care of Grace? *How?*"

"Lexi . . ."

"Please," she whispered. "Don't make it harder, okay? I appreciate all you've done for me, but I'm going to Florida tomorrow morning. Eva got me a job. I'll be able to save up enough to come back in a year. My bus leaves at 9:25."

"Oh, Lexi . . ." Scot said. "I wish you'd listen to me . . ."

"Make sure they send me pictures," she said quietly, trying not to cry. "I'll write to her every week."

He went to her then, took her in his arms. She had a hard time letting go. "Thank you for everything," she finally said.

"What about Zach?" Scot asked.

The question hurt so much she didn't even try to respond.

"Do you need a ride to the bus station tomorrow?"

"No." The last thing she wanted was to tell him good-bye again. "I've got it covered. I left Jenny's suit in the conference room. Tell her thanks for me."

"You can tell her yourself. Come to dinner tonight?"

"Okay, but there's something I have to do later."

"Do you need help?"

"No. I need to do it alone."

※

Jude sat on the sofa in Zach's quiet living room. She hadn't bothered turning on any lights, so the lavender evening crept through the windows. A fire danced orange in the black hearth, and for once she felt warmed by it. Every now and then she heard a giggle coming from down the hall, where Miles and Grace were playing something on the Wii. Grace was like a light that had suddenly been switched on; she talked nonstop, and she hadn't told a lie all afternoon. Jude had no doubt that the last few hours with her granddaughter would become one of the anchor memories of this new part of their family's life. The start of After.

But even as she'd joined in, Jude had felt a rising sense of urgency. There was more to be done, she knew, more wrongs to right.

Finally, at about seven, the front door opened and Zach walked in, with his heavy backpack hanging off one shoulder.

"You're late," Jude said, rising to her feet.

"The last test was a bitch," he said, tossing his backpack. He looked utterly exhausted. "I think I blew it."

"You have a lot on your mind."

"You think?"

"I tried calling you."

"My phone died. Sorry."

She got up from the sofa and stood there, staring at him. Even now, she wasn't sure quite how to say all the things on her mind. The last few days had been so startling; she felt like a glacier that had begun slowly to melt and move again.

"I stopped by the lawyer's office, too," he said, meeting her gaze. "I agreed to the modified parenting plan. It's done. I know you don't like it, but I can't hurt Lexi anymore. I won't. And if she needs to have Grace by herself for a while, I'm going to say yes." He paused, and then said quietly, "I shouldn't have gotten drunk. If I had stayed sober—"

"Don't, Zach, I—"

"You can't run this thing, Mom. I know how much you care about everything, but this is about me and Lexi and Grace. I have to do what's right."

"I know," she said. It was time. "And I'm proud of you."

They were like soldiers who'd fought on a common battlefield, she and her son. There were things to say, but they were just words, and they would come in time. What mattered was that they had survived and that there was still love—between them and around them. Everything else was a postscript. There was really only one thing she needed to say to him now. One question to ask. "Do you still love her?"

Zach seemed to crumble at that. In his eyes, she saw both a fragile youth and a terrible maturity. "I've always loved her. I never even tried not to."

She gathered her son in her arms and held him as she should have years ago, when he was young and hurting and afraid. She wished she'd known then what mattered most. "I love you like air, Zach."

He held her tightly. "I love you, too, Madre."

It was the first time he'd called her that in years, and with that little endearment, she melted more, moved just that much closer to who she'd been. She drew back slowly. "I think she's leaving tomorrow. Going to Florida maybe."

"Why?"

"She thinks Grace will be better off without her."

"But that's crazy."

"Lexi has always tried to do what was right for everyone else. That's who she is, isn't it? I should have remembered that, Zach . . . how much Lexi meant to us . . . to me."

Zach looked at her. She saw both hope and worry in his eyes: hope that she meant it and worry that she didn't. "What are you saying?"

"Go find her, Zach. Tell her how you feel." She pushed the hair from his eyes and smiled. "She's a part of our family. She needs to know that."

"She won't care, Mom. I let her go to *prison*."

"You can't claim all the blame, Zach."

"Enough of it. How could she forgive me?"

"Can you forgive me, for being such a bad mom in the last few years?"

"There's no need."

"That's how we do it, Zach. We just . . . forgive. I used to worry that you and Lexi were too young for love, and I still think of you as young, but you're not, are you? None of us are, and life doesn't take the straight road."

"Where is she?"

"I don't know that."

Zach gave her a hug and then hurried out of the cabin. She was still in the open doorway, staring up the empty driveway when she felt Miles come up beside her.

He put an arm around her. "He went to find Lexi?"

"Yep."

"Change comes fast."

"It can." She turned into him, slipped her hands around his waist, and gave him a kiss.

It was a quiet miracle, really, the durability of their love.

"Nana, Papa!" Grace slipped between them like a little eel. "Let's play Candy Land. Nana can be Princess Frostine."

"Your Nana doesn't play—" Miles started.

"I'd love to play Candy Land again," Jude said.

It was strange how a sentence could free something inside of you— such a little thing.

They sat around the coffee table, in front of the fire. With the board set up, they played and talked and laughed. They were finally putting it away when the front door burst open and Zach walked in.

"I couldn't find her," he said, looking miserable and pissed off. He tossed his car keys on the entry table. "I don't even know where to look."

Grace ran to him and he picked her up, kissing her cheek.

"Hey, Daddy. Look what my mommy gave me." She held out the ring.

Jude thought her son was going to crumple to his knees right there. "The promise ring," he said, letting Grace slide down to the floor. "She didn't want it anymore."

"Daddy?"

He walked over to the window, stared out at the dark Sound. "Where could she be?"

"Who?" Grace said, coming up beside him, putting her hand in his back pocket.

"I looked at the park, at that place in the woods by her old trailer. I looked in every window downtown. I even went to the cemetery and the . . . place on Night Road. It's like she vanished." He turned to Jude. "Did she say *anything*?"

Jude tried to remember. She'd been so focused on the journal, she'd barely been listening to Lexi. Another mistake to atone for. "I think she said something about a last good-bye. Something she should have done a long time ago. I should have stopped her. I should have—"

"A good-bye?"

"Yeah, that's right. She said she had one last thing to do. A good-bye she should have said a long time ago."

Zach grabbed his keys and ran out of the house.

Lexi tried to wait until midnight, but she couldn't do it. She was anxious, sick to her stomach about what she had to do. Finally, at about nine-thirty, she couldn't stand it anymore. She left Scot's warm, love-filled home and rode the bicycle out to LaRiviere Park. There she stood at the water's edge. The sound of waves whooshing forward, reaching for her and receding, would forever remind her of first love. But finally, it was time to go.

She walked the bike up the hill and pedaled onto the main road. Even this late on a summer's night, Main Street was full of people milling about, and Lexi dodged between and around them with the ease of a local girl in a tourist town. A faded melancholy assailed her as she passed the places that would forever define her youth. She would always remember the girl she'd been on this Main Street, the girl who laughed with her best friend and waited for a boy in a white Mustang.

On Beach Drive, she slowed down and coasted up to the Farradays' driveway. Hiding her bike in the salal, she stayed close to the tree line until she was close enough to see that the house lights were off.

No one was home.

Breathing a sigh of relief, she walked down the driveway and around the side of the house.

Night claimed the backyard. A single porch light glowed above one of the doors, splashed light onto the glittery gray stone patio. Moonlight illuminated the waves and turned the grassy lawn blue.

She eased past the barbeque area and around the pair of chaise loungers that overlooked the Sound. Flicking on her borrowed flashlight, she pointed a beam of yellow light toward the giant cedar tree that guarded this bit of land from the encroaching water.

At the base of the tree, she scanned the ground with her flashlight, wondering exactly where she should dig first.

"We should have used a marker," she said to the ghosts of the kids they'd been.

It'll be a pact.

We'll always be friends.

Never say good-bye.

They should never have buried the stupid Thermos, should never have let themselves get so caught up in nostalgia.

Or maybe she simply shouldn't have remembered it. Who could have known how heavy a pact could become, how precise a promise could seem?

She dropped slowly to her knees, feeling the shock of cold sand on her bare skin. She dug through the sand, pushing mounds of it to one side and then the other.

It wasn't here.

She dug faster, feeling desperation rise. She *had* to dig this up, had to say good-bye to Zach . . .

"Is this what you're looking for?"

She heard his voice in the darkness, and when she looked up, there he was, standing at the edge of the trees. She must have walked right past him . . .

"I guess you beat me to it." She got awkwardly to her feet.

"You can't have it," he said. "It stays. Just like the promise we all made."

"That promise died in a car on Night Road," she said.

"Did it?" He moved toward her slowly.

"Stay away from me, Zach. Please."

"Why?"

Words were impossible with him this close. She started to turn away.

"Don't go," he said.

He couldn't know what those words did to her. "Don't, Zach. It's too late. I can't take it again. Just . . . let me go. Say good-bye. Throw the Thermos in the Sound."

"I miss her," he said, and Lexi felt the start of tears.

How was it they had never had this conversation? She started to say how sorry she was, but he shook his head and said, "But I miss you, too, Lexi."

"Zach . . ." She could barely see him through her tears now, but she wouldn't wipe them away.

"I don't see how you could forgive me . . . I can't forgive myself, and I'll get it if you hate me. But Lex . . . oh, man . . . I'm so sorry."

"*You're* sorry? I killed your sister."

He looked at her. She saw how uncertain he was, how afraid. "Could you ever love me again?"

She stared at this blurry version of him, shadows and moonlight, and remembered the first time he'd kissed her, the first time he'd held her hand, the day he'd stood up in court and said he was guilty, too, the day he'd taken their daughter in his arms. It was all between them in this instant—the good, the exceptional, the sad, the horrific. Everything that they'd been as kids and the adults they were trying to now be. She could no more deny loving him than she could carry weights into the Sound and drown herself. Some things simply *were* in life, and her love for him was one of those things. It didn't matter that they were young or that there were a dozen reasons for them to be apart. It only mattered that his blood had somehow found its way into her veins and without him she was lost. "I do love you," she said quietly. "I tried to stop . . ."

He took her in his arms and kissed her. At the touch of his lips, so sweetly, achingly familiar, she felt as if her soul, bound in chains for years, broke free, stretched and opened its wings. She was flying, soaring. She clung to him, crying at last for the best friend she'd killed and the years she'd lost in prison and the daughter whose babyhood would forever be hidden from her. This moment was more than she'd ever dared to hope for, and the love she'd tried so hard to extinguish overwhelmed her.

She drew back and stared at him in wonder. Tears spiked his lashes, made him look impossibly young again, like the boy she'd given her heart to all those years ago on a night like this, with the lights of the highway rushing past them. "How?" was all she could say, but she knew he understood. How could they go back, really?

"I love you so much, Lexi," he said. "That's all I know."

"So, what do we do? How do we start?"

He handed her the dirty Thermos as carefully as if it were an artifact from a lost civilization, which, in a way, it was. "We keep our promise."

Lexi held the time capsule in her hands, picturing the gold earrings, the Saint Christopher medal, and the fraying friendship bracelet within.

Lexi felt Mia with them—in the warm summer breeze, in the rustling of the trees, in the steady heartbeat of waves. She kissed the sandy curve of the Thermos and buried it again. When she was done, she patted the sand in place. "She's here," Lexi said, feeling her best friend beside her for the first time in years.

Zach finally smiled. "She always will be."

Then he took her hand and they stood up. "Come home with me, Lexi," he said, and all she could do was nod. *Home.*

They walked quietly toward the house, and she thought: this is how we do it; this is how we talk to our daughter. Holding hands.

❧

The next morning, Grace woke up early. In her footed pink jammies, she walked sleepily down the narrow hallway to her daddy's bedroom, dragging her yellow blanket along behind her.

His door was closed. That was weird. She pushed the door open and started to say, *Wake up, sleepy head,* but all she got out was, "Wa—"

Mommy was in bed with Daddy. They were kinda stuck together, sleeping.

Grace got a little flutter in her heart.

Her *mommy* was here.

She shuffled forward and climbed up on the bed, squirming between them. Before she could say anything, her daddy started tickling her, and she giggled until she couldn't breathe. Then she lay there, between her mommy and daddy, feeling like crying even though she didn't know why.

"Are you okay with me being here, Gracie?" her mommy asked.

"I thought you were leaving."

"Your daddy changed my mind," Mommy said. "Is that okay with you, Grace? Can I live with you guys?"

Grace giggled at that. She felt so happy she forgot to cover her mouth. "Of *course* it's okay."

After that, Grace had a lot to tell her new mommy. She talked nonstop until the alarm beside Daddy's bed rang; then she sat up suddenly and said: "I gotta go to school. It's the last day. Will you drive me, Mommy?"

"I don't drive," her mom said, looking nervously at Daddy.

"That's weird," Grace said. "*All* mommies know how to drive."

"I'll get my license back," Mommy said. "By first grade, I'll be ready. Now, how about breakfast? I'm starving."

Grace launched herself onto Daddy's back, and Daddy carried her into the kitchen, plopping her down in her seat at the table.

All the time she was eating, she couldn't help staring at her mommy. She could tell that Daddy couldn't help himself either. It felt like being a family.

And Grace could think of a *lot* more to say to her mommy now. Through breakfast and out to the car, Grace talked. She told Mommy about how bendable Barbie was and how cool Hannah Montana and Cinderella were and how long she could hold her breath, and before she knew it, she said, "An I c'n waterski like Ashley Hamerow."

They were in the car now, driving to school.

Mom turned in her seat and looked at Grace. "Is that true?"

"It could be."

"But is it?"

Grace slumped in her car seat. "No." It was hard to *only* tell the truth. How would anyone like her for who she really was?

At school, Dad pulled out of the carpool lane and parked under the big trees off to the side of the school.

"Can I walk you into class?" Mommy asked.

Grace got that fluttery feeling again. She smiled. "You could be my show and tell."

Mommy smiled. "I'd like that."

They walked through the crowd of children, and Grace started to feel sick. Mommy was gonna notice that she had no friends.

But all the way to the classroom door, Mommy held her hand, and when they got there, she knelt down and looked at Grace.

"You remember when I told you about my best friend, Mia?"

Grace nodded. She wanted to suck her thumb, but the kids would just make fun of her for that.

"I was so scared the day I met her. It was the first day of school, and no one liked me. I ran out of the lunchroom 'cause I couldn't sit with anyone. And then I saw this other girl sitting all by herself. And I just went up to her and started talking. That's how we became best friends. You have to take a chance, Grace. Talk to someone."

"Okay, Mommy."

Mommy pulled Grace into a fierce hug and kissed her cheek. "I'll be here to pick you up when school's over."

"Promise?"

"I promise," her mommy said, and then she backed away.

Grace looked nervously into the classroom, where kids were busy doing all kinds of things. She saw Samantha standing by the cubbies, all by herself. "Ariel? Are you here? I need you."

Go on.

Grace looked down at her wrist; she saw a flash of yellow and heard a sound that was like laughing, or maybe like the waves in front of Nana's house. "I'm scared," she whispered. "What should I say?"

You know what to say. You don't need me anymore, Gracerina.

"I do! Don't go." Grace started to panic. Her cheeks got hot. She was afraid she was gonna cry.

Go on, Gracerina. You have your mommy now. Trust her.

Grace looked at her mom one last time and then walked into the classroom.

Her heart was beating like crazy. Taking a deep breath, she walked over to Samantha and just stood there beside her. "My mommy came home last night," she said finally.

Samantha turned to her. "The spy?"

"She's not really a spy."

"What is she?"

Grace shrugged.

"Oh."

"You wanna sit by me today?" Grace said, biting her lip.

"Are you gonna punch me?"

"No."

"Do you like hopscotch?" Samantha finally said. "Cuz I do."

"Yeah," Grace said, smiling. It was a lie. Really, she didn't know how to play hopscotch, but she wanted to learn. And anyway she didn't think it was a bad lie. "I *love* hopscotch."

❧

The day woke Jude gently. She lay in bed with Miles, feeling his body along hers, hearing the catch in his breathing that meant he would soon start snoring.

She kissed his stubbly cheek and peeled back the covers to get out of bed. Through her bedroom windows, she saw a brilliant salmon-pink sky glowing above the steel blue Sound, and, for the first time in years, she went in search of a camera.

Standing outside in her terrycloth robe and bare feet, she took several pictures of the black cedar tree silhouetted against the pink sky. It looked new to her all of a sudden. Dew sparkled on the dense green lawn and on the stone patio. She thought about the parties they used to have in this backyard, the laughter that used to fill it, and she hungered for a time like that again. She'd bought that huge outdoor table for her future, assuming that she would have grandkids clustered around it one day. It hadn't been used in years.

She walked purposefully outside and pulled the plastic covering off the table, exposing it to the sunlight again.

Then the garden caught her eye.

In bare feet, she walked across the dewy grass and stared down at her runaway garden. Everything was a mess; the rows she'd once clipped so carefully were impossible to distinguish in the riot of color. There were flowers everywhere—blooming in spite of her absence, their colorful blossoms tangling up with one another.

Before, she would have seen disorder here, plants that grew where they weren't supposed to and bloomed with abandon. She would have gone in search of her tools—clippers and trowels and stakes—and set about the task of re-creation.

Now, though, on this bright morning, she saw what she hadn't seen before. There was a beauty in chaos, a wildness that hinted at things gone wrong and mistakes overcome. She stood there a long time, looking down at her ruined and yet still beautiful garden. Finally, she knelt in the grass and began pulling up weeds. When she'd cleared a space, she got shakily to her feet. It was a start.

She went to her glass-sided greenhouse, where once she'd poured her heart and soul into trays filled with black soil. Things were forgotten in here now, draped in cobwebs. A watering system had kept everything alive; plants, like people, learned to grow in rocky terrain. Up on a high shelf in the back, she found what she was looking for: a small white packet of wildflower seeds. She'd bought them years ago, from a friend of Mia and Zach's who'd been selling them outside of Safeway. For a trip somewhere, she thought. She'd never intended to plant them, not wildflowers that could sprout anywhere.

Taking the packet of seeds from the shelf, she walked out and stood in the center of her overgrown garden.

She poured the mismatched seeds into her palm and stared down at them, reminded of how small things were in the beginning. With a smile, she threw the seeds across the garden. Someday, she would be surprised by what would grow from these seeds. And soon, maybe tomorrow, she would plant a white rose right there, where Mia had lost her first tooth . . .

Returning to the house, she made a pot of coffee. The smoky, roasted scent of it filled the house, drew Miles stumbling into the kitchen with his hand outstretched, mumbling, "Coffee."

She handed him a cup, black. "Here you go."

"You're an angel."

"Speaking of that . . ."

"Speaking of what?"

"Angels."

Miles frowned. "You know I have trouble before coffee, but were we talking about angels?"

"I'm going to the cemetery today," she said quietly. "I decided yesterday."

"You want me to come with you?"

She loved him for asking. "This is something I need to do by myself."

"You sure?"

"I'm sure."

"Call me when you get home?"

"Afraid I'll throw myself in some open hole?"

He kissed her and drew back. "Been there, done that. Not worried anymore. You've come back."

"Call me Frodo."

"Not Frodo. Sam. Sam came home and got married and had a life."

"You're right. I'm Sam."

She stood by him in the kitchen for the next half hour, sipping coffee and talking. When he left her and headed for the shower, she was struck by the extraordinariness of it all: that they could stand around and talk about little things again. A potential dinner party. The newest coffee maker. A movie that was getting good reviews.

She had gone a whole hour without thinking about her heartache. That might not sound like much to some people, but to her it was monumental, like swimming the English Channel. It offered her a glimpse of something she'd given up on: the possibility of being herself again, of even someday being happy with her life. She knew she could never let go of her sadness, but maybe Harriet was right: maybe she could go on. Maybe time didn't heal wounds exactly, but it gave you a kind of armor, or a new perspective. A way to remember with a smile instead of a sob. Maybe someday when a stranger asked how many children she had, she could simply say one and talk about Zach.

God, she hoped so.

She met Miles in the bathroom and went into the shower as he was coming out. He patted her bare butt, and she smiled and scooted out of his reach and ducked into the hot water. She was rinsing the conditioner out of her hair when the glass door opened.

"You sure you're going to be okay?" Miles said again.

"I'm fine. Call Zach and remind them that we're going to the aquarium tomorrow. Mom is meeting us there."

Miles paused, and she knew him well enough to recognize that he was thinking about something.

"What?" she said, stepping out of the shower, wrapping a towel around her body.

"We had a pretty big anniversary a few years ago. We didn't celebrate it. We didn't celebrate any of them . . . after."

"We'll do better this year. Dinner at Canlis."

He held out a familiar blue velvet box.

She was shaking as she reached out for the small, soft box. The velvet was worn on top; that was how often she'd held it, but she hadn't touched it in years. Releasing a deep breath, she flipped open the lid. One a bed of stark white, Mia's graduation ring stood up proudly, the gold glinting in the light. The once-empty prongs had been filled with a sparkling pink diamond.

Jude looked up at this man she loved, and the full power of that emotion, of their commitment, surged through her like a tide carrying her home. He knew her better than she knew herself; he knew that she needed this reminder of their daughter, something Jude could wear, see every day.

"I love you, Miles Farraday."

He touched her face, smiling. "You're a warrior. You know that?"

"I wish."

He kissed her again, whispered, "Tell her hi for me," and then went back into the bedroom.

After he left the house, she dried her hair and dressed in a pair of old, comfortable jeans and a white hoodie. Ordinarily, she'd take the time to put on makeup, but today she didn't feel the need to hide anything. She was who she was: a woman who'd survived a war of the heart and had the wrinkles to prove it.

She meant to leave right away, but somehow she couldn't do it. She spent the next few hours doing chores, picking things up around the house, doing laundry, making a casserole for dinner.

Stalling. Finally, at just after one o'clock, she drew in a deep breath and stopped moving. *It's time, Jude. Now.*

Slinging a purse over her shoulder, she went to her car and drove away. As she came to the corner, sunlight skittered along the blue water below and winked from windows along either shore. Such a beautiful, beautiful day.

At Night Road, she slowed down. It had been years since she'd dared to turn onto this stretch of asphalt where her life had changed. It was time to face it at last.

She turned and kept driving. Then, after about a half a mile or so, she pulled off to the side of the road and parked. Slowly, she got out of the car and crossed the street.

The remnants of the memorial were barely visible.

She stood at the hairpin turn.

The forest was dark here, even in midday. Ancient, towering evergreens grew in dense thickets on either side, their mossy, spearlike trunks rising high enough into the summer sky to block out the sun. Shadows were knee-deep along this worn ribbon of asphalt; the air was still and quiet, like an indrawn breath. Expectant.

She shouldn't stay here long. If someone saw her on this lonely roadside, the talk would start up, people would worry about her. Still, she closed her eyes for just a moment, remembering that night, so long ago, when the rain had turned to ash . . .

Letting it go.

At last, she returned to her car and drove off the island.

It took her less than thirty minutes to reach her destination. That surprised her. Somehow, she thought it should have been farther away. It had taken her years to get here, after all.

The cemetery was a rolling landscape of manicured lawn studded with the decorations of death: headstones, monuments, stone benches.

She took a deep breath. "Come on, Judith. You can do this." She reached into the backseat for the three pink balloons she'd bought at the florist's shop yesterday. Clutching the strings, she herded them up and left her car. In her mind, she clicked through the directions she'd gotten yesterday, but it didn't really matter. She could have found her child blindfolded . . .

And there was the marker. A smooth granite headstone with an etching of Mia's face in its center.

MIA EILEEN FARRADAY.

1986—2004

LOVING DAUGHTER AND SISTER.

NEVER TO BE FORGOTTEN.

There was a small gift-of-life symbol there, too, memorializing the lives she'd saved.

Jude held her ridiculous balloons, staring at the image of her daughter's face. Even in granite, Mia's smile shone brightly.

"I'm sorry it took me so long to get here. I got . . . lost," she finally said, and once she started talking, she couldn't stop. She sat down on a granite bench and told Mia everything.

For years, Jude had worried that she would forget her daughter, that time would somehow sand away her memories until nothing solid was left, but now, sitting here in the sunshine, holding her balloons, she remembered everything—how Mia used to suck her thumb and stroke her stuffed puppy's satin paws, how she used to break into a run just before she saw Jude in the carpool lane, how she ate her oranges in sections, tearing away every tiny speck of white, how in a hurry she was to grow up.

"I bought you this ring . . . a long time ago," Jude said, feeling the tug of both sadness and joy. It was strange how those emotions could coexist at a moment like this. "I bought it for an eighteen-year-old girl who I thought was my future." She stared down at the pink diamond. It sparkled in the sunlight, danced.

Every time she looked at this ring, she would remember something about her daughter. Sometimes she would cry, but that was okay, because someday, maybe she would smile. Or even laugh.

That was something she had learned the past few weeks. In the sea of grief, there were islands of grace, moments in time when one could remember what was left rather than all that had been lost.

She stood and released the balloons into the sky. The pink dots swirled and bounced on an invisible current of air, as if an impatient girl had grabbed at them and missed. A sound like laughter came through the trees, and Jude experienced a profound sense of peace. She'd been wrong before; her daughter *was* here, with her, inside of her. She'd always been here, even when Jude was too broken to look for her. But it was time now to say, "Good-bye, baby . . . I love you."

For the first time in years, she believed that her daughter could hear her.

Acknowledgments

A special thanks to Amanda DuBois, family lawyer extraordinaire. Your help in maneuvering through the maze of legal issues in this novel was invaluable. Any mistakes are most certainly mine.